Lieutenant and Mrs Lockwood

by

Mark Bois

A Novel

Lieutenant and Mrs Lockwood

by

Mark Bois

WWW.FIRESHIPPRESS.COM

Lieutenant and Mrs Lockwood by Mark Bois

ISBN-13: 978-1-61179-309-3 (Paperback)
ISBN -978-1-61179-310-9 (e-book)

BISAC Subject Headings:
FIC0012000FICTION / Action
FIC014000FICTION / Historical
FIC032000FICTION / War & Military

Cover work by Christine Horner

Address all correspondence to:
Fireship Press, LLC
P.O. Box 68412
Tucson, AZ 85737
Or visit our website at:
www.fireshippress.com

AUTHOR'S NOTE

This is a work of fiction. While the 1/27th Foot, the Inniskilling Regiment, is very real, the persons created in this novel are creations of the author.

That being said, the situations in which the regiment and the author's characters are set are as close to historical as the record allows. The history of the Inniskilling Regiment during the Napoleonic Wars is nothing short of fascinating, and the reader is encouraged to pursue some of the histories of the regiment and their role at Waterloo. For those fortunate enough to visit Enniskillen, Northern Ireland, a visit to the regimental museum is a true pleasure, as the displays are uniquely informative and the kind staff is exceptionally knowledgeable.

The author is trained as an historian, but admits to a wholly unprofessional admiration for the officers and men of the Inniskilling Regiment of 1815. The demands of an interesting novel require that numerous fictional elements be created; the author has, for example, inserted a very disreputable character into the regiment, though there is no hint of such a rogue ever inhabiting the Inniskilling officers' mess. The story of the Inniskilling's gallant stand at Waterloo, however, is told as accurately as this author is capable, and requires no dramatization.

Mark Bois
Cincinnati, Ohio
August 2013

Do mo bhean, mo chuisle, mo mhile stòr.

Acknowledgements

I must humbly thank so many people. Among them: Michael James at Fireship Press, for taking a chance on me; Major Jack Dunlop for his kindness at the Inniskilling Regimental Museum; Dr. Wayne Lee, who taught me to be an historian; the Cincinnati Writers' Project, who taught me to write more like a novelist than an historian; Lt. Colonel Brad Luebbert, who taught me a soldier's voice; Mark and Julie Wurster, who taught me how to be a friend for a lifetime; my children, who taught me what love is; and as always to Charmin Bois, who taught me, frankly, everything.

Reviews

"The lives of soldiers are filled with bored endurance punctuated by occasional moments of great excitement if not outright terror. Bois has here enlivened both while telling a rich tale of the complex bonds between Englishmen, Irishmen, and their Atlantic world at war. His characters live and breathe while simultaneously conveying the real history of the Inniskillings and their wars. Lovers of Patrick O'Brian will revel in the rich details of life and warfare, here in the land forces."

Dr. Wayne E. Lee, Professor of History, University of North Carolina

"Both military and historians will love this novel. Bois makes history comes alive, telling a story that few others are able to do, making you feel you are there with the regiment. He truly is a gifted story teller and readers will be happy they discovered him. Bois' meticulous research and command of historical detail makes this novel a must read. He sets the standard for research and understanding, enabling a mixture of fact and fiction setting. Bois establishes his reputation as a serious writer and the audience will demand more novels from this new author. Historical fiction welcomes Mark Bois with open arms."

Lt. Col. Brad Luebbert, US Army

Chapter One

Bermuda, April 1815

Captain Barr desperately wanted to kill Lieutenant Lockwood. He thought constantly of doing so, though he had long since given up any consideration of a formal duel. Lockwood, after all, was a good shot and a fine swordsman; a knife in the back would do. And then Barr dreamt of going back to Ireland, and of taking Brigid Lockwood for his own. Or perhaps he might kill her as well. He had so many options open to him.

*****

Lieutenant James Lockwood, while of a generally cheerful nature, was conscious of his reputation. As a gentleman and an officer, he was sensitive to anything that might be seen as a slight. Thus, when Lieutenant Thomas Mainwaring referred to him as "an odious recluse," an impartial observer might have feared their discussion would conclude with pistols on the secluded beach below their quarters.

Still, many good friends abuse each other with the same freedom as established enemies. Tom Mainwaring had long been James's closest friend, so James's response was only a

1

civil, "Come, that is coming down a bit hard, don't you think? This is my first letter from home in seven weeks, and I intend to read it. When you are thirsty you are very prone to irritability; in the future I must keep a bottle at hand, to fend off these bursts of petulance."

They were taking their ease in the room they shared at the Officers' Quarters above St. George town. The extent of their ease was somewhat restricted, as they were lodged in a cramped, whitewashed room that contained only two short beds, two battered trunks, and a dilapidated chair that had first served the British army in the days of Queen Anne.

James was in high spirits; though he had been sampling the island's dark rum, his mood was largely due to the arrival, the long-awaited arrival, of the letter from home. He folded his face into a scowl, which might have been more convincing if had managed to contain the playful tone that crept into his voice, as he added, "Besides, I am not a recluse, odious or otherwise. I would, in fact, contend I am an exceptionally social creature. My stock in trade is interaction with my fellow man: did I not spend the entire day with a hundred of my fellow beings, marching and drilling in the most heartfelt fellowship?"

Tom slipped on the better of his two uniform coats and said, "I hardly think this indisputable command over our men can be considered social contact, and it is certainly not of a refined nature. Every year that passes sees you grow more solitary; I believe you Irish are by nature sullen and morose."

"Am I Irish? I was not aware."

"Well, you were born there," said Tom, "certainly there must be some degree of... 'contagion' is an unkind word... perhaps an unwitting absorption, of the Irish character."

"Brother, I do not care to discuss the Irish character, or my adherence to same. I wish only to lie on this ridiculous little bed and read a letter from my wife and children. My desire to do so does not equate to a general loathing of you,

2

our friends, the regiment, or mankind in general. I shall be just a few minutes, I promise, Tom."

"Very well, then: one reading. I shall roust out Pitts and Davies, and will be back in five minutes. I am the most patient of friends; if I were any more supportive of you I would demand a ring."

They were perhaps unlikely friends. Tom was an exceedingly handsome man, and while he was far from vain, he was aware of the fact that women found him attractive, and he had on occasion applied that knowledge to advantage whilst engaged in negotiations with ladies of undecided natures. James was a very tall, solidly built man, with a likable, usually cheerful face, but he was not beautiful.

His wife, Brigid, however, was beautiful; James smiled as he read her account of a battle with a bat that had invaded the drawing room of their home in Clonakilty. The bat, which by all accounts was the size of a moderate eagle, had eventually been subdued with the help of the children, who all desired their mother to mention their valour in her weekly letter to their distant father. The occasional bat excepted, the family was very comfortable in Fáibhile Cottage, the modest house they leased near Brigid's family in the south of Ireland. They had taken the house just as James left for foreign service, and for those three years it had proven to be a good home for Brigid, their five children, and their large black dog.

Brigid went on to request the lieutenant's assistance, his very firm assistance, in convincing his children that the dog should sleep outside, as was standard practice in Christian homes. She closed with an elegantly written, "With great love, Brigid." But in a hurried, scrawled postscript she added, "Pray never forget how I love you. As much as you hate him, you must remember your promise; you **must not** fight him."

Before he could dwell on his wife's plea, James was interrupted by Tom's voice from the doorway.

"If you continue to lie about like that, you will certainly contract some horrid tropical disease, and I shall be forced to debauch myself without you." Gesturing toward the letter, he added, "All well at home, I trust?"

"The children were mentioned in dispatches; valourous conduct in the face of flying rodents."

Tom noticed, but did not comment upon, the break in James's voice, saying only, "Well, there's glory for you; they shall likely be made captain before either of us. But for now we can enjoy Price's Vile Dotage. A French brig came in this morning, and Price bought six dozen of a capital burgundy. Now I really must insist we go down and drink our share."

"Insisting, are you? Our friendship has sunk to this level, where we insist, for all love?" James sat up with a smile and carefully tucked his letter into an inside pocket with as much composure as he could muster. "The wars were all well and good," he said, "but now they're over, we shall at last have access to some decent wine. Down with Napoleon, but *vive la France*." Noticing Tom's pink perfection James ran a hand over his chin and added, "I hope I needn't shave for this affair. Old Price will make allowance, certainly; he has never been one to stand upon ceremony."

"Price is a forgiving creature, but pray allow me to brush your coat; it would shame a collier. That villain Doolan should be flogged for letting you out like this. Two minutes, and I shall render you fit for decent company. Oh, I should mention those awkward fellows in the 99th are hosting a welcoming dinner for us Saturday week."

James stretched enormously and said, "We no longer know anyone in the 99th, do we? Collins was with them, but I believe I read of him buying into the 4th. I only hope the 99th does not have anyone who is deceived regarding the quality of his voice. If I am forced to dine with one more fool who tearfully croaks out 'Barbara Allen,' I shall be driven to heinous murder."

4

They belonged to the First Battalion, 27th Regiment of Foot, otherwise known as the Inniskilling Regiment. Having arrived in Bermuda only days before, they were pleased with their newly-assigned barracks, as the four large white-stuccoed buildings sat atop a hill overlooking St. George town on one side, and Fort St. Catherine and the turquoise sea on the other. All of the barracks buildings were squat, two-storied affairs that lacked anything like comfort or convenience, and the Inniskillings soon found the limestone-slabbed roofs leaked badly in the frequent tropical downpours. In laying out the barracks, however, the army had made certain concessions to the tropical weather, one of these being the deep covered verandas that graced the officers' living quarters. The officers of the 1/27th dragged a motley collection of tables and chairs out onto their breezy upstairs veranda, the veranda that looked out across that exquisitely beautiful sea, and made the best of it.

It was an April evening, the freshly-scrubbed sea breezes providing a cool, delightful contrast to the day's drumming rain. The brutally hot days of summer, and the fevers that typically claimed the lives of so many British troops in the Caribbean, were yet to come. The officers who gathered on the veranda were dressed in such a wide variety of clothing, only a well-informed observer would have been able to identify them as British infantry officers.

"I tell you, gentlemen, it will not do," said one of the senior captains, the very thin, pinch-faced Charles Barr. Of all the battalion's officers, he alone wore the regulation uniform upon every occasion, his wardrobe of a quality and quantity that set him far apart from his brethren. He was addressing three other officers, the unpleasant handful of the battalion's more abrasive and less competent gentlemen.

Pausing to ensure he had the full attention of his cronies as well as a few of the other men on the veranda, Barr continued, "To promote a man from the ranks is an error of the first order. A man who is raised in the gutter is incapable

5

of assuming the burden and responsibility of a British officer. True officers are driven by honour, an impulse that cannot be expected of the lower classes, and I need not mention the concept is unknown to Irish peasants. Only a gentleman, a man of superior social origin, is capable of leading men; it is the natural way of things. The sheep must have their shepherd. The analogy can certainly be found in Scripture."

"Oh, yes!" cried one of Barr's most devoted adherents, a pimply ensign named Elphinstone. "I heard our parson at home speak of the natural order! But I believe he spoke of asses, not sheep..."

Barr, not pleased with the interruption, glared at the blushing ensign. "It was certainly sheep, Ensign Elphinstone. But at any rate, it is my opinion that the colonel is mistaken in granting Sergeant McBride an officer's commission. The man is incapable of intelligent conversation; he speaks as if he just wandered in off the bog, and his table manners would not recommend him anywhere. I wonder if the colonel did not promote him simply because of his birthplace!" This prompted some simpering amusement, as regimental tradition called for only Irishmen in the enlisted ranks.

Most of the men on the veranda, however, made pains to distance themselves from Barr. James and Tom sat at the far rail, side by side, enjoying the view and the breeze, leaning back in their chairs, their feet up. James had a moment to think about Brigid's letter, and he mused upon his own moods. The letter had done a great deal to raise his spirits, but then he had been oddly downcast by her warning. Tension and unhappiness were never far from his mind, as fate had been pleased to place upon him requirements which he considered shameful, nearly unbearable. He knew he was drinking too much. He had changed; of that he was sure, and in quiet moments he wondered if Brigid would recognize him, whether she would truly be glad of his return. He had served in His Majesty's forces for eighteen years, the last three without once seeing his wife and children. Once again, James was tempted to unburden himself to Tom, to ask his opinion, but James had given his word. A gentleman did not break his word, even when his word was given to the worst sort of man: in short, he had given his word to Charles Barr.

Without looking about, James waved his empty glass over his head and muttered "Oh, where is that felon..."

The felon in question was his servant, Private Diarmuid Doolan, who had in fact never been proven guilty of anything more infamous than stealing three pounds of potatoes in his emaciated youth, charges that had prompted his enlistment into the Westmeath Militia. He and Lieutenant Mainwaring's servant, Private O'Mara, were long familiar with the ways of their officers, and soon both those gentlemen were awash in that fine vintage. Two bottles into Lieutenant Price's burgundy, Tom closed his eyes as he leaned back in his chair, the picture of contentment. James was sharing Brigid's tale of the invasive Irish bat (both he and Tom loved a good story, though after a few glasses they each had a regrettable tendency to embellish) when he was interrupted by a roar of laughter from Barr's table. Barr was known for his coarse jokes, and while James could not make it out he had heard the word "Teague" as part of the punch line. Doolan was pouring his lieutenant another glass, but froze at the mention of the word. It was an ugly word, enough to raise the ire of any Irishman, and a damned fool thing to joke about in an Irish regiment.

James caught Doolan's eye and very subtly shook his head, then said quietly, "That bottle, I think, is not quite up to snuff. You may take it back to the mess room." The glaring Doolan went to share the bottle with his friends while Barr launched into another ribald story.

Tom had been raised in England, but he had served in the 27th long enough to understand what "Teague" meant. Without opening his eyes he muttered softly, "If you'd like, I'll go over and shoot that damned fool."

7

James laughed softly and said, "Oh, would you, please? He quite interrupted my story of the mad Irish bat, and I was just reaching the stunning climax. I should take your shooting him most kindly."

"Not at all. But that would necessitate me getting up and walking over there, which seems, at this moment at least, quite a lot to ask."

"Why, can't you shoot him from here?" James asked as he held up his glass, watching the waning light filter through his wine.

"Certainly not. You know my aim is not what my friends might wish. You might recall the incident with that mad hussar in Spain. What was his name? He called me out, and put a hole in my best cloak."

"Stapylton. You might recall that at the time your cloak was lying on the ground, ten feet from you. He was a worse shot than you, brother, as difficult as that is to imagine."

Some quiet, companionable laughter. "Besides," muttered Tom, "Barr is always going on about his important family connections. If I shot him I might get a stern letter from Horse Guards."

"Or a note of thanks," James said quietly. "The army might be pleased to be spared the presence of a man who beats women with such fury."

"Barr was fortunate we left Canada when we did; a magistrate was making inquiries."

"Yet he has his admirers; he does put on a good show. His thralls might be disappointed to find their hero is the son of a customs officer, not a gartered lord."

"True, true," said Tom, "but then we Inniskillings have never been noted for the elegance of our birth. As the fifth son of a clergyman, a Leister clergyman at that, I stand a case in point. If any of us could boast of family connections, it might be you, my dear James."

"Much good it has done me," said James dismissively, then loudly to Barr, "I say, Barr. My apologies. I'm afraid I wasn't attending. What was that you were saying about Colonel Nelson and asses?"

At the mention of the colonel's name, Barr's audience grew more restrained, though Barr bristled at the interruption. "Nothing of the sort, Lockwood. If you can't attend when your betters speak, then you had best mind your own affairs." Barr then cursed Lockwood in a snarling undertone, still loud enough to make Elphinstone jump, startled wide-eyed by its viciousness.

On that evening, Lieutenant Price was responsible for entertaining his fellow company officers in accordance with regimental tradition, by ruefully celebrating the fact that he had been a lieutenant for seven years, and would henceforth receive the lofty sum of one additional shilling per day in his pay. It was a dubious honour, as any officer who remained a lieutenant for seven years was most likely destined to remain in that rank for his entire career.

When all of the battalion's captains, lieutenants, and ensigns had arrived and had been given ample opportunity to sample Price's burgundy, ritual required that the gathering be addressed by the senior lieutenant, in this case Rawdon Campbell, a small, wiry Highland Scot of good family and a propensity for drink and dark moods. Normally taciturn, he relished the role of marking the somewhat painful passage of a brother officer into seven years of seniority.

"Gentlemen!" cried Campbell, calling the chattering throng to order. "In accordance with the epic traditions of the Inniskilling Regiment, the most effective, if least fashionable, regiment serving His Majesty," much cheering and raising of glasses, "I am called upon to note the Vile Dotage of our own Lieutenant Henry Price!" A crescendo of cheering, and slaps on the back of the grinning Price. "Och, it's true, gentlemen! Handsome young Price has crossed that loathsome mark of military obsolescence, the much-dreaded seven years of lieutenancy! He has joined that noble brotherhood of fighting men, poor of pocket and lacking of influence. But is he destined to serve unnoticed and unrewarded!?"

"No!" cried his enthusiastic, inebriated brothers.

"Then," called Campbell, "Let each man come forward and proclaim his march to join Henry Price in Vile Dotage!"

As tradition demanded, each officer then stepped forward and dropped a shilling into a prized regimental trophy, an ornate silver chamber pot captured in Spain from the baggage of Marshal André Masséna. They came forward by rank and seniority, calling out their years in rank as they tossed in their shilling. The ensigns were first, the most junior nervously piping out just months in that noble rank, none of them able to claim more than two years. These young gentlemen were, of course, greeted with good-natured cries of "Baby!" and "Puppy!" while Campbell called "Wee bairn!" The only exception was the hulking Ensign McBride, whom no man would casually tease, and whose shilling was welcomed with only spatters of applause.

The lieutenants were next, a few calling out two or five years of service, but most of them had long preceded Price into the ranks of Vile Dotage. Tom had celebrated his Dotage a year before, as his seniority dated from February, 1807. James was slightly senior, his lieutenancy dating from November, 1806, so he could proudly boom "Eight years a lieutenant!" as he dropped in his shilling. The captains came last, almost all senior men, though Barr made a point of returning to his quarters before his turn came. The mood on the veranda had lifted with Barr's departure, and with much good will Major John Archibald closed the ceremony as the senior company officer, calling "Ten years a captain!" The evening ended with more congratulations for Price, as the officers eagerly attacked the remaining bottles of wine.

James was not the only officer to drink to excess that night. He was, however, the only one whose sleep was ruined by nightmares of unsolvable puzzles, impossible mazes, and a laughing, screaming, Captain Charles Barr.

Chapter Two

Bermuda

The next morning, rain fell hard all across the islands of Bermuda, though it seemed to fall with particular vehemence on the nine hundred men of the 1/27th, who were drilling on the sodden parade ground outside Fort St. Catherine. Rain was not a great discomfort to the soldiers of the battalion, however, as most of them were Irish. They had been born in a wet country, they had grown up wet, and their service in the 1/27th had often required them to stay wet.

To the men of the battalion, that sleepy cluster of islands seemed a paradise, if perhaps a rather damper version of paradise than is commonly cherished. Despite the rain coming down in torrents, wholly unlike the mellow Irish rain of their collective youth, there was only a moderate degree of grumbling, as the battalion had a reasonable hope of a roof over their heads and a decent meal at the end of their day; those two considerations being, by long experience, of great import to soldiers and the Irish.

After the lengthy drill, the officers gathered for their scandalously tardy dinner with few smiles, and more than a few stiff joints and hacking coughs. The seniority of the officers of the 1/27th meant experience and skill in the ranks, but old wounds and harsh conditions had compounded the effects of advancing age.

As the officers assembled, Barr was exceedingly irritated with Lieutenant James Massey, saying, "Massey, why can you not control that mob of yours? Those damned fools were frolicking like a pack of schoolboys, and cost us all an extra hour of drill."

Massey was a short, round-faced, rather jolly man, who also happened to be a very capable officer. He had endured Barr's jibes for years, and, like most of the other officers of the battalion, he had learned not to take offence easily.

"My apologies, sir," said Massey, "but it is good to see the men back in good spirits, after all that time aboard ship."

James had a high regard for Massey, and he hoped Barr was not going to be more than usually unpleasant. Barr had grown increasingly volatile over the past months, though he was conspicuous about maintaining a mask of civility to those senior to him. The worst of his venom was usually reserved for James or McBride, though Massey was by no means exempt from Barr's rage. But Barr was currently more concerned with tearing into the loaf of bread on his table, and he contented himself with commenting, "Some good floggings would soon eliminate any concern about 'spirits.' The only way to control those damned Irish is to use the cat, and often. The only spirits that interest those bastards come in a bottle."

The 27th Foot was one of the few British regiments to be headquartered in Ireland. They were known as the Inniskilling Regiment, after their home in Ulster's County Fermanagh. The regiment was proud of its Irish heritage, and nearly all of the enlisted men and non-commissioned officers were Irishmen. In fact, a majority of them were from Ulster, and many from County Fermanagh itself.

While the men were Irish, most of the officers were not. Of those few born in Ireland, most, like James, were of

English stock. His branch of the Lockwoods had been in Ireland since Cromwell's excesses in the early 1600s, and had a long history of service to the British crown. James's father had served in the 43rd Foot at the taking of Quebec in 1759, and as the second son of the family, James, who lacked any inherent knowledge of religious truth, preferred to follow his father's example of military service rather than seek religious orders.

The mood in the mess tightened when Ensign Gerald McBride entered and saluted Barr. "All bayonets in One Company have been inspected and found satisfactory, sir," said McBride in his thick Donegal accent.

"Very well," said Barr with a look on his face that might have been interpreted as a smirk, "that is all." There were less-constrained smirks on the faces of the two men who sat with Barr, but McBride made a soldierly about-face and moved toward the door.

"McBride!" called James, "Come have a glass of wine with us."

Ensign McBride was tall, broad, and exceedingly strong. He was in his mid-thirties, with dark, brooding features; a somber, not over-kind man who had been in the regiment since he had enlisted as a seventeen-year-old private.

Studying that stoic face, James thought he caught just a hint of fury behind the façade, but McBride's voice was very controlled. "Thank you, no, sir, I still have some duties to which I must attend, and I believe I shall then dine with my wife in our quarters." McBride was hardly out the door before some of the younger officers began to laugh and mimic his massive build and thick Donegal brogue.

"I've heard," said Tom to James in a muted voice, "that McBride is having some trouble with his men. Nothing obvious, of course, but it's the usual nonsense, as the rankers expect only gentlemen to command them, not some labourer's son from Baile na Finne. Promotions from the ranks are rare, and growing more so. No one has ever been able to define 'gentleman' to my satisfaction, but the qualifier is being applied with increasing frequency."

"There's the truth of it," said James. "And it is a pity that McBride is married. It is bad enough that his birth, faith, and speech separate him from every other man in this mess. But being married and spending all his free time with his wife, his very - " the angels whispered in James's ear and kept him from saying *his very Catholic wife*, " - Spanish wife, does not allow him the opportunity to become familiar with us, to blend in, as it were."

"That, and his intimidating visage; I do not think I have ever seen him smile. I will not comment upon his imposing size, as some of my best friends are Brobdingnagians." With a growing smile Tom went on, "But I quite agree that no officer of His Majesty's army should ever be married; a most unfortunate attribute, a lamentable state of affairs."

"Oh, you know what I mean. Wives at home are perfectly acceptable, better than acceptable, I mean, damn it all; but a wife who travels with the battalion could make a fellow's life damned difficult. And I am not a Brobinger." Then, his face softening, "Still, for a man to have his wife with him might be a true comfort. A true comfort, I say, when one's best friend calls one untoward names, and taunts a fellow over every honest little slip of the tongue."

When he had finished his dinner, James paused at the table occupied by the battalion's ensigns. As he leaned over the table, James put his hand on the shoulder of Ensign Coakley, perhaps rather more firmly than he might have; he had forgotten how thin boys could be. James addressed them in a voice that would have been very familiar to his sons at home, and the ensigns immediately recognized the tone. The giggling very quickly ceased, and they were paying full stony attention as Lieutenant Lockwood said, "A suggestion, please, gentlemen. If some of the officers of this mess make ungentlemanly comments regarding Ensign McBride, then that is their business. You young gentlemen, as officers in

His Majesty's army and the sons of gentlemen, will not engage in such behavior. I might also make so bold as to point out that while Ensign McBride may not reply to most of the officers of this battalion, if he hears one insult from you, his fellow ensigns, he has every right to call you out. McBride has been in a dozen battles, and I advise that you not toy with him. I trust that we understand each other?"

James was pleased to see every one of the young men say "Yes, sir," without hesitation. Amongst them was a new ensign whose name James could not recall; he was delicate enough to pass for a girl, and he seemed particularly horrified with the notion of fighting the massive Gerald McBride.

"Very well, then," said James, now patting Coakley on the shoulder, "you will please consider what I have said. Enjoy your evening." He strolled out to join Tom and his other friends, thinking that in thirty years or so, one or two of those boys might make an acceptable officer, though Elphinstone's face would certainly pose a hindrance.

James had always tried to treat the ensigns fairly, and he did what he could to help them with both their duties and some of the more enigmatic aspects of army life. James did his duty and considered himself a rather average fellow; he would never have suspected that the battalion's ensigns held him in exceptionally high regard, as Lieutenant Lockwood's fighting record earned him something very like awe in their eyes. A few words from him carried a great deal of weight amongst the young gentlemen; they could always tell when the lieutenant was speaking in earnest, as his accent took on a decidedly Irish edge, inherited from his boyhood at Malahide, though they would have died a hundred deaths rather than mock him.

Driven by that concern for Lieutenant Lockwood's opinion, the next day a deputation of the ensigns called on that gentleman to tender their apologies. The ensigns had nominated the new boy, John Blakeley, to be their spokesman, as they considered him to be the most genteel. Gentility, however, did not seem the most accurate description of a thin, pale, doe-eyed boy, in a uniform coat purchased by a frugal widowed mother who intended that her son should grow into it. Mrs. Blakeley evidently expected her son to grow into spectacular manhood, as Blakeley's hands were buried in his cuffs, and what little of his face that was visible above his collar was buried beneath an equally outrageous shako. While his inelegant appearance did little to recommend Blakeley, his brother ensigns hoped that, in the not-unlikely event they found Lieutenant Lockwood in a foul humour, that unpredictable gentleman might not tear Blakeley's head completely from his shoulders.

"Please, sir," piped the nervous Blakeley, "on behalf of myself and my fellow ensigns, we apologize for yesterday's iner... ere..." sputtering to an embarrassed pause.

"Erection," whispered a grinning Ensign Digby.

"Indiscretion!" urgently whispered Ensign Coakley.

"Indiscretion," continued Blakeley, "and we beg your pardon, sir. We will apologize to Ensign McBride, if you feel we really must, sir."

The boys sounded earnest, so James decided to let it go. "Well said, sir. Ensign Blake, isn't it?"

The other ensigns would have known better, but Ensign Blakeley was so unversed in military courtesy and common sense as to suggest, "My name, please, sir, is Blakeley."

Lieutenant Lockwood looked the young fellow in the eye for a moment, then went on, "Of course. I do not believe an apology to Ensign McBride will be necessary, though you all might make an extra effort to support him. In the future you must all remember to adhere to the tenets of gentlemanly behavior, and you will recall that you serve in an Irish regiment. They may not be welcome in Hyde Park, but these men fight."

Encouraged by the lieutenant's evident good mood, Ensign Coakley took the long-awaited opportunity to ask, "Please, sir, were you really in the fighting in Ireland in '98, back when you were an ensign, like us?"

"Why, yes, youngster," replied James, feeling rather more ancient than he had just a few minutes before, "back in my days in the militia. How ever did you come to know about that?"

Feeling that some of the barriers of age and rank were down, Ensign Digby risked adding, "Oh, sir, we know all about it. What was it like, sir, fighting the rebels? Was it as bloody as everyone says?"

The lieutenant's good humour dissolved, and in an instant he reestablished the wall between them. "The Rebellion of 1798 was a singularly unpleasant experience. My role in the suppression of the rebellion was not noteworthy. If you gentlemen wish further information on the subject, I am sure that one of the published histories will answer any questions you may have. Good day, gentlemen."

*****

As a senior lieutenant, James commanded one of the battalion's ten companies. The company, number Six, technically belonged to an elderly captain named Balneavis, but that aging gentleman had been on leave for more than two years, before the end of the war in Spain. James enjoyed the command, and considered it good training for the golden day he received his captaincy, and his own company.

One of the duties required of each of the ten company commanders was to take a turn acting as Captain of the Day, a duty James frankly loathed. Every tenth day found Lieutenant Lockwood at each meal served up to the men, inspecting the kettles and approving the quality and quantity of the food. James's culinary skills ended just above an ability to roast wild pork over an open flame (a necessary skill in Spain), and thus his review of the battalion kitchens was perfunctory at best.

Another irksome responsibility assigned to the Captain of the Day required James to go by the Fort St. Catherine guardhouse several times that day, and to be constantly available to respond to any problems that were above the province of the Sergeant of the Guard.

No exceptional issues had cropped up during James's turn as Captain of the Day, for which he was thankful. The day before, the unfortunate Lieutenant Elliott had been called in the middle of the night to deal with a drunk and combative drummer named Quinn.

Before going to bed, James walked down to the fort to ensure things were in order. Numerous lanterns lit the bastions, so the man standing watch at the guardhouse door, a grizzled old sinner named Cassidy, saw James's approach.

"Lieutenant's coming," he whispered harshly.

"Shite," said the Sergeant of the Guard, James McCurdy. Addressing the men who were relaxing in the guardroom before taking their turn on the walls, McCurdy, in the kindly manner typical of infantry sergeants, said in Irish, "If you devils turn out like Christians, rather than a pack of God damned *omadhaun* straight off the feckin' mountain, perhaps I'll not suggest to Daidi *a grah* that you all be flogged at dawn."

The men were not especially concerned, since they were all from Six Company, and Lieutenant Lockwood was their officer. Amongst themselves they called him Daidi, the Irish version of daddy (‘*a grah*’ being a term of endearment often used amongst the Irish), and while he was demanding he was not cruel, and he watched out for them. They did indeed manage to turn out like Christians, or at least a rough approximation of Christians, and James was not displeased.

The men who were assigned to guard duty were expected to make an effort to look presentable, and thus avoid bringing shame to the regiment. The men James reviewed may have done their best, but they were far from the army's ideal. One or two might still be described as young men, but many were veterans of ten or even twenty years' service. They were mostly small men, in uniforms that were worn, patched, and faded. But they were experienced soldiers: their weapons were clean and well cared for, they were alert and serious about performing their duty, and many had a smile or brief greeting for Lieutenant Lockwood.

Drummer Quinn was the only man in the custody of the guard that day. He was consigned to the Black Hole, under the strictest guard, and was to be given only bread and water, though James suspected he was living rather better than regulations dictated. James took no joy in seeing soldiers, particularly Inniskillings, being punished, but he was far from naïve. Soldiers were even more prone to sin than the rest of mankind, and discipline, discipline, was the one element that kept an army intact and under control. While that discipline often required some exceedingly harsh punishment, James would not have prisoners on his watch unnecessarily brutalized, especially valuable men like Quinn. "Sergeant McCurdy, we will please inspect the Black Hole."

McCurdy unlocked the cell door, and James bent low to pass through, filling the door with his large frame. Peering in, he found Quinn standing at attention in the centre of the small cell, the cell neat and tidy, lit by a small candle. James carefully avoided noticing the laden plate and mug that had been quickly kicked under the rough bunk.

While eyeing Quinn, James asked over his shoulder, "Sergeant McCurdy, pray, how is our Drummer Quinn behaving?"

McCurdy was standing at attention behind him, but smiled a bit as he answered, "Sure and he's penitent as a Franciscan, sir. Hair shirts ain't in it."

"He should have thought of that last night, the fool."

"Begging Your Honour's pardon," replied McCurdy, "it was his birthday, sir, and he's a great favorite, the creature."

"Yes, yes, Lieutenant Hancock told me all about it. A new twist on the same old yarn: his friends treat him to their rum allowance, and he ends up in the Black Hole after stripping stark naked and attempting to swim home to Tara and claim his true place as High King. He is fortunate Lieutenant Elliott has an appreciation for the absurd, but I wager Colonel Pritchard will give him two dozen, *Ard Rí* or no." James knew just a few words of Irish, the title of the High King recalled from Brigid's bed time stories to the children, and he relished the opportunity to show off a bit. No other officer of the regiment had ever deigned to learn any Irish, and while the amazed McCurdy and Quinn didn't say a word their eyes stretched wide at the same instant, a curiosity sadly missed by Lieutenant Lockwood, who was gazing about the cell, looking nonchalant.

Warming to the occasion, James went on, "We mustn't have the *Ard Rí* swimming home to his *tóin tinn*, as it were."

The Inniskillings had a hard-won reputation for steely discipline, which in this instance enabled both McCurdy and Quinn to silently nod in agreement in spite of Lieutenant Lockwood's unfortunate confusion over the terms for *home fire* and *sore ass*.

James and McCurdy locked the cell door behind them, and James was cautioning McCurdy not to be so obvious with the illicit rations when Private James Higgins burst into the guard room. "Thank God you're here, sir," he gasped. "Captain Barr has arrested poor Loughlin." Private Lancelot Loughlin was the company fugleman, a steady, reliable, popular man.

"Whatever for?" asked James.

"Asleep on the guard, sir, the sorrow and woe," answered Higgins, obviously shaken.

"Take us there, man."

James, Higgins, and McCurdy walked quickly toward the far end of the fort. "If Your Honour doesn't take offense at the liberty," said Higgins confidentially as they walked quickly along the wall, "Captain Barr does not perhaps seem quite himself."

They found Private Loughlin and Captain Barr standing under a lantern at a barred gate. Barr called, "The great Lieutenant Lockwood! Here at last." Even from a distance James could tell Barr was spectacularly drunk.

James strode angrily up to Loughlin, who was standing at strict attention, wide-eyed and pale. "Private Loughlin, were you asleep at your post?"

"Jesus, no, sir!" said Loughlin, aghast.

Silence then, as Barr stood there grinning, swaying.

"Loughlin, Higgins, McCurdy," said James quickly, "you are dismissed. Return to the guardhouse." All three soldiers walked quickly away, ignoring Barr. McCurdy led Loughlin and Higgins thirty yards down the wall, where in the deep shadows the three men stopped, quietly loaded their muskets, fixed their bayonets, and peered back at the two officers facing each other under the pale light of the gate lantern.

"You may recall," slurred Barr, "that I have placed that Irish dog of yours under arrest. For now, I shall gracefully suspend the charges. But stand thee warned, Lockwood, if you cross me I shall see he gets a thousand. I saw a man get a thousand, once; he died at nine hundred forty... such fun."

As Captain of the Day, James wore his sword, and unconsciously his hand went to its hilt, hissing, "God damn you, Barr, don't you have even a shred of decency left?"

Barr laughed wildly, driven by more than drink. "We each hold a knife at the other's throat. What fine gentlemen we are, each keeping our word for so long. We have held our little bargain for, what... is it seventeen years now? My, how the time flies by. If you expose me, I expose you. Just know I have another arrow in my quiver: I have your man's life in my hands. All the more for you to lose if you betray me."

James was desperately angry, but there was nothing more he could do. "I hold my tongue as long as you hold yours." With this he turned and stalked off, still futilely clutching his sword.

"Oh, why can't we be friends, Lockwood? I was at your wedding, you know!" called Barr after him, his mad laughter echoing off the dark stone walls.

Chapter Three

Clonakilty, Ireland

Brigid Lockwood, alone again, walked quickly up the lane toward Fáibhile Cottage. She had been in town shopping with her sister, and the cold rain that had threatened for most of the day now began to fall, large drops that beat around her with increasing frequency. When she had left the house that morning, she had put on her best bonnet, the one that James had sent from Madrid itself, and she had no intention of seeing it ruined. The late-winter branches of the lane's beeches offered little shelter, and when the rain came in earnest, she gave up all pretense of lady-like propriety and broke into a run for the last few yards to her door. As a girl she had once won a ribbon in the barefoot races at the West Cork Fair, and though it may have been some years since her last sprint, she took surprised pleasure in her dash along the low stone wall, past the white gate, and through the green door into her slate-floored front hall.

Her five children were watching from the front windows, loudly cheering her dash through the rain. An excess of childish noise was not normally tolerated in the Lockwood home, but for that moment at least all sins were overlooked. The survival of the Madrid bonnet was duly celebrated, though the cheering brought Sergeant, the family's lumbering black dog, charging in from the kitchen, wagging a tail that threatened to knock over Lucy, the frail youngest. The cheering only increased when Brigid triumphantly produced a letter from James she had picked up in town. Both the older girls noticed their mother had two letters in her bag, but she quickly stuffed the second deep back out of sight.

The children craved letters from their father, as he always included a few lines for each of them, only to them, special. Brigid had also brought home a small bag of taffy to celebrate the arrival of the letter, which incited more jumping up and down than was absolutely necessary, prompting Sergeant to bark, bringing the noise level up to a standard that would normally rouse the militia. In this case it brought only Mrs. Cashman, their housekeeper, with a spoon in her hand and murder in her eye. But seeing that dear Mrs. Lockwood was home her mood quickly softened, and she helped Brigid in matching each child to their respective quarter-sheets from the letter and a bit of the candy.

"But Richard got more than I did!" cried Mary.

"God loves the poor, *a chroi*," replied Mrs. Cashman, shooing the children off so Brigid could be alone with her letter. Sergeant, unhappy he had been deemed unworthy of a share of the candy, was reluctant to move until Mrs. Cashman gave him a quick, practiced whack with her spoon, adding a sharp, "*Tar liom, mhadra amaideach*," in her broad Munster Irish. It is well known in Cork that babies and dogs are born with an innate understanding of the Irish language, and while babies typically outgrow the gift, many dogs have sense enough to retain it. Thus Sergeant, who was at heart a sensitive soul, had cause to look wounded as he retreated into the kitchen.

As Brigid sat down to read her letter, she briefly wondered if Mrs. Cashman would wash her spoon before she started their dinner, but that concern was quickly replaced

26

by the excitement of hearing from her husband. With her legs folded under her, she broke the seal and paused for a moment to bask in the familiarity of his hand. She quickly, anxiously, scanned the letter for any sign that the worst had happened, but seeing no obvious indication of calamity she settled in for a slow, affectionate read.

Port Royal, Jamaica
January 14th, 1815

My dearest Brigid,

My fondest love from the warm shores of Jamaica. I pray this letter finds you and the children well and happy. Your last letter told of Lucy's illness, and I have thought of her a great deal over the past few weeks. I ache to see all of you again, but I am especially anxious to make her acquaintance. I wonder: are her eyes as blue as yours, Dear?

I have received no letters from you since we were in Halifax, on December 10th. I do not mention that as a slight to you, honey, as I know you are so diligent in writing, but the battalion has been on the move so much that no mail has yet caught up with us. I confess I grow somewhat irritable when I have no word from home; just this morning I savaged Doolan when he mentioned that Corporal Cavanaugh once lost a two-year-old daughter to just such a fever. Of course Doolan meant no harm (you know how fond of the children he is), but there are times I wish I had an idiot deaf-mute for a servant instead of a meddling gossip-monger. He desires me to mention that the shirts you sent reached us safely, and they were a welcome addition to my "fiesteas", whatever that may be. He delights in using his Irish to sly purpose; I wish you

*were here, my Dear, to keep him honest. I wish you
were here for that, and for so many other reasons.*

To say Brigid Lockwood loved her children would be a
criminal understatement, but there were times she would
have sold them to the Rovers without three minutes' barter.
In a fit of taffy-induced madness, her sons had coaxed
Sergeant into Mrs. Cashman's room, into her very bed, a
genuine heresy if one considered that good woman's
obsession with cleanliness. Thus Brigid's reading was soon
interrupted by the pounding of eight felonious male feet
tearing out of the kitchen, quickly making for the front door
as they were pursued by two aging female feet that were not
above kicking some naughty bottoms. As Mrs. Cashman gave
up the pursuit and returned to the kitchen, Brigid gave a
silent whistle: the Irish language arms its adherents with
some truly harsh curses, and while Mrs. Cashman never used
the worst of them *to* the Lockwood children, she occasionally
said them *about* them.

*You are no doubt astonished to find me in the
Caribbean. Trust me, your astonishment is shared
by every member of the First Battalion, 27th Foot,
your devoted husband included. When last I wrote,
I mentioned we had arrived in Canada after a good
passage from France. We were under the command
of General Prevost, who had the reputation of being
a ~~God-damned~~ complete fool, and his conduct only
proved that, and more. The whole army is
disgusted, and as the Americans have offered a
hundred acres of prime land to any man who
would desert to them (which seems rather
unsporting) we had about fifty of our battalion
desert, three men from my own company amongst
them. I do not mourn the loss of those three villains,
as all three were new men from Belfast who had*

not blended with my veterans. It is perhaps treasonous to say so, but I hope never to see them again, for if they are caught I shall be obliged to have them flogged, and they will hold a grudge and cause trouble until the next time they find an opportunity to take Dutch leave.

Brigid saw a knot of people quietly pass her window, followed by a hesitant knock at the kitchen door and the gentle murmur of voices. Mary stepped halfway into the drawing room and asked, "Mama, may we do without that white cheese, and a loaf of bread?"

Brigid had to swallow the first response that came to mind, instead saying, "Of course, dear." But then as Mary passed back into the kitchen her mother called, "But no more than that, please!"

Even before they reached the road, the rain-soaked beggars, two women and three children, were passing around the bread, heading toward the hills north and west of town where the cottiers lived in horrid squalor. After a moment of anguish, Brigid managed to convince herself one woman could not cure all of the world's ills; she blessed herself, said an Act of Contrition in Latin, then another in Irish, and returned to her husband's voice.

The politicos have deprived us of the opportunity to redeem ourselves, as peace has been declared; still, we were fortunate not to have been involved in that debacle at New Orleans. You are doubtless pleased your husband will not be shot at by any ill-mannered Jonathans, but I have lost another opportunity to gain my step. Since then your lowly lieutenant of a husband has been treated to a cruise through much of the Caribbean, finally settling at least temporarily here in Jamaica. Bermuda may be next.

Lieutenant and Mrs Lockwood

Speaking of being a lowly lieutenant, the Annual Army List is arrived, though as far as I am concerned they can quit printing the fool things if they cannot convey any better news. There is almost no movement since the wars ended, and yes, my dear, I know it is evil to hope for a war, but there are still nine ahead of me on the lieutenant's list with little hope of moving up this side of eternity. But it may be down to eight: Tom is in receipt of a letter from Mason, who says Stone is very ill and is despaired of. (I am sure that you would scold me for saying such a thing, but he is widely loathed for his conduct at Badajoz; another fellow who needs to be called to account, in this life or the next.)

Doolan is with child to get this letter in the mail bag before it is carried off for the packet that sails on this tide, but I have ordered him to stand over the bag with bayonet fixed while I finish. I must ask, my dear, if you have reconsidered your thoughts regarding the girls going to Malahides School in the fall. It will be difficult for all of us (yes, dear, me as well), but if the girls are to get ahead in this world they must be prepared as best as we can afford. And yes, I promise to write to my father to ask if the monthly allowance might be increased; perhaps age has softened his earlier resolution.

I have already written out the quarter-sheets for each of the children, so I enclose them now, with my dearest love. I miss you, dear Brigid. I live for the day ahead when we shall once again share the same roof.

All that truly matters to me is that I shall someday return home to you.

With great hurry and greater love,
James Lockwood

30

James loved her habit of biting the right side of her lower lip as she read. A strand of fine dark hair fell astray against her cheek, and she frowned a bit as she read the end of the letter. She had hoped James was not going to insist on Mary and Cissy (whose given name was Bridget, but known as Cissy since birth) going away to school. James and Brigid disagreed on few things, and both of them always phrased their views in the kindest of terms, but both were of decidedly firm opinions on this matter.

When she was a girl, Brigid had been educated at Miss McCarthy's School in Cork, just a few miles up the road. She had come home every weekend and holiday, and she had received quite a good education. James might have countered that Brigid's handwriting was not all that it could have been, or that her letters were written with only a perfunctory nod toward punctuation, but after seventeen years of marriage he had grown sufficiently wise to keep such comments to himself. James had grown up in Malahide, near Dublin, but had gone to school in England. He had received the education due a gentleman, but even he had to confess that some days in faraway Surrey were difficult for a tall, shy boy with an Irish accent.

There was, however, another reason Brigid hesitated to send her girls to Malahides School. Most of the Lockwood family lived near the school, and they had promised to look after the girls.

"Be damned to that," she whispered.

While she knew having closer connections with James's family would give the girls opportunities she could never offer them, Brigid was determined not to lose her children to that world of rank, wealth, and spite. To keep her family whole in the presence of such opportunity was a game that Brigid had played with the Lockwoods ever since she and James had married in the year of the Rebellion. She would continue do her best to play the role required of her, for

James and for her children, but she would not allow society to break Brigid O'Brian.

"Missus, *a grah*," called Mrs. Cashman from the hall, "the rain is gone, and the children were asking if I might be taking them down to town to post their letter to himself, and then to see the kittens at Hurley's farm."

"That is a fine idea," answered Brigid, "and please give Mrs. Hurley my blessing. She must be due any day now."

"You're in the right of it, I'm sure. Eight little boys, and Liam Hurley as ugly a man as ever walked. That Mary Hurley is a saint, and it's no mistake. But she's carrying this baby high, so God may bless her with a daughter at long last."

James's letter had given the children his address in Jamaica, and the letter they had written together could now be posted to their father with a reasonable hope of it reaching him before the end of the decade.

The children took special interest in posting their letters, as they had recently decided they should help with household expenses by earning the cost of postage. They were thus learning about the value of money, as well as some of the inequities normally experienced in its accumulation. The older children were annoyed that Lucy had earned a penny for making a curtsy to Mrs. Cashman, while the boys were enraged that Mary and Cissy had each earned a penny by playing with Mrs. Butler's mean, hopelessly nervous cat. Together Richard and Joseph had earned a groat by mucking out the Reverend Butler's stalls, a Herculean task when one reflected upon that Anglican worthy's unique notions as to what constituted a proper diet for his four Belgians.

If postage taught the Lockwood children lessons about money, they also learned something about rank. A letter to their father, an officer in His Majesty's army, cost 6d. to post, though a letter to a private soldier cost only 1d. postage. When writing to their father the children typically also spent the penny to post a letter to their old friend Private Diarmuid Doolan, though their father would have to read the letter to

Doolan, as his familiarity with the written word was roughly equivalent to Lucy's.

Brigid watched Mrs. Cashman lead the children down the lane toward town, doubtless filling their heads with tales of Oisín, Niamh, and Tir na nÓg. Sergeant, who was not above a clichéd dislike of both postmen and cats, was nonetheless allowed to join the company on this excursion, as he had long before come to terms with the implacable postmaster, and he had proven oddly tolerant of the Hurleys' wildly affectionate kittens. Mrs. Cashman, who had seen some of the more unpleasant aspects of life in Ireland, was also glad to have the company of a large, protective dog even on such a short trip. As soon as they began their walk, however, that four-legged bastion of security broke into a gallop down the hill, happily pursued by Mary, Cissy, and Joseph. Mrs. Cashman carried Lucy, and since Joseph wasn't watching, Richard took the opportunity to hold Mrs. Cashman's hand as they followed.

"Nana Kay?"

"Yes, *a chroí?*"

"Were you ever a mama?"

"Why, of course, silly Richie. Isn't it three of my fine sons who you see every Sunday at Saint Brigid's?" She grinned at him from the corners of her eyes, the same grin that had won her the heart of Kevin Cashman a lifetime before.

Richard gave her a puzzled frown, so Catherine explained, "Sure and you know Paul, David, and Stephen Cashman?"

"But they are the great men of the world!" answered Richard, astonished.

"My sons, grown to fine manhood, as one day your Mama shall see you grow to a great fine man, with the blessing."

"So, you had three babies?"

"*Wisha,* I carried six babies, *a grah.* Two went to Heaven early, so great was God's love for them. Four were allowed to grow to men; three you know. The fourth is my John, gone these many years."

"You don't you know where he is?" asked Richard, armed with the innocence of youth.

"He got into trouble, and rather than bring those troubles to his family's door he went away, and he has not returned to my sight these many years." Catherine Cashman typically avoided any circumstances that would test her hard-won resistance to tears, so she told Richard, "Oh, that black thief Sergeant is gone wholly wild; would you run now and call for him, Richard? He always listens to you."

Catherine Cashman had been with the Lockwoods for six years, after raising her four boys, then losing her fisherman husband to the sea. Paul, David, and Stephen lived nearby, working the sea, like their late father. She had four grandchildren, and a fifth was coming. But she had not seen or heard from John, her oldest, since 1798. He had been amongst the rebels who had battled the King's forces at the Battle of Shannonvale, and branded as a rebel, he had been forced to flee Clonakilty. For months after '98 the Crown had ruthlessly searched for escaped rebels; they had John Cashman's name, and threatened to arrest the other Cashman boys in his stead. But Government eventually slaked its thirst for vengeance on other men, and other families, and John Cashman quietly dropped from the thoughts of everyone in Clonakilty. Everyone, of course, except Catherine Cashman.

In quiet moments Catherine often thought of her missing son, though most of her day was dedicated to the Lockwoods, and she was well loved in return. She ensured they spoke fluent Irish, and on fine days she often led them off on marvelous adventures to nearby ruins and beaches and dells, though she knew better than to lead them past the wretched cottiers' homes in the hills above. Brigid wished she would speak English more often, and perhaps not fix potatoes with quite every meal. But in the end Catherine was part of the family, and the Lockwoods' lives were much the better for it.

If one could put aside the affairs of men, the Clonakilty through which Catherine Cashman led the Lockwood children was a place of surpassing beauty. The little town was nestled among the low green wooded hills of the County Cork, above glimmering Clonakilty Bay. The entrance to the bay was guarded by the steep cliffs of Dunowen Head to the west and Seven Heads to the east, and in front of the town sat low, sandy Inchydoney Island, home to ten thousand and one sea birds.

The harbor and hills had been home to the Irish for a thousand years or more, and many of the native Irish still called it by its ancient name: Cloch na Coilte, the "Stone of the Woods". Twenty miles to the northeast lay bustling Cork city, Corcaigh in the Irish, while five miles to the west lay the ancient stone circle of Drombeg, a strange, silent place that gave a perceptive mind a glimpse of the old world and its strange domain of nature and magic. Mrs. Cashman would sometimes arrange for old Hugh O'Flynn from the Bandon Arms to drive them out to picnic at Drombeg, where the children would play and Catherine and Brigid would take a few minutes to pray a rosary for the lost souls who dwelt there still. O'Flynn was a master piper, and he always brought his pipes along to serenade the Lockwoods. His were Irish pipes, challenging and piercing, which required the piper to sit like a civilized being, without the strident marching required of a Scottish piper. The warm life of his music was an odd contrast to the cold stones of Drombeg, stones that never warmed even in the brief Irish summer. Every trip to Drombeg ended with Hugh sitting alone at the far side of the circle, playing "Aisling Gheal," a warm, lovely tune, playing to the ghosts, *at* them being perhaps a better term, and at the end of his tune Hugh would lean forward and coarsely whisper, "Take that, ya bastards."

Fáibhile Cottage was a well-kept little house that lay on Scartagh Lane, a narrow road lined with dry stone walls and whispering old beech trees a little north of Clonakilty proper. Its slate roof marked it as the home of a gentleman, as thatched roofs were the province of the common folk. Turning left from their front gate took a determined walking man to Ballinascarthy in an hour's time, while a right turn lead back down into town, and then to the sea, the sea that had carried James off to war.

After reading her letter, Brigid sat alone in the silent house. Even as a child she had disliked being alone, and the house that so often echoed to the sounds of lively children now seemed uneasy. The tall case clock ticked away the gray minutes of late afternoon. But for now, at least, Brigid was relieved to be alone, as she stole the other letter from deep in her bag. She stared at it first with a look of fear, then of anger, and eventually, defiance. She would not open it, and though she glanced over at the fire she would not destroy it. Instead, she pulled the loose board from the back of the bookcase, and slid the unopened letter into the narrow little space that held all the other letters from Captain Charles Barr.

Chapter Four

Bermuda

Satan offered him a bargain: his own life for Lucy's. "Come, Lockwood, you do not even know the child; there is no disgrace in such an arrangement. Your feeble notions of honour are laughable."

It had taken James hours to fall asleep. It was perhaps unfair, then, that he was destined to wake from his reeling nightmare less than an hour later with a shout, sweating and breathless. From across the dark room Tom said sleepily, with only a touch of annoyance, "Are you all right, James? Is the Devil afoot again?" Tom was all too aware that the Devil often took centre stage in James's dreams.

James was tempted to answer truthfully, but instead he gathered himself and said only, "It is nothing. I am sorry, truly, Tom. All is well." James hated himself for having a mind that could devise such wickedness. He sat on the edge of his bed, trying to steady his heart and his hands, until he heard Tom's breathing settle.

He slipped out of bed, dressing quietly so as not to wake Tom again. He would be needed at the guardhouse at dawn to supervise the changing of the guard, so he decided to stop by the mess to have a quick glass of something to clear his mind and wake him properly. Walking down to the mess, he was surprised to see a lantern burning, as it should have been empty at that hour. Lieutenant Lockwood, however, had not considered the ubiquitous Private Diarmuid Doolan, who had laid out coffee, biscuit, and oranges.

"*Dia agus Mhaire duit*, God and Mary to you, now, Lieutenant dear," said Doolan. "A lovely country this is, with oranges to be had for the asking, and the same coffee as they serve in Heaven on Saint Patrick's Day."

"Thankee, Doolan, but I have no stomach for it this morning. I'm needed at the guard house. I'll just have a quick dram."

"Ah, I'll not be hearing that, sir, if you please, after the great trouble I went to at this unholy hour. Sure and it was dark as the Devil's arse out here, and me stumbling about to get your breakfast, to have it thrown in my face. You'll not be having a glass of gin for breakfast today, please. Can I not see you wasting away like a Burrens wraith? If your poor mother that's dead was to see you now, sure and she'd call me a damned poor excuse of a man, after me promising Mrs. Lockwood, your own wife she is, a solemn vow to a good Catholic woman, now, God bless and keep her, that I'd watch over you..."

Rather than suffer any further under this barrage of righteousness, James sat down and ate his breakfast, his stomach warming to the challenge, the oranges indeed being a great luxury.

Doolan disappeared muttering out the back and brought back the pot to refill James's cup. "Did you know, sir," he said in a harsh half-whisper that could be heard in Carrickfergus, "that there be *slaves* here? Me being at work long before you woke, I went back to the cookhouse, so as to brew your coffee, me being so dutiful, and it being so dark, and with my great brogans not as dancing spry as they once were, I tripped over three women, three! sleeping on the hard kitchen floor. Old creatures, mind you, now, sir, so you need not question my moral intent, and black as ink, all three, though sure that's not their fault, and helpful dears, God bless them, as truth be told in the end it was they themselves which brewed your coffee. Once they got past their fear of me, me being such a fine martial figure of a man, we got to chatting, and they're slaves, sir! Born in Africa itself, sold like cattle, worked like dogs, torn from their children and their husbands."

"Oh, what stuff, Doolan. Slavery was outlawed years ago, '07, I think. Someone is making game of you."

"There is no more law here than in Ireland, sir. The rich rule, and all an honest man can say is it's a hard world, Lieutenant *a grah*, from top to bottom. Top to feckin' bottom..."

The instant, full-light dawn of the Caribbean surprised James, who was accustomed to a gradual, filtered gray start to his day. The combined effects of the sunlight and coffee did their work, and it was a fully awake Lieutenant Lockwood who strode down the hill to Fort St. Catherine. But despite the glory of the day, his mind was still full of an irrational mix of what he had said the night before, what Barr had said, and the thousands of possible outcomes of their twisted relationship.

James was thus taken aback when he arrived at the guardhouse and found his men drawn up in razor-sharp ranks. Soldiers coming off guard were typically tired, disheveled, and ill-tempered after their time on duty, but this group was as crisp and soldier-like as any infantry officer could ask. Full dress: shako cords, plates, red-over-white tufts, McCurdy with his pike, Cassidy had even washed his face and hands. The formation was straight, still, and silent, eyes front, no grins or greetings. This was a soldierly salute of the first order, and for a moment James was confused as to what this was all about. But then he noticed Lancelot

Loughlin standing ramrod straight, his eyes locked but gleaming. It required a conscious effort for James to pull himself straight and formally inspect the retiring guard, stoically accepting the soldierly compliment.

It was well known in the company that Private Patrick Ryan had shamed himself and his comrades by selling his brass belt plate in Montreal to buy liquor, but somehow during the night he had managed to acquire another, now gleaming on his chest in the sharp morning light as Lieutenant Lockwood walked slowly past. James reached the end of the formation, and received the brief formal report of Sergeant McCurdy.

"Very well," replied James, "prepare to retire the guard." No more was said; all of these men were experienced soldiers, and they knew what a turn-out of this nature was meant to convey.

James marched the guard back up the hill to the barracks parade ground and dismissed them. The effects of the coffee were wearing thin; sleeplessness and worry clouded his mind as he walked over to have a word with McCurdy, but he was sidetracked by Quartermaster Sergeant John Kennedy, who said, "The Colonel's compliments sir, and, he'd like a word when you are at ease."

The invitation was politely offered, but knowing Colonel Pritchard as he did, James knew he was expected to report immediately. His first thought was that Pritchard had heard of his confrontation with Barr at the gate, and was asking questions. As he walked to the headquarters building, James fretted over what else the colonel could want. He prayed Barr had not gone to the colonel.

James was shown into the colonel's office and made his salute, but Pritchard only asked, "Lieutenant Lockwood, Drummer Quinn was in your custody yesterday. How did he comport himself?"

"Sober, well behaved, and penitent, sir. It was evidently his birthday."

"Damn all birthdays. In a battalion of nearly a thousand men I can expect that excuse at least twice a day. No, unless I can be convinced otherwise, Quinn is very much going to wish he was at Tara. Pity. But enough of that. I have been meaning to ask, James, how is our young Richard coming along, eh? How old is he now?"

"Thank you, sir, at last report he was coming along fine. He is seven this year, but I confess he is so fond of the sea that he is thinking of a career in the navy." The potential sailor being discussed was Richard Pritchard Lockwood, Lieutenant Lockwood's second son. Colonel Pritchard had never married, and young Richard was his only namesake.

Pritchard paused for a long moment, looking out the window, his eyes oddly unfocused. James, anxious to be on his way, stood watching. The colonel had once been an imposing figure, but now his belly hung over his painfully thin legs, and his sparse white hair barely covered his splotched scalp. Pritchard eventually gathered himself and said, "As interested as I am in your son, Lockwood, there is another reason I wished to speak with you. I intend to assign you extra duty."

"I hope I haven't displeased you, sir," replied James, assuming the worst.

"Oh, no, nothing like that. Byrne is fallen ill, quite ill; the surgeons have ordered him to bed for a fortnight at least. Dr. Howard is fascinated, and is hoping for a chance to open him up, the ghoul. Major Archibald and Sergeant Kennedy will handle most of Byrne's duties, but I will rely on you to assume one important task. As you well know, the adjutant is responsible for training new officers, and we are in possession of a new ensign, fresh from the womb. You are hereby appointed dry-nurse to the infant Ensign—oh, damn it, what's the boy's name... here it is—Blakeley... John Blakeley."

"It will be my pleasure, sir," answered James with hardly a flinch. James had long had a reputation for being a good

41

training officer, for both the men and young officers, though he had trained so many of His Majesty's soldiers that the duty had lost much of its charm. "I had the opportunity to speak with that young gentleman yesterday. May I ask, sir, if said infant will be assigned to my company?"

"Yes," said Pritchard, "he is your boy, and of course you will keep Coakley." Pritchard muttered, "God knows we must keep the boy clear of Captain Barr." Then, more clearly, he went on, "I have asked Blakeley to wait for you in the officers' mess; Kennedy has his particulars. He seems a decent enough young man, though we must not let him be seen in public until we can do something about his God damned coat. He looks like a tot who got into his father's trunk, and is playing dress-up. These ensigns get younger every year. Though perhaps it is simply me, getting older. I have never thought of myself as old, you know, but lately age seems to be in my mind constantly. Pray give Richard Pritchard my regards, won't you, Lockwood? You'll not forget?"

Lieutenant Lockwood was in no hurry to meet his new charge. A great deal had happened in a short time, and he took a few minutes to sit on a low stone wall that was out of sight of the headquarters building. The anxiety of his meeting with the colonel was gone, replaced now by weariness. James had always been a man who needed his sleep, and he promised himself to take a nap at the first opportunity. Despite his weariness, the back of his mind continued to churn with thoughts of Charles Barr. While their enmity had never been a secret, the open rift the night before had fully exposed his men to the issue, and it would be through the entire battalion before long.

In a thoroughly bad humour, James wearily got to his feet and headed off to meet his new pupil.

While Ensign John Blakeley was expecting to meet Lieutenant Lockwood in the mess, it was soon obvious he did not realize the gravity of the occasion. When the lieutenant came striding through the mess door, Blakeley leapt to his feet, propelling a large black rabbit from his lap, the rabbit landing in an ungraceful tangle, claws scratching at the hard tile floor as he righted himself and dashed for cover under a bench. "Good morning, sir!" screeched the disconcerted Blakeley, striking an impressive range of octaves in those three words.

James felt his temper surging, consciously holding it back, but this boy might get hell for breakfast, oh yes, he just might. "Good morning, Ensign Blakeley." A long pause, for maximum effect. "Pray, Ensign, what was that creature in your lap? Yes, that one, the quadruped that is currently engaged in soiling the floor of His Majesty's mess."

"Begging the lieutenant's pardon, sir, but he is not a quadruped. That is a rabbit."

James looked sharply at Blakeley, wondering if for a moment this boy would dare make game of him. Likely not. Certainly not. "Why, Ensign, would you presume to bring a rabbit, a *rabbit*, for Christ's sake, into the officers' mess?" James had long before learned to utilize his imposing size and a grim visage to advantage whenever he interrogated felons, lunatics, and teenaged boys. While such tactics rendered him a formidable opponent to those notorious disturbers of the peace, in this case they were rather too much for a small boy who had left home and a doting mother just a month before.

Blakeley's lip quivered, and his voice broke again. "He is my pet, sir. When my ship landed the other day, the old black woman at the quay said he would be a true friend to me. But Ensign Elphinstone said he'd make a wallet of him, so I daren't leave him in the barracks. Please, sir, I didn't know what to do." This was accompanied by hitching breath and a couple of very unmilitary tears, hastily wiped away.

"Ah," said James. "A pet, is he?" Another pause, but not for effect this time, as the lieutenant was somewhat at a loss, stumbling across a corner of his mind that held the memory of a very young, very similar, Ensign Lockwood. Without a conscious thought the black fury faded. "Well, come now, that is a perfectly acceptable explanation. Yes. Quite. But let us not have him in the mess, as some thoughtless brute might toss him into a pot. Further, you will please explain to Ensign Elphinstone he is not to make a wallet of the rabbit. The same instructions apply to all of your brother ensigns. You will please explain to those young gentlemen that I expect to see the rabbit at every inspection of your quarters, and that the rabbit is to be kept in top condition, per the high standards of the Inniskilling Regiment, and their long-held respect for, ah, mascots, and such. One cannot ask fairer than that. When next you encounter those gentlemen, you may also care to mention the date of your commission." James roughly rubbed his face with the open palms of both hands. "Now sit down, son, and tell me how you come to join our noble band."

James got them each a mug of small beer from the communal keg. He was pleased to see that Blakeley managed to gather his wits quickly, and after a moment the new ensign began a cogent summary of his life to date.

"Well, sir, my father was a barrister in London, but he died so long ago I scarcely remember him. My mother moved us—I have four older sisters, sir—to our home in Sussex, and I grew up there. For a short while I attended the Duncan School for Boys, but I had some problems there, and I came to be tutored at home by Madame Seras. She was very kind to me, and she was very pleased with my progress in music, language, and literature."

Blakeley paused for a moment to take a drink from his mug, and from his gasping reaction James guessed the boy had never tasted beer before, at least not at that hour of the morning. Blakeley choked out, "That is very fine, sir, thank you."

"I fear that perhaps the beer has gone bad, Ensign. It is this heat, certainly. It seems to have turned you rather green. Please do not feel compelled to drink any more."

Blakeley's color eventually returned, and he continued, "Yes, sir. Thank you, sir. Well, sir, my Uncle Latimer, my mother's brother, who managed our finances and holdings and such, was not much pleased with me. He suggested I be sent to the army on my sixteenth birthday. My mother and sisters were shocked by the idea, but he insisted, and he made all the arrangements for my commission. There was an opening here with the 27th, and I was shipped out very quickly, though my family was very unhappy about it. My mother wept a great deal, and she is afraid I will never see her again. Do you think that true, sir, that I shall never see her again?" Blakeley had calmed down during his recitation, but the mention of his mother made him seem quite the lost boy once more.

"It is a hard service," answered James, "and one must do one's duty, and not be distracted by thoughts of home. But still, don't be downhearted, son. We are not at war, for now, at any odds, so with the blessing you shall see your mother eventually. We shall likely be in garrison for years, bored to death. That reminds me, though; as you are not likely run into your mother in the near future, I shall have Private Scully look at your coat. He was a tailor in Tyrone before he took the shilling. And speaking of your duty, have you been studying the Regulations? There is a great deal to learn, very quickly."

Blakeley flushed and answered, "Well, sir, I was rather ill all through the crossing, so I'm afraid I couldn't start my studies until I arrived here in Bermuda. I was frankly hoping to finish a novel, *Historie Armoureuse des Gaules*, before I started to read the Regulations, sir."

"A novel, sir? A novel, for all love? Ensign, you will bury that book at the bottom of your chest, and with it you will bury any romantic notions. You are a soldier. Romance will not save you; nor, more importantly, will it save your men, when you have a squadron of cuirassiers thundering down on you. Romance, indeed. You will put your nose in the Regulations every spare moment, until you have made yourself more a danger to the enemy than to your friends. Your novel days are over."

"Yes, sir," said the wide-eyed ensign.

"Further, I will have Sergeant McMullen draft you a copy of the Company Order Book, and you will please commit to memory the General, Garrison, Brigade, and Regimental orders. You will attend every roll call, spend every morning at drill, and every afternoon will be spent with Sergeant McCurdy, who will explain the handling of a firelock, and the Manual of Arms. You will not, however, attend the firing of a weapon until I am convinced you know which end is to be pointed at the enemy. You are now a soldier, Ensign Blakeley, an officer in His Majesty's service, and it's time you realize the magnitude of that responsibility."

*****

As a married man, Gerald McBride had mercifully been granted separate quarters, but the balance of the Inniskilling ensigns were banished to live in a single large room, known as the Rookery, far from where they might disturb their elders. The room had a tall, beamed ceiling and was furnished in heavy, uncomfortable furniture that had survived three generations of rambunctious ensigns. It was to that communal den of iniquity that John Blakeley returned, finding his brother ensigns devoted to various states of sloth. The only two young men not lying in repose were Ensigns Digby and Coakley, as Digby was sitting atop Coakley's head, threatening to retain that dignified pose until Coakley cared to retract his earlier comment regarding Digby's poetry. When Blakeley came in, Digby maintained his position atop Coakley but looked up to ask, "Blakeley, did you really go to speak with Lockwood with that fool rabbit under your arm? I'm surprised he didn't eat the bunny *a la tartar*, ears and all."

That comment brought a muffled guffaw from Coakley, but a grind of Digby's posterior changed it to a howl of pain, and finally a muffled but impenitent, "I was mistaken... there is such a word as emprize, and it does indeed rhyme with rise."

Honour satisfied, Digby rose and flopped onto his cot. Coakley sat up, rubbing the side of his head, and asked, "So, Blakeley, did the colonel decide to send you back to your mama? If so, you really must leave your bunny here, so Elphinstone can do something unnatural with it. Isn't that right, Elphinstone?" Ensign Elphinstone, deep in slumber after having eaten eight potatoes with his breakfast, was incapable of response.

"The colonel says I am to train under Lieutenant Lockwood, and Lieutenant Lockwood says you all are to leave Blackie alone. He is to be a mascot."

Digby sat bolt upright. "What! A bunny as our mascot! We'll be laughed out of the service!"

Pleased to have gotten a rise out of Digby, Blakeley added, "The lieutenant also said I should mention the date of my commission." Even an officer as inexperienced as John Blakeley realized that the King's commission was of vital importance to an officer. It was his tangible proof of his status as an officer and a gentleman, a material manifestation of his position, and his claim to honour. Blakeley's was a typical example, finely printed on heavy paper, even if its grandeur was cheapened a bit by the sections that had been hastily filled in, or indeed left entirely blank, by a busy War Office clerk.

Concerned by Blakeley's sudden self-confidence, Digby and Coakley scrambled to pull their prized commissions from their trunks, and a hurried review made Digby return to his cot with a sullen flop. "Damn!"

That was enough to finally waken Elphinstone, who thickly asked, "Damn it, what's wrong now? No pudding again today?"

"No," replied the deflated Digby, "Blakeley is senior."

Uncle Latimer must have had some powerful friends, for while he had forced Blakeley away from his comfortable existence in that feminine Sussex household, he had at least sent his nephew to the army with two years seniority under his belt. Such things had once been done routinely, but crackdowns by the Duke of York had made such favoritism rare.

The aspects of military life that puzzled Ensign Blakeley numbered well into four figures, but one in particular came to mind. Blakeley eventually grew confident enough to confess to his new brothers that he did not really understand all the fuss over seniority and promotion. Digby and Coakley, who were, unlike Elphinstone, not prone to more than the usual amounts of adolescent wickedness, pulled out the most recent copy of the Army List, and tried to explain things.

"Look here, boyo," began Digby. "You see, under First Battalion, 27th Regiment of Foot, the names of all of our officers. Here's me and Coakley, proud as peacocks, the pride of the British Army, destined for greatness, ensigns with seniority of July 23rd, 1813, and July 30th, 1813. Your commission shows that your date, you lucky sod, is April 22nd, 1813, so that makes you senior, see?"

"That's easy enough," answered Blakeley. He wanted to ask next if that seniority allowed him to order the others about, or at least if it kept people from sitting on his head, but he contented himself with asking, "But what about promotions and such? How does all of that work?"

"Well, old cock," said Coakley, "let's look at an example or two... here's our dour old Scot, Major Archibald."

"Yes!" said Blakeley, "Everyone calls him Major Archibald, but when we dropped our shillings into that silver pot he said he had been a captain for the past ten years."

"Shillings in the shilver shitpot from Shpain!" called Coakley.

"Shillings in the shilver shitpot from Shpain!" loudly echoed Digby and Elphinstone, waking the other ensigns, who added their voices to the chant.

Blakeley looked startled, and Digby explained, "Whenever anyone mentions... you know, the article... we all have to yell 'Shillings in the shilver shitpot from Shpain!' as loudly as possible."

"But whatever for?"

"Oh, no reason," said Digby, "we just do. The regiment, in fact the whole damned army, is loaded with traditions that make no damned sense, so we made up one of our own. At any rate, some general heard about Captain Archibald doing something brave in Spain, so Archibald was awarded a brevet rank... it's like he's an honorary major, see, and so we call him Major Archibald, but he's still a captain in the regiment."

"It's the same with Colonel Pritchard," Coakley said, "as in the regiment he's a major, but he has a brevet lieutenant colonelcy, and doesn't he love it, drilling us like Frederick's God damned Prussians, while Colonel Nelson is home on leave."

"So, then," asked Blakeley with a rational degree of dread, "being brave is the only way to get promoted?"

"If it were only that easy. Elliott and Mainwaring, and your new friend Lockwood, that lot, are mad brave, and what reward have they gotten? But you'll find that much of the army don't make much sense, most of the time."

Digby held up a finger to claim the floor and said, "I got to be Major Sparrow's runner when he went to call on the governor, and on the ride back he told me about Lockwood in the breach at Badajoz. That's where old Sparrow lost his arm, see, and a pack of Frenchies was closing in to finish him, when Lockwood dives into 'em, slashing left and right, roaring like a lion, and saves Sparrow. Bugger promotion, give me that kind of glory any day. Still, it's the shame of the army not to promote such men."

Blakeley sat wide-eyed at the thought of his lieutenant performing such feats, until he finally asked, "So, how do we get promoted?"

Promotion was of keen interest to every officer in His Majesty's service, the youthful Digby and Coakley included, and while typically willing to show off their detailed knowledge of the system, Coakley only said, "That, boyo, is a subject that can take hours, and young Digby and I have an appointment with a pair of buxom amazons down in town. So you just ask old Lockwood about it, but be sure to ask nice, or he may turn ugly on you."

*****

The next day was a sun-dappled treasure, but it was wasted on John Blakeley. He had been shaken awake before dawn by a very insistent Irish private, and he was too shy to inquire into even such mundane matters as to where he might piss. The day did not improve as it progressed.

"You will now ask me an intelligent question, Ensign." Lieutenant Lockwood could typically call Tuesday mornings his own, but his assignment to tutor Blakeley had put an end to that. "I am to act as your training officer, but your success or failure is up to you, sir. I will hear an intelligent question; I will not have my time wasted."

John Blakeley was not accustomed to such challenges, particularly so very early in the morning, particularly as they were delivered by a very large gentleman who looked to be on the verge of a very foul temper. The ensigns' berth of the Inniskilling Regiment could rarely merit any type of blessing, but Blakeley silently did so as he asked, "May I inquire, please, sir, how an officer might expect promotion?"

Lieutenant Lockwood, who had been musing upon the fact that the back of his head was doing its best to exit his skull through his ears, sometimes found that distracting his mind served to make painful mornings more bearable. Blakeley had happily struck upon a topic that rarely strayed far from Lieutenant Lockwood's mind, a topic that now engaged that gentleman's attention to their mutual benefit.

"Promotion. Yes, I think that a worthy subject for your first training session. It is the goal of every officer of any merit whatsoever. You may find a handful of dandies in the Guards who only serve for a year or two to dress up and play soldier, but the backbone of this army is made up of career officers. And career officers, sir, wish to progress in their careers, for a number of reasons." Then, ticking off the count on the fingers of his right hand, the Lieutenant winced, and went on, "First, the higher the rank the better the pay, though God knows if a man wants to get rich there are a thousand better ways. Second, if you go lame, get mangled, or grow ancient in His Majesty's service, a man can retire on his half-pay, and the amount of that half-pay is based, of course, on rank. And lastly, any officer of quality wishes to improve his martial skills and earn the respect of his brother officers. One would not want to see one's fellows go on to do great things while he is left behind."

"Yes, thank you, Lieutenant. I shall certainly seek promotion at every opportunity."

"Now," said James, warming to the work, his tone growing conversational, "as to how this miracle of promotion is to be attained. Most of the promotions in the British army are made through purchase, and a wealthy, well-connected man can rise in rank very quickly. Take Lowery Cole—you may not know of him—he is a great friend to the regiment, as his father is Lord Enniskillen. He enlisted in 1787, and by 1806 he was a brigadier. A general, Ensign. Money can carry you very far, very quickly. Years ago it was possible for a mere boy to command a regiment, but there are rules in place now requiring a level of experience before the next step is purchased. Still, rich men have a very great advantage."

Ensign Blakeley felt a response was expected, so he asked with a bit more confidence, "How much money is required, please, sir? When I turn eighteen I shall inherit a hundred pounds from my father's estate."

"That was good of him to think of you, but I am afraid you shall need to turn eighteen several times. Take me as an example: my lieutenancy is worth five hundred fifty pounds, while a captaincy costs one thousand, five hundred pounds. I trust your Madame Seras taught you enough arithmetic for you to realize a purchase of my next step would thus cost nine hundred fifty pounds, which you may understand is difficult to gather when a man earns five shillings eight pence a day, of which some four shillings twelve pence is deducted to pay his mess bill. And of course one is also responsible for such personal necessities as horses, uniforms, and weapons. Many regiments require their officers to have private means to supplement their pay, but I suppose one could categorize the 27th as an unfashionable regiment. Only a handful of our officers have any income beyond their pay, and few prospects beyond their military careers."

Lieutenant Lockwood had generously used himself as an example, but that example went only so far. He did not mention the awkward fact that he was the second son of an Ascendancy family, the powerful Anglican elites who essentially ruled Ireland. He received a small allowance from his family's holdings, but barring an extremely unlikely series of family deaths and changes of heart, James's only real inheritance was an Anglo-Irish burden of tradition, honour, and unacknowledged guilt. James's asthmatic and perpetually unhappy father had arranged for James to be granted his first commission, as an ensign in the Westmeath Militia. But despite the fact that the family estates were extensive and lucrative, his father had come to assure his son, with particular emphasis, that in light of certain choices made by James, he could expect very little financial aid from his family.

Ensign Blakeley looked somewhat deflated at the notion of paying for every step of his new career, so James went on, "There are, of course, options for officers of limited means, and I for one have made the most of them. I started as an ensign in the militia, and I made the jump to the line by convincing twenty-one men of my militiamen to volunteer into the line with me. There have been times when militiamen were 'persuaded' to join the line through some very harsh and disreputable means, but I believe the men who volunteered with me went willingly."

Again, the lieutenant did not bother with the full story: how Charles Barr had gained his line ensigncy in like manner, but had kept his men of the Westmeath Militia standing in formation for nineteen hours in a winter rain at attention until twenty-one gave in and submitted to volunteer, thus ensuring Barr's posting to the Inniskillings.

"Were the militiamen pleased to volunteer to serve His Majesty, sir?"

James smiled knowingly and said, "You were raised in England, Ensign, so perhaps you are unaware that there are very few Irishman who would give a groat for His Majesty, and there are quite a few who would be pleased to knock him on the head. No, it is more poverty than patriotism that brings Irishmen into the army. Again, your life in England would not familiarize you with the miserable conditions under which most of the common people of Ireland suffer. When a man is starving, army life might seem quite appealing, even if it is for a king of whom you may not be overly fond."

Lockwood's twenty-one volunteers. James had a list in his portmanteau of the names of each of them, and their fates. Most were no longer with the battalion; killed in battle, dead of disease, or returned to Ireland as "unfit for further service" because of illness, wounds, or age. James's soldier-servant, Diarmuid Doolan, was one of the twenty-one, and had remained with his officer for all those years.

"No, Ensign," said Lieutenant Lockwood in an odd voice, "poverty, raw need, is the primary motivation for most of our rankers, but especially for the Irish. When I was on recruiting duty in Ireland I'd see it over and over, where we'd recruit some scare-crow for life, and as we marched him off he'd hand his enlistment bounty to his ragged wife and children, twelve pounds to feed them... how long? Men go into the line because they need the enlistment bounty, a chance at a line soldier's pension, and the hope of regular rations." Lockwood took a long pull of small beer, and went on a more normal tone, "Still, I suppose there are other reasons to take the shilling. Since line regiments are likely to be posted overseas, some fellows volunteer to satisfy the dreams for adventure that fill the heads of so many men, young and old. Traveling the world as strong men, armed; there's some romance for you, Ensign," he added, not unkindly. Then with an open grin, Lockwood said, "And some men go to escape an unpleasant family situation; when I enlisted Private John Kerrigan, for instance, he was fleeing the brothers of an amazingly unattractive woman who he had got with child after unwisely downing eight pints of cider. You must remember, youngster, not to drink cider; lethal stuff. Goodness, what a row we had, getting him out of Omagh in one piece. Sergeant Murray had to knock one fellow on the head, and I recall throwing one cheeky fellow into a pond. Happy days."

Ensign Blakeley, who had been paying close attention, said, "Purchase, then, sir, and gaining one's commission through volunteers. Ensign Digby explained brevet rank; are those all I should remember?"

"One more for you to keep in mind: advancement through war." Blakeley watched the lieutenant's good humour wane. "When an officer is killed in action, all the men behind him in the regiment move up a spot; no interest, no purchase, no discussion. Thus, if a captain in the Second Battalion is so foolish as to step in front of a ball, all of the captains below him move up one spot, and the senior lieutenant of the First Battalion is now the junior captain in the Third. It is an indication of how many years of war this regiment has seen: I have been a lieutenant for eight years, and in that time I have moved from junior man in the Third Battalion to one of the senior men of the First. So many dead men; so many of them my friends." The lieutenant found it difficult to keep his eyes steady. In John Blakeley's heart, an unconscious decision was made that he should grow to love Lieutenant Lockwood. "That is enough for this morning, please, Ensign. Sergeant McMullen should have the copies of the orders written out fair for you; we shall discuss them tomorrow."

After serving His Majesty as a lieutenant for eight years, James Lockwood had become one of the battalion's senior lieutenants. But his chances of gaining his captaincy, and the long-awaited glory of being given his own company, were remote. For him, there would be no purchase: he used the allowance, the niggardly, penny-pinching allowance, from his family to support Brigid and the children. Lieutenant Lockwood's best chance for advancement was war, but now the wars were over, and the opportunity to advance through seniority was essentially gone. Peace, for all its charms, was not always welcomed by British infantry officers, James Lockwood included.

*****

The next day brought more of the activities that marked the battalion's return to a well-known and comfortable routine: the guard, a general parade, drill, and a review of the men's equipment. Six Company had their usual turn with the armourer, Sergeant Francisco D'Amato, a jovial, capable young man. The Inniskillings had lured the young man, an apprentice gunsmith, away from an abusive master in Palermo three years before. As the only Italian in an Irish regiment D'Amato might have had a rough time, but he was such a genuinely likeable young fellow that he was soon adopted without constraint. Serving in a veteran regiment made D'Amato's service less burdensome than it might have been, as most of the Inniskillings took good care of their weapons, and the experienced officers were wise to the tricks of the handful of slackers who might allow rust on their locks. D'Amato examined nearly a hundred muskets during the day he spent with Six Company, and other than replacing a few worn springs, he spent most of that time gossiping and trading stories. He brought over stories of some of the goings-on in the other companies, and he carried back to them the happenings in Six Company. The news about the growing animosity between Lieutenant Lockwood and Captain Barr was spreading.

*****

The April weather in Bermuda being what it is, in their free time many of the Inniskilling officers took strolls along the breezy ramparts and the narrow sandy paths that ringed the harbours of the eastern islands. James and Tom preferred the walks to evenings of Barr's pontifications.

Tom had noticed a rapid deterioration in the relationship between James and Barr. For years he had been curious to know what had sparked their long-standing enmity, but as a gentleman he could not question the conduct of another gentleman, even if that gentleman was his closest friend. James and Tom could chat and joke about thousands of mundane topics, so long as they did not delve into areas that might be viewed as insulting to a man's honour. Tom knew that James and Barr had had a bitter disagreement during their days in the Irish militia, but that part of James's past was not up for discussion unless James raised the topic. He never did so. But Tom could bring up a related subject, one that did not question James's conduct.

"I think," said Tom as they walked, choosing his words carefully, "Barr is losing his mind."

James said nothing for several steps, then without looking at Tom he quietly replied, "I am surprised to hear you say so."

"Are you indeed? I thought his conduct spoke for itself," said Tom, his words suddenly flowing unchecked. "If it continues I may have to speak to the colonel, if for no other reason than the safety of his men. I have never seen so many floggings in this regiment. Since Archibald is senior to him, I may go speak with him first; nonetheless, I am concerned about looking the coward. Are you telling me you don't find Barr's conduct to be well beyond the bounds of rational behavior?"

Tom had halted, and with that direct question James stopped as well. James made no response, and only looked at his friend with slightly raised eyebrows and a slight inclination of his head. "I am sorry, brother," said Tom hurriedly. "I am tied in knots over this; I did not wish to question."

"Never in life," replied James with a quick, pained smile, "never could there be any offence between us. All I can say is that I cannot in good conscience make any comments regarding the conduct of Captain Barr."

"Very well, then, I shall respect your decision. But your silence on the issue aside, all of the rest of us have voted, and we have resolved that we have been pushed beyond reason. Barr is to be sent to Coventry. There are a number of issues with his conduct, but the letters he sent to Colonel Cole and General Power have impugned the honour of the officers of this battalion, and he must be called to task. He will not be spoken to except as required by duty. As you do not choose to voice an opinion, you may of course choose your own way of dealing with that son of a bitch."

Tom rarely swore, doubtless the lingering effects of his religious upbringing, and James was shocked to hear him speak with such an edge. James considered his course, his own delicate course.

Grass grew only in scant patches, and gusts of wind kicked up stinging wisps of the loose sand as they walked on in silence. The silence was not awkward, as they had been friends, very close friends, far too long for that, but both of them knew James's replies had bordered upon rudeness. Putting his own concerns aside, James eventually came to comment in a conciliatory tone, "It just came to mind, that it is already April 16th. We must 'Beware the Ides of April', and all that, you know."

With a grin Tom replied, "I believe the usual cautionary tale refers to the 'Ides of March', brother. In either case, I feel compelled to mention that the ancients made it clear the Ides of a month was the 15th day. That, James, was yesterday. Indeed, if I were to flaunt my classical education I should add the word comes from the Latin *ides*, meaning "half division", which would be the 15th day in some months, perhaps the 14th in others, but certainly not the 16th."

"But I didn't think of it until today," continued James. "If you were somewhat less argumentative, pedantic being perhaps too strong a term, you might stretch the point, and allow the analogy to be made without this barrage of ridicule."

"Well, that is hardly fair. It is as if I should wish you a Happy Christmas on the 26th of December; it surely does not convey the meaning it might have conveyed the day before."

"Yes, I suppose I see what you mean," replied James, pausing, overtly reflective. "Rather like kissing one's sister."

"Precisely. The motion, the delivery, the essential mechanism, is present, but the feeling, alas, is quite different, the flame of emotion lacking." They both looked quite smug, eminently pleased with themselves. For years they had reveled in mock arguments, silly but lucid; while they would never say it aloud, their friendship was a key part of who they were as men.

As they were in no hurry to return to the barracks, and as they were each of an inquisitive nature, their feet carried them up the sandy road that edged the north side of Castle Harbour. They came upon the battery that overlooked the entrance to the harbour, where they were saluted by a sentry from the 99th Foot.

"Stand at ease, Private."

That soldier may have assumed the stiff, unnatural stance that passed as ease, but he was far from easy, thinking, "They both look like right bastards, and wouldn't that big one tear a bloke's head off for the sport of it, like."

The scene below them was picturesque, as the harbour was filled with merchantmen of every size and description. A Royal Navy ship of the line, HMS *Blenheim*, was anchored somewhat apart from the merchantmen, as if to emphasize the Navy's status as real seamen, not mere shopkeepers. The two-decker had her gun ports open to allow the fresh breeze to air the gun deck, while most of the crew was aloft, performing a spectacularly complicated renewal of their rigging.

At the far end of the battery, they found Ensign Digby leaning against a massive twenty-four pound gun. That gentleman was intently studying the warship's activity through a brass telescope; so concentrated was his study that he jumped a foot when James came up behind him and wished him good evening.

"Good evening, Lieutenant Lockwood. Good evening, Lieutenant Mainwaring." replied Digby. "I was just watching the Blenheims swaying up their new spars, and right lubbers they are, sirs."

"I had forgotten," replied James, "you served some time in the Royal Navy, did you not, Digby?"

"Oh, yes, sir. My grandfather had me on the books for years, though I was afloat as a midshipman for just six months. I was just a little squeaker, sir, and when I got knocked about in an action with a French privateer my mother made me quit the navy, and join the army, as a less hazardous pursuit."

Tom and James laughed aloud, amused with Mrs. Digby's notions of army life. Tom asked, "You have been with us now for, what, nearly two years, Digby? With the battalion going on garrison duty, life should be as dull and safe as a mother could wish. I trust you have been writing to her, and—"

He was cut off by the sharp report of a gun firing from off the point, and a gun from Castle Island sounding in return. Various signals were hoisted from the castle, and Digby swung his glass to Castle Roads, saying, "Begging your pardon, sirs, but that was the private signal." He scanned the sea for a moment, and then added, "There's a brig-sloop coming into the harbour, and she's in a mighty hurry." He turned to James and Tom, and reluctantly offered his glass, "Would you care to see, sirs? It's an old glass, but it's clear."

"No, youngster, you have the sharp eyes," answered Tom. "Just tell us what you see."

Digby's excitement grew as he watched the brig draw closer. James could see that the crew of the *Blenheim* was also intently studying the new arrival. "Oh! Sirs!" cried Digby. "God's my life, it's the *Scout*! I was aboard her for dinner at Gibraltar once. Eighteen guns, and a right flyer, sirs. Her signals show she is carrying dispatches, and they are in one hellfire hurry! She's carrying more canvas than she ought to, in this breeze. Topsails, sirs, topsails!"

Soon James could see the *Scout*, all billowing canvas and spray. She threw a great bow-wave as she bore past Paget Island and the entrance to the harbor.

"Lord!" cried Digby, forgetting military propriety, "they are going to try to weather Gurnet Rock on this tack!"

There was great tension as hundreds of eyes across the harbor watched the *Scout* near the point, then triumphantly tear past the rocks within biscuit-toss of her destruction. The Blenheims cheered her, as did Digby and every sailor in the harbor. James and Tom, while impressed with the brig's nerve, could not understand what would bring her to risk such an entrance.

"She's hoisting signals, sirs!" cried Digby, the glass glued to his eye. "Urgent dispatches... yes, we know that, you buggers," muttered the impatient ensign. A gun fired from her windward side reinforced the urgency of the brig's next hoist. "She's hoisting the next signal alphabetically... B... O... N... A... P..."

"Bonaparte," said James. "Christ, it's Bonaparte again."

Chapter Five

Clonakilty

There were instances when an impartial observer might have concluded that, prior to her domestic career, Brigid Lockwood had served as an infantry colour sergeant. Her efforts to prepare her children for Sunday Mass were a case in point: "Joseph, if you continue to torture your sister, you will certainly not go sailing with the O'Learys this afternoon. And Mary, it is no wonder your brother pesters you, when I witness that very unladylike tendency to stick out your tongue. Cissy, that porridge is to go into Lucy's mouth, *le te thoil, a grah*, not onto her pinafore. It is the only piece of clothing remaining to her fit to be seen at St. Brigid's. Oh, Sergeant, you must stop licking yourself in that unseemly manner; there are ladies present. And Richard Lockwood, if you do not return that frog to the pond this minute I shall run stark raving mad."

In the end, Brigid got her children out the door and marching toward town without losing her mind, despite Richard's surreptitious concealment of the frog in his pocket. They were handsome people, and as they walked down Scartagh Lane in their best clothes, the six of them made a pleasant sight. Joseph and Richard, possessed by the blind optimism found only in the minds of young boys, led the way, quietly devising the Machiavellian strategy that would convince their mother they really did deserve their own horse. Brigid carried Lucy, periodically kissing her daughter's forehead, checking for a return of the fevers that haunted her. James had never held this, his youngest child, conceived just before he left for Spain. In a private way, Brigid considered Lucy to be her very own.

The older girls walked beside their mother, explaining in great detail the convoluted relationships that dominated the lives of the young ladies who attended Madame de Berruyer's School for Young Ladies. Madame de Berruyer was unique in Clonakilty, a penniless émigré who had fled Calais during the Revolution, the same Revolution that had claimed the lives of most of her immediate family. An odd series of events had carried her to the south of Ireland, and lacking youth, beauty, money, and wit, she had resorted to teaching young ladies the only two assets remaining to her: the French language and a languid sense of entitlement.

"Oh, Mama, that Elizabeth Innis is certainly the most evil creature that God has ever placed upon the earth," said Mary with unrestrained passion.

"Come, my dear, that is a bit harsh, surely?" offered their mother, who always struggled to hide how desperately she wanted her girls to fit in.

"When Mary did well in her French exercise, so much better than that know-all Elizabeth," cried Cissy, "she said Mary had an unfair advantage, as everyone knows that France is a Catholic country, and other Catholics can learn their nasty old language whenever they please. Oh, you should have heard her say *Catholic*, Mama, you would have thought she was saying *manure*."

Mary could not wait to add, "Elsie Fitter laughed that horrendous laugh of hers, and then so did the other girls, and Madame de Berruyer wasn't cross with them at all, and then she laughed as well!"

Mary and Cissy were both good, kindhearted creatures, but they were young women, and as such they had mastered at least the basics of manipulation. They had waited all morning to get their mother all to themselves, and they intended to make the most of it. Elizabeth Innis was the youngest daughter of Henry Innis, the Earl of Bandon, the wealthiest and most powerful man in Clonakilty and, indeed, the whole of West Cork. The Earl and his family constituted the pinnacle of local society, bastions of the Protestant Ascendancy, and the family of Lieutenant James Lockwood operated only at the fringes of their lofty concerns. Bandon was a diehard Tory, long opposed to any reform that would even marginally empower the Catholic majority. There were few people in Clonakilty and its environs deemed worthy to mingle with the Innis family, and while every one of those people had to be careful to avoid their wrath, the Lockwoods had to be especially cautious.

"I am acquainted with Madame de Berruyer," said Brigid, "and I must agree she is a lady of... unusual character, though as gentlewomen we must make allowance for a degree of eccentricity. As much as I wish she would stand up for you, knowing her past, and her current situation, I suspect she will always side with the aristocratic families."

"Oh! It is so unfair!" said Cissy. "Madame is always harping about the Three Estates, and the Divine Right of Kings, and of course that Elizabeth Innis just sits there so smug, expecting all of the rest of us to bow to her."

Mary couldn't wait for her sister to finish so she could add, "The other girls all go to church with Elizabeth, and their fathers go fox hunting with Lord Bandon, so we are always the butt of their jokes!"

"I am so sorry, my dears," said Brigid. "There are instances, I know, when Madame and some of your classmates might not be as agreeable as we would wish. All I can ask is that you bear it, and make your way as best you can." Then, after a slight pause, she said in Irish, "It is the world that is full of those who would judge you. You must do all you can to placate some, and to others you must give the back of your hand. But you can always—always, mind you—trust those who love you."

"If only Father were here!" said Mary, exasperated, immediately regretting her words. There was an unspoken rule in the family never to complain about their father's absence, and to hear Mary do so shamed Cissy into a hollow, wholly false end to their story.

"But we did get even with Elizabeth, Mama," said Cissy lamely, with a significant look at her sister. "Just before we left for home we tailed her."

Brigid sniffed a little laugh and replied, "You tailed her, dear? Whatever is that?"

"You see, while she was reading that horrid Jane West book... self-righteous claptrap... we tied a long hairy piece of red yarn to the bow at the back of her dress, and she walked all the way home wagging her tail. All the girls thought it was the funniest thing."

On any other day Brigid might have detected the faint note of falsehood in Cissy's voice, but she was eager to hear a happy ending to the story. The family continued their walk toward St. Brigid's, Richard looking back once, wondering why his mother was holding Lucy up close to her face and secretly wiping her eye with the corner of the little girl's blanket. Brigid did not hear the whole story, as unpleasant as it really was, and now her daughters would never tell her, never in this life.

Clonakilty was like every other town in Ireland in seeing more rainy days than not, but a surprising number of Sunday mornings were dry, and that April Sunday morning was a sparkling glory. The Lockwoods' route lead them down McCurtain's Hill onto George Street, then a right turn up Sovereign Street to St. Brigid's. Sovereign Street was narrow as it passed through town, though the sun was high enough to shine on the shops that lined the north side of the street. It was on that side of the street the Lockwoods traveled, enjoying the steady sunshine. All the shops were closed, of course, and most of the other people on the street were also headed to St. Brigid's. As a general rule, Clonakilty Sundays were marked by carriages bound for Kilgarriffe Anglican Church and by pedestrians bound for St. Brigid's. The only exception was the tiny handful of adherents heading to the new Methodist Church, who were quietly regarded as flaming radicals by both the Anglicans and the Catholics. Some very nontraditional music had been heard coming from their church, and rumors of some unusual practices had been floating around Clonakilty. It was said some Methodists waved their arms during services, which was, in Clonakilty at least, akin to reading goat entrails.

The eminently traditional Father McGlynn was standing at the door of Saint Brigid's, greeting his flock, his square figure instantly recognizable. Saint Brigid's was a small, plain cruciform chapel that lacked the stained glass and ornate pews of the Anglican church, but despite its austere appearance God dwelt there as well, in perfect comfort. The roof was thatch, and the recent repairs by the Hurley men had done away with the worst of the leaks. The walls were rough and the floor was dirt, worn to a dull sheen by countless feet and knees. A fine Persian rug that had been salvaged from a wrecked ship at Dunowen Head graced the floor at the altar, but the faithful knelt on the hard dirt, like true penitents.

Father McGlynn smiled broadly as the Lockwoods reached St. Brigid's. While the Father followed Church doctrine and would never advocate open opposition to British rule, he did stick a thumb in the eye of convention by speaking Irish at every opportunity. "God and Mary be with you, Brigid *ni* Brian *a grah.*"

Brigid, who had known the good father since she was a girl, always took comfort in his kindness, and his understanding. Father McGlynn, too, knew some of the details of the marriage of James Lockwood and Brigid Marie O'Brian. "God, Mary, and Patrick be with you, Father McGlynn *a grah*."

The boys made their bows, the girls made their curtsies, and Father McGlynn blessed Lucy, who promptly buried her face in her mother's shoulder. "Brigid," said the priest, "I'll be telling you we are once again collecting a fund for the poor. You'll know of course the potato crop is nearly failed again this year, and I hope we may rely upon your generosity once more?"

"Of course, Father, it shall be our pleasure to help," Brigid added without flinching, knowing she would likely to be short again that month.

Brigid was all too familiar with the poor. Her branch of the O'Brians was one of the few middle-class Catholic families in the area, struggling to make their way in the shadow of the Ascendancy families. Early in her life Brigid had been instilled with a deep-seated fear of poverty, as starvation was a specter that haunted the rough cabins and filthy hovels that lay just miles from Fáibhile Cottage.

The Lockwoods filed in and sat on the same rough pew they had known for years, though only after Brigid had to hiss at the boys, who had displayed a marked lack of reverence for the Holy Water. The Latin Mass was the same Mass said all across Christendom, but St. Brigid's was blessed with a small but very skilled choir. Father McGlynn was a great scholar of ancient Christian music, and he had trained his small choir to near perfection. Their *Pater Noster*, for example, was a joy to those who reveled in the magic of such music. Brigid was one such person, and so was James; it was a shared love of choral music that had first brought them together. When the choir sang *Media Vita* she closed her eyes and imagined James was there beside her, floating with her on the deeply evocative waves of song.

The Lockwoods were one of the premier families at St. Brigid's. Many of the parishioners viewed them as unspeakably rich and powerful; the Lockwoods, after all, rubbed elbows with the Innis family, the landlords of nearly every Catholic family for thirty miles around. While many Catholic families had a son, brother, or husband in the British army, those were all enlisted men; only the Lockwoods could boast of an officer, even if he was only a Protestant. Further, Brigid had been born an O'Brian, one of the most respected Catholic families in all Munster, and she had many good friends and relatives amongst the McCarthys and O'Learys, other families of ancient lineage.

There were, however, some St. Brigid parishioners who were jealous of Brigid and her family. There was also a bitter handful who hated them.

Some of those were found among a pack of old widow women who watched the Lockwoods walking home after Mass. Helen McNamara, who had lost her husband and her only son to the British during the '98, bitterly pointed out Brigid to her clucking cronies. "Ah, sure, the pretty trollop, the shame of the O'Brians, who caught herself a Proddy gentlemen, she did. Her, with her fancy clothes, her ill-bred children, and her haughty ways, when decent folk, her own kind once afore, go hungry, forced from their land while she lives like the feckin' Queen of Sheba."

"And not just any Proddy gentleman," added the aged Maggie O'Conner, "but a bloody-handed Redcoat officer, the Devil take his soul. And wasn't it him, sure, with his Westmeath Militia who butchered our men at Shannonvale? And wasn't it that Proddy bastard Lockwood himself who put his sword through my young Eamon's neck, and him gone to die? And yet here on our own streets walk Lockwood's whore and her pups, proud and mighty, while the best of us lie cold in the ground."

Such conversations had been murmured off and on by Clonakilty's disaffected for more than fifteen years, and if Brigid could not hear what the old women were saying, she could guess. Whenever she went into town there seemed always to be old widows in the background, staring, their black shawls drawn over their heads, their dark eyes following her wherever she walked.

The Lockwoods walked home with a purpose, as the children were anxious to change out of their church clothes and spend the rest of the sunny day outdoors. They were nearing Scartagh Lane when the Earl of Bandon's coach-and-four came clattering up alongside them. The earl lowered a window and called out, "Good day, Mrs. Lockwood!"

Brigid made her curtsy, and answered, "Good day, My Lord." The Earl's florid, vinous face filled the coach window, though Brigid could see two other men in the coach as well, all of them dressed for a hunt. One of the hunters peered luridly over Bandon's shoulder down at Brigid, and muttered, "What a remarkably fine woman," to his companion, loudly enough for Brigid to hear. She blushed and made as if to continue home, when Bandon asked, "I say, Mrs. Lockwood, I wager our hero Lieutenant Lockwood shall be leading the fight against that scoundrel Bonaparte, eh? eh?"

Brigid was increasingly certain the Earl and his companions were drunk, perhaps very drunk, and she was not happy about speaking with them. "Perhaps you are confused, My Lord?" she asked, "I believe Bonaparte was defeated some time ago."

There was some harsh laughter inside the coach, one of the men mimicking a woman's voice, "Oh, you are confused, My Lord!"

Bandon flushed with annoyance, and said, "Certainly not, madam. You may wish to consult the newspapers. Bonaparte has returned to France, armies are being assembled, and the nation is again at war. Good day, madam." To his coachman he called, "Drive on, Jenkins!" As the coach moved off, Bandon slammed the window shut and huffed to his companions, "God's my life, I am insulted wherever I turn."

One of Innis's friends turned completely around in his seat to watch Brigid through the coach's small rear window, and said, "By God, Innis, that woman can insult me any time she may choose. Does that mob of children truly belong to her?"

Brigid was not immediately concerned that she was being leered at in such a fashion, or that she had just annoyed the most powerful aristocrat in southern Ireland; she was thinking of James, and the possibility that the Inniskillings would once again be sent to fight the French.

Mary and Cissy, quite terrified that Bandon would wish to address them, had stayed well back from the coach, but Joseph had come close enough to hear about Bonaparte's return. "Mama," he asked, "will Father have to go fight the French again? I thought Napoleon had been exulted."

"Exiled, my dear, exiled," answered his mother. "He was, but it seems he has escaped, the black thief. I am going back into town to find a newspaper. Mrs. Cashman will be at her sister's, so I will rely on you girls to see everyone home and get them something to eat. Mrs. Cashman baked us some nice bread, and there is enough cheese left, I think."

"But Mama," asked Cissy, "Father is in Jamaica. Surely he won't have to come all the way back to fight again. Surely he will stay there, away from the French?"

"I hope so, my dear. Now off you go, please. I shall bring a newspaper home if ever I may find one on a Sunday."

As expected, Brigid found all the shops still closed, and no one she met on the street had heard anything about Bonaparte. She grew increasingly anxious and frustrated, until she finally thought to go see Reverend and Mrs. Butler, who should be home after their services. Youghals Hall was a mile south of town, though Brigid covered the distance with the ease of a woman who had never owned a carriage. She found quite a crowd gathered there, all speaking at once about Bonaparte and war.

Brigid, as the wife of a serving officer, suddenly had a special status amongst the elites of Clonakilty. Several nearly frantic women, women who would normally not have bothered with her, whisked her inside and treated her like their closest friend. She was welcomed to the drawing room with great fanfare, and Lady Bandon herself, a tall, aging, moderately elegant woman whose face was remarkable only in its complete lack of kindness, now had patriotic tears in her eyes as she greeted the wife of a *bona fide* British hero. Brigid, who was growing increasingly uncomfortable, was granted pride of place on the settee beside Lady Bandon, who held Brigid's hand while Reverend Butler read aloud from the London papers. A number of other ladies drew chairs up as close as possible to bask in the glow of Lady Bandon; Brigid took a brief private pride in thinking of the perfect word to describe them: "obsequious." She would have to remember that, to use in her next letter to James.

The reverend's piercing tenor was the perfect tool to broadcast the news that was electrifying Europe. *The Times*, Thursday last:

> *Brussels. With a speed that can only be described as spectacular, France has once again thrown herself prostrate at the feet of Napoleon Bonaparte. The exiled Emperor, through means as yet to be uncovered, has escaped from his island exile on Elba. On or about February 26th, with only a handful of his Guard, he landed at the Golfe de Juan in the south of France. Troops ostensibly loyal to the rightful King Louis XVIII, dispatched to apprehend the Outlaw, promptly deserted to Bonaparte en masse. The pusillanimous, treacherous, and duplicitous nature of the French Soldier, from private soldier to Marshal, at great cost exposed and vanquished by His Majesty's Army and Navy in the late wars, has once*

again broken from the reins of duly constituted authority, and once again imperils the entire globe.

The true extent of the conspiracy that engineered Bonaparte's escape, from under the very noses of the Allied Commissioners posted to observe his every move, is yet to be discovered, but the perceptive Reader must conclude that incompetence, treachery, guile, and black cunning have combined to free the Corsican Ogre, and WAR once again is laid at the doorstep of the Europe that had thought itself at last at peace!

At this juncture many of the ladies were overcome with emotion, as the good reverend read from *The Times* as if it were Holy Writ and the Apocalypse had come in spades, with Bonaparte cast as Antichrist. Two or three ladies fell faint; after some skilled maneuvering, the plain, unpleasant, but buxom Miss Caldwell fell into the hesitant arms of Ensign Peters of the militia, managing to do so in a manner that best displayed her ample bosom.

Brigid, not much given to histrionics, was anxious for Reverend Butler to continue, but the distraught ladies were given time to recover, more tea was served, and several loud discussions erupted amongst the gentlemen regarding the likely outcome of a return of a Napoleonic France. Mr. Boffut gruffly argued that the Austrians would certainly ally themselves with France, as Marie Louise, daughter of the Austrian emperor, was married to Bonaparte, and was mother to his son and heir. Brigid knew that was so much stuff; she would have countered that Austria had aided in Bonaparte's fall in 1814, and that Marie Louise and her son were virtual prisoners at Schönbrunn, and forbidden any contact with Bonaparte. But as a lady, particularly a lady of precarious social standing, Brigid dared not differ with such knowing gentlemen, prating fools though they might be.

A heavy woman with whom Brigid was not familiar boldly drew a chair up very close beside her. She was soon introduced as Mrs. Holt, the stumpy, heavily powdered wife of a wealthy Kerry land owner who sometimes came to Clonakilty on business, obviously a woman who was used to getting what she wanted. She did her best to speak only with Lady Bandon. The conversation in the packed room raged at a great pace, while Brigid spent most of her time sitting bolt upright, to allow Lady Bandon and Mrs. Holt to speak across her.

Several new guests arrived. The room grew more crowded, and more chairs were carried in from the dining room for all the ladies to be seated before the next reading by the reverend. In that close-packed atmosphere the air soon became stuffy, and the room took on a discernible funk. That was life, and Brigid, who had a sensitive nose, simply took it in stride. But she soon picked up another unpleasant smell, and she had her suspicions confirmed when a low but staggeringly long rumble came from Mrs. Holt's chair. Shortly thereafter Mrs. Holt, pleading a sudden fit of emotion, had to be led away by her knowing husband, the very fat, very dissatisfied Mr. Holt.

Lady Bandon leaned close to speak into Brigid's ear, and in a low confidential voice she said, "Pray do not mind Mrs. Holt. I have known her since we were children, and while she comes from a fine family, wealthy as Midas of course, she is cursed, the poor dear. I am afraid that her bowels cannot withstand nervous excitement. She was quite excited today, it seems. Oh my, yes." Brigid, shocked into silence, said nothing as Lady Bandon gazed about the room and added airily, "I suppose that is why she and Mr. Holt never had children."

Reverend Butler finally called the crowd back to attention. "Ladies and gentlemen, please, if I may continue. No, Mrs. Blackwood, I am afraid that there are no more crumpets. We were quite unprepared for this number of guests; Bonaparte caught us unawares as well. Now, if I may.

"Bonaparte has marched on Paris with lightning speed, gathering strength with every passing mile. Faced with a complete lack of support by his traitorous army and the cowardly French upper classes, King Louis has withdrawn to Brussels, where he awaits the aid of the legitimate European Powers to reinstate the rule of law in France.

The safety of Britain, indeed, all of Europe, is in the balance. The Congress of Vienna is the last best hope of peace and prosperity. With the wisdom of long experience the Congress has declared Bonaparte an Outlaw, and every legitimate nation now gathers its strength to renew the struggle with France.

Every Briton may, however, take hope and pride in hearing the news that echoes as loudly and stridently as the news from France. The Congress of Vienna, with singular sagacity, has appointed His Grace the Duke of Wellington to be the Commanding General of all the Allied Armies.

While The Iron Duke is no doubt pleased to be given armies of every description, he will certainly command in person that most lethal instrument of war yet devised: a British Army. Confidential sources at Horse Guards report that troops are being recalled from all across the Empire. The veterans that drove Bonaparte and his minions from their despoiled conquests gather once more; the Royal Navy, master of the oceans, is bearing them back to Europe with astounding speed. Ships from America are expected to arrive at any time.

God save the King!"

Brigid was accustomed to military gatherings, and she and the few militia officers present stood and echoed the customary "God save the King!", but the civilian crowd exploded into passionate discussion. The men who had been densely packed along the walls now migrated into the centre of the room, and as she sat down Brigid's view from the settee now consisted of overfed, wool-clad, male backsides, at no great distance. These were rich men, and much of their conversation centred on how the new war would affect their fortunes.

"The price of corn, gentlemen! The price of corn!" declared Mr. Boffut. "The price of corn is the flawless barometer of trade's ebb and flow. With the return of Bonaparte the grain shipments from America are sure to be interrupted, and prices will rise like never before!"

"Nonsense!" cried Mr. Chambers. "Bonaparte has always failed to interrupt our overseas trade; how, sir, can you expect things to be any different this time round?"

"Because, sir, I am personally in possession of knowledge that most of the Royal Navy is disbanded! The bulk of our fleets are decommissioned, our naval officers reduced to half-pay and sent home, and our seamen cast ashore. Go, sir, down to any port, little Clonakilty included, and you will see, for the first time in twenty years, unemployed seamen! Prime hands cast aside by Government in an ill-advised, poorly managed attempt to save pennies! Penny wise and pound fools!"

Brigid had had quite enough for one day, and Mrs. Butler, who was a good soul, rescued her from the settee and kindly offered to have their man take her home. The Butler's man was the elderly Padraig O'Brian, and thus family to Brigid. He had been married to a Donegal woman for fifty years and had thus long since learned the art of supportive silence, so the only sounds that intruded on Brigid's thoughts were the grinding of the trap's wheels and the steady noise of the horse's hooves. When they arrived at Fáibhile Cottage he handed Brigid a copy of *The Times* that he had "found in the trash, as it were," while from beneath his seat he produced a basket of food prepared by Mrs. Keefe, the Butler's cook, a welcome gift for a woman who faced a house full of hungry children. Brigid was genuinely touched; she patted the top of Padraig's battered old hand and gave him a tired smile. "*Go raibh maith agat, a ceathar a grah.*" Thank you, dear cousin.

As old Padraig swung the trap around and urged the Butler's mare back toward home, Brigid saw a man sitting on the stone wall a little further down the road. It looked to Brigid as if he was watching the house. She did not know him; in his short blue jacket he looked like a sailor. There was no reason for anyone to be sitting there, particularly a sailor, as the Lockwood cottage was the only house along that stretch of road. Crime was not a common concern in Clonakilty, but times were hard, and she was a woman alone with a house full of children. She hurried to her door, trying not to look as if she was hurrying, and quickly bolted the door behind her.

Of course the children were anxiously awaiting her return, and the rest of that day was spent in explaining the news, dissecting the newspaper, and praying for the safety of their father. Joseph pulled out the worn atlas with which they followed the movements of the Inniskilling Regiment across Europe and America, and the children saw that the ship carrying their father from the Caribbean to Europe would doubtless pass just miles from the southern tip of Ireland; in other words, just miles from home.

Brigid left her children arguing the likelihood of a ship at sea seeing five children waving kerchiefs from atop Dunowen Head, while she slipped into the kitchen to get some supper together. She was absently slicing some apples when she cut her finger, and as the blood dripped onto the dark slate floor she abruptly began to cry, racking sobs of frustration, loneliness, and fear. She held a kitchen towel to her face to muffle her weeping, the children just in the next room, but the tears came hard, the towel slowly growing red with her blood.

Chapter Six

Portsmouth, England

James drained his cup in one long pull and said, "What a God damned mess."

Tom poured them each another measure of Navy grog and said, "I have never seen its equal. I have two dead, and twenty very nearly so." They had been drinking for some time, but it had yet to blur the memory of the past month.

"I lost three," James said. "One of them was Kelly's little girl. Children should not die in such a fashion." He had visited the girl on the ship's tossing orlop deck just before she died, and her death cut him deeply. She had looked so much like his daughter Mary.

They leaned on the rail of His Majesty's Transport *Clarendon,* a miserable little brig of dubious ancestry. *Clarendon,* eighty feet long and twenty-two wide, was packed with fifteen crewmen, a handful of women and children, and ninety-four officers and men of Six Company, First Battalion, 27th Foot. She was the smallest and slowest member of a convoy that *Scout* had escorted from Bermuda to Portsmouth, that crowded, corrupt, stinking bastion of British naval power. Three other small transports full of

Inniskillings, *Mary, Bacton,* and *Doncaster,* anchored near *Clarendon,* though the largest, *Strathmoor,* was missing.

After a few minutes of silence, Tom quietly said, "I spoke briefly with Elliott. He was with Barr aboard the *Bacton.* It seems for the entire crossing Barr rarely left his cabin, foully drunk the whole time. At night Elliott could hear him talking to himself, alternately cursing and weeping."

James was silent for a moment, them softly said, "God between us and evil."

Drinking steadily, the two lieutenants stared into Portsmouth, relieved by the sight of land, even that if that land bore more than a passing similarity to Gomorrah. They watched as *Mary's* jolly boat carried two red-coated gentlemen ashore, though neither Major John Archibald nor Assistant Surgeon Patrick Kennedy did the regiment much credit, as both were rumpled, pale, and exhausted. To compound matters, Kennedy was in a high state of fury. Archibald was on his way to report to the commander of Gosport barracks, which lay directly across the harbour from Portsmouth, while Kennedy was in a blinding hurry to arrange for the most critical of his many patients to be transferred to the barracks hospital.

The convoy's Transport Agent, a Calvinist, still commanded the convoy, and had unkindly ordered that the men were to stay below deck, and no boats were to be allowed alongside. Nonetheless, entrepreneurial bumboats pushed off from the quay, some to sell food and liquor, some full of whores, cackling and lifting their skirts. "When I was very young," said Tom, "my father taught me to say 'This blessed plot, this earth, this realm, this England,' but I doubt that he ever saw Portsmouth at low tide. But then, one might argue that it is always low tide in Portsmouth." He then bellowed in a tone that would have surprised his father, "Ahoy, the boat! Come any nearer this ship and you'll be fired on, you poxed harpies!"

The ladies aboard the boat had been called much worse, by worse men. Their pimp, a vicious-looking brute at the stern, urged the oarsmen on, and one of the whores, surprisingly quite pretty, held up her arms and called up to James, "Come, husband, give us a kiss!"

It had been a very long time since James had kissed anyone, a very long time indeed. But before he could dwell upon that notion, *Clarendon's* bosun and his mate came trotting over to the side and tossed a large bucket of filth into the boat below. Howls of laughter echoed across the convoy, and with shrieks and curses from the whores the bumboats retreated.

James gestured to the boat and said, "If that young lady had garnered sense enough to bring a newspaper with her I would have given a guinea for it, and she might have kept her damned kiss."

Tom frowned and said, "I should think that for a guinea she'd supply the kiss *gratis*, a bonus, as it were. Still, it is very unpleasant, not knowing what is going on. War or peace? And if war, where?"

"My men have a betting pool going, possibilities ranging from 'Bonaparte is dead, back to garrison duty' to 'Expect the French in Sussex by Michaelmas'. I had Doolan put a penny in for me, under 'Britain fights the whole damned world', which I thought was prophetic."

The two lieutenants raised their battered tin cups to their native kingdom and drained them again. As Tom poured another, James looked toward the quay and said, "I was wondering if the Second was still here, but yonder comes my answer."

A double-oared wherry pushed off from the quay with a Redcoat in the stern. The officer in the boat was Lieutenant Charles Gooch, Adjutant of the Second Battalion of the 27th, who was, sadly, less than popular across the regiment. When he abruptly stood in the small boat to wave, he quickly became very unpopular with the boatmen as well, the stroke asking, "What was the gentleman thinking, standing in this little boat? Did he wish the lot of them to wind up in this cold old water, aswim with shit and dead puppies?"

Both James and Tom were acquainted with Gooch from their service in Spain. Tom cringed, threw the boat a wave, and said to James, "Oh, Lord, it is Gooch. I am no mood to speak to that silly fellow."

"I shall see to him," said James. "I suppose that I have enough of His Majesty's grog aboard to face the challenge. Still, what shall you give me if I keep him away from you?"

"All that I have left to my name is my immortal soul."

"Which, at last bidding, was worth, what, four guineas?"

"I was once offered five, but that was some time ago," replied Tom.

"Your soul it is, then. Perhaps I shall use it as a doorstop."

As he ducked below Tom added, "But do try to get some news from him, won't you?"

James had an unfortunate belief that a man's handshake was an infallible indicator of his character; Gooch's grip only confirmed his earlier opinion. Gooch was of average height, yet he still wore tall heels that were long out of fashion as he stood splay-footed, his hands clasped behind his back, a weak, nervous man who did not realize that he was either. He was, instead, convinced that he was deathly ill, whether the surgeons concurred or not, and his greatest pleasure in life was informing the balance of humanity of the fragile nature of his health.

"James, I am pleased to see you once again. I trust that you do not object to my use, my most affectionate use, of your Christian name. I allow myself this liberty only in light of the intimate nature of the brotherly relationship in Spain, however briefly we served as comrades in the field, due to the terrible illnesses that so unfortunately confined me to the rear, and which haunt me to this day." As Gooch spoke in a low, wandering mutter, James had to lean down to listen to

Gooch's breathless recitation of his current symptoms, all of which puzzled even the civilian doctors, "Cambridge men, James, Cambridge men!"

James managed to give Gooch his full, if somewhat swaying, attention, which was so rare an occurrence that Gooch felt encouraged to continue with his monologue. James spent most of the next ten minutes blinking and trying to clear his head, though when Gooch paused to draw breath James ventured, "Pray, what news of Bonaparte, Charles?"

"I do not wish to 'show away,' if you will allow the use of so informal a term, but I confess to be singularly well informed in such matters, as my studies of world affairs are quite exhaustive. The Emperor Napoleon has reached Paris, acclaimed by the mobs, while the unfortunate Bourbons have fled to Brussels. Austrian and Russian armies are slowly mustering in the east, while a Prussian army under Blücher is gathering in eastern Belgium."

"Old Blücher is a scrapper..." offered James.

Gooch loosed a fawning, simpering little laugh. "I am in possession of an amusing anecdote, in which Marshal Blücher believes himself pregnant with an elephant, fathered by a Grenadier of Napoleon's Guard, but perhaps such manly banter is left for a more discreet environment. Our very own Duke," Gooch said in a shrill voice that sent a jet of pain through James's head, "is based in Brussels. He will command all of the Allied contingents; Dutch, Belgians, Germans of every stripe, while we British will compose less than half the army. If you ask me, it sounds rather like the 'dog's breakfast,' if you will once again excuse the use of such a rough, soldierly expression, but if anyone can pull things together, it would be 'Old Nosey.' Goodness, how full of cant phrases I am! But now tell me, James, may I be so bold as to inquire as to the location of Colonel Pritchard? You might understand that I am not anxious to see him."

Gooch might well be wary of Colonel Pritchard, as there had been a time in Spain that Pritchard, in no uncertain terms, had accused Gooch of feigning illness to avoid duty. "Oh, you need not concern yourself with the colonel, Charles," answered James. "The colonel, the battalion staff, and three of our companies are aboard *Strathmoor*, a great hulking thing, but we were separated shortly after leaving Bermuda. We had hoped to find them here waiting for us, as we have been more than a month at sea."

"There has been no sign of this *Strathmoor,* but James, a month in transit!" cried Gooch, "From Bermuda, you should have been here in less than two weeks!"

"We saw storms nearly every mile of the way. I can't tell you how many times that this old hooker rolled and I thought that we'd never right ourselves. A solid month of cold, wet, and never a moment to rest, the ship tossed about like a child's toy. I used to get quite seasick, but now I could roll down a mountain in a barrel without a blush. On top of all that misery a fever broke out across the convoy. Half the battalion is ill, and there have been numerous deaths."

Gooch backed closer to the rail, and asked, "I saw your surgeon go ashore with Archibald; tell me, James, is he a man of some skill? Our surgeons have very limited familiarity with advanced medicine."

James had expected Gooch to ask about the battalion medical staff, as Gooch lusted after medical opinions as most men lusted after women. "West is still our surgeon, but he is aboard *Strathmoor* with Pritchard. Both his assistants are with us, though: Kennedy and O'Donnell. You may wish to consult them, as they are both men of experience, though they could hardly be more different. Kennedy is senior, an Irish gentleman with some formal medical education. I understand that he found it expeditious to join the army after he had skewered an Anglican minister in a duel. O'Donnell has been with us for years, but is a rather rough character, having worked his way up from hospital assistant."

Still close to the rail, Gooch said, "I shall certainly consult Mr. Kennedy at the first opportunity. Now, James, where has our friend Thomas gotten to? I suppose that I really should tender my regards."

"Let me go below and find him for you," said James. "He has broken out in some horrible red things... what do you call them... buboes? At any rate, he would certainly value your opinion, Charles... Kennedy was so pessimistic... mind the side, Charles, it is a long way down to the boat... you have torn your coat... but yes, I shall certainly give him your regards."

*****

It was late afternoon before all of the Inniskilling officers were called across to *Mary,* where they were addressed by Archibald, newly received orders tucked under his arm.

"The battalion will not disembark," said Archibald. There was a buzz of discontent, as every man aboard was desperate to make the crossing a distant memory. Archibald went on, "Any man judged by the surgeons to be incapable of immediate service will be detached to the barracks hospital. As you all know, our Second Battalion is here at Gosport barracks. The War Office dictates that whatever men we lose to the hospital shall be replaced by a draft from the Second, to bring each of our seven companies up to full strength, after which we will sail with all dispatch to Ostend and service with the main army, under the Duke of Wellington." That drew further murmurs from the officers, as the incorporation of new men into long-established companies was at least difficult, and at worst entirely disruptive of the battalion's cohesion. James was disappointed that Archibald did not immediately squash the derisive comments. A good battalion commander would not put up with such chatter; the battalion was not a democracy.

"All officers may spend the night ashore," continued Archibald; that was standard procedure upon reaching port, but he sounded conciliatory, as if he heeded the murmuring. "In the morning all company commanders will assemble at Gosport barracks to select men for the draft. Tomorrow afternoon those men will be brought aboard, and we sail for Ostend the next morning." That, thought James, came off rather better; orders, not suggestions.

"Any word of *Strathmoor*, sir?" asked Lieutenant Elliott in a respectful tone, for which James silently blessed him.

"None. Until such time as she comes in, the War Office has authorized us to operate with seven companies; I will continue to command."

Kennedy and O'Donnell had been quietly consulting by the starboard rail, comparing notes. Kennedy did some final addition, and then stepped forward to say, "Major Archibald, Mr. O'Donnell and I have a concluded our consultations, and at this point we have one hundred twenty-seven men, four women, and seven children who must be committed to the hospital, or we shall not be responsible for the consequences."

The rest of that wet day was spent in getting their invalids ashore, lifted over the side on stretchers in a cold mist. Those who were delirious with fever often cried out mad rantings, many in Irish, a language uniquely capable of conveying anguish. Most of the invalids who still had their senses were passed over the side shamefaced, looking out to sea, leaving their mates when there was fighting to be done. The sick women and children made for the most painful departures, as their husbands and fathers were not allowed to leave their companies to join them ashore. Eileen Goodwin was the good-hearted wife of Private Robert Goodwin; she was terribly ill, but even as she was lowered down into the boat she whispered, "Sure and I'm feeling so much better now, Doctor Kennedy *a grah*. Now for pity's sake let me stay; if I go ashore I'll never find my Bob again, not if it's ever so. If I die in England, I die alone, without a priest, a husband, or a friend." She reached the boat weeping weakly, her anguished silent husband at the rail compulsively running a hand through his hair, his friends at his side, calling down that she'd be fine, and they'd buy her a dram of the finest brandy in all of France, just wait and see.

Six-year-old Andres Moran, the dark-eyed son of Private Denis Moran and his wife Maria, was passed over the side with a spiking fever. He was to be joined ashore by his mother and two-year-old sister. Maria was a native of a small village in Catalonia, a war bride who had never set foot on English soil, now turned adrift with a toddler and a desperately sick son in a military hospital. The men of Four Company and most of the officers of the battalion had contributed to a modest collection to support her, but she looked terribly lost as she was rowed ashore, vainly looking back the whole way, searching for Moran at the rail, but he sat inconsolable on the deck, openly weeping.

*****

James found Gooch's office to be a tiny, inconvenient cell that gauged the level of that gentleman's standing with the Second Battalion. Still acting as unofficial adjutant to the First, James sat on a rickety chair, balancing the battalion rosters on his lap, as Gooch offered comments of some of the men who were to be drafted. "Hugh Argue was made corporal, once, in Malta, but he has too short a temper. A humourous coincidence, don't you think? Robert Adams, now, is a steady fellow, in the right company, but is easily led astray. This draft may pose a problem for Andrew Buchanan, as he is married, with a large number of children. I understand that his wife is a woman of some...," then in a low, disdainful tone, "appetite." James made no reply, so Gooch continued, "I sense, James, that you took offence to some of Colonel McCullough's earlier comments regarding the manner in which this unfortunate draft is being conducted. Without fear of recrimination I must privately attest, in a tone that I must moderate so as not to risk the feelings of the other officers of my battalion, that I have the honour of being a close confidant of Colonel McCullough, a gentleman of remarkable affability and condescension. Being acutely familiar with the extensive depth and width of the colonel's mind, I perhaps might translate his thoughts upon this topic. Archibald has taken every experienced sergeant, corporal, drummer, and private of the battalion, as well as the best of the young recruits. Of our veterans you have left us only Malone and Malarkey, who are, again to use an expression I heard in the mess, 'barking mad,' a descriptive if vulgar term."

"Charles," replied James, "as I have said a dozen times, we are only carrying out our orders. For McCullough to refer to us as 'vultures' is certainly uncalled for. It is fortunate that we are under orders for the Continent, or Archibald may have felt obliged to call him out."

"If I may speak in the most frank terms, James, you gentlemen in the First have always been quick to fight; a most lamentable trait. You will, please, consider the loss of two hundred eighty of our men. Every seasoned man we had. Men past fifty years of age, or whose wives are ill, or who have four children in the barracks, surely you don't need them all? And I particularly wish to ask, James, as a personal favor, that you ask Archibald to leave my servant behind. Carter, Robert Carter. Surely you are not so desperate for men that anyone would consider him? He is over sixty, and more fit for discharge than active service."

"I shall make note of it," said James, though he had no intention of doing so, partly out of annoyance with Gooch and partly out of a hardness that would have disappointed Brigid.

Officers' call sounded, and James and Gooch hustled down narrow stone step to the yard. Gentlemen of both battalions were gathered there when Barr, who had been very withdrawn during the draft process, suddenly grew verbose, drawing several incredulous looks. Addressing a group of Second Battalion officers, he said, "So, gentlemen, what cheer? Have you considered the consequences of the loss of our gallant command staff? A colonelcy, a majority, three captaincies, and three lieutenancies suddenly open! We are all likely to move up two or three places!" Every officer in the regiment was very interested in promotion, and many might secretly calculate how the loss of the command ship would impact his career, but to say it out loud was very distasteful. To broadcast it in jovial terms within earshot of many brother officers was very ungentlemanly indeed.

"Captain Barr," said Archibald, "there is no evidence that the command ship is lost. We all ardently hope that Colonel Pritchard and the rest of the staff will rejoin us as soon as possible. I believe that the officers of the First Battalion shall return to the ships. Lieutenant Lockwood, as you are well with Adjutant Gooch, you will please remain here and finalize the transfer of the new men. Captain Barr, you will walk with me, please."

James grinned, imaging what Archibald might say to Barr, but he was quickly swallowed up in the blur of activity around Gosport barracks. The enlisted men were scrambling to pack their kit, the veterans taking the bare minimums, selling or giving away any garrison luxuries. The wise recruits followed their example, but there were many who stuffed their packs with all manner of nonsense, most of which would eventually be discarded along a distant roadside.

James and the officers of the Second were soon very busy with the massive paperwork that detailed a man's life in the regiment. All of the information from the Second's rosters had to be transferred to those of the First, while the paymaster had to bring their pay up to date, and their quartermaster scrambled to issue any equipment or uniforms that the men were owed. An endless stream of men came to their NCOs and officers to ask for a loan, help in writing a letter, or with questions about the thousands of other details that encompassed their lives in the army.

As adjutant of the 2/27th, Gooch was assigned the odious duty of determining which of the battalion's wives and children would be allowed to accompany the 1/27th to Belgium.

"James," Gooch asked, "I must beg your assistance with that pack of, I shall not use the term 'slatterns,' as unworthy of a gentleman's utterance, but you are aware of the wholly unwarranted disdain with which common women regard me. They will surely tear me to pieces if I displease them."

"Oh, very well, man." James had reached the point of surfeit with Charles Gooch, but he had a vested interest in seeing that the allocation was done fairly. Even in such an exclusively male society as a British army battalion, the manner in which the families were treated was closely observed by even the hardened bachelors in the ranks. The battalion was allowed only a few women and children, and while the lot of the families was a hard one, the men expected them to be treated fairly, and woe to an officer corps that did not take that responsibility to heart.

All of the married men who had been drafted were gathered on the parade ground, their anxious wives and children standing with them. James, Gooch, and a Second Battalion drummer marched out to the crowd with considerable formality, in part to show that they took the affair seriously, and in part to take a degree of shelter behind the bulwark of tradition and ceremony.

James looked to Gooch to address the silent crowd, but Gooch was terrified into silence by the pack of tense, emotional women. "Adjutant Gooch," said James loudly, "has given me the honour of managing the process to select which of the women and children will accompany the First Battalion on active service on the Continent."

James had a loud, confident voice, and his presence went well with the women, as they were suspicious of Gooch, a man who so obviously despised them.

"Know this!" continued James, "The lives of army wives and children on campaign are hard, and fraught with danger. I would advise you all to consider that, before putting in for such a life, particularly if you have children." No one moved; they were all determined to stay together, come what may.

"Very well. War Office regulations dictate that only three wives accompany each company overseas. Those women have to be on the Married Roll, be of good character, with no more than two children, and they have to be willing to work for the other men of the company, doing laundry and such. I trust that this is not news to you; we all understand what is at stake here."

The crowd was silent, all their eyes and hopes focused on James. Clearing his throat, he continued. "The First Battalion left Bermuda with a full complement of wives. The seven companies that are here had twenty-one wives and their children, but due to illness, seven will remain here at Gosport barracks. There are, of course, many more than seven wives here, so, we will use the traditional method to determine who shall go, and who shall stay. Drummer, come forward."

The drummer, whose profession required a talent for theater, dramatically marched forward, unhooked his large brass drum, and set it on the ground at James's feet. James dropped two dice onto the drumhead, and called, "Each eligible woman shall come forward and roll the dice. The highest seven rolls will go. You can't ask fairer than that. Chance, or God, will decide."

There was no argument as to which women were eligible, as the established wives would have brutally called out any woman who would have dared try to bluff her way into the proceedings. The women on the battalion's Married Roll jealously guarded their status, and even if they had some sympathy for the unofficial wives, they would not risk lengthening the odds by allowing them into the lottery. The several Portsmouth doxies, crude, drunken slovens, merited no compassion, but many of the wives could not bear to look at Susan Ullum and Deb Dissell, decent, desperate local women who were living on the meager incomes of Privates Shaw and Toole, who stood abashed at their sides. There was also some sympathy for Mrs. Buchanan, an older woman of great standing amongst the wives, but if she and her sergeant husband had opted to have four children that was their concern.

In the end, twenty-six women stepped forward and rolled the dice. Most were Irish, the balance English, Spanish, or Portuguese. Mary Rooney, unlucky all her life, tentatively stepped up, rolled twelve, and burst into tears. Colleen Costello handed her baby to her husband, stepped forward, rolled a three, and turned back to them, her hands shaking. Helen McManus had both her little girls and her husband blow on the dice, quietly said an Act of Contrition, and rolled nine, hopeful.

The ceremony, held with an almost religious reverence, ended with seven relieved families, trying to not show away, and nineteen shattered families, trying not to show their fear and disappointment, most tearfully failing.

James, Gooch, and the drummer marched back to the parade ground gate. Gooch was clearly relieved to be done with it, though James was surprised to see the drummer's face wet with tears. James went alone to the adjutant's office and quickly drank half a bottle of Gooch's brandy, not tasting it, rubbing his hands roughly across his face.

A shuttle of Royal Navy barges rowed two hundred eighty-one men, seven women, and eight children out to the transports. A sergeant's guard was posted to maintain order as the men, women, and children who were to stay behind lined the stone jetty, calling their farewells. The loading was done professionally, though all concerned knew what these separations meant.

The last boat was ready to pull away, and James shook hands with the officers of the 2/27th. He went down the wet stone steps slowly, trying not to look unsteady. The boat, ten oars to a side, was packed with forty Redcoats and their gear. The boat pushed off and was rounding the end of the jetty when a frantic woman broke through the guard and ran calling to her husband in Irish. She was weeping, young and pretty, a baby in her arms, and it was her obvious intention to leap from the jetty into the boat. Her husband screamed for her not to try it, and she and the baby would most probably have been killed in the attempt, but Gooch was up to the task and caught her just at the edge of the jetty, the woman, baby, and adjutant sprawling on the cold stone pavers as the boat pulled away.

The next morning the transports made sail for Belgium, escorted by the loyal *Scout*. In the thin rain falling on Gosport Barracks, a nervous Charles Gooch quietly padded down to the Orderly Room. There he made an entry in the Orders of the Day that dictated that all battalion wives and children whose husbands and fathers had been transferred to foreign service were to vacate the barracks within three days. The order quoted directly from Regulations: "*Pursuant to the Act of the 51st of Geo III ch. 106, will be granted, to enable them to proceed to their Homes, or to Places at which they intend to reside during the Absence of the Husbands on Service, their government-mandated mileage travel allowance, such Allowance not exceeding two-pence per mile*", where if they lacked other means they were to go on the parish. Most would disappear into the anonymous multitude of Irish paupers.

Chapter Seven

Clonakilty

The kitchen of Fáibhile Cottage, always a comfortable room, was especially warm and inviting on the days that Mrs. Cashman baked. That particular May morning found that worthy woman carefully tending the oven fire, as even year-old turves need gentle prompting to be brought to a baking heat. She then turned to knead the dough on the great oak table that dominated the room, her strong hands pressing and folding in a motion that came to her without conscious thought. Next to the table stood a tall chair that was usually occupied by one of the Lockwood children, in this instance young Richard Pritchard Lockwood. He sat with his head resting in the crook of his arm, watching Catherine work, sharing a comfortable silence.

"Nana Kay, why do the beggars come to our house? We are not rich. Mightn't we ask them to go to the Big Houses?" Richard almost added that many of the beggars, brittle and haggard, frightened him, but he was too proud a boy to say so.

"Ach, Richie, don't be daft. At the Big Houses the poor are driven off if they are lucky, and beaten like dogs if they are

95

not. God desires that the people should suffer, and so they do. Make no mistake, they shall be rewarded someday, though it looks to my eyes like the rich want to hurry them to their reward faster than God intended." She thought of her cousin Moira, who had returned from a visit to Kerry with tales of potatoes rotting in the fields, people starving, and disease taking many more. There was little work there, and while a healthy man might be able to keep himself alive, and perhaps a bit of a family as well, the young, the old, and the weak suffered most, in rough cabins on cold dark hillsides.

Such things were largely kept from the Lockwood children. Instead, a few minutes passed as Catherine again bent to tend the fire, and Richard asked, "Nana Kay, why is there going to be another war?"

"*Wisha*, such things are far beyond the ken of an old Irish woman, *mo stor*."

The silence returned, the only sounds being the crackle of the turf fire and the song of a chaffinch in the kitchen garden. "Is it your papa that you're thinking of, Richie?" asked Catherine quietly without looking up from her work.

"I wish that he would come home, and not be in the army anymore. Sometimes my mama cries, when she thinks we don't see, but we see."

"It is good, I think, that you worry about your mama, *mo cuisle*. But your papa is the great soldier of the world, a lieutenant, for all love! It's the French who should be worried, when Richie Lockwood's own da turns his hand to war."

Richard made no reply, but Catherine, long familiar with the hearts of boys, said, "Now I wonder if I might be asking you a special favor, Richie. I need for you to go out and whisper to the bees and the cows that little Maura Hurley may be going to the angels soon. Off you go now, *a grah*, but remember to whisper, so that the Devil won't hear."

Richard Lockwood had executed such missions before, and he ran off into the fields with great earnestness, carrying his message with the pureness of heart found only in the young. He knew that he could find the bees on the patches of clover on Mr. O'Leary's pastures, their hives in the hedges above. O'Leary's fields were like many in Ireland, in that they bore names that had been bestowed when the world was young. In *gortcolmán*, the doves' field, the swirling bees grew quiet, settling on the leaves of trinity, as Richard lay in the grass and whispered, "Mrs. Hurley's baby girl is going to Heaven soon; will you help her?" As if in response, several bees soon took wing, whirring off into the measureless skies above.

Richard then ran to the cow pastures, though he made a wide detour around the fairy fort that dominated the crest of the hill, knowing that those foul creatures would betray the baby's soul out of pure spite. He found the dairy cows on the south side of the hill, sunning themselves in the fledgling spring sun. The cows did their best to maintain their phlegmatic demeanors, but they cocked their ears forward and listened intently as Richard crouched low amongst them, speaking softly.

"Mrs. Hurley's baby may be going to Heaven soon, will you ask the angels to show her the way to Heaven?" Richard saw one young cow wink in an obvious fashion, and he caught a glimmer of understanding in the depths of their great brown eyes.

His mission complete, Richard soon reverted to the boundless manner of boys, climbing trees, collecting rocks, keeping the good ones and chucking the bad ones at the fairy fort. At one point he wandered as far as the Fourcuil Road, where he waved to Mr. Heaney, that impossibly old man who taught the cottiers' children in the hedge school. Richard was not to play with the cottier children, but Mr. Heaney was a friend of Mrs. Cashman. Once Mr. Heaney had taken a meal in their kitchen, and Richard took some pride in remembering, "*A bhonnán bhuí, is é mo léan do luí,/ Is do chnámha sínte tar éis do ghrinn.*" Richard had some talent for verse, and as he wandered toward home he worked out the English, "The yellow bittern that never broke out,/ In a drinking bout, might as well have drunk."

Richard was nearly home, following the hedged path that twisted between Mr. O'Leary's pastures, when he came across a man walking furtively along the overgrown, cow-trodden track. The man was not Mr. O'Leary, and Richard had never seen any other adult use that secluded way. Richard was not a bold child, but he found the man wholly fascinating; tan and lean, wearing a short blue jacket with shining brass buttons, a gold earring, and a plated pigtail that went to his waist. The man seemed shy as well, at first, but as they drew closer the two came to smile at each other, and the man said, "Well, my fine fellow, a grand day to you now."

"And to you, sir."

"I suppose that is your house, down there. Can you tell me now, if you know Catherine Cashman?"

"My Nana Kay? She is in the kitchen, baking bread."

"Oh, is it Nana Kay she is to you? And is it the finest bread in all Munster that she bakes?"

"Oh, yes sir. My mama says that Nana's bread would make the angels give up their wings, even without the butter."

The man had been very friendly, but he was more serious when he asked, "Is your mama home now, boyo? And your da?"

"Mama and everyone else went into town to talk to Colonel Simon about Napoleon. I had to stay home because I called my brother a turd. My papa is not at home, because he is fighting the French again."

"Then I might just sneak down to the house for a bit, to pay a call on your Nana Kay."

The man said that with great feeling, and Richard, recalling Nana Kay's broken heart, thought to ask, "Please, sir, but is your name John?"

"You know me, clever boy? Johnny Cashman himself, come home at last. God forgive me," he added with an emotional, perhaps hesitant, sigh.

Richard Lockwood, who loved his Nana Kay very much, loved surprises as much as any other child. So he quietly led the uncertain John Cashman down the path to the warm kitchen that smelled of fresh bread, both of them hoping to surprise and delight that deserving woman.

Richard held back as John tentatively stepped into the kitchen, hat in hand, as he quietly said, "God be with you, Mamaí."

She knew him before he spoke. Through all of his years, and all of hers, she saw the good, kind eyes, the little boy who always called her "Mamaí."

She was a strong, proud woman, but all pretense was lost to such a flood of joy as she had never known before. She wept and clung to him for long minutes, John and Richard weeping as well, as she kissed her son and stroked his face. John finally got his mother settled in a chair, him kneeling by her side. "Seventeen years," she gasped, "dear, dear, John, seventeen years. You'll know that I never gave up on you, but you'll explain yourself now to a mother who wept for you many a night."

John wiped his eyes, turned to Richard and said with a smile, "Friend, it wouldn't do for your ma to find me here, me being such a wandering rogue. Might I be asking you now to watch from the garden and give the good call if I need be on my way?"

Enchanted, Richard ran out the front to stand watch while Catherine held her son's hand, and John told his tale. "Where shall I start, *a grah*? You'll remember me with the Whiteboys, Mamaí... what a joy it is to say that again... my own Mamaí." He leaned over and gently kissed her cheek.

"So, we were intent on righting wrongs and settling scores. What boys and bunglers we were, but we raised some hell, still, and the people were ready to fight the English. Tadg An Asna O'Donovan led us, our little army with homemade pikes and a handful of stolen muskets."

"Oh, that artful dog O'Donovan, with his glib tongue, a carpenter with dreams of changing the world."

John offered another quick grin and said, "It's been tried at least once before, Ma."

Catherine gently slapped her son's arm and said, "You'll not be teaching me the faith, young man. Such manners, after all these years. And you'll know that after your battle Mary O'Donovan could never recover her son's body, he and all those other boys left to rot in the crab hole at the quay, and she died with a broken heart, tormented by his wandering ghost." Her heart was so open, so full, that the thought of that other mother's suffering sent a jet of pain through her.

John was quiet for a moment; he had heard that the bodies of his dead comrades had been abused, but he had never heard of such a horror. "Still, Mamaí, you cannot deny the rightness of our cause. When we joined up with the United Irishmen, it was a chance for a new Ireland. Independence! Think of that, now! But Government always wins; hundreds of arrests snatched up what leaders we had, and the militia searched every village for weapons. You'll remember that Da's friend, the blacksmith of Lissavard himself, was accused of forging pike heads for us. Tortured in the main street he was, a cap of hot tar on his head, his home and forge burned, his wife abused."

Catherine knew that her husband had been sympathetic to the Rising, but she would not say that to her rebellious son. "If only your father had lived to see this day. You know John, that your da..."

"Yes, Mamai, I know that Da is gone to the angels."

They were quiet for a moment, until Catherine squeezed John's hand and said, "And so you followed Tadg O'Donovan to Shannonvale itself. Death and disaster."

"But the rising was all across Ireland Ma, and we had to do our part, but yes, a glorious, brutal, tragic failure. It was so damned close. We had turned many of the Westmeaths, and they nearly brought the whole of their regiment over to join us. But it was their officers, including your Lockwood, who held them in place. When the Caithness Legion arrived to reinforce the Westmeaths our fates were sealed."

The bitterness of the defeat had burned in John Cashman for years, and it took him a moment to continue. "I knew that I could not go home, as they were burning the homes of anyone even suspected of sympathy for us. So I made my way to Galway and returned to the sea, my father's son."

"Poor men take to the sea; the rich to the mountains," said Catherine. It was a very old saying, and dear to the families who drew their livings from the sea.

John smiled and went on, "I was lucky and met the captain of a merchant ship, the *Young Emily*, who didn't ask too many questions, and I was aboard her for nearly two years before I was pressed off Flamborough Head by HMS *Active*. Can you imagine that, Ma, me pressed as a sailor for the English? Them without a clue as to who I was, as I go by John McCarthy now. It was a hard life, but I was bred to the sea, and I was a foretopmastman and captain's bargeman in no time at all. We had a chaplain aboard who had a good heart, and it was he who taught me to read and write as well as any priest."

Catherine smiled and nodded her head at the notion of a literate Cashman, and with some excitement in her voice she asked, "Is it the world that you saw, John? Faraway places?"

"Up and down the Med, mostly, *a grah*, wonders as you'd never imagine, pyramids! and more fights than I can remember. I did bring you a little something," handing her a beautiful little jade elephant that she received with a delight that made him flush with pleasure. The elephant had been carved in Java two hundred years before; it had come to a bleeding John Cashman when he looted the pocket of a dead French privateer in 1811.

The elephant, long since washed clean of French and Irish blood, lay in Catherine's hand as John went on, "So, with the wars ending, I was cast up on the beach, my humble services no longer required. I'd a few pounds of pay and prize money in my pocket, and after scratching my head on it, I decided that really I had nowhere else to go. So your John is returned home, but still looking over my shoulder with every step I take in Ireland."

Catherine suddenly remembered that Mrs. Lockwood might come home at any minute. The normally unflappable Catherine Cashman was confused, nearly overwhelmed, but she knew that John would have to go. She could not ask Mrs. Lockwood to be involved in harboring a fugitive from the King's Justice.

"John *a stor*, where can you go now? Is there a safe door in all of Munster?"

"Don't you worry, Mamaí *a grah*, as I have enemies here, I have a few friends as well. I can't tell you who and where, but I'm as safe as the saints' virtue, and I'll come to see you as often as the angels allow. God bless, now, *a grah*, and I'll see you soon."

With more tears, a kiss, and a quick embrace he was gone again, back across the fields. Before he passed out of sight he gave a confidential wave to the vigilant Richard. Catherine spoke to Richard about the need for secrecy, and he swore that he would keep the secret for the sake of his new friend John, his Nana Kay, and his mother as well. He was young, but he was growing up in Ireland, and he knew that no Catholic could have even a remote connection, even the rumor of sympathy, to anyone suspected of rebellion.

*****

Brigid and the other children were visiting Colonel Simon, an elderly retired cavalry officer who purported to be an expert in world affairs, but who was primarily motivated by gossip and the opportunity to wistfully gaze at beautiful women. Brigid craved information about the war that James seemed destined to fight, and the colonel, however enamored, was the best source available. Brigid had long before developed considerable skill in deflecting the attentions of amorous gentlemen, so she had little trouble in keeping that aging gentlemen on his best behavior. Her adept handling of the colonel was good training for her attentive daughters; a blunt observer may have considered the occasion analogous to an experienced lioness training her adolescent daughters to hunt, using a hamstrung old boar as a training aid.

"May I offer you a glass of Madeira, my dear? Or perhaps these other young ladies would care for a glass?" asked the colonel, forgetting that Brigid had already twice declined a glass of wine, and that the other two young ladies, despite appearances, were barely into their teens.

"Thank you, no, Colonel. My daughters, you may recall, take no wine. But may I ask, Colonel, that you continue your comments on the French army? Will they be able to reassemble their army quickly, and how effective do you think the Royalists will be in resisting Bonaparte's control of the more distant provinces? I assume that the Vendee will once again remain loyal to the Bourbons?"

The colonel, always the soldier, was not easily dissuaded from his assault. "Oh, come, my dear, you must not worry your pretty head over those poxed Frenchmen. Our army will soon put paid to that lot. But it is a pity that our brave warriors are so long away from home. You have not seen your husband for what, nearly three years now? Surely that is very hard on your children, and of course, you must be terribly lonely yourself."

Both Mary and Cissy looked down into their laps, embarrassed at the obvious gambit, but Brigid easily responded, "It is so kind of you to think of us, Colonel. You are so like my grandfather, though he passed so long ago. I say, Colonel, is that not a new uniform coat? Your silver hair goes so well with the blue of your regimentals."

*****

Joseph Lockwood, mercifully, was not witness to his mother's clinical dissection of Colonel Simon, as early on he had been dispatched to spend his afternoon with Simon's long-time servant, Corporal Archibald M'Vicar, late of the 10th Hussars. M'Vicar was a serious cavalryman, and even if he also was getting on in years he knew horses as well as any man in Ireland, and that is high praise indeed.

"So, Master Joseph Lockwood," began the corporal, "where is your younger brother? Arthur, was it?"

"His name is Richard, please, sir. He called me a turd, and my mother said he had to stay at home."

"Well, come now, that is a good cavalry insult, but your mother is quite right in keeping discipline in the ranks. Confined to barracks, and all that. Yes. Also, you will remember, please, that you will not call me 'sir.' I am a corporal, a title earned at considerable expense to my delicate hide, so you will please address me as such. Now, then, Master Joseph, do you recall the crux of your last lesson?"

"The crux, Corporal?" answered Joseph, somewhat puzzled. "Is that the strap that—"

"No, the crux, boy! The crux! The important part!" snapped M'Vicar, the sharp-edged cavalry NCO once again.

"Oh, yes, sir! Corporal! You told me all about the combination of heel, toe, and bit."

"Good. Aye, good boy," replied M'Vicar, placated. "You will keep that in mind, and today we shall get you up on old

104

Joanna's back, and we will work on the importance of posture. Posture, Master Joseph, is the *crux* of today's lesson. Without your proper posture you will never swing a sword from a horse's back, oh no indeed."

"Yes, Corporal. Thank you, Corporal. My father rides very well. He is on his way to Belgium to fight Napoleon; I wish I could be with him when he buys his horse there."

"Flanders, eh? I was there in, what, 1794 or so... good horse people, but they do draft beasts, mostly; fine animals. They don't raise many saddle horses, but what they have are quite fine."

"What countries have good horses, please, Corporal?" asked Joseph.

"Well, let me think. The Italians have mules, never a horse with four legs to be found. The Spanish are capable of some good mounts, but most of them have been eaten by now, I wager. Never trust a Frenchman with a horse. They can't breed, and what nags they do produce they treat shamefully. No, I lie. The Normans know a fair bit about horses, Percherons from St. Lo and thereabouts. And in the south they have a few capable studs; I knew a Comtois once, a fine, good natured beast. But on the whole, the only way that the French cavalry can keep from walking is to buy or steal mounts from Flanders and the Germans. Austrians, Prussians, that lot, breed some fine cavalry mounts; good blood, there. The Saxons are famous for their mounts, big, strong, spirited beasts; you must shake the hand of any Saxon you ever come upon. But never let any man blackguard an English or Irish horse. In fairness we may have to concede that they are a bit pampered and might not campaign over well, but for size, strength, and speed, get me a hunter from the south of England, or better yet, one of the light hunters that we're breeding here in Ireland. I just brought back a mare from the County Down; Christ, boy, the speed, the jumping, she'll carry you all day and ask for more."

By late afternoon Joseph Lockwood was much the wiser regarding horseflesh, and Colonel Simon was reduced to the role of doting grandfather. The colonel, who would have nothing to do with carriage horses in his stables, had arranged for the carriage from the Bandon Arms to take the Lockwoods home. When they returned to Fáibhile Cottage, they came through the door with a steady rattle of conversation, and if Richard and Mrs. Cashman seemed rather strained, no one noticed. Sergeant, who was a notorious gossip, was perfectly willing to discuss the appearance of John Cashman, but he was unable to convey more than a general sense of enthusiasm.

"Richard, would you let Sergeant out, please?" asked Brigid. "He seems rather agitated."

*****

John Cashman made a wide swing around Clonakilty, working his way round to the west side of Inchydoney Island, where one of his friends was waiting for him in a small fishing boat. Liam Collins was another survivor of the Whiteboys of '98, wiser now about trusting anyone outside his class and his close circle of friends. He had been very pleased with the return of John Cashman, and they had quickly thrown in lots together. The two of them masterfully tacked the curragh out of Clonakilty Harbour, west to the secluded safety of remote Rabbit Island. That seclusion consisted of a dry-stone hut, long days of rich fishing, and the care of a chest full of expectant, well-oiled muskets.

Chapter Eight

The English Channel

As an officer, Lieutenant Lockwood was allowed to walk the deck of *Clarendon* at his leisure, and it was from that heaving platform that he saw continental Europe for the first time since the Inniskillings had left Spain nearly two years before. The increasingly discontented enlisted men of the battalion were still huddled below, and it was only through the few portholes and scuttles that a fortunate handful were able to glimpse the distant coast of Belgium, relaying their observations and opinions to their fellows. At that point, at least, Belgium was a profound disappointment, as the coast was an unvarying line of low, flat, dun-colored sand hills. The shore may have been desolate, but the sea was not, as there were many other ships in that patch of the Channel bound for Ostend. Numerous small fishing craft and luggers also populated the choppy sea, and it was from one of those luggers that the port pilot came aboard.

An old hand with channel traffic, the pilot wore a large badge in the shape of an anchor affixed to his old woolen coat. Everything about him was dirty, hairy, and wholly unpleasant.

"Steer south-southwest, God damn anyway. *Mon Dieu* this is scow. I seen redbacks they come like sheep for Bonaparte to kill, he kill these bastards too, no? Maybe we sink this damned tub now, save Bonaparte the trouble, no? Maybe it sink by itself anyway, God damn anyway."

In response to this encouraging oratory *Clarendon*'s captain, anticipating the likelihood that the infantry officers were not accustomed to the uniquely loathsome habits of channel pilots, called, "Infantry officers to the wardroom, please, gentlemen!" Rather than returning to the tiny wardroom the three displeased Inniskilling officers opted to join their men below, throwing angry glances back at the pilot, who continued to insult the ship, the crew, the passengers, the Commandments, and the world in general at a fantastic rate.

The pilot was a necessary evil, as the entrance to Ostend, like most channel ports, required an intimate knowledge of its strong tides, shifting bars, rocky outcroppings, and generally malevolent physical features. The pilots had to know the weather as well, as the coast was notorious for its fickle fogbanks, and the local winds shifted with such caprice that an unwary ship could be cast up on the rocks in an instant. Just weeks before, the first British transports arriving at Ostend had been delayed for days when the wind had blown foul. Even the Royal Navy could not command the wind to shift from the southeast, no matter how Wellington and the army howled. When the wind had finally shifted, there was such a pressing need to speed the assembly of the army that the pilots were ordered to hazard any risk to get the transports into Ostend while the wind stood fair.

The wind stood fair, but it was a wind that was steadily increasing in velocity. The transports were scattering, each now making her own way as best she could for the shelter of Ostend. One of *Clarendon*'s many failings was a scandalous tendency to fall off to leeward. In short, a breeze that struck her from any point but from directly astern pushed her sideways at nearly the same rate that it pushed her forward. It was this significant fault that was being discussed with some vehemence by *Clarendon*'s captain and the opinionated pilot while *Clarendon* wallowed closer to Ostend. The harbor itself was guarded by a great stone mole, the seaward side of which was being pounded by waves of increasing size and power.

James, who was an indifferent swimmer and who lacked the wings that might otherwise be required to survive an untimely encounter with the Belgian coast, stood at the bottom of a ladder that led to the deck. He was listening with a great interest, and he was not alone in his concern. Ensigns Coakley and Blakeley stood beside him, the men of the company beyond them, occasionally trading a look or a quiet word. Looking up the companionway, Coakley muttered, "Damned squids," with considerable contempt.

Aboard that crowded brig no conversation was ever private, and the hundred men of Six Company watched and listened to their officers with great interest, many of them looking very concerned. With some effort James smiled and said lightly, and rather loudly, "Ensign Blakeley, is it your intention to remain by this ladder for the rest of the voyage, in case of emergency?"

"My respects, sir, but if this vile tub begins to sink, I intend to be the first man off."

"Begging your pardon, Blakeley," said Coakley, giving Blakeley a solid nudge, "but you'll be the second man off." This prompted some good-natured laughter, especially amongst the enlisted men who stood nearby, but they all continued to stare up the companionway, listening. James was pleased to hear Blakeley speaking more like a soldier now, even after such a short apprenticeship. But war was another step entirely, and it lay just beyond those dun-colored hills.

Clarendon approached Ostend from the north-northeast, and any wind south of west should have seen any sailing vessel afloat into the harbor without issue. But *Clarendon's* horrid leeward motion was soon apparent to even the stubborn pilot, who began to run around the deck like a man possessed, ordering a hawser to be coiled at the bow. James could restrain himself no longer, and he came up on deck in time to see the stone mole on the port side grow closer with every minute as *Clarendon* angled for the small fort at the end of the mole. The wind had increased to nearly a gale, and tremendous surf was pounding the jetty. There was great excitement and effort on the deck until the last instant, when every head was turned and silent to see if *Clarendon* would clear the mole. She did not.

A great wave and a blast of wind conspired to toss *Clarendon* onto the rocks at the very end of the mole. The port bow of the wallowing ship struck a hard glancing blow, nearly bringing her to a complete halt. The frantic crew raced aloft to reduce what little sail she had on her yards, as the howling wind now tried to drive them further onto the rocks. Below decks, Six Company was hanging on for dear life, and there was a great deal of shouting and cursing. Belgian soldiers from the fort above them, thankfully used to such scenes, scrambled to receive the hawser that had been prepared on *Clarendon's* deck, and using stanchions and a capstan they strained to pull *Clarendon* around the final feet of the breakwater.

James dashed below and called, "Six Company! Drop your packs and firelocks! Coats off! We may get wet, so any men who can swim, help your mates! Give the women and children something that floats!" But a huge, merciful wave came and lifted rather than smashed *Clarendon*, and the mass of retreating water allowed her stern to swing round. The hawser went taut and pulled her bow away from the rocks, and *Clarendon* finally made her undignified entrance into the harbor.

She was badly damaged; the planking that had sullenly leaked for most of *Clarendon's* life now allowed the cold dark water to pour into her hold at an alarming rate. All that water slowed her progress into the long, narrow harbor, so more sail was raised to catch the wind that roared over the city's defenses. The harbor was full of vessels, but there was one open stretch of shallow water beside *Mary*, and *Clarendon* finally nosed up onto the sand below Ostend's walls, her final crossing over.

Clarendon's survival was of key importance to those aboard, but beyond them her dramatic entrance was hardly noticed, as the harbour was in a frenzy of activity. Even before the tide had fully receded, many of the vessels in-harbour had begun to offload their cargos onto the sand. Aboard a nearby transport, a light dragoon regiment was forcing its horses to jump off the deck into the cold water, while naked troopers splashed about, dragging the frightened beasts ashore.

The transport's jolly boats were soon lowered, and the Inniskilling officers were pulled over to *Mary*. Shortly thereafter, a launch with a Royal Navy captain aboard pulled away from the port office to view the damage to *Clarendon's* bows. He was then pulled over to *Mary*, where he climbed aboard, saluted her captain without a word, (the pilots had long since made a discreet departure) then curtly turned to the Inniskilling officers. He threw them a salute, saying, "Captain Hill, Royal Navy." Archibald stepped forward, returned the salute, said, "Major John Archibald, First Battalion, 27th Foot," and made as to shake hands but Hill was not interested.

"Major Archibald, you will please have your men disembark as soon as the tide has receded. Sooner, if they do not have an aversion to wet feet. The Duke's orders allow no delay. If you, sir, and a couple of other officers will accompany me, I will escort you to the fortress commander, Colonel Gregory. There is not a moment to lose."

"Colonel Gregory of the 39th?"

"I believe that is the gentleman, yes."

"We had the opportunity to serve with Colonel Gregory in America," said Archibald. "Lieutenants Lockwood and Drake, I believe that you are well acquainted with the colonel?"

"Yes, sir," answered James. "At one point our companies were detached to serve under Colonel Gregory for a boat attack. He is a very capable officer."

"Very good. Captain Pratt, you will please see the battalion disembarked, drawn up, and ready to march in two hours' time. Lieutenants Lockwood and Drake, you are with me, please. Let us bring Ensign Digby as well; we may need a runner."

Hill led the four Inniskillings hurriedly up into town. They peppered him with questions about Bonaparte's activities, though the indignant Hill was less than willing to discuss such things. "Gentlemen, you will please reserve such questions for Colonel Gregory. All I know is that I am a captain in His Majesty's Navy, reduced to the duties of a glorified longshoreman. My seniority should see me in command of a first rate, but here I am, directing the unloading of transports! Transports, gentlemen, most of them contract vessels that would otherwise be hauling corn, most of them floating disasters, commanded by puppies twenty years my junior. As to the end use of this army that I am so gleefully seeing ashore, I am evidently not held worthy to possess any knowledge of the enemy's intentions. A God damned longshoreman, gentlemen!"

Hill, still the picture of indignation, left them at the door of a tall, narrow mansion that overlooked the harbor. Colonel Gregory had eschewed the unfortunately named Fort Napoleon as both uncomfortable and inconvenient, instead establishing his headquarters in the imposing granite-faced house that had been built in 1637 for a wealthy textile merchant. A steady stream of civilians and the officers of numerous nations were coming to the house, to complain, enquire, cajole, and beg.

"Ensign Digby, you will please wait here in the street," said Archibald. "We may need you to carry a message back to the battalion, so please do not stray."

As the three senior men passed inside, Drake added, "Digby, if you continue to stare at young ladies in that fashion, one of their fathers may find it necessary to put a hole in you."

"He speaks from experience," said James *sotto voce* as he and Drake pressed into the crowded foyer, getting a brief grin in reply. A harried sergeant directed them to a harried lieutenant, who directed them to wait in line to speak to Colonel Gregory's secretary, a harried civilian behind a desk that was much too small for the mountain of applications, notes, and letters that had to be processed.

"I am sorry, gentlemen," said the secretary after a twenty-minute wait, "but the colonel is wholly taken up with his duties. If you might come back tomorrow, I may, *may*, mind you, find you some time in the afternoon."

"I appreciate the press of business," said Archibald, who was maintaining his Scots temper in admirable fashion, "but I have seven hundred men who—"

"Lockwood!" came a high-pitched voice from the inner office. "God's my life, Lockwood himself! And Drake as well! The Inniskillings! At last some fighting men!" Narrow at the shoulders and wide at the waist, Colonel Gregory had a soft face and a mop of graying hair, but despite appearances he was a soldier of great skill and experience.

A silken Belgian aristocrat, raging about the trampling of his lawn, was next in line to speak to Gregory, but he was diverted to a conciliatory captain. Major Archibald was introduced, and the three Inniskillings were shown into the resplendent office. Gregory was never one to stand on rank or ceremony, so after some warm handshakes Archibald, James, and Drake were settled on comfortable chairs.

"As I recall, the Inniskillings were never opposed to a glass of wine in the afternoon," said Gregory, already pouring four glasses.

"That would be most welcome sir, thank you," said Archibald.

"You gentlemen would not believe the chaos we have here. Our troops are pouring in, all in need of food, fodder, shelter, and direction. I am tasked with providing all four, and precious little with which to do it. Then the civilians, damned nuisances, each more demanding than the last. Yesterday I had a general's wife, I won't bother you with her name, come in without an appointment to demand a berth aboard a man-of-war in order to be in Bath in time for the Season. Impertinent ninny. But enough of my burdens; my latest orders from Horse Guafrds told me to expect you, but you were last in America, were you not?"

Colonel Gregory's claret was excellent; James was glad to be junior, so that Archibald had to do the talking. Archibald briefly explained the voyage and the draft, ending with, "So, sir, we had hoped to find that *Strathmoor* had sailed directly to Ostend, but it seems that we were mistaken."

"We have had no word," said Gregory, "so it seems, Archibald, you shall have to carry on without Pritchard. And you shall have your work ahead of you, incorporating all of these new men into your battalion. After all this time at sea, I wager that your other men are worn mighty thin. Three companies short as well, and your command group. My, my. I wish that I could do more to ease your way, but all I can do is to get you under a roof for a night or two."

"We're coming ashore with three day's rations, sir," said Archibald, "but we'll need access to billets or stores soon."

"You'll see no billets here, sir," replied Gregory, now reminded of his predicament, and ready to take offense. "You will move to join the duke near Brussels as soon as I discover to whom you are to report."

"Aye, sir, aye," replied Archibald quietly, and James was relieved to see Archibald's temper recede. Gregory could make their lives a misery if he wished.

"Very well, then, I'll do what I can. The army will need your Irishmen very soon, and many more like them, if the rumors that I hear from France are true. Bonaparte is gathering his army, all veterans, damn them; though what he intends to do with them, and where he intends to do it, God only knows."

*****

Colonel Gregory did them very handsomely. A Belgian officer guided the battalion to some extensive stables on the outskirts of town, and they arrived just as rain and darkness began to fall. The stables were comparatively clean, and the three days that the Inniskillings spent there went a long way towards restoring their strength and spirits. The officers were lodged together in a large inn that stood nearby, an inn which at any other time would have seemed rather shabby, but which at this stage in their lives seemed like shameless luxury.

One sign that the battalion's morale was rebounding was apparent the next evening, when Ensign Blakeley strode into the inn for dinner. James was sitting with Tom, anticipating the delivery of a brandy-soaked Crème Brûlée, when he noticed the grins on the faces of several of his brother officers. Looking up at the source of their mirth, he saw young Blakeley looking pleased with himself. Blakeley ventured a brief glance toward his lieutenant, who held up one deliberate finger and beckoned Blakeley to join him.

Lieutenant Lockwood took a long look at his protégé and sighed.

"Ensign Blakeley, what is that on your face?"

With more than a little pride Blakeley answered, "I wasn't able to grow a mustache yet, sir, so I drew one on with grease pencil."

"Whatever prompted you to do so, Ensign?"

"Ensigns Digby and Coakley helped me, sir. They explained that all the officers of Six Company wear mustaches. From your days in Spain, when General Cuesta called you the '*Banditos de los Muertos*.'"

"Ensign, your brothers are once again amusing themselves at your expense. In the future you must overcome this remarkable capacity for gullibility. While I confess that the '*Banditos de los Muertos*' sounds terribly romantic, you are an ensign in a centre company of a line battalion, and much to our collective dismay, such a position does not typically engender romance. To the best of my knowledge, none of the officers of the 27th Foot are intelligence agents, natural sons of foreign princes, or undiscovered heirs to vast fortunes. We are soldiers: very capable soldiers, but no more. I have a mustache and whiskers because we are on campaign, and I care to; you may grow them or not at your leisure. But, mind you, only when you are able; I loathe a six-whisker mustache. That, sir, is the extent of our tenuous connection to romantic fancy."

Reality slowly dawned upon the heretofore innocent features of John Blakeley, who flushed and replied, "Yes, sir."

"Abandon ye romance, young Ensign. Now, tell me, have you worn this grease pencil abomination all day?"

Quietly, "Yes, sir."

"And no one else has said anything?"

"No, sir. Sergeant McCurdy did seem to have something on his mind, but he never said anything. By the way, sir, the men of the company seem to be in very good spirits. After drill Lieutenant Drake and Major Archibald were very complimentary, and asked if you had helped me draw my mustache."

"Oh yes, I am sure they did, I am sure they did. Did those hounds in the ensigns' quarters not see the List? They understand that you are senior?"

"Yes, sir, but why does it matter that I am senior? Am I their superior?"

"Superior? Oh, goodness, no. Outside their duty they may be mindless apes, but within the confines of their duty they are occasionally useful. In that respect, at least, you will emulate them. In that respect only, the lizards. Your only hope is that someday you are made lieutenant ahead of them, and you will then be able to make their lives a misery." The entrance of the Crème Brûlée restored at least some of Lieutenant Lockwood's spirits, and with moderate good humour he quickly told Blakeley, "Off you go, now, Ensign; eat your dinner, though the waiters may mistake you for one of Bonaparte's Grenadiers. I will confess that you carry off a mustache quite well, but you will wait to come by one the old-fashioned way. You will please scrub it off by morning roll call. Go now, and sin no more."

*****

On the second morning of their stay in Ostend, James and Tom left a meeting of the battalion officers, drew a corporal's guard, hired a local cart, and marched back to the anchored, disgraced *Clarendon*. The harbor was still a hub of activity, so a small group of soldiers who looked like they had a purpose went unnoticed. The tide was out, and the sad hull of *Clarendon* sat unmoved on the sand, her bows stove in. The tides had left her deep in the sand and she looked wholly abandoned, so James and Tom climbed straight aboard, only to be met by two guilty-looking Royal Marines who clambered up from below deck.

"Beg pardon, sir," said the taller marine, "we was just patrolling the ship, like. Orders from the Port Admiral, sir," this more officially, "and this vessel is to be held for inspection by the port commissioner, who will determine her value for compensation to her owners, and no one allowed on board."

Skipping only half a beat, James, said, "Yes, Marine. We have heard the news, and have come to say goodbye to the dear old girl. She carried my company across many miles, through many storms."

"Come now, sir," replied the marine, whose breath would not bear close inspection, "it's not often we hear soldiers with such a fondness for ships, sir."

"Oh yes," said James, "we were shocked to hear that she'll be turned over to a pack of foreign grass-combing vultures, sold for firewood, the grand old barky." In the background Tom surreptitiously rolled his eyes.

"Aye, it's a right pity, sir," said the marine. "Oh my, yes, sir. And here we are guarding her corpse, it's right creepy, sir."

"So her carcass is to be sold to those Belgian dockyard mateys, but what of her stores, Marine?"

"Her stores, sir?" replied the marine, who was slow to comprehend, in the manner typical of marines.

"It would be a shame to see her stores handed over to those foreigners, do you not think, Marine? In all fairness, you would think they should be enjoyed by His Majesty's loyal soldiers and marines, don't you think?"

"Oh, her *stores*, sir," a smile gradually dawning. "We have no orders regarding her *stores*, sir."

With a smile and a nod, James leaned over the rail and motioned for his men to get to work, and in a trice a dozen firkins of rum had been carried up from the hold, eleven for the Inniskillings, and one, oddly already tapped, consigned to the care of the Royal Marines. When *Clarendon* had left Portsmouth she had been stowed for another cross-Atlantic voyage, and James, who had an eye for such things, noticed she had received a generous rum allotment. The British army had very strict rules regarding the distribution of government stores, though James and his brothers were willing to interpret those rules to best meet the needs of the service. The rum was meant for His Majesty's soldiers, and if the Inniskilling officers conspired to have it consumed rather more quickly than regulations suggested, that was the merest technicality.

That night the enlisted men of the First hosted a welcome for the men drafted from the Second, the rum giving the occasion great momentum. After addressing the men, the officers turned the affair over to the Colour Sergeants, whose imposing presence kept things from getting out of hand. As with any body of hard-drinking men, particularly Irish men, there were a few fights, but there was also a great deal of singing, storytelling, and shared memories of a common home. The clear tenor of Private John Campbell, formerly of the Second Battalion, proved to blend perfectly with those of First Battalion favorites Corporal John McCourt and Private Arthur Toole. They combined on several comic and bawdy tunes that were very well received, and their rendering of "Do Bhi Bean Uasal" brought tears to every eye in the stable. The affair proved a great success, though the squalid battalion that crawled out from under the stable straw the next morning was incapable of any military function beyond shakily gathering for roll call.

James had assigned Blakeley to take every Six Company morning roll in order to learn the men's names, and so that they could come to know him. For the same purpose, James made it a point to attend as well, and he also required Coakley to rise early, if for no other reason than to prevent a backslide into indolence. That morning, the enlisted men of Six Company were of unique countenance, ranging from ghastly pale to a quite discernible green.

Blakeley, who had limited experience with soldiers in such a state, was less than patient with their distracted responses. "Devine!" he called. No reply. Blakeley checked his roll, "Corporal Benjamin Devine!" Still no response, other than a number of very discreet smiles as Devine stood with his eyes closed and a decided sway to his stance. Blakeley's voice grew shrill as he yelled, "Corporal Devine! I know you are present, say something!" The only response that Devine could tender was an exquisitely timed fall, crumbling into the soft dirt of the stable yard.

"I believe that Corporal Devine is present, Ensign," said James straight-faced. Discipline required that during the taking of the roll the men in the ranks remained straight-faced as well. James looked closely to ensure that there was no nonsense, and was pleased to see the expected iron discipline. There were, however, many eyes that sparkled in merriment, which pleased him as well.

Later, an annoyed Ensign Blakeley approached his lieutenant in the stable yard and said, "Begging your pardon, sir, but I wonder at the wisdom of allowing the men such access to drink. This morning they were quite surly, and many could barely stand."

"Ensign, we did not allow the men to debauch themselves without a purpose. Here beginneth the lesson: You will please remember that under normal conditions, a disparate body of men may or may not evolve into a unified whole, and it certainly does not happen quickly. It requires an unusual situation, either pleasant or unpleasant, to draw men together. The men you saw this morning were mean, crapulous, and foul, but they were beginning to bond; there were the first signs that they were members of the same company, and the same battalion."

"I see, sir. What form of unpleasantness would draw the men together, sir?"

"There is nothing like a battle to shape a company and a battalion. Now, mind you, pushing a unit that is not wholly united into a battle is a risky proposition: battle can meld it into a cohesive whole, but it can wholly shatter it as well. And certainly it would be a great sin to wish for a battle, as battles are, on the whole, very unpleasant things. But I think that our battle is just over the horizon, and we cannot afford to face the French with some of our men not feeling a close bond with the rest. It is all about cohesion, the bonds between men, Ensign. Here endeth the lesson; I believe you are required at drill."

As Blakeley headed off to work with the third section of their company, he was glad Lieutenant Lockwood had been so friendly. Some days he was very nice, but other days he was as sullen as the men at that morning's roll call. He could not understand why.

Later that day, word came that the Inniskillings would move out and join the 10th British Brigade under Major General Sir John Lambert. The brigade was forming at Ghent, where the Inniskillings were to be brigaded with the 1/4th, the King's Own Regiment, and the 1/40th, the Somersetshire Regiment. The news quickly filtered through the battalion, and it was greeted with a general sense of approval. The Inniskillings had served with both the 1/4th and 1/40th in Spain and had learned to respect their steadiness. No battalion wanted to be brigaded with unreliable battalions that might break at a critical moment and leave them in the lurch. The conversations amongst the men caused Blakeley to search out Lieutenant Lockwood again, hoping that the lieutenant was still in a good humour.

James was in the stable offices that were serving as battalion headquarters, filling out his Company Books. He was notorious for being tardy with his paperwork, and the absence of the Quartermaster Sergeant, lost somewhere with the rest of the battalion staff, allowed him to nearly forget it completely. But Archibald had mentioned it with an official tone in his voice, so James grudgingly spent his afternoon completing the considerable paperwork that came with commanding one of His Majesty's infantry companies. James kept a Day Book in his pocket, in which he kept track of all the myriad items for which his men would be charged against their pay. Private Jack McHail, for example, had managed to misplace his bayonet, and he would be reimbursing His Majesty for the replacement over the next several months. Such details were to be transferred to the Company Ledger by the 24th of every month, and Lieutenant Lockwood was now three months in arrears. Looking up from the Ledger, James glanced at the equally overdue Order Book, the Description Book, the Clothing and Accoutrement Book, and the Weekly Mess Book, all of which still demanded his attention.

Walking into the stable office, Ensign Blakeley quickly realized that the Lieutenant's good humour had dried up, but it was too late to alter course, so he forged ahead with a tepid, "Begging your pardon, sir." James did not raise his head from the paperwork, only looking up impatiently from under arched eyebrows.

"Another question, sir, if I may?" asked Blakeley, not admitting to himself that he craved more fatherly words from the lieutenant. James grunted, still looking up impatiently, so Blakeley continued quickly, "The men are talking about Skins, Lions, and Exellers, sir, and I didn't want to look foolish in front of them. Can you tell me what they are on about, please, sir?"

James relaxed, flipped the Day Book shut, leaned back in his chair, and laced his fingers behind his head. "Yes, I suppose that would puzzle a new man; those are old nicknames from Spain. Skins is a corruption of Inniskilling, so that refers to our glorious band of brothers, forever bound together by rum, battle and mountains of God damned paper. The 4th Foot has a lion on their shako plates, so there are your Lions, and the 40th Foot has the Roman numerals XL on their shako plates, hence the Exellers."

Blakeley was not going to risk being more of a bore, so he said, "Thank you, sir; that was all that I had to ask."

Blakeley had already started for the door when the Lieutenant added, "John, I can understand your not wanting to look foolish in front of the men, but there are times when you should ask them such things. It would show that you are coming to trust them. I can see them coming to know and respect you, and you can use such questions to show you trust them as well. Pray keep that in mind; you are showing the first signs of becoming a fine officer."

The lieutenant had never before used his Christian name, and Blakeley had a broad grin on his face and a fresh commitment to his new profession as he returned to his duties, the praise ringing in his ears, his feet scarcely touching the ground.

*****

Another bit of news that pleased the Inniskillings was the rapidly circulated report that the battalion was to move to Ghent by barge. The Inniskillings had always marched to war, and the thought of traveling those fifty miles by barge was akin to being carried by royal carriage. The barges normally carried grain from the heart of Belgium down to the channel ports for export, and they easily carried grinning Irish infantry back up the canal to Ghent. Each barge carried a company, pulled by one great horse with apparent ease. The horses were changed at well-managed intervals as the battalion silently slid through the flat, prosperous Belgian countryside. The fields were verdant with new grain, the numerous herds of dairy cows were fat and content, and the widely spaced farms were large and well-kept. The Belgians were not overly interested in the red-coated Irishmen, as large farms in late May brook no delay, but they were friendly enough, and returned the waves as the laden barges glided past.

As many of the men were still feeling the effects of the draft party, the barges were filled with napping soldiers, lying on the warm planking of the shallow hulls, the soft May sun on their faces. Their officers thus felt free to leave them to the sergeants, and Archibald commandeered one small, gaily-painted barge as their exclusive conveyance. Several smoked the cigars they had garnered in the Caribbean, chatting along the rails, taking sips from the bottle of brandy that Lieutenant Reddock had purchased at the quayside.

Scattered about the deck were four captains, eleven lieutenants, five ensigns, two assistant surgeons, the quartermaster, and a single black rabbit. From Bermuda, across the Atlantic to Portsmouth, and now Belgium, Blackie had survived the carnivorous attentions of soldiers, sailors, and marines, and his survival skills had earned him acceptance amongst the officers of the 1/27th. He had been napping at Blakeley's feet, but after a bit his awkward, loping half-hop bore him across the deck to accept an apple core offered by Lieutenant Massey and a gentle scratch behind his imposing ears from Lieutenant Pitts.

Of the battalion's twenty-three officers, twenty-two were enjoying themselves. The only negative note was again the jarring behavior of Captain Barr, who sat alone in the shadows at the stern, wrapped in his elegant cloak, his shako pulled down over his eyes, silent. None of the other Inniskilling officers had spoken to him regarding anything but service matters since Bermuda, and to all appearances that situation was entirely to Barr's liking.

The officers' barge passed a picturesque village as James stood alone at the rail. Barr silently came up beside him and hissed, "When will you stop your God damned prating?"

James had been daydreaming, and in a startled tone he turned and said, "What? Whatever do you mean?"

In a low, vicious voice Barr said, "You never shut your fucking mouth. I see you talking to the others, playing the great man. Just you watch your mouth, damn you. I am watching, listening. If you let anything, *anything*, slip about me, I will see you and that family of yours dragged through the mud. So just shut your God damned mouth." And with that, Barr strolled casually back to the stern, where he lay down and went to sleep.

Stunned to be addressed in such a fashion by anyone, let alone by a man in the King's uniform, James made no reply. As Barr lay sleeping James grew angry, disgusted with himself for bearing such abuse, abuse that he *had* to bear, as he wracked his mind searching for a solution, a solution that had eluded him since 1798.

*****

Ghent, Belgium
June 1st, 1815

My dearest Brigid,
I dearly hope that you and the children are well and happy. We have been constantly on the move, and I have received no letters from you since Jamaica. I confess to having read that letter so many times that it grows quite worn.

I suppose that you have heard of the return of that villain Bonaparte. We have been hustled across the ocean to join the army here in Belgium. The voyage was not very pleasant, but we have finally reached Ghent, and at last we have time to catch our breaths, and hope that our mail catches up with us.

Before I forget, Doolan asks whether you and the girls would each like a silk scarf, and if so, what colour? He has made friends, and I trust that is all, with a woman whose brother owns a shop on the Place de Armes. Tom and I have had a few opportunities to stroll around Ghent, and have been struck by the abundance and prices of items that would seem impossible luxuries at home. I shall keep an eye open for something for the boys as well, as I would not want them to feel slighted.

The town itself is quite lovely, and it is interesting that all the signs are in both Flemish and French. While both factions appear to do very well, there is a certain level of disdain between them. Our men are billeted in a neighborhood on the western side of town, not far from their citadel, a silly, crumbling thing full of trembling militiamen. The Belgian civilians are thus far friendly and generous, and the men are settling quickly, especially as some of them have some French that they picked up when we were in the south of France, not so very long ago. Even Doolan has a few words, though most of them are not fit for polite society.

Tom, Elliott, Campbell, and I are all billeted together on a grain merchant named DeVore. We drew straws, and Tom has been awarded the finest room, a lovely little apartment on the ground floor that opens up onto a small private garden of great beauty. I, of course, drew the short straw, and have an enormous attic room that has very little furniture, no carpets, and even on sunny days it is as cold and gloomy as the average cave, and less cheerful.

James paused to sharpen his pen, and as he did so he cut the palm of his hand.

"Damn," he muttered, which woke Tom, who was napping on James's bed with an empty bottle of Madeira cradled in his arms.

Tom noticed the blood on James's hand, and asked, "Suicide attempt?"

"Stigmata."

"Blasphemous dog," Tom said before rolling over and going back to sleep.

Tom is here, and while currently indisposed he would certainly want me to forward his love. I also remember to mention that Elliott's younger brother Peter has attached himself to us. He is an ensign in some other regiment (I forget which; pray witness the first signs of my impending dotage) and happened to be in Portsmouth on leave when we passed through. Horse Guards looks favorably on young officers who show initiative, so young Elliott has come along as a Volunteer, in hope of seeing some action and distinguishing himself. I hope that he does not come to regret it, and Elliott has quietly asked some of us to keep an eye out for Peter, who I hope will be a friend to John Blakeley.

Pray tell the children not to worry about the war. Bonaparte is unlikely to attack us, as we grow stronger every day, and the Prussians aren't far away, and they are very numerous as well. The people here are deathly afraid of the Prussians, as they well should be, as the Prussians are notorious looters and vandals. The few that I have seen here in Ghent seem to meet the Belgians' prejudice completely. Dirty, undisciplined devils, who think they own the world. Perhaps after the French occupation of Prussia they feel that they are owed, but the Belgians are their allies, though that does not seem to make much difference when they see something that they desire.

You must not worry, either, dear. I am eating and resting more than a serving officer ought, and Doolan is having a grand time shopping here, as everything is so cheap and plentiful. My only concern is finding an acceptable horse. All of us are looking, of course, but so far only a few have made a purchase. Towne has found a lovely gray mare, and Barr has purchased a great black thing that bites; it suits him. I got a good price for the horse and tackle I sold in Canada (you may recall Robert the Roan) so I think I will be able to afford a decent mount. I hope not to be the only company commander who has to walk.

It is very late now, and the candle here in this empty old cavern is sputtering, so I had best close, with my dearest love. I shall write again in a few days; pray write to me as soon as you may, as there is no telling when your past letters shall reach me.

James paused for a moment, and then with a serious, nearly desperate, look on his face, he went on.

Barr's abuse grows worse; every officer in the battalion wonders at my patience with him, and while no one has hinted at it, I wonder if they think me shy. I shall bear any rumour to keep you and the children loved and honoured. In the end, all that matters is our love for each other, and that I return to you. It must be soon, or I shall go mad.

With all my love,
James

*****

The garden room Tom had won in the drawing was indeed a prize. The room was pleasant unto itself, but its true worth was in the private garden upon which it opened. It was walled on all four sides, and shaded by a great chestnut that grew to immense height. The garden's glory was a mad collection of flowers, seemingly all in bloom that day, their blossoms impossibly perfect in the sharp light of early morning. Tom, who had a deep, private love of flowers, sat amongst them with great contentment.

There was a sharp rap on his door, as James had come down from his melancholy attic through the kitchens, bearing two large cups of coffee and a grim look.

"Is this garden not the glory of the world, brother?" asked Tom, sipping his coffee, sweeping his arm towards the riotous flowers.

"Eh? Oh, I hadn't noticed. Yes, they are quite pretty, I suppose."

"You are in a study this morning, I find. Not bad news from home, I trust?

"Oh, no, nothing like that. In a way, perhaps, but that is foolish to think. Last night I had another one of my dreams."

"Dear, dear, I am concerned to hear it. Shall I call for the doctor?"

"Ah, Tom, I didn't come down here to have you flog me. This damned dream has already made me so very low. If you won't give me an ear then I may very well go back upstairs and hang myself, and then you will have to live the rest of your life in soul-wrenching regret."

That got a bark of laughter from Tom, who replied, "You know, back in Leicester there are some old country people, pagan heretics, of course, who interpret dreams. In the Middle Ages they were burned at every opportunity. When this war is over I shall take you to find one; they would have a field day with you. So, pray, James, what dream had you last night?"

"I was at the great Dublin fair, at one of the grand horse races they run every day for two weeks. It's a grand way to spend a day; I'll take you there some day, after we see your dream-witch. At any rate, in my dream there were thirty or so other people there at the tables, dressed up to watch the races. They were all friends from early in my life. People from my boyhood in Malahide and from school in Surrey, and friends from when Brigid and I were first married."

"That does seem the most horrible of dreams, brother."

"But you see, Tom, in the dream they were all older now, not the young, happy, ambitious people I loved. They had become old, bitter, and disappointed. Two of the boys I grew up with in Malahide, David Boyer and Kevin McMaster, were there; Lord, the fun we had as boys! But now they were old, complaining about their careers, their wives, their children, not a drop of joy left in them, heavy, bitter men. Girls I loved, after a fashion, as a boy: the Curnes sisters, and that McKenzie girl. Old now, heavy, matronly, caked in rouge, dressing like they were twenty years younger and fifty pounds lighter. Righteous, angry, spiteful creatures, none of the grace and laughter I loved them for. Christ, what a blow to see them all, now."

"The Devil, or should I say, your Devil, is usually involved in these things; did he make an appearance last night?"

"No," said James absently, "he told me once he does not care for racing, as they are too unpredictable for his tastes. He concentrates on people; far less element of chance."

Tom sat back and folded his arms, gazing into the flowers. "Damn, James, I may go hang myself now as well. Come, was I in the dream, at all?"

"Yes, I am happy to report you were there, but young and dapper as ever. And now that I think of it, you didn't say a word the whole day. I had forgotten that. Everyone else chattered away, but you were as silent as a tomb. I wonder why that is."

For some time they sat there together, ignoring the beauty of the garden, time slipping past them, ignored as well, to their peril.

James broke the silence. "One other bit: I rarely wager, you know; it is a luxury not afforded to men with large families. But at that race I bet a hundred pounds, I remember thinking it was a fortune, it was every penny I had, on a mare named Gliondar. It's odd, but I remember the name distinctly: Gliondar. I have no idea what it means. At any rate, I bet on her, knowing, *knowing*, that she would win, but she lost miserably, disgracefully. I can't describe what a blow that was. I feel it even now."

"But still, just a dream, James."

"Yes, thank God. But it seemed so *real*. That race, and all those people I had such affection for, young and happy, turned so bitter and disappointed. Disappoint*ing*. Thank God that Brigid and the children weren't there, that way. I would not have been able to bear that."

Only then did James notice the exquisite smells of the garden, as lavender, rose, and a dozen other scents tumbled together in a heady mixture. They served to clear his head of most of the effects of the dream, but there still lingered in his mind the end of the nightmare, the finale he would not discuss. Of how Charles Barr had been at the race party, young and lean and fierce, of how he had sat far apart from the others, on Brigid's worn pew from St. Brigid's. He wore his uniform, but it was the uniform of the Devil's army, every bit of the uniform black, black. On the pew beside Barr lay a hundred letters, addressed but not yet posted, each capable of destroying the Lockwood family, as Barr sat sharpening a long thin knife, a hellish glitter in his eyes.

Chapter Nine

Clonakilty

Of all the people of the world, young women and the Irish are the two segments of humanity who feel love most keenly. Mary Lockwood, a fifteen-year-old Irish girl, was thus more susceptible to heartache than most. The object of her affection was in many ways an unfortunate one, as George Boffut, the eighteen-year-old son of a prominent local Protestant family, was tall, handsome, and insufferable.

Ordinarily Boffut would not have bothered with a girl as young as Mary, but she was the very image of her mother, and thus an exceptionally attractive young lady. A further consideration, a consideration of prime importance to Boffut, was the fact her father was absent.

Boffut had been away from the quiet Clonakilty social scene for more than a year, as he had gotten one of the family's servants, Helen McCarthy, with child, and he had been hustled off to his uncle's home in Scotland until the girl's family could be bought off. Ordinarily a girl in such a situation would have been dismissed from service without ceremony or compensation, but there were still a few parts of Ireland where the old clans merited a grudging respect: there

133

were many McCarthys in Munster, and they were a proud lot. Young Boffut's situation was further complicated by two other local men who complained that George had ruined their daughters. While they lacked the backing of a powerful clan, it still required a few pounds of Boffut senior's substantial wealth to silence their complaints. Servant girls were considered fair game, but village girls were another matter, and George was provoking some considerable ill will, by necessity concealed but present nonetheless, amongst the people of Clonakilty.

No one in town was aware of an incident in Scotland in which George had badly beaten the daughter of his uncle's gamekeeper, a young woman who had been so bold as to laughingly reject his advances. George's escape from a dozen vengeful McGregor claymores was due solely to a fast horse and a dark night, though his parents were gullible enough to believe his return home was due to a longing for their company.

The family's official explanation for young Boffut's absence from Clonakilty was a term at Trinity College, but anyone who was acquainted with George Boffut would no more connect him with Trinity than Lucifer with Christmas. George had been home for just a month when he first noticed Mary Lockwood at a dinner at the Butler's home. Boffut was most particular in the attention he paid her, commenting on the purity of her blonde hair, and Brigid soon found it necessary to make her excuses and get Mary home. Brigid paid no calls on the Boffuts, and she hoped she could avoid them altogether until George could find some other girl on whom he could lavish his attentions.

Brigid managed to avoid the Boffuts for more than a month, and it had been some time since Mary had last mentioned her *beau idéal*, until an afternoon came when they heard a carriage coming up their lane. Carriage traffic was very rare there, as their lane frankly led nowhere to which a moneyed family would care to travel. Brigid listened intently, biting her lip, as both girls ran to the window to see if they indeed had visitors. A quick glimpse around the room made it clear the Lockwoods were not prepared for company. Brigid and the girls were sewing shirts for the boys; cloth and thread were scattered across the settee, and all three of them were wearing old frocks that were far from their finest. Sergeant was soundly and massively asleep atop Brigid's feet, and the house smelled distinctly of fish, as Mrs. Cashman was preparing a fine salmon that had come as a gift from her son Stephen. Thankfully, Joseph and Richard were off building a creditable fort in the woods, but construction of such an edifice rendered them completely unfit for society.

"It is a beautiful carriage, Mama!" cried Cissy.

"Mama, the Boffuts!" added Mary in a scream laden with delight and horror.

"Oh, dear!" cried their distraught mother. "Quickly girls, we must hide this horrid squalor. Mrs. Cashman, visitors! Sergeant, *mo cara*, get up, please!"

At the first glimpse of the carriage, Mrs. Cashman threw open the kitchen windows to alleviate the worst of the salmon, and was hustling about the drawing room, straightening the clutter and quickly brushing out the girls' hair. The girls were not so panicked that they could not mount a brief, silent struggle over who would wear the red barrette, and who the blue.

Brigid was not much help in the preparations, as she remained pinned to the settee by the slumbering Sergeant. No amount of tugging or pleading could rouse him, despite the stampede of frantic activity. Finally Brigid twisted his ear and wished his soul to the Devil, whereupon Sergeant leapt to his feet; sensing the anxiety in those he loved and feeling he had been somehow remiss in his duty, he began to bark ferociously and indiscriminately, hoping to make amends.

Outside, Mrs. Boffut was pointing out the glory of the lane's towering beeches to her two children, giving the Lockwoods a few minutes' grace, since she was visiting without invitation, a sometimes precarious proposition. She was a tall, graceful woman with a good heart, who had married a man her exact opposite. To her dismay, her son and his younger sister Mary had grown into tall, graceful, overtly cruel, selfish creatures.

"Mother," said George testily, "are we here to visit, or stare at these damned trees?"

"George! How dare you speak to me in such a fashion!"

George was about to make a scathing reply learned from his father, but was brought up short by the sound of Sergeant's fierce barking. In addition to a litany of other faults, George hated and feared dogs, so he assumed Sergeant's ferocity was directed at him. This prompted him to feign an interest in the beeches for a few minutes until the dog was silenced and his mother led them to the door of Fáibhile Cottage.

Mrs. Cashman answered the door with a natural graciousness, and as the Boffuts passed in she looked over George with an appraising eye. "As they said," she told herself, "a devil and a rogue, that one."

Brigid and Mrs. Boffut greeted each other formally but with the underlying understanding that they liked one another. Mrs. Boffut had dressed carefully, wanting to look as if she felt a visit to the Lockwoods was an occasion of some note, but also hoping to avoid any appearance of flaunting her vastly superior wardrobe. George made a leg to the Lockwood ladies, glancing up at Mary, who blushed extremely.

"Will you sit, Mrs. Boffut?" asked Brigid, "and perhaps you should care for a cup of tea?"

"You are very kind, Mrs. Lockwood, but we shall trouble you for only a moment. I really must apologize for not warning you of our visit. We are hosting a dance to celebrate George's return from Trinity, and we were most anxious to deliver a personal invitation for you and your lovely daughters to attend."

"That is very kind, of you, Mrs. Boffut, and we do bid you welcome home, George. But my daughters are still rather too young to come out." Brigid avoided looking at her girls, feeling their pleading eyes on her.

"I quite understand, my dear, but please allow me to qualify my invitation. Our little event is intended for just the young people of the area, not at all a formal affair. Just a chance for them to practice their social skills, and dance a bit, and for George to reacquaint himself with some of the finer young people, such as these two fine young ladies."

Brigid made the mistake of looking at the girls. Their glee and hope, and her own desire for them to fit in, overcame her caution and she soon relented. The Boffuts hurried off, pleased, George looking optimistic, making eyes at Mary, she demurely making eyes back at him.

The three Lockwood ladies stood in their front garden, waving goodbye as the Boffuts' carriage clattered off. As soon as it was out of sight, the girls screamed in delight and hugged each other in delirious rapture. They hugged their mother, effusive in their thanks, hugged the stoic Mrs. Cashman, and ran upstairs to see if they had anything suitable to wear to such a grand affair. The ball was more than a month away, on Saturday, June 17th, so there was time to carefully prepare. As Brigid passed back into the house she avoided Mrs. Cashman's eye as deliberately as she avoided looking into her own conscience.

"With your pardon, Missus, that George Boffut is a devil, for all his looks and ways. You know his kind; Hell is lined with them, thirteen deep."

"I will be at the dance," answered Brigid as she stood looking out the window, "I can keep them apart."

"I am no bearer of tales, but this day I shall tell you, Missus, that in town that young man's name is poison. *Wisha*, whether he forced himself on those three girls is not for me to say, boys and girls being as they are, but I would not give ha'pence for his life if he ever finds himself alone on a dark road, with the McCarthy men at hand." Then, in another tone, Catherine added, "Father McGlynn is hosting a country dance at the Linen Hall next week, with never the likes of George Boffut to be seen."

"You might recall the Father's last dance. The men got to drinking, and of course their talk turned to rebellion. I can still remember their faces when they looked up and saw me standing there; friends of my family, men I've known all my life, now look at me with suspicion."

"Oh, Missus, it's just a few fools' babble."

"John O'Leary, Tom Callaghan, Liam Fitzgerald, my own cousin Patrick? No, times are changing, and people are choosing sides: it's the green or the orange." Brigid still stared out the window, her voice growing bitter. "Just look at my name: O'Brian Lockwood, each half hated by the other. So what am I to do, when neither side truly trusts me, when both think me capable of betraying their precious cause to the other? And what they think of me, they think of my children. Until the lieutenant comes home I need to consider any chance that offers itself, to show both sides that we can be trusted, to build friendships that might protect us if the damned blood flows again."

*****

A few days later, at a morning hour long before the Lockwoods would normally expect company, there was the sound of several horses outside the house. The boys, at the table in the drawing room, were more than willing to be distracted from their copy books, and after peering through the windows they ran calling to their mother, "Mama, Mama, there are soldiers coming up the lane! Please, *please*, may we go outside to see them?"

Brigid distractedly waved her permission for the boys to go out the back, and as they bolted into the kitchen there was an aggressive knock at the front door. Sergeant growled and barked, and the very startled Brigid Lockwood did not wait for Mrs. Cashman to come in from the kitchen, but opened the door herself. She had been around soldiers for many years, and even before they spoke she knew them: two Yeomanry cavalrymen who wanted to look jaunty, but instead looked sloppy, careless, in expensive uniforms that were badly cared for. There was rust on their scabbards, and the pistol in the officer's belt was poised to neuter him at the least provocation.

"I am Lieutenant Bookey of the Camolin Yeomanry Cavalry," said the cocksure young officer. "Last night a barn on the estates of Lord Bandon was burned, and a number of his cattle were houghed. We are searching the vicinity for any suspects."

"You will find no arsonists here, Lieutenant Bookey, nor will you find anyone who lames livestock. My husband is Lieutenant James Lockwood, a line officer of His Majesty's First Battalion, 27th Foot. I am an officer's wife, and I know a soldier, particularly an officer, of quality removes his shako when speaking with a lady."

Her manner was so assured, so versed in military and common courtesy, that Bookey immediately removed his hat, though his arrogant sergeant stepped back and strolled out into the front garden, looking about as if he expected to find a Whiteboy behind every flower. "Beg pardon, ma'am," muttered Bookey.

"Not at all, Lieutenant Bookey. I welcome you to Clonakilty. Colonel Simon of the West Cork Yeomanry is a friend of the family. Perhaps you are acquainted with him as well?"

"I have yet not had the honour, ma'am." Bookey was rude, but not completely stupid, and he quickly took Mrs. Lockwood's point: she had powerful friends, and was a trusted member of the better class of people. "We arrived only yesterday, at the specific request of Lord Bandon. We had good results in quelling this type of mayhem back in Wexford, and it appears we have arrived none too soon."

"I hope Lord Bandon's losses were not severe," said Brigid. "Are there any suspects? Can the Whiteboys be assembling again?"

Some of Bookey's confidence returned as he replied, "There are no solid suspects yet, madam, but we intend to knock a few papists about, burn a few cottages, and they'll turn on each other like mad dogs. These papists have no stomach for English steel."

At that point Brigid had a distinct choice to make, but she did not pause to ponder her options, instead quickly replying with an edge in her voice, "It may disappoint you to learn, sir, that I am an adherent of the Catholic faith."

Brigid had intended her comment to check Bookey once again, but instead it prompted a suspicious look to cross his face. "Very well, then, ma'am, I shall then ask you about a man who has been seen skulking about the fields hereabout. Average height, trim, perhaps a sailor? What have you to say about that?"

"There has been no such person in this house, and I will thank you to leave now. I shall certainly discuss this with Colonel Simon at the first opportunity," she said angrily, forcefully closing the door. She had been so distracted by Bookey that when she turned she was startled to see Mrs. Cashman standing at the kitchen door, holding Sergeant's collar and a kitchen knife. Catherine was prepared for the worst, as she was very aware of the shades of red coats. In any given situation, His Majesty's regulars could be relied upon to do as they were told, the militia may or may not have done so, but the yeomanry typically did as they pleased. They were men who were capable of exceptional brutality, who protected their class and their superiority as they saw fit.

The boys stood at the roadside and watched the yeomen with something like adulation, blissfully unaware of their mother's anger and Mrs. Cashman's panic, while their three sisters were upstairs in the small room they shared, each involved with concerns of her own. Lucy had been playing with her doll, but when she had one of her coughing fits her sisters had laid her in her little bed and she immediately went to sleep. Relieved of the need to watch her baby sister for a while, Mary began to brush her hair, staring out the rear window, dreaming of George Boffut. Cissy had no desire to discuss George, as she had heard nothing but sighs for George Boffut from her sister for days on end, so she contented herself with curling up on her bed and rereading the last letter she had received from her father.

> *My dearest Cissy,*
>
> *In your last letter you said you are to begin watercolors with Madame de Berruyer, and you would like to make a painting of a soldier of my regiment. I am very pleased you are learning to paint, and doubtless you have already surpassed your old father in many of the social graces. I very much look forward to seeing you again, and to see how you are growing into such a fine young lady.*
>
> *My first instinct is to suggest that a soldier is not much of a subject for a genteel painting, but if you are determined, please allow me to make some suggestions.*
>
> *There are, I think, too many artists who portray soldiers as tall, straight, handsome, clean, happy, and well dressed. Average people see such paintings, and think a soldier's life is something it surely is not. Instead, you may wish to paint a soldier as he really is. The choice is yours, of course, but if you should care to follow my advice, here are a few points to follow:*

Our basic uniform is much like every other British infantryman. The coat is a red wool affair, and our trousers are gray. You must not use a bright red, as the dyes in the uniform coats fade quickly, and a soldier of any time at all has a brick red coat, and his trousers fade to a worn gray. (Campaigning can be very hard on the uniforms. In Spain, which is mostly covered in thorns and very sharp rock, almost every man in the battalion had patches on his knees, elbows, and seat, which can look very odd indeed.) The facings (the cuffs and collar, my dear) of our regiment are buff in color, but again, they fade as well, so perhaps a pale tan is best. Some regiments have their drummers wear reversed colours, such as a buff coat and red facings, but we did away with that practice some time ago, so that everyone wears the King's red. Drummers are typically big, brave, showy fellows, not boys as so many silly people suppose, particularly as the drums are great heavy brass brutes.

Cissy paused for a moment as she listened to her mother's steps hurry up the stairs and down the hall to her room. She was afraid that she might hear her mother crying, so she read the rest of the letter with great concentration.

Our shakos (the caps, sweetheart) are of course tall black useless leather things that won't keep you warm in winter, or cool in summer, or keep the rain from running down your back. They do make some of the shorter fellows look a bit more fierce, and they look well when they are mounted with the plume and cords, and the brass plate is quite fine, but on campaign they are covered by a black oilskin cover, all hint of fashion extinguished.

As for your average soldier of the Inniskilling Regiment, you will find him to be rather lean, not very tall, and brown as a nut. The hair is usually cut short, though while on campaign the opportunities to shave are rare, and we officers grow outrageous mustaches. You will not go far wrong by making your man look at least a bit dirty, tired, and hungry. Not overly happy, perhaps, but confident, and consigned to his duty.

But I must not make things quite so grim, as we are having a fine time of it here in Belgium. We are fed like prize cattle, and you would laugh to see my whiskers, which I tend with great vanity. Private Doolan asks me to forward his fondest regards, and wishes that you might pay his duties and respects to your mother.

Good luck with your painting, my dear. I doubt that you will be able to put such a treasure in the post, but do please keep it so that I might see it when I come home. We shall have so much to talk about, and I hope to bring home a few things from my travels.

Your Most Affectionate Father
James Lockwood

In truth, Cissy Lockwood really wished to paint a picture of her father, but she would not admit to the fact that she could not remember his face as clearly as she used to. She did remember his size and strength and kindness, and she saw his blue eyes looking back at her with every glance in her mirror. But his face and the sound of his voice were lost to her, and when late that night she came to realize that, she silently cried herself to sleep.

Lieutenant and Mrs Lockwood

*****

Two nights later was the new moon. Into that exceptional darkness, a low shebeen in Baile an Chaisleáin emitted a few dim slivers of light across a line of small fishing boats that were drawn up on the hardscrabble beach. The tavern was populated by a handful of local men, landless laborers and coastal fishermen, worn men with hard hands. Baile an Chaisleáin was an isolated little village, but its location on a quiet inlet some twenty miles southeast of Clonakilty occasionally drew in fishermen from up and down the coast and from the desolate islands that lay beyond, men looking to sell their catch, pick up a few supplies, and to buy a drink under a dry roof. It had been some years since anyone had spoken English in the shebeen, and even a man who might offer to stand his round in English would have been eyed with great suspicion.

"Sure, they put Bandon's nose out of joint, boys," said John O'Sullivan, a laborer who had gone up toward Clonakilty in search of work, and who had come back with the latest news.

"Out of joint, John," said Tom McCarthy, "but it's brought the yeomanry down on our necks. Up at Fahouragh it was Kevin Flynn's cottage they burned to the ground, his cow killed, and it's him and those three babies sleeping in the fields with shite to eat, and him no more a Whiteboy than Saint Colm. Burning for nothing more than feckin' spite. Imagine what they'll do if they actually find a real Whiteboy. Jesus, Mary, and Joseph."

"Well, now," said the thirsty O'Sullivan, "a poor welcome home this is to a weary traveler, and me covering those miles home in a great wearing hurry to bring the news to my own, and here I sit ignored and forgotten, my throat as dry as Noah in the desert."

"I think you've got that wrong, there, as sure wasn't it Jesus in the desert?" asked young Liam McCarthy, Tom's nephew, who had yet to learn the subtle conventions of shebeen banter.

In the ensuing silent air of general disapproval, Tom McCarthy poured O'Sullivan another drink, telling his nephew, "Never you mind about correcting your elders, and them old and wise as Fiachadh of Munster himself." Then, to the rest of the house he said, "It's that the lad was an altar boy at Limerick, for a time, and the learning pours out sometimes, unchecked, like. But now, John O'Sullivan dear, you'll be telling us more about the Big Lord, if it pleases, with your throat soothed by my bottle, and us all ears for the hearing."

Appeased, O'Sullivan made as to begin, but first had a cautious look about the room, surveying the crowd. All locals, friends for the most part, good trustworthy lads, though he called over to Liam Collins, "Liam *a grah*, it's your friend there I've not come to know."

"Ah, its manners of a Saxon I have, John *a grah*, not to introduce my friend to this worthy house, though sure it's many of you men of the sea who have seen me hauling in full gleaming nets with my oldest and closest friend John McCarthy, him back from long years in the Navy, but at last home to his friends and comrades."

This last word was a hint to the knowing, but again young Liam McCarthy transgressed, calling, "A McCarthy, is he! Well, he shall drink from my Uncle's bottle, and sit with us and tell of his people, as Uncle knows every branch of the clan McCarthy from the Tuatha de Danaan to this day. Tell us now, were your born hereabouts? Are you a Cork man, or a Kerry man?"

"You are good and generous man, Liam McCarthy," said the man called John McCarthy, "but as sore and worn as I am from making Liam Collins a rich man with the cod filling his boat, sure I shall drink from his bottle, he owing me the great debt of the world." Three men there knew John Cashman as John McCarthy, but they would never say so, in a seaside shebeen, in Cork gaol, or before the King's Bench. One of these men was Tom McCarthy, who silenced his nephew with a hard kick under the table and a wide-eyed scowl.

While this was going on, John O'Sullivan had taken the opportunity of drawing off another glass or two from the elder McCarthy's bottle, and now, properly inspired, he proceeded, a welcome diversion. "As I was saying, it's the Big Lord who's had his nose tweaked, a slap for him that slapped the common folk. They're saying it's ghosts who are houghing the sheep and cows of the landlords and their puppets, and the fairies who are setting light to their barns, as no one sees a soul, though the earth says that it's the Whiteboys who are returned to do the people's will."

"If I had a hundred pound I should give them all up to be a Whiteboy, and do the people's will," said Liam McCarthy with boyish enthusiasm. His uncle raised his eyes to heaven, not bothering to kick him again.

"Well might you say so, young Liam," said O'Sullivan, "with your valiant heart, but sure the yeomanry and militia are stirred, the landlords howling so, and it would be your own mother's grief to see you carried to Clonakilty in a gaol cart, to be hung like a common thief, even with your elegant education, the sorry and the woe."

"I don't give a shite for these cowardly yeomen, and sure isn't it our own people who fill the ranks of the militia, even with Proddy officers?"

"You'll change your tune, lad," said Liam Collins, suddenly angry, "when the yeomen kick in your door in the middle of the night and drag you away, laying their hands on your wife and children, burning cabin and rick. And don't think for a minute that the militia won't be just as hard. Sure the rankers may be Catholics, but isn't it from Dublin, Carrickfergus, or Sligo that they come, far from their homes, strangers to us, and Kerry looking like the far end of the world?"

There was an awkward lull in the conversation, as many there knew the loss that Collins had suffered in the '98. Finally O'Sullivan offered, "And won't the yeomen and militia be thick as Clare grass soon too, as I heard in my travels that another militia company is coming down from Kerry, and another troop of yeomen from away north somewhere. There will be more than cows' blood on the grass before long, as I see it."

If anyone had been looking, they would have noticed both John and Collins listening intently to O'Sullivan, and then exchanging glances with the older McCarthy.

Much later, McCarthy met Collins and John on the dark strand, nearly invisible, only the crunching of the beach rock betraying their presence. "What the hell were you thinking, McCarthy," said Collins softly, still angry, "saying that boy was ready to swear in. Stupid, naïve, and he can't be quiet for two minutes."

"Och, Liam, he's usually not like this. It must have him being nervous, and him having the drink."

"Well, he's not to be given the oath, and I'll be asking for your word not to swear him, and that you won't be having him on any of your operations." John was silent, intently watching Collins, learning. McCarthy was insulted, that much was obvious, as his own nephew had been rejected. Collins calmed himself, then continued, "It's especially cautious I am with you, Tom, as I count on you and your men to continue your good work. And in token of the regard I hold for you," leaning into the curragh, Collins pulled out a French musket and handed it to McCarthy.

"Jesus," muttered McCarthy, awestruck.

"If the yeoman and militia raise the stakes and start putting our folk in the ground, we must be ready to strike back. Hide it well, but if the need should arise the Whiteboys will have the means to respond in kind."

John had nothing to say during the exchange, but he wondered how well an aging Kerry farmhand, a simple man who didn't know one end of the musket from the other, would strike a blow against their oppressors. Still, a musket would bring McCarthy a great deal of stature in little Baile an Chaisleáin, and perhaps he might do some good with it. But as John Cashman was a man of some discernment, he knew that in Ireland there were infinite definitions of good.

Chapter Ten

Ghent, Belgium

The first morning after their arrival in Ghent was a cool, cloudy, breezy dawn, as the battalion NCOs gathered the men from their scattered billets and marched them down to the parade grounds that bordered the citadel. Morning parade was spent in extensive drilling of the companies, the first time that the men from the Second had formed ranks with their new mates. The new men, not wanting to look like green recruits, *earcach glas* as they were called in the 27th, did their best to look sharp, and the companies maneuvered crisply. There was a small crowd of Belgian civilians watching, the ladies in ornate bonnets and low-cut white dresses, so the men were determined to put on a good show.

Pleased with their precision, Archibald dismissed the battalion for dinner. Most of the officers stood chatting until they too broke up and went in search of their dinners. Tom came across Captain Pratt and asked, "By the way, Pratt, I've been meaning to ask you something. I heard a word recently whose meaning escapes me; I'm sure it is not English, and my mediocre French did not recognize it either. I know your Spanish is quite good. I have heard of a horse named 'Gliondar'... pray, do you know the word?"

"'Gliondar'?" Pratt knitted his brow in concentration. "No, I can't think of such a word in Spanish. I also have enough Italian to endanger my virtue, and I don't believe I have ever heard it there either."

Tom, who was looking forward to the *coq au vin* that Messr. DeVore's cook was preparing for them, was about to head off to find James when he was stopped by Sergeant Dunne of Four Company, who had been standing nearby in his role of interim battalion quartermaster sergeant. "Not meaning to intrude, sir, but I believe the word you're thinking of is '*gliondar*'," giving it a soft Irish pronunciation, "in the Irish it means 'joy', sir."

"Joy, is it? Why, thank you, Sergeant."

"Joy," Tom said to himself. He turned back into the park and saw James out on their parade ground, still working with young Blakeley, and stood watching them. He loved James Lockwood, and a deep sadness crept over him, wondering if James would indeed lose his bet.

*****

If Lieutenant Mainwaring looked upon Lieutenant Lockwood with affection and concern, Ensign Blakeley was looking upon him with increasing annoyance. Blakeley was anxiously awaiting his dismissal, as he was to accompany Coakley, Digby, and Peter Elliott in a sortie to a local café, a café that was frequented by young ladies rumoured to enjoy the company of dashing young officers. But Lieutenant Lockwood was not to be rushed.

"Very well, Ensign, it appears that you are sufficiently familiar with the various parts of the firelock: lock, stock, and barrel." Blakeley's hopes soared, then came crashing down as James continued to ponder young Blakeley's professional competence, saying, "Let us now see how you load and fire the weapon. You will please call out the steps as you perform them."

James knew, of course, that Blakeley was anxious to go, but he was purposefully drawing out the lesson. The boy had to learn that duty came first. Discipline, discipline.

"Load," said Blakeley, bringing the weapon to port arms.

"Mind your cock, Ensign."

"Sir?"

"You must begin with the firelock at half-cock."

"Oh. Yes, sir," said Blakeley, pulling the hammer back with some difficulty until it reached the half-cock position with a satisfying click.

"That weapon has a strong spring and a solid lock. That is something to check on every firelock in the company, as springs and locks can wear out or bind up. Worn locks can release early, and it is damned unpleasant if your firelock were to discharge when you'd rather it didn't. Pray proceed."

Blakeley opened the pan and said, "Handle cartridge." With that he reached into the cartridge box that hung at the back of his right hip, and awkwardly retrieved a cartridge. The manual dictated that at this point the end of the greased paper cartridge, including the ball, be bitten off, but the inexperienced ensign bit off rather too much, getting his lips black with powder. Wincing at the taste, Blakeley muttered, "Prime." He sprinkled a bit of the powder into the pan and flipped it closed.

"Cast about," mumbled Blakeley as he set the butt of the musket inside his right foot, poured the rest of the powder down the barrel, and then spit out the paper-wrapped ball and stuffed it into the muzzle.

"Draw ramrod... ram cartridge."

James was satisfied to see the boy force the ramrod all the way down, giving it two solid taps at the bottom of the barrel, seating the charge properly. "One point here, Ensign," said James. "A lazy, tired, or demoralized soldier may not bother to tamp the load all the way down, or he may drop the ball down without the paper wadding. Those tricks make loading faster, but the main reason for a man to load like a felon is to reduce the recoil. Our Bess does kick like a Donegal mule, and after a dozen shots you'll be black and blue. Some men will deliberately spill some powder onto the ground; such fellows will never see Heaven. But those tricks often result in misfires, and if by some miracle it does fire, the ball does not carry far, or hit hard enough to knock over a moderate kitten."

"Make ready," bringing the firelock up, Blakeley pulled the hammer back to full-cock. "Present." At this point he paused, not sure if the fashionable inhabitants of Ghent were prepared for a sample of the soldier's trade, but most of *le beau monde* had wandered off to their dinners as well.

The parade ground was bordered by one of the endless canals that laced through Ghent, and pointing out to the water James said, "There is a duck out there. Can you hit it, do you think, John?"

"I shall try, sir," Blakeley said nervously, the duck being in midstream about a hundred yards away.

Blakeley had never fired a musket before, and he held the weapon tentatively to his shoulder. "Hold it close," said James, "it shall knock you to Thursday, else."

The firelock was heavy, and Blakeley had a hard time trying to hold it level, let alone aiming it at the duck. He got it at least close, said "Fire," closed his eyes, and pulled the trigger. It seemed that the firing took an eternity: the hammer cracked forward, its flint striking the frizzen, sending a shower of sparks down into the pan. The ignition kicked the butt back into Blakeley's tender shoulder with great force, driving the ball down and out the barrel in a hot cone of fire and smoke. Blakeley was spun halfway to the ground with a shocked look on his face, amazed, *amazed*, at the amount of smoke and noise that one musket could make.

The duck, in no danger at a hundred yards from a smooth-bore musket in the hands of a green ensign, took to the air as James helped Blakeley to his feet with a smile.

"Welcome to the infantry, John. You will never carry a musket—that reminds me, though, that tomorrow we need to put an edge on your sword, and flints in your pistol—but it is important that you know what it is that we ask our men to do. The taste of powder and greased paper is very unpleasant; it will make them thirsty, when they can't spare half a minute for a drink, even if they have a drop left in their canteen. The firelock is heavy and hard to aim; there is not even a rear sight. The large charge and a large ball makes it kick hard, as you now know. You can see the smoke from our one discharge is amazing thick. Now think of thousands of men firing dozens of cartridges, each. All that noise, all that smoke. With so many balls in the air the laws of probability dictate that men are hit, and those heavy, soft lead balls cause horrid wounds. It's as close to hell as a living man can come."

Blakeley stood silent, holding the musket, rubbing his bruised shoulder, shocked into silence. "But for now," said James rather more cheerfully, "go catch up your brothers, before the locals think the French have arrived, and call out the gendarmerie."

James found Tom at the narrow footbridge that crossed the canal, looking displeased. James gave him an apologetic look and said, "I am sorry that I've delayed our dinner; I hope that you are not unhappy with me?"

"Do not concern yourself, brother, it is about something else entirely, I assure you." Tom made an effort to rally and continued, "Now let us step out sharply; a perfectly lovely dinner awaits us, which has been growing cold and congealed while you tormented that poor boy. Elliott and Campbell are certainly there by now, wolfing down Jacqueline's *coq au vin* without giving a thought to we two lost souls."

Madame Jacqueline Maurin was the attractive red-haired widow of a sergeant who had fallen in Napoleon's wars years earlier, now the capable cook for Messr. Devore's household, and at the mention of her name James colored a bit and said "Yes, of course."

As they strode up Theresianenstratt Tom suppressed a smile and said, "Madame seems very fond of you."

James stopped, held his right hand aloft, and said, "Upon my honour, Tom, upon my honour, now, I swear that I have done nothing to encourage that woman."

"Doubtless that is why she finds you so charming. I made my position very clear to her, but she is beyond disinterested. Perhaps if I had a wedding ring on my hand she would find me more palatable."

At their billet they found Elliott and Campbell standing in the dining room, discontentedly chewing on crusts of bread. "Here at last!" cried Campbell. "That madwoman wouldn't give us a bite to eat until you two came in. Perhaps now we will get something that might keep body and soul together."

Jacqueline was with them an instant later, serving with efficient kindness, with perhaps a special smile for Lieutenant Lockwood, who flushed yet again. The other three officers smiled discreetly at James's discomfort as Jacqueline served him the tender breast meat; her subtle display of its human equivalent made James even more uneasy. She served some of Messr. DeVore's best wine, a noble merlot, and before she returned to the kitchen she coyly filled James's glass, placing the bottle down beside his plate, and as she passed through the door she gave James a secret, particularly winning smile.

*****

The next morning broke cloudy but warm, the scent of verdant summer in the air. The Inniskilling officers assembled at Major Archibald's billet, across from the park in a lovely coral-colored house that was quickly being converted to battalion headquarters. The wealthy family that owned the house had prudently retreated to their country home, but had left their attentive staff to see to Archibald and his officers. Antoinette Lenoire, the very young, very nearly pretty junior maid of the house, was posted at the door to direct the red-coated gentlemen to the dining room, where they were to meet and enjoy their *petit déjeuner*.

On most occasions Archibald played the role of the dour Scot, and was thus not typically the most demonstrative of men. But that morning he could scarcely contain a boyish grin when he announced to his officers, "I am in receipt of an order from General Lambert, requiring that the Inniskillings provide a guard of honour for Louis XVIII." There was a general cheer of surprise and delight, as such plums were typically the jealously held prerogative of the Guard regiments. The Bourbon court had fled Paris just ahead of Napoleon's triumphant return, and Louis and his entourage had settled in Ghent, under the protective wing of Wellington's Allied army.

"Each guard," continued the smiling Archibald, "will consist of one officer and thirty men. I shall take the first rotation, marching out tomorrow morning, and then each company commander will take a turn, and eventually each of the subalterns. We will do our best to get every officer an opportunity to wait upon the Bourbons, but I must stress that our priority remains a flawless performance and an impeccable appearance."

In the following days, while waiting for his turn with the mobile Bourbon court, James made a deliberate effort to avoid Madame Maurin, instead trying to amuse himself with the spectacularly varied rumours that filtered down to the battalion. The dapper Messr. DeVore, for instance, shared the news that Bonaparte had been converted to Islam, and that a massive Turkish army was sailing to his aid. Then Ensign Blakeley, who for all his naïveté still spoke an elegant French, came back from a *rencontre* at the café with word that the French army, three hundred thousand strong, was expected in the streets of Ghent the next day. He was somewhat deflated when Lieutenant Lockwood replied, "Three hundred thousand tomorrow, eh? That is concerning. I shall have to ask Madame to set another place or two at dinner."

Diarmuid Doolan, who was capable of vast sin but who knew one end of a horse from the other, was charged with nosing about town to test the equine market, and he returned to the billet with two good leads and word that the war was as good as over. Before Doolan could set sail, James held up a finger, poured himself a glass of Messr. DeVore's brandy, found a comfortable chair, and finally, hesitantly, waggled his fingers. "Sure and the horse fair here is run by thieves and felons, sir, though sure that's the case all the world over, as I've seen most of the world, in one form or another, always in your service, protecting your honour from such coarse brutes, *wisha* I've never seen the like. But my Stephanie, *mo mheile stor*, the kind woman who has befriended me, alone here in this foreign land with all its hardships, has taken me to see her cousin the drayman, it's his bay gelding I'm thinking of, sir, and while he's no foal he's a steady, goodhearted creature, not like that Norman stallion, the ill-tempered monster. Sure and it's the bay, sir, now, that is up your weight, not to be casting aspersions, though this rich food will drive you to your grave, and don't I see how that Judas-haired cook has her eye on you, oh, wouldn't the Missus put a cork in her wanton ways."

"Doolan, one more word and I'll have Quinn give you a dozen, and then another six out of pure spite. A cook, forsooth."

Doolan held up an open palm in surrender, adding, "As I said sir, casting no aspersions, now, but I know her type, her flirting ways, and *nuair atá an cat amuigh bíonn na luch ag damhsa.*"

"What was that, Private?"

"The merest blessing, sir, now."

"No, I distinctly caught something about a cat, and what, mice dancing?"

Doolan, thoroughly annoyed that Daidi was picking up the Irish, a great blasphemy, sure, as no other officer had ever bothered to do so, deftly changed topics. "Ah, speaking of cats, now, Lieutenant *a grah*, I came upon a row in the market today, two Belgies fighting like a pair of Kilkenny cats, and I paused, briefly, now, sir, in my wearisome duties to watch for half a moment, and I got to chatting, like, with a whitecoat Frenchie who had just come up from Liege, you know Liege, sir, where they make all that lace, not a stitch of which can stand next to the worst that they make in Fermanagh on a cloudy day. Sure and this Frenchie had taken Dutch leave from old Boney's army, as his sergeant was an *aisteach*," meeting with a puzzled look, "a sodomite, sir, and even if my Frenchie was a Frenchie, he didn't care for such shenanigans, and so he's come up here to join Fat Louis's army, and *wisha* won't he be flat to find whole regiments of *aisteach* with Louis, if the rest of that lot are like the other whitecoats I've met."

"Is there a point to all of this, Doolan?"

Doolan, who, like many Irishman, prided himself on his elegant oratory, was briefly put out, but consoled himself with the knowledge that Daidi was at heart only an Englishman and thus not capable of truly civilized conversation. "Well, now, sir, as you're in such a tearing hurry to attend to your pressing duties," casting a discreet glance at the soft chair and the brandy snifter, "I'll say two things and then say no more. First, my Frenchie brings news that Boney has lost his touch, and what men he's got are throwing in the towel, and Boney will be hustled back to his little rock pile kingdom in a fortnight. No fighting, no unpleasantness ever at all, and home by Samhain. Shall I pack your things, now, sir?"

"No, Private, you may not. You may tell your Frenchie to go back to Liege and make lace. What more?"

As he cared for James with such devotion, albeit an odd, loquacious, nagging, intrusive, meddling, heavy-handed devotion, empowered by an understanding with the sainted Mrs. Lockwood herself, Doolan rarely had the need to ask the lieutenant for anything, and finding himself in that unenviable position had a remarkably pained look on his face. "I am come, sir, now, to ask a favor."

Fearing the worst, James cried, "Don't tell me you want to marry that woman!"

"Jesus, Mary, and Joseph, no, sir! Jesus, you nearly stole the life from my soul with that. Jesus, no. I'm after asking, sir, please," straining at that word, then spilling out quickly, "if you'd think of taking me as part of the guard you'll stand at Fat Louis's palace. There, I've said it."

"Why on earth would you want to go out on guard, Doolan? You've never given a tinker's curse for such duty."

With a mildness that would have shocked any man in the company, Doolan quietly said, "It's for my old mother, sir. When I was a wee thing she always told me stories about kings and queens, and if I saw a real king, and stood guard for him with a man's musket in my hand, I could face her in Heaven, sir, and tell her all about it, is the way of it."

James had a biting reply on the tip of his tongue, but he let it go, replacing it with, "Very well, then, Doolan, I'll put your name on the list. But for God's sake practice your Manual. And if I see a spot of dust on your uniform or on your firelock I will leave you on the parade ground, and you may go whistle for your king."

*****

In the gloomy attic room, James and Tom shared a plate of baked apples that Jacqueline had sent up. Tom took a voluptuous bite and said, "I forgot to mention that I received a letter from my father. He cautions me against sloth and gluttony. I have made an informal study, and it seems that each letter he sends contains admonitions on two of the seven deadly sins."

James spooned a bit more cream onto his plate and said, "My father never writes to me. In fact, I think that since you are fortunate enough to have such a supportive parent, you should honour your father's sage advice and put that fork aside. To support your resolution, I shall finish those last two apples."

"You are the kindest of friends, but perhaps I shall commence my filial devotion as soon as I finish this plate. Or perhaps after the next. But we should consider going out at least occasionally, seeing the town and such. Elliott and most of the others are going out shortly, and I promised to join them. But do pass the cream, won't you? It seems to have migrated to your side of the table and taken up residence there."

They lapsed back into silence. James was still angry with himself with the way that he had allowed Barr to handle him aboard the barge. He had very nearly decided to tell Tom the details of their history. He was contemplating a way to broach the subject when six or eight officers (their exact number could not be determined, as the noise they made was roughly equivalent to a squadron of heavy dragoons, at the gallop) came thundering up the stairs, roaring with laughter over some old joke. Tom looked at them affectionately, and as he threw his coat on he said, "Here, witness an example of social intercourse, of true military brotherhood: the brothers Inniskilling, we few, we happy few, we band of brothers, ready to taste the best the eager city of Ghent has to offer."

"I am not sure how eager Ghent is to intercourse with us," replied George Elliott, "but I cannot express how eager we are to intercourse with Ghent!" Roars of laughter, and James threw half a stale biscuit at Elliott. "Come now, Lockwood," continued Elliott, "and join our merry band!"

"Go!" roared James, "Leave me in peace. I remain the only married man, and I shall remain here, alone and embittered, while you eligible young bucks go forth and conquer."

They were eager to be on their way, so after some brief, strident urging for Lockwood to tag along, they gave up on him. Tom turned at the top of the stairs and gave James one last tilt of the head and a raised eyebrow, but James gave a dismissive smile and waved him on. James heard them pouring out into Kerkstraat far below, their newly-issued pay burning holes in their pockets, thirsty, numerous, amorous, confident, and carefree.

Darkness had not yet fallen, but in James's gloomy garret he already had four candles lighting the rickety table that served as his desk. He had been elated earlier in the day when a letter from home had at last caught up with him. Its date was very recent, and while doubtless there were many others that were chasing him across America, the Caribbean, and the north Atlantic, this was the first to find him in months. Oddly, elated as he was, he had not told anyone about the letter, not even Tom. He had developed an entirely irrational notion that the letter had bad news, and he wanted to be alone, completely alone, to read it.

As was his habit he first read the sheets written by the children, each nearly bursting his heart with joy. He was convinced that every one of his children was a genius, as each letter was a study in affection, intelligence, artful phrasing, and elegant penmanship, though he was a bit taken aback when young Richard mentioned that they had "a mouse named Cornflower, and they put him in the gravy, as he was dead." It required some further reading and cross checking with the notes from the other children to determine that the word that eluded his son was "grave", and he made a mental note to explain that spelling at the earliest opportunity, so as to avoid future misunderstandings.

His spirits buoyed by the good news from the children, James told himself, "What a perfect old fool you are, there is nothing wrong at home," but still he opened Brigid's portion of the letter with hesitancy.

Her handwriting was worse than usual, some parts written in an emotional scrawl, others written with great forcefulness, but worse there were spots on the paper, obvious tears, blotting out some words, and the thought of her crying at home nearly unmanned him.

My Dearest James;

We have heard here about Bonaparte's return, and we are all so afraid that you shall have to fight the French <u>Again</u> is there no end to this constant war You know that I <u>pledged</u> myself years ago not to beg for you to shirk your duty but you must preserve yourself at all costs you must come home to me. The children are bearing up well but I fear that I am not raising them in the manner in which they deserve but rather in the manner of a foolish Irish Country girl not a <u>gentlewoman</u> of breeding and education and without your wise kind guidance they may make some foolish rash <u>decisions</u> or <u>actions</u> that might ruin their chances. Mary worries me so with this <u>Boffut</u> boy the back of my hand to him and his gentle manners and his tight breeches if he lays one hand on her I shall put Sergeant on him he knows he's a bad 'un and I have loaded your pistol. I do not want to worry you I know that you have trouble enough of your own but I have no one else to whom I can speak <u>frankly</u> I pray you forgive my weakness I try to send on our <u>Dearest Love</u> but I am so alone and so afraid please come home safely. Your father has not sent the allotment to Mr. Bettany, so we are very short again, might I beg you to write to your Father and remind him? I know how it pains you afraid to act the beggar but you <u>deserve</u> your share of the family estates if only you hadn't married me and ruined *your relationship with your family you could have a better wife a respectable, Protestant wife but never, never one who loves you more.*

Lastly, Know how much I <u>love</u> you and treasure our dear <u>dear</u> marriage but I must tell you something that I have been keeping from you. Ever since you left for Spain, I have received letters from that beast Barr you <u>Must Not</u> fight him though I know your heart demands that you must. I tell you this only because I cannot bear to think that I have withheld anything from you ever in my life and as the time seems to go by so swiftly I must unburden myself. No Honour will protect you from a pistol ball, and we both <u>know</u> what he can do to us even if you should kill him. I believe him when he says that he has secreted letters that will expose us if he should die. I know it was my foolishness and stubbornness that has caused us such a burden, and every day how I regret it, and wonder how I could have been such an ignorant fool. Do not fight him, do not fail us, do not forget how I cherish you.

Forever.....
Brigid

P.S. I will wait until morning to decide if I should sent this letter or not I cannot bear to put a greater burden on you.

P.P.S. It is now the morning and I shall go mad if I cannot share this with you.

Brigid was right, his first impulse was to find Barr and finally kill him. But she was right, what could he truly do? For years he had fought the impulse to tear Barr apart, and now he would have to swallow his rage yet again. And no money in the house, damn his father. The old man must be toying with him, punishing him, making him beg. And whatever could she mean about this 'Boffut boy'? He knew Boffut senior, of course, a fool, but he couldn't recall if he had a son. Mary was just a child, who would lay a hand on a child? But she had loaded the God damned pistol? And what did she mean by 'if only you hadn't married me'?

She had never sent him such a letter before. He normally handled her letters very carefully, but this one he nearly crushed. "God damn it," he said in a voice full of frustration, and only seconds later he said "God damn it!" in a voice black with rage. He was exceedingly angry, with that son of a bitch Barr, of course, but also with Brigid for letting things get into such a God damned mess. And the children for causing such trouble, and his miserly old father, and that God damned Boffut and his God damned son. He'd put thirty inches of Sheffield steel through his heart if he should think that he could toy with his daughter, the little son of a bitch.

He stood quickly, grabbed the back of the chair, and lifted it off the floor as if it had no weight, about to dash it against the wall before he caught himself. He set it back down, hard, then wadded up Brigid's letter and furiously threw it into a dark corner. "I live this miserable God damned life," he hissed into the darkness, "to provide for our futures, and now the first letter in six months tells me that my home is falling to pieces. What will I go back to? Barr and my wife, my children, my father. What the God damned hell can I do from here?" He gave the chair a kick that knocked it, shattered, well across the room. He then strode out into the hall to the back stairs, and quickly, loudly, down the many flights of narrow steps to the wine cellar. He carried a small lantern, and in its weak light he searched quickly, finding the last two bottles of laFite 1795. He took one and turned to the stairs, then went back and took the other as well.

On his way down the stairs the kitchen door had been closed and dark, but as he carried the bottles back upstairs he now saw that the door was ajar, inviting, a gentle light issuing forth. The warm smell of baked apples and cinnamon filled his senses, a comforting warmth. In his mind's eye he opened that door and passed inside and satisfied his hunger, but he found himself standing stock still, deliberately breathing.

He had sense enough to wait. After a moment he quietly reached out and pulled the door closed. Upstairs, he retrieved the letter and carefully smoothed it flat, arranging it neatly on the table with the letters from the children, and with shaking hands he read them again and again.

Chapter Eleven

Ghent

The march to the Palais was the stuff of boyhood dreams. At the head of thirty hardened men, James marched through the most fashionable streets of Ghent, his sword drawn, carried at his shoulder, the drum snapping the cadence in the sharp morning light. The few people in the street stood aside and watched the Redcoats with subtle appreciation, while from the windows above, fashionable women, languid and *négligé*, watched with dreamy eyes.

The Palais itself was an imposing edifice on Veldstraat, the premier street in all Ghent. Broad stone steps led up to ornate mahogany doors, where the white-coated Frenchmen who stood guard to the right of the steps contrasted with the faded red coats of the Inniskillings to the left. James's guard relieved George Elliott's guard in the traditional ritual, the retiring guard looking pleased with their time with the French.

Elliott took James to the officers' guard room, in fact an elegantly appointed suite of rooms, and introduced James to his counterpart in the French service, Lieutenant Dumon of his His Most Catholic Majesty's army, who would command the French portion of King Louis's guard that day. On the whole James was not impressed with the Frenchmen that he had seen outside, as they seemed a pack of misfits and outcasts. There were uniforms of several different regiments evident in just the few men on guard, less an army than a collection of deserters. Their uniforms were disheveled, with only a few real soldiers in the mix. Fortunately Lieutenant Dumon was one of these, an older fellow who spoke passable English. This was fortunate, as James spoke little French, and he was of the regrettable opinion that if any Frenchman should wish to speak to him, he had best learn to speak English beforehand.

"Am I correct in recalling, Lieutenant Lockwood," asked Lieutenant Dumon, with a slightly awkward air, "that your regiment, the 27th, was in Spain, at the Battle of Badajoz?"

"Yes, Lieutenant," replied James, somewhat guardedly, "you are quite correct; our Third Battalion served there, in General Kemmis's brigade of the Fourth Division."

"You were yourself present, sir?"

"I was."

"I was there as well, serving in my father's battalion, the First of the 58th. He was killed the night of your army's gallant assault."

James searched Dumon's face for anger or resentment, but saw only a fond remembrance. "I hope," said James, "that you will allow me to convey my condolences, sir, and I only pray that it was not the Inniskillings who caused you such a loss."

"*Merci*, Lieutenant, but a soldier could ask no better death. To fall at the front of his battalion in a moment of triumph was a most glorious death." James, who was no friend to glory, only nodded, and Dumon continued, "I hope that you did not suffer the loss of friends there, Lieutenant?"

"Our regiment suffered very much; sixteen officers and more than two hundred fifty men. A good friend of mine, Frank Simcoe, died at my side."

Dumon had been on the walls of Badajoz, and he knew what hell the British had advanced through on the night of the assault. The approaches to the city had been full of surging Redcoats, lit by the flashes of the guns that flogged them. The Frenchman saw that experience in Lockwood's eyes, and they both knew that having that experience, even if seen from opposite sides, bound them.

They were both silent for a while, each with his own memories of Badajoz. Dumon broke their reverie: "I must beg you tell me, please, Lieutenant, the meaning of your battalion's... what shall I say? The sobriquet? The *nackname*? Pray, what does 'Inniskilling' mean? It sounds most fearsome."

James smiled a bit, warming to his Frenchman, "Yes, monsieur, it does have a rather ominous tone, but Inniskilling is the town in northern Ireland where our regiment is head quartered. 'Inniskilling' is from the Irish, '*Inis Ceithleann*' or 'Ceithleann's Island'. I suppose he was the fellow who first put two rocks together there, back when the world was young."

"You fascinate me, Lieutenant. Pray, these Irish of yours, are they Catholics, speak Celtique, and are stubborn to the point of madness?"

James laughed and said, "They are indeed, Lieutenant. You are acquainted with Irishmen, I suppose?"

Dumon made an exaggerated frown, saying, "When first I joined in the *armée* I served in the Vendée, fighting the Royalists, defending La Revolution, before that fellow Bonaparte corrupted it. The Vendée was filled with the cousins of your Irish... mad Celts... we had to kill nearly every one of them before they would bend. An impossible people. Still, I am pleased that Inniskilling is a place. I had feared that the name was... how do you say? Ghoulish? Like those Prussians barbaric, and their 'Death's Head Hussars', may God strike them dead."

James agreed with Lieutenant Dumon's opinion of the Prussians and a wide variety of other subjects, and his time with the Frenchman proved to be exceptionally enjoyable. They both shared a love of good wine, and after a bottle or two Dumon even managed to slip James upstairs to sneak a peek at Louis during that notable gentleman's dinner. There were over twenty guests at table, but peeking through a side door James got a good look at His Most Catholic Majesty.

"He is quite an imposing fellow," whispered James as he peered out into the scene of opulence.

"He is a fat pig," whispered Dumon in a blasé tone. "Six hours to eat dinner. *Mon Dieu.*"

James was enchanted. The entire scene was immaculate, men and women in perfectly powdered wigs, in the finest uniforms and the latest Parisian fashion. Not being above such things, James noted the presence of several exceptionally lovely women there, their opulent bosoms barely constrained.

Louis himself, however, was a great disappointment. Protruding eyes dominated a sallow complexion, with a chin so weak that it was nearly swallowed by his corpulent bulk. He had no table manners to speak of, and he ate like a man possessed.

"At each sitting, he will eat one hundred of oysters. One hundred! Every day!" whispered Dumon, his head under James's, his eye at the edge of the door.

"I should hate to empty his chamber pot," cracked James, which earned a stifled bark of laughter from Dumon, and an annoyed glance from a marshal, a bishop, a countess, and an exquisitely bored Parisian prostitute. The two lieutenants snuck away from the door giggling like boys, and few of the servants in the busy back halls of the Palais D'Hare-Steenhuyse would have guessed that only three years before those two gentlemen, and thousands of others like them, had desperately tried to kill each other in the hellish darkness of Badajoz.

The rest of the evening was spent on wine and conversation in the officer's guard room. When Dumon heard that James was in need of a horse, he sold him a powerful bay mare at a very modest price. They strolled down to the stables to see her, and James was pleased with her name: Mémoire. After James and Mémoire had been properly introduced, and each had taken an instant liking to the other, the two lieutenants stayed up most of the night drinking the fruity red wine from the Terrasses du Larzac of which Dumon was particularly fond.

The next day James look leave of Dumon with a fond embrace, kisses on the cheeks that made James only briefly uncomfortable, and a promise to bring Brigid and the children to Languedoc for a visit after the war. As the guard returned to their less-fashionable corner of town, James rode at the head of his men, to the great annoyance of Doolan, who argued that this bay with the fancy name might look well, but she was too young for a rider with James's modest riding skills. "Nonsense. She will do very well. Just remember who brought you along on this guard. You have seen your king, and you will now care for Mémoire as you care for your own hide. We have a great deal to do."

*****

Having enjoyed a splendid dinner at the Hôtel de Flandre, Tom returned to his room late, just before storms rolled in from the west, lightning on the horizon. He took off his coat and transferred the flame from the night lamp to a few candles on his desk. He glanced out the door into his garden and with a start he saw James sitting amongst the flowers, looking very serious. "Back from the Palais, brother, I see," Tom said gaily, knowing that he had hit the wrong note. "You missed quite an evening. Lambert had us stay for dinner after brigade drill, and that lizard Elliott plied me with absinthe. I am somewhat addled... What brings you to my humble abode this night, brother, on the verge of storm and tumult without?"

James silently handed Brigid's letter to Tom. He accepted it with a curious look on his face. Seeing then that it was from Brigid, he quickly carried it back into the room, sat at the desk, and read it by the golden candlelight. After several minutes, much longer than it would have taken to read it two, even three times, he returned to the garden and sat beside James. "Will you go home?"

"As soon as I can," replied James. "But of course I will wait until this business with Bonaparte is seen to. As that looks more and more likely, I feel that I need to explain several things to you. You will understand that this is difficult for me, but should I get knocked on the head, I need to ask that you do what you can for Brigid and the children."

"I swear it."

After a moment a bolt of lightning split the darkness, immediately followed by an epic roar of thunder. "It appears that God is angry with us," said Tom.

"With me, at least, I think," answered James, and Tom offered no response. James took a deep breath. "I have resolved to deal with this damned life differently, to deal with things from my past, things that have haunted me for years. Thus I have a great deal to tell you, brother, but I will be as brief as I am able. You know that Barr and I served together in the Westmeaths in '98, when we were posted to the barracks just north of Clonakilty. I was seventeen, the junior ensign, an absolute puppy," and James smiled a bit at the memory of himself. "Barr had just purchased his lieutenancy, I suppose he was twenty or so, wealthy and worldly, and I confess that I admired him very much. He was a regular at the country dances; you wouldn't believe it now, but he was a fine dancer, a great wit whom the ladies found charming. Even then he was cruel with his men, but I was a young fool, and I thought that was the way things were supposed to be."

"But you came to fall out, it seems?" asked Tom, but he then added, "I am sorry, James, I ask too many questions."

James smiled and replied, "No secrets, tonight, Tom. Yes, we fell out. After one dance in Clonakilty, Barr came back to the barracks and told us all about a girl he had met there: Brigid O'Brian."

"Brigid!" cried Tom, "So that is why he writes to her. It sounds is if he is tormenting her, the bastard."

"Yes. Yes... Now, at that point I had not yet met her, I only knew that the officers' mess had proclaimed her the most beautiful girl in Munster. In the following weeks Barr called on her often, and they were on the verge of coming to an understanding."

"Barr and Brigid," gasped Tom. "I never would have imagined that."

"Believe me, I try not to dwell upon it. Then one evening our battalion surgeon, Charles Oades, came to me and asked that I serve as his second in an affair of honour. I was flattered, and agreed to serve before I thought to ask who had crossed him. He had challenged Barr, which amazed me, as Oades was a meek, timid little fellow, and rumour had it that Barr had been out a dozen times or more, but Oades was determined. I begged him to allow me to see if I could get some form of apology from Barr, but he would have none of it, nor would he tell me what had sparked the quarrel. They met the next morning, and Christ, Tom, it was pure murder. Barr had chosen swords, and in two passes he had his point in Oades's chest. He could have left it at that, a wound that would have ended it, but with a smirk that I can remember to this day Barr thrust the blade clean through Oades, out the back, determined to kill him."

"Christ. So he was mad even then."

"Yes, that was the first time I saw it. Vicious bastard. As Oades's second, I stayed with him while his assistant dressed the wound, but it was hopeless. I had never seen anyone die before, and it affected me very much. But before he died Oades told me why he had fought Barr."

Characteristically, James rubbed his face with both hands, and continued, "It seems that Lieutenant Barr was overly fond of the brothels in Dublin and Belfast, and some time before had contracted the French Pox."

"My God, syphilis!" cried Tom, and after a moment he said, "That explains everything. My God, if that got out he'd be driven out of the service... out of society entirely!"

"It was Oades who diagnosed Barr, and he was treating him for the worst of the symptoms, but Barr continued to press his suit with Brigid. Oades was a decent fellow, and he had confronted Barr, telling him that honour dictated that any man with syphilis had to remove himself from any consideration of marriage, particularly to a lady of such quality as Miss O'Brian. Oades had met Brigid at one of the dances, and was quite taken with her, I think. But Barr laughed and called Oades a sniveling little papist lover, and told him to keep his mouth shut. Oades felt himself bound to keep his patient's condition private, but even so he felt equally obligated to call Barr out, and he died for it."

"What an honourable fellow," said Tom.

"Yes. I wish that I had known him better, but I cherish his memory. You might not recall my son Joseph's full name: Joseph Charles Oades Lockwood. After seeing the manner in which Barr had killed Oades, and hearing Oades's noble story, I was furious, and later that day I confronted Barr myself. He had already been snubbed by several other officers for how he had killed Oades."

"I should think so. Even without word of his disease getting out, he must have become a pariah for killing a harmless little surgeon in such a fashion."

"Yes," said James, "and he was unhappy with me for having stood up with Oades, but even so he seems to have realized that he had gone too far, much too far. He went quite pale when I told him that Oades had told me the truth before he died, and he swore to me that he regretted Oades' death, and that he would withdraw from his relationship with Miss O'Brian. And he did so; Brigid later told me it came as a great relief to her, as she had begun to see the horrid aspects of his nature. She was very young at the time you know, entirely innocent."

"Yes," said Tom charitably, "young ladies are so often deluded by a veneer of kindness, and only later do they find the true character of their spouse. It is so fortunate that she was spared Barr's attentions."

With a quick grin James said, "Yes, she was instead doomed to a life with me. I met Brigid shortly thereafter, at a concert given by a local church choir, and we grew fond of each other very quickly. Ireland was in a great state of upheaval, and many militia regiments were moving to far ends of the island in response to the uprisings that were springing up everywhere. When we heard a rumour, unfounded in the end, but all the better for me, that the Westmeaths were to move to Mayo, Brigid and I decided to marry before we could be separated. Her family was unhappy about it, as they had no love of Anglicans, and after their experience with Barr they nearly convinced her that I was no kind of match for her. I need not mention my father's reaction to the match was apoplectic."

Another bolt of lightning lit up the sky, and the rain began to fall. The big chestnut could shelter them for a while, but it was only a matter of time before it failed them.

"I have been rambling on too long," said James.

"Nonsense. I confess to having wondered about this for years; I thank you for trusting me enough to share it."

"One last thing. You must know this as well, please, Tom. Brigid and I decided to marry, family concerns be damned, without waiting another day. When I went to ask my colonel's permission... do you know Colonel Sykes? A grand gentleman. Well, Sykes quickly gave his blessing, but he insisted that the Officer of the Day accompany me and serve as one of the witnesses, as an honour to the regiment, and by the Devil's own chance the Officer of the Day was..."

"Don't say it was Barr."

"Exactly. So that vile beast was at my wedding, eyeing my bride, and while we knew his secret, he soon knew ours."

"Secret? What secret?" asked Tom, puzzled, on edge.

"Understand, now, that Brigid was under great pressure from her family. And under the circumstances, it was perfectly reasonable for her to ask that a Catholic priest perform the service."

"Not an Anglican minister, at all?" asked Tom, realization dawning.

"No. I should never have agreed to it, but her family was insistent, and she would not defy them. I think now it was their way of determining just how devoted I was to her. I knew that it was technically illegal, of course, but so many of the Penal Laws were being quietly winked at before the Rebellion. When I agreed to the priest, I never knew that Barr would witness the whole thing; when I walked into the chapel with Barr at my side Brigid went quite pale. But we carried on, trusting in Barr's discretion."

"Barr's discretion. My Latin Rector at St. George's would call that an oxymoron. Now, tell me, James, I know something of English law, but what does a Catholic marriage in Ireland entail? In England it is no great issue, but I know that in Ireland things are far different."

James sat hunched over, looking only at the ground, compulsively rubbing his fingertips together. "I have become quite a student of the issue. At one point it was a felony, but around, say 1760 or so, the law was softened a bit, and it was deemed that the marriage was to be considered null and void."

"So, then, legally..."

"Yes," said James, "in the severest application of the law, we were never married; my children are illegitimate."

Tom well knew how the fractious nature of society, particularly the bitterly divisive Irish society, might use even so tenuous a threat to shred a family's reputation. "So Barr has never revealed your secret?"

"A few days after the ceremony he came to the little apartments that we had rented. Brigid and I agreed that we would never speak of his affliction, and he agreed never to disclose the conditions of our marriage. It was perhaps the worst day of my life, making a compact with that snide, insinuating son of a bitch. Every bit a deal with the Devil. We have lived with it, and been tortured by it, every day since. And every day I hate myself for not having called Barr out for the way in which he murdered Oades. I try to remember all that happened, but I can only conclude that I was shy: a coward and a fool. Oades had hardly known Brigid, but still he died for her, and I failed to meet the standard of honour that he set. If only I had killed Barr then, or died trying."

*****

James returned to his room tired and still very dissatisfied with himself. As he gratefully crawled into his bed he did, however, muse on what Tom had said; such unreserved support from such a trusted source, coupled with the relief of having at last shared his story, eventually gave birth to a faint optimism. James was hesitant to give even that flickering optimism much credence, but it was a pleasant notion by which to go to sleep.

His reverie was interrupted by a thunderous pounding at his door. Sergeant Dunne rumbled up the steps with a bright lantern, followed by Tom, Campbell, and Elliott, disheveled, throwing on their coats. "Major Archibald's compliments, Your Honour," said Dunne, in a great hurry and flow of excitement, "There is a staff officer come, is the way of it, and his fine horse near dead with the hurry, and we are to be formed and ready to march within the hour, unholy darkness or no, as the French are coming, and all hell is coming with them."

Chapter Twelve

Clonakilty

"All well, John?"

"Aye, all well, Liam."

And it had gone well thus far. They were rank amateurs, for the most part, but Liam Collins knew his craft, and with John Cashman at his side they had begun to organize the West Cork Whiteboys.

The hills north and west of Clonakilty provided ideal places to meet, as few roads ran into those secluded heights, and they were easily watched by the locals who were friendly, if not completely affiliated with, the Whiteboys. In a remote dell in those hills John and Collins crouched in the dense darkness at the edge of a clearing. "He'll be up in a few minutes," said John, gesturing toward the sky, "and we'll finally have some light. Reidy and his boys are at their posts, and I heard some fools tripping around down in the glen; Clerkin's gallant band of heroes is arrived."

Liam Collins was a grim man, wholly grim after his family had been killed in the round of reprisals that followed the '98. "You're sure, then, it's not the militia in the glen, and we here with muskets in our hands?"

"Not to worry, Liam, I slipped down and had a listen, and I heard Clerkin telling Charlie Moy to shut the fuck up, in that gentle way of his."

"All right, then, but be sure to keep the groups separate. Reidy would never sell out his own, but he'd give over Clerkin for a song and a tot."

Reidy and his six men were to provide security and screen the dell from any intrusion, while Clerkin and his four men were to be in the dell at moonrise. Bob Clerkin was an older man, a tough, hardened leader of the Clonakilty men in the faction fights that often marked the local fair days. In the shebeens and on Clonakilty Quay he was revered, a hulking figure who ruled the lowest layers of society with his fists, his blackthorn cudgel, and his not inconsiderable intelligence.

"I don't know how you can handle that pack of brutes," said John. "As nasty a bunch of bruisers as I've ever met, and I've met my share. Christ may have died for us, but likely he wasn't thinking of Bob Clerkin at the time."

"Aye, John, Clerkin is a mad dog, but it's me holding the leash, and won't I choke him if need be."

The waiting was difficult, listening for every little noise in the woods, until the light of the gibbous moon began to filter down to them, and they passed silently into the glen.

"*Cia sud thall?*" whispered Collins. Who goes there?

"What did he say?" came a puzzled voice from ahead.

"It's the fucking challenge, Charlie. Now, we give the fucking password," harshly whispered another voice. "*Mise Tadhg.*" I am Teague.

After the long wait in the dark woods, the moonlight in the glen seemed like midday. John and Collins stepped out into the grass from one side, Clerkin and his gang from the other. John looked up to see one of Reidy's hilltop guards sharply silhouetted against the now-bright sky. Amateurs.

"Who the holy fuck is that, now, Liam Collins?" said Clerkin, pointing his cudgel at the shadowy John. "I agreed to work with you, and no one else."

"You know John McCarthy. He's my right hand now, Clerkin, as he's a veteran of the '98 who skewered a Redcoat and saved my life at Shannonvale, and a true friend of the Cause."

"Cause," said Clerkin derisively, with a smirk back toward his men, adding as he grabbed his crotch, "I've got your Cause, right here. And sure I've met this rogue a few times, but even with you trusting him, why should I? I'd as soon open his skull as trust him with my life."

"Handsome and charming as always; it's a delight you are, Bob Clerkin," said John without a smile.

"You have the Irish, but sure and you sound like an Englishman to me."

"And you sound like a sheep-fucking Connaught *spalpeen* to me."

Before John had finished his reply, Clerkin raised his cudgel and lunged toward him, but in an instant John had a double-edged knife in each hand, crouched, every muscle taut. Clerkin was used to bullying farmhands and shop boys, and he quickly realized that John Cashman was a different type of man. In the slanting moonlight Clerkin saw the knives gleam, and caught the murderous set to John's face. Swerving awkwardly away from the knives, Clerkin barked out a false, nervous laugh, calling, "*Wisha*, your friend isn't shy, Collins. He may just do."

"Enough of this shite," said Collins angrily. "Clerkin, take your men and fulfill your mission. You'll burn Andrew's barn and kill twenty of his sheep."

"After what he's done we should be burning his house and cutting a few Proddy throats. That son of a bitch drove off the Devlins without—"

"No, damn it," snapped Collins. "None of our people were hurt, so none of theirs will be hurt. A measured response. A barn and twenty sheep will teach him the lesson he has to learn, and if you go any further you'll have regulars, dragoons, down on us."

"Are you after thinking that Bob Clerkin fears the likes of their dragoons?"

"Enough. The moon won't last long. Carry out your mission, and nothing more."

With more muttering, Clerkin and his men moved off into the darkness, to the fields managed by Collin Andrews, Lord Bandon's land agent for the area, who had forced the Devlin family off their land. The Devlins were six months behind in their rent, as were many of Bandon's tenants, but Andrews coveted the Devlins' plot for his sheep, and so they were turned out with no notice. The Devlins had no recourse but a life in the hedges.

"That one will be trouble before long," said John.

"Shite, and don't I know it. Clerkin and his lot are tough as they come but it's a burning fuse they have, and woe to whoever is about when it blows. Then on the other hand I have Reidy and his people, an old tavern owner, his sons and his stable boys, quiet, biddable lads, but they balk at houghing a cow. Simon's yeomen would cut them to pieces."

John and Collins withdrew to the trees and waited for the next group to arrive. When the moon was at its height, four men and an old woman cautiously worked their way down into the glen to be sworn in: the four Devlin brothers and their mother. With their callused hands upon their mother's head, the brothers took the oath of *Na Buachailli Bána*, The White Boys, in deadly earnest.

With orders to return to the glen at the full moon, the silent, solemn Devlins filed back into the night, lacking hope, clinging only to a dim dream of retribution. Collins gave two sharp whistles, the signal for Reidy and his men to disperse and return home. John and Collins made for the coast and the curragh that they had hidden in a shallow, narrow inlet. Whether they admitted it or not, they were nervous, and in their hurry they reached the boat well before their time. As they waited for the tide to turn John said, "Tell me the way of it, Liam. The Devlins swore their oath on their aged mother's head. Liam, tell me, honestly, now, that if one of her sons betrays us to the English, would she die?"

Collins looked him straight in the eye, and said, "I would kill her with my own hand."

"The years have made you a hard man, Liam. Christ, what a business."

A few minutes went by, the waves gently slapping against the skins of the hull, when John continued, "The Devlins could lose their mother, and Reidy and his lot have their inn and their families to lose, God help us, if ever they would turn traitor. But what do we have to hold over Clerkin and his gang? They're all Connaught men, wandering *spalpeens* without a penny to their names, living together like a pack of wolves in some mud hut. Whatever family they might have is off in the wild north, though I for one would doubt that lot had mothers. Sure and they crawled out of some bog, unbidden and unwelcome."

"Aye, they are the weakest leg in the organization," admitted Collins. "The Castle is offering ten pounds for information, and any one of those bastards could rat us out, ten pounds being a fortune to any man who lives in a hole, eating a goat's leavings. The only thing that holds them is their hate. *Wisha*, all they want from life is to drink and kill... no, not just kill, but to murder. They are like us, sure, in wanting nothing more to do with the United men and their damned Irish Republic, but where we fight to keep some justice in the landlords' dealings, Clerkin won't be happy until he's murdered every Proddy and burned every big house."

"God between us and evil," said John, staring out to sea.

Lieutenant and Mrs Lockwood

*****

The evening of the ball found the chaise from the Bandon Arms clattering up Scartagh Lane, Hugh O'Flynn in his finest coat, wearing a powdered wig only slightly askew, his four horses dandied with ribbons and bows. It was a grand vehicle, but a vehicle any less grand would have been unfit to carry the three Lockwood women, each in her glory. Mary wore pale yellow with white trim, while Cissy mirrored her in white with yellow trim. Brigid wore a royal blue gown that she had owned for years but had opportunity to wear only once before. Each of them was a lovely sight in her own right, but collectively they made a wholly pleasing picture, a most complete study of loveliness.

The Boffuts lived in a fine house which stood a few miles east of Clonakilty, significantly re-named "Fort Dominion" by Boffut. By the time O'Flynn turned his team up the pea gravel drive, darkness was beginning to fall. It was soon obvious that the Boffuts had spared no expense, as the house was brightly lit and liveried footmen helped the guests from their carriages. Mrs. Boffut was there to greet their guests, giving Brigid an especially kind, genuine welcome. Passing inside, all three of the Lockwood ladies were dazzled by the opulence. The girls of course had never been out before, and while Brigid had been to dozens of country dances, none of them could compare to the Boffuts when they meant to show away.

As she adjusted to her surroundings, Brigid grew concerned that only ten or twelve adults were in attendance, chaperoning nearly sixty boys and girls, many of whom were not from the area. The affair was beginning a bit awkwardly as the young people did their best to remember their manners, with many stops, starts, and laughter. Their dancing was also somewhat erratic, though everyone seemed to be enjoying themselves as the skilled eight-piece orchestra, from Dublin itself, filled the brightly lit ballroom with invigorating music.

Brigid was pleased to see that Mary and Cissy were asked to dance by two shy, nice young men, neither an Adonis, but polite, respectful, and friendly. Her first hour or so was spent in chatting with some of the other parents and watching the girls dance. Eventually Mrs. Boffut worked her way over and quietly said, "Mrs. Lockwood, I am so glad that you and your girls are here, but I feel that I really must tender my apologies, and an explanation for how this 'little dance' grew so imposing."

"Please, Mrs. Boffut, no explanation is necessary. Your home is so lovely, and the music is simply wonderful."

Mrs. Boffut hesitated, and her smile faded. "As soon as Boffut heard that Lord Bandon might attend, he insisted on the best of everything, and he would not heed one word from me. I wonder sometimes if he..." She stopped abruptly, her smile instantly, artificially returning, as a Mr. Beamish approached, with two glasses of punch and an insidious smile. He was youngish, unmarried, and moderately handsome.

"I saw you two ladies speaking so seriously," said Beamish, "that I told myself, Beamish, you really must go over and rescue them from themselves. Now, Mrs. Boffut, I am certain that Mr. Boffut is monopolizing your dance card, but I would wager that Mrs. Lockwood is most eager to dance."

His manner was so self-assured, so knowing, that for an instant Brigid wondered if he had any right to speak to her so confidently. No, he did not. "Do I look so lonely?" she asked herself, then, aloud, "As much as I should love to dance, Mr. Beamish, I shall not stand up until Lieutenant Lockwood returns. On that happy day, I shall most happily dance with him, and with you, and with any other gentleman who should ask, until the dawn itself."

Beamish, looking thoroughly put out, mumbled something, handed over the two glasses of punch, and beat a rapid retreat. Brigid and Mrs. Boffut exchanged an amused look and took a sip of their punch. Its taste made both women start; they both stared into their glasses, until Mrs. Boffut said, "Oh my God. Brigid, please excuse me." She hurried away to go speak with her husband with a determined look on her face. Mrs. Boffut approached her husband, who was standing with a group of his friends, all of whom appeared to be sharing the same joke. He had little to say to her, and she hurriedly walked out the elegant French doors to the garden with an anguished look on her face.

Brigid turned to follow her out, but she first looked to check on her girls. They were both still with the younger, less popular part of the crowd, and she was pleased to see them there; one step at a time. She wanted no part of the punch, and she put the glass down on the edge of a planter, then thought again, and quickly dumped the rum-soaked drink into the foliage. As she moved toward the garden doors she watched a group of boys, including George Boffut, gathered around the punch bowl, their laughter growing loud and harsh.

Brigid was in no way a real friend of Mrs. Boffut, but still she felt compelled to follow her out into the garden. Outside there were only a few lanterns burning, and it took Brigid some minutes to find Mrs. Boffut in Fort Dominion's ornate formal garden, distraught but appreciative of sympathetic company.

Brigid was conscious of not being able to watch her girls, and it required some artful disconnection before she could pull herself free and return to the ball, her anxious, hurried footsteps clicking on the garden flagstones, the glorious light and music of the ballroom beckoning. Passing through the open doors, Brigid was startled to see that the mood in the room had noticeably shifted. Lord and Lady Bandon had arrived, with their insufferable Elizabeth, fashionably late,

184

looking aloof, drawing a crowd, Boffut senior fawning their favor. Cissy, still dancing with the awkward, honourable boys, found her mother's eye and gave her a significant look. Many of the older boys and girls were missing, including Mary, and Brigid was just stalking off to look for her when the strays came through the main hall in a herd, loud and raucous. George Boffut was in the lead, trying to get his very confident arm around Mary.

George and several of the others boys were clearly drunk, their yelling and the resulting chaos in the ballroom prompting the orchestra to tumble to a dissonant halt. Brigid strode out onto the floor and told Cissy that they were leaving, and as she furiously sought out Mary in the noisy crowd, she heard the boys calling out that only the girls who would give them a kiss could dance, and one plain girl did give one of them a quick, desperate kiss. Mary was still at George Boffut's side, looking thrilled, and she may have been tempted to kiss Boffut until Brigid took her by the arm and unceremoniously steered her to the door.

In the general turmoil several other families were exiting as well, gathering their possessions in the hall. Brigid, livid, did not speak to anyone on her way out, but she heard Bandon tell his wife, "A bawdy house! But what can one expect from God damned tradesmen."

The deteriorating nature of the ball had evidently reached the waiting coachmen, as Brigid found O'Flynn at the bottom of the steps, and she silently hustled the girls into the chaise. Her fury was obvious, but Mary, who was braced by two glasses of punch, said, "Mama, please calm yourself. We were just having fun; we did nothing wrong."

"Nothing wrong?" replied Brigid angrily, "Drinking, wild behavior, sure and it was like the Skibbereen Road shebeen in there. You will see no more of that George Boffut, I tell you right now, young lady."

"But Mama! He said that I was the prettiest girl there! He said that he should like to call on me!"

"I wager that he should like that very much, the rogue. I forbid you from ever seeing him. How could I have been so foolish?"

The moon had set, so the narrow roads east of town were lit only by starlight. O'Flynn had two lanterns mounted on the front of the chaise, a small circle of light as they moved through the thick darkness. Not far from Fáibhile Cottage, O'Flynn had to flick a rein at Bláth, his offside leader, who was unhappy about being out so late, and thus he did not notice the shadowy men who crouched in the ditch just yards away.

Clerkin and his gang, their hands red and sticky, watched the coach pass, then trotted after it, keeping their distance, and watched as it drew up in front of Fáibhile Cottage. As the carriage pulled away they saw the three women, with never a man in sight. Mrs. Cashman stepped into the yard with a lantern to see them in, and in the flickering lamplight of the cottage Brigid, Mary, and Cissy Lockwood were eyed with brutal lust by the drunk, bloody, angry men.

As the women went inside the gang gathered around Clerkin, eagerly anticipating his command. Undecided, Clerkin ran the back of his hand across his mouth. "Ah, the proud, rich sluts...," he began, but he was startled into silence by the door of the cottage banging open again. Brigid strode into the front garden with a lantern in one hand and the collar of a snarling Sergeant in the other. Clerkin could also see that she had a pistol tucked into the band of her apron, and it was she who harshly called out in Irish, "Who lurks in those hedges, like a thief in the night?!"

Clerkin did not expect to be challenged in such a fashion, especially in Irish. He waved his men to stay quiet, and called in response, "What would you say, Missus, to an honest man come to beg a bite?"

"An honest man, is it?" Brigid cried. "An honest man, with a pack of his friends, crashing through the hedges in the middle of the night, making a racket that would rival the *Shee*? Tell me your business, man, or I'll put my dog on you!"

Some of Clerkin's men chuckled appreciatively. Still unsure of what path to take, Clerkin called, "What would you say, then, to honest men who fight to bring justice?"

"Whiteboys, then, are you?" called Brigid. "Then I will tell you that my name is Brigid ni Brian, a daughter of the greatest clan of the south, and I'll not be hearing one more word from you lot, I can tell you that." As she turned to her door, in a scolding tone she added in a dismissive tone, "Sneaking about in the dark; shame on you! What would your own mothers say!"

There was now open laughter from the men, as one muttered appreciatively, "A hellcat, that one."

Clerkin felt the mood shift; shaking his head, he said, "Like my grandfather said, boys, 'Better a good run than a bad stand'. Let's get home."

Inside Fáibhile Cottage the wide-eyed Mary and Cissy stood amazed at their mother's handling of the Whiteboys, but Brigid only said, "Never mind those silly men; tomorrow I shall go to see my Uncle Brian, and we shall see no more of such foolishness." Only Mrs. Cashman saw the way her hands shook as she put away her pistol. "Instead," continued Brigid in a rallying voice, "we shall discuss with Mrs. Cashman the manner in which my daughters comported themselves tonight in company."

It was nearly dawn before the girls got to bed, though only after Fáibhile Cottage echoed with considerable scolding, tears, anger, and the requisite amount of adolescent theatre. Eventually Brigid sat and wrote a few lines to James, hoping that thinking of him would give her some idea as how best to deal with Mary. She would not tell him of Whiteboys in the night; she was determined to send no more weak, plaintive cries for help. She had been damned silly that one night, but she had her wits about her now, and she wrote a lucid, if rambling, account of their time at the ball.

Since the first days of their marriage she and James had a running joke, in that whoever could first cross off the previous date in the calendar made that lucky soul the boss of the house for the next day. Midnight had long since passed, so with a slight smile she allowed herself to cross off Saturday, June 17. It was Sunday, June 18, 1815.

Chapter Thirteen

Ghent

Six Company stood drawn up along the broad Burgstraat, a hundred men just a blur of shadows in the faint clouded starlight. Further up and down the street the other six companies of the 27th were gathered, invisible, their presence discernible only by the low murmur of conversation, most of it in Irish.

In a cluster of Six Company men, old friends and comrades, Private Diarmuid Doolan stood holding Mémoire's reins. For reasons known only to God, the mare had quickly come to love Doolan, and she gently placed her muzzle on his shoulder and closed her eyes in equine bliss. Even Doolan was not immune to such overt affection, and he gently placed a hand on her nose as he told his friends, "It's always the same, boys. Hurry up and stand about, roused from a cozy billet, all in a panic, drop everything, all the more pity, as my Stephanie had just started to polish Daidi's own boots. But it's the good soldier I am, sure, so while the moon was still up, did you see her up there, white and bold as a Dublin whore, I went to roust poor Mémoire from her warm stall," a gentle pressure from the irrational mare at the sound of her name, "so that we might obey our lords and

189

masters and stand about in the road, even if it's dark as Satan's arse out here, for hours uncounted while we wait for the dawn, when we all might have stayed in bed like Christians."

"I like your horse, Doolan," said Peter Cunningham, who was renowned in the company for his profound lack of looks, eloquence, and intelligence: hence his nickname, *Rí Sasana*, "King of England".

"Ah, you're a fine judge of horseflesh, Rí, sure, as she's the great creature of the world, as I told Daidi, and didn't I get him a grand price for her, as fine as she is, just twenty pound, and she worth eighty if a penny, but that Frog lieutenant didn't know that he was dealing with an Irishman born and bred in the trade, with an eye for fine flesh, on two legs and well as four." At that Doolan felt a twinge of regret, as he had parted with Stephanie Ferroux in a blinding hurry, lacking the time, ability, and will to confess any particular affection for her.

"It's not Bobby Slatter," said Lancelot Loughlin in his sharp Ulster Irish, "who will mind being told to come to the road, dark or no, even with the King of the World's own million Frenchmen waiting, as he was to be at the court martial tomorrow morning for fighting with that evil Michael Feighery, the Three Company hound."

"Sure it would be the pity of the world," chimed in Alexander Toner, who was standing nearby, "to be punished for losing a fight in such a fashion. Feighery could teach Satan a trick or two, the great monster, him the size of Donn Cuailnge, and twice as fierce."

"Daidi told me," said Doolan with a knowing air, "that it's the *deamhan caol* who will be having his turn this week as judge of the court martial, and wouldn't half the lads in the battalion have red backs."

Nearby, Private Robert Carter, lately Lieutenant Gooch's servant in Gosport and now a member of Six Company, nudged William Smith, and asked in English, "What is that lot going on about, Bill? In the Second Battalion the officers didn't like the men speaking Irish, thinking that they were up to no good."

Smith, who was born John Keegan and who had enlisted in the 27th using that rather unimaginative alias after stealing a gentleman's watch in Dublin town, answered, "Ah, those boys are harmless. If you were in need, Alex Toner there would lend you his arse and shite through his ribs. And that other fellow, the one holding the reins, is the lieutenant's servant, Doolan. He's not a bad sort, once you get used to his damned jabbering. It's him telling how this week it's the turn of the *deamhan caol* to oversee the battalion court martial. As you're new to the battalion, Bob, I'll tell you this: there's an officer named Barr, the lean demon, as what that means, as commands Three Company, and hasn't he turned it into a hell for those poor bastards. It wasn't long ago that there were lads in Three who would do anything for Barr, as he played favorites, and kept at least some of them on a leash. But now Barr is gone all bad—flogging and cursing—and there's not a man who will speak up for him. You're an old campaigner, Bob, so I don't need to tell you what that means."

Carter was a timid old man, but he had indeed been a soldier for many years, and his eyes burned a bit as he said, "It gets dark at night."

Smith smiled grimly in the darkness, and replied softly, "Aye, Bob, you're in the right of it. It gets dark at night."

Doolan heard them and said sharply, "What is it you're thinking of, William Smith?"

"I was just telling old Bob here about our lean demon."

Appeased, Doolan replied in English, "All right, then. It's a wise man who might liken Charles Barr to Dermot MacMurrough, and no man can say worse than that." With the speaking of that name all of the Irishmen within earshot spit on the ground, though its import was lost on Carter.

"But, aye, Bob Carter," continued Doolan, "sure and it gets very dark at night,"

It was an old soldiers' expression, rarely uttered above a whisper, repeated with increasing frequency in the 1/27th, especially in Three Company. Any officer who abused his men had better watch his back, as on campaign the nights were dark indeed, and anything could happen if men were pushed to desperation.

James had been at the head of the column, but he soon came stalking back, calling for Coakley, Blakeley, and the Six Company sergeants: McCurdy, Irwin, McCoy, and Jameson. He was very angry, but tried not to show it as he drew them off a short distance, trying to make out their faces in the ridiculous darkness. James, indeed most of the battalion, knew that Archibald had erred in calling out the battalion at midnight, when the moon set at two, and the sun did not rise until after four thirty. But it could not be helped now. "We march at first light. That is not for another hour or so, so have the men get what rest they can. We all had a long day yesterday, and I doubt that anyone got any sleep before they called us out."

With only the slightest hint of anxiety, Coakley asked, "Any word of the French, sir?"

"None, though if they have an ounce of sense they are sound asleep, wherever they are." James did not mention his opinion of Archibald's mistake. "As to the order of march: Captain Pratt and our lights will join the other light companies of the brigade to lead off, followed by the 40th, the 4th, and then us. For now, we are moving on Brussels, though it's likely that we'll move well beyond it. Look for halts ten minutes every hour, but nothing more. And at the halts we musn't let our guard down; we need to keep the men away from temptation. You can't go far wrong if you manage to keep them out of cellars, kitchens, and bedrooms. Ensign Blakeley, this is of course your first campaign march, but the rest of us have seen this all before. Take the roll again now, if you please, and again at dawn. Dismissed."

As James headed back to the head of the column, Blakeley quietly asked Coakley, "Why do we keep taking the roll? Is Lockwood afraid that the men are going to desert rather than fight the French?"

"Oh, he's not thinking that anyone will run," answered Coakley. "This lot isn't shy, but a few of them are over-fond of loot, women, and liquor. If we aren't watching, the Devil might whisper in a few ears and persuade some fool to sneak off in search of one or the other. So let's take a quick roll and tell them to take a caulk."

Dawn found at least some of the men of the 1/27th asleep. Cobblestones are sometimes referred to as Irish Confetti, but in this instance they served as pillows, to surprisingly good effect. At the head of the column the officers stayed awake, and as the light grew there were some handshakes and quiet good wishes as they broke up and headed back to their companies. James returned to Six Company and gave the word to form up. As the company shook itself awake the men gathered in their ranks, waiting for the word to move, and the growing light revealed several local people coming down to say goodbye in French, Dutch, and scraps of English.

Ever since their days in Spain and Portugal, the British army had insisted that their men treat civilians fairly, with the cat and the noose to ensure that they did so, but James had long before found that the Scots and the Irish did so largely by nature. In the cool half-light James saw that an intriguing number of women came down to say goodbye, some smiling coyly, some teary-eyed. Stephanie Ferroux was not there to see Doolan, but Kaat and Paulien Claes and their friend Uiljke Janssens were waving their kerchiefs at several smiling Irishmen, and Sylvie Gagnon, who was not at all happy with her choice of a husband, had slipped out to slyly kiss Lancelot Loughlin goodbye. Jacqueline Maurin was there as well, though perhaps she would have been at a loss to explain why, as she stayed out of sight and watched Lieutenant Lockwood only from a distance.

The working-class families upon whom the enlisted men had been billeted were not wealthy people, but many brought a bottle, a loaf of bread, or some other simple parting gift. The childless Ferdinand and Marie Couder had spent the hours since midnight baking two pies for "their boys" Garret Costello, Dan Moriarty, and Jimmy McConvill, who wolfed down the pies laughing as the doting Marie tried to keep them from getting crumbs on their uniforms. An elderly butcher and his wife, Sint Joris and Baertie Peeters, brought a smoked ham to give to the six men who had shared their roof. A few days later, Tim Hammican and John Quick would die, each with a carefully wrapped piece of ham in his pack.

*****

The march began, the horses behaving badly, every man on edge. Even before they had left Ghent there was a delay, the entire brigade standing in place as the Belgian carters hired to haul the brigade's baggage and ammunition had decided at the last minute that they would rather not risk the lives of their drivers and horses, and only an angry aide-de-camp with a drawn saber and a purse of guineas convinced them that the risk was not so great after all. Finally moving, the battalion had not marched more than a mile when there was another long halt, as the three light companies that led the brigade's advance made a wrong turn leaving the city, and the Inniskillings at the tail of the column stood in place for nearly half an hour, a very frustrating half-hour, as the accordion-like column was redirected.

Free of the city, the column stretched a mile in length, a ribbon of red that snaked steadily across the verdant Belgian countryside. At the rear of the long column came the baggage wagons, the ammunition carts, and the unformed mass of wives, children, sutlers, and camp followers. With maddening frequency the Inniskillings came to a halt as there were delays up ahead, while at other times they were urged to "Step out, step out, now," hurrying to catch up if a gap appeared between One Company and the 40th.

Most of the Inniskillings were veterans long accustomed to road marches, and while this road was reasonably level, the day was getting warm, the humid air thick as banks of black clouds scudded across the sky. The welcome call "Drop packs! Ten minutes!" came down the column more than three hours after the brigade had set out, as Lambert had wanted to clear Ghent before they took their first break. As the men sought out the nearest patch of soft ground, their officers drifted back to the rear of the column to meet at the battalion baggage wagons, where a keg of fresh water mixed with wine was kept for their use. Blakeley's rabbit had a comfortable billet in a slotted box aboard a wagon, and as they had a few minutes at the halt, Blakeley set Blackie out to munch on the lush roadside grass. All of the officers made their way back to the baggage except the outcast Charles Barr, who, for a reason known only to himself, contented himself with trotting his snorting black stallion up and down the resting column.

Lieutenant Reddock strolled up to his brothers and asked, "Did any of you happen to speak with that gentleman in the phaeton and the handsome gray team? A Dutchman, poor fellow, but he spoke passable English, and he told me that the frontier is in chaos, the French are drubbing Blücher right, left, and centre, and the latest rumour in Brussels is that the Duke is seeking an accommodation with Bonaparte, in an attempt to save his army after getting clawed somewhere south of Brussels. Complete nonsense, of course," he added calmly.

"Why do civilians always behave so badly?" asked Lieutenant Pitts with elegant nonchalance as he took a drag on his cigar. "It's always the same: panic, rumours, and wholesale flight."

Normally the ensigns maintained a studied silence in the presence of their seniors. Ensign Coakley, however, was about to offer up a rumour that he had heard from a squat, hirsute Belgian farm girl whose acquaintance he had cultivated at the last halt, when he was interrupted by Barr trotting past the baggage wagon, looking down on the other officers with a look that could only be interpreted as unveiled contempt. But an instant later Barr's vicious façade was replaced by a surprisingly human look of startled fear when Blakeley's rabbit, spooked by the dancing stallion, dashed out into the road between the horse's hooves. The stallion skipped and nearly fell; an observer unacquainted with Captain Charles Barr might have concluded that only a miracle had kept him in the saddle. Enraged and humiliated, Barr saw the rabbit dash madly into the field and spurred hard after him, yelling "Tally Ho!" He ignored the voices that called for him to "leave the poor little fellow alone" as he galloped after the rabbit with a will, while the stallion, who was by nature already prone toward evil, needed little prompting to pursue the wildly scrambling Blackie.

Barr watched as the exhausted rabbit soon went to ground in a patch of tall grass. He reined his horse up, drew his pistol, and slowly walked his mount forward. He spotted the rabbit quivering in the grass, and killed him.

Barr trotted further out into the field, laughing, triumphant. Archibald, displeased, not knowing what else to do, called "Fall in! Fall in!" as the disgusted officers returned to their companies. James walked Mémoire back up to Six Company, his hand on Blakeley's shoulder, as Reddock called out to Barr, "Badly done, sir!"

Since Six Company was near the end of the column, many of their men had seen what had happened. "I'm right sorry, sir," said Sergeant Jameson quietly as Ensign Blakeley silently took his place with his platoon. There were several other murmurs of condolence from the ranks, as Blakeley was well liked. When Barr trotted past on his way up to

Three Company there were several hoots from the men, and one anonymous voice called "Bastard!" Blakeley stood with his head down, Coakley did nothing to quiet the company, and it was only Lieutenant Lockwood, stalking along the road scarlet with rage, who called, "Silence in the ranks, you pack of God damned mooncalves! This is not a God damned republic! Sergeant McCurdy, take that man's name!"

*****

The long day dragged on. As the men grew tired there was no singing and little conversation, as they had their heads down, their thumbs tucked under their shoulder straps, mile after mile getting down to the serious business of soldiering. It was nearly dark when James and Tom finally had an opportunity to ride beside each other for a mile or two. "I spoke with Archibald," said James, "and we will halt for a few hours at a town about three miles ahead, called Asse."

"In any other circumstances, I would have had great fun with that. But I'm too damned tired."

"According to his map," continued James as he stretched his back with a grimace, "we've made about thirty miles. Thirty miles in fifteen hours, which is convenient, as any calculation any more complicated than that would be quite beyond me. An average pace, I suppose, but I'm just about worn through as well."

"I noticed that you let Blakeley ride a while; you are going to spoil that boy. You realize, of course, that we godlike company commanders have a lofty image to maintain. When the men see you walking they may get wild Jacobin ideas about equality and the rights of man."

"You should have seen the blisters on that boy's feet. His boots are far too big for him. I had him ride for an hour or two, but when the men from his squad heard that he was gimpy Private Meaze quite kindly gave him a pair of thick wool socks that his Gosport brute had knit for him."

"You amaze me," said Tom, "do brutes indeed knit? I would have thought their domestic skills were limited to endless coupling."

"This one does, evidently; I suppose that they were all someone's daughter, once. At any rate, Carrigan got some salve from O'Donnell, and they tended Blakeley as gently as his own mother, so you can go stuff your Jacobin ideas. Besides, I saw you let Mrs. M'Mullen ride for some hours."

"Well I had to, didn't I?" said Tom. "To say that she is large with child would constitute a criminal understatement, and I couldn't have one of my best men falling out to see to her. I can't get over how huge she is: when she walks past she quite blots out the sun, a mobile eclipse."

James Lockwood, the father of five who had long since had any humour regarding the size of pregnant women excised from his psyche, ignored the opportunity to further comment on Mrs. M'Mullen, only adding, "It is a pity that Archibald is such a stickler for orders. Pritchard would have had a pregnant woman up on the baggage wagon, orders be damned."

"But the orders come straight from the Duke: no women or children on any army vehicles."

"Oh, bugger the Duke."

"Doubtless Brigid has told you this more than once, but you will allow me to mention that when you are tired you are very irritable."

"Humpf."

They rode on in silence for a while, almost soothed by the sounds that they had heard through most of their adult lives: the steady footfalls of men who knew their business, the gentle rattle of equipment, the lulling sound of Irish voices.

At the next halt, Sergeant McCurdy double-timed up from the rear of the company to tell James, "Begging your pardon, sir, but it looks as if Shanks will have to be falling out here, crippled as the returned Oisín he is." That was unfortunate, as Corporal William Shanks, who for some reason was known as Brúitín, or "mashed potatoes", in the longstanding, complex, private culture of Inniskilling soldiers, was a seasoned regular and a steady man. James found him lying behind a hedge, being tended by Kennedy. "Shanks, I hear that you are not doing well. Mister Kennedy, what do you make of his condition?" James was asking only out of form, as for the past hour James had seen Shanks struggling to keep up, and he now lay in the grass looking wholly destroyed.

"Well, sir," replied Kennedy, "Private Shanks's arthritis has flared, and has rendered him unfit for any duty beyond battalion paperweight. I have dosed him, but I would suggest that he be left behind, as rest is the only truly effective treatment. The worst of it should subside within a day or two." As he packed up his bag, Kennedy added, "I might also mention that Private Guggerty from One Company is also unable to continue." That solved one problem, at least: battalion tradition dictated that no man was ever to be left behind alone.

As Kennedy returned to the column, Shanks finally burst out, "Lieutenant *a grah*, you'll not be leaving me here, with only that dog Guggerty as company? I am no dirty informer, sir, but I'll tell you that Guggerty is a slacker, a fake, and a rogue. The black thief will get us both sent up a ladder for a rest." Seeing the Lieutenant's puzzled expression, he explained, "He'll get us both hanged, sir." After a pause, in a different tone he added, "It's pitiful sorry I am, sir, to be playing the cripple when there's trouble brewing"

"You are an old campaigner, Shanks, and you know that we can't leave healthy men behind to see to our stragglers. So use those stripes: don't let Guggerty stray, and join up when you can. Besides, I wager you'll be back with us before there is any real scrape with the French. Now, have you any money?"

Shanks eventually confessed that he had spent his every penny on the daughter of a Ghent grocer, and James left him with a few coins from his purse. As the men formed up, the news that Brúitín was falling out spread through the company, and a few men trotted up to the hedge to wish him luck, check that he had enough food and water with him, or lend him a shilling or two.

As the battalion formed up, there was a commotion from up near One Company, where Private Henry Stewart had snuck away from his company, intent on breaking into a nearby barn. Instantly and loudly accused by a Belgian peasant, he was seized up, and in a drumhead court martial Archibald ordered three dozen. As a new recruit who was yet unfamiliar with the harshness of military discipline, Stewart was fortunate not to have actually stolen anything. In the British army, thieves were handed over to the Provost to be hanged, as capital offences were numerous and strictly enforced. Instead, the sergeants of his company made an upright triangle with their pikes as his company quietly drew up around him, and as the rest of the battalion marched past, he was stripped to the waist and flogged by the thick-armed One Company Drummer, James Bunton, who conveyed his company's collective disapprobation by laying on with a will. Stewart, who had never been flogged before, bore it poorly, and after twenty strokes a disgusted Archibald ordered him cut down. The men of his company handed him over to the surgeons without much sympathy, as they had warned him of the costs of straying, and if he was fool enough to try it, he was to be man enough to bear it. Worst of all, One Company was to pay for Stewart's criminal levity by being posted to march at the very rear of the column, behind the wagons and baggage, an obvious and thoroughly humiliating reprimand.

The march continued. After the battalion had settled into their route pace, James and Tom rode together again, Mémoire and Tom's bay Porthos having grown fond of one another. After long consideration, Tom said quietly, "I am

200

going to speak to Archibald, and suggest that Barr is unfit for command. I hope Kennedy will support me."

"I hardly think," James said softly, "that the willful murder of a rabbit is tantamount to mental incompetence."

Tom edged his mount into a side lane, James following, away from the men. "Listen, James. I will, of course, respect your wishes, and I will not share any of what you have told me about Barr's syphilis. But I will tell Archibald this: your Irish is better than mine, but every officer in this regiment knows what '*tá sé dorcha san oíche*' means."

James's head snapped around to face Tom, his tension passing on to Mémoire, who tensed and tossed her head. "Christ, Tom, you've heard them say that? 'It is dark at night'?"

"Yes," Tom said quietly but urgently, "I thought that I heard it this morning, but I'm certain that I heard it just before the last break. There is scarcely a man in this battalion who I wouldn't trust with my life, but if Barr continues with this madness he shall certainly drive a wedge between the men and the officers. Neither of us would mind if Barr met his end some dark night, but if this kind of thinking spreads through the battalion we could lose control very quickly."

*****

It was well after ten o'clock and nearly dark when the order to halt finally came. As the men fell out, James walked through the company, ordering, "Road march camp: no one is to be more than ten steps from the road, unless he is using the latrine. That clump of bushes is hereby designated as the company latrine." That was well accepted; for such a hardened lot of men they were modest about where they would tend to their business. "Each mess will have a man go down to that farmyard and fill their kettle and his mess's canteens from their well. And no nonsense down there, or you'll go hungry and thirsty, and be damned to you."

There is nothing like exhaustion as a prophylactic for nonsense, as the men of Six Company thought of nothing more devious than food and rest. There was an established routine amongst the veterans that the new men were expected to learn quickly, so that they might get a quick bite and as much sleep as possible. Each man in the six-man messes took a turn carrying the heavy kettle for a day, so those unfortunates threw their messmates' canteens over their shoulders and headed down to tend to the water. The others quickly gathered dry grass and twigs for a quick cook fire to boil their beef. Flints, never a rare commodity in an infantry battalion, were struck, the fires blazed, and up and down the road the hedges and ditches took on a decidedly homey feel. A quick if plain dinner in their stomachs, the Inniskillings spent the few remaining hours of darkness wrapped in their blankets on what dry ground they could find near the road.

James and Tom took their ensigns to a nearby cottage, where for a few sous they garnered a bowl of *soupe* and the privilege of sleeping with a roof over their heads. The one bed in the cottage was occupied by the dirty young master of the house and a large number of fleas, while the floor of the front room was filled with sleeping ensigns. Tom and James, lieutenants in all their grandeur, slept fitfully in rickety chairs in the filthy kitchen, which sadly also proved alive with fleas.

At three o'clock the drums sounded at the head of the column, the call in turn picked up by each of the battalions, calling the men to duty. The stars in the eastern sky were just beginning to fade as the men yawned, stretched, pissed, grumbled, and prepared to march.

Doolan had spent much of the night tending to Mémoire, and at dawn James found him holding her reins at the head of the company bivouac. Doolan could see that Daidi was obviously still tired, a condition that prompted a degree of circumspection. He also saw the lieutenant irritably scratching, and wisely thought better than to make hay of his long night with Mémoire, instead saying, "Top of the morning to you, now, Lieutenant *a grah*." He then gestured toward the lieutenant's coat and asked, "Is it the light troops on the march, now?"

James shook out his coat in a thoroughly bad humour. "God damned fleas," he groused, "tonight I shall sleep in a wet ditch if all I get indoors are fleas and the tepid dirty water that these bumpkins call *soupe*. Damn it all anyway." He was fully prepared to kick the first man to cross him, but Mémoire gave him a delighted morning nicker, the first rays of the sun began to light the sky, and he took a few swallows from the bottle of brandy that he kept in his valise. After rubbing his face with both hands James felt a modicum of humanity creep into his consciousness. He could have left the call to "fall in" to his ensigns or his sergeants, but he wanted to review the company's condition and to plumb the collective mood. Walking Mémoire to warm her, back through the company in the half-light: "Fall in, there, men, fall in. Loughlin, pray check the contents of that fellow's pack. Cunningham, isn't it? Yes. Check Cunningham's pack; it looks as if he is carrying a hundred of bricks. Some of these fellows think they need to bring half of Ireland with them. Fall in, fall in. Good morning, Mrs. Carmichael; might I beg you to return to the rear of the column, please? No, children, you must not worry about Bonaparte; we shall chase him back to Hell presently. Now back to the rear with you. Little beasts. Ensign Coakley, take the roll, please. Ensign Blakeley, pray do not scratch in such an obvious fashion; it ain't genteel. Good morning, McCann. Yes, I'm sure that there will be plenty of Frenchmen left for us. It seems that is one commodity that the world does not lack for, is Frenchmen. Sergeant Irwin, I believe that Private Toner has mud upon the lock of his weapon; pray correct his sinful ways. Fall in, there, men, fall in."

Up to that morning, the Inniskillings had been prudent in their choice of weather, as it had been warm and humid but it had not rained. Soon, though, the dark clouds that had been haunting them organized into an ominous, black mass that hung just above their heads. For the first hour of the march, and with growing apprehension, the battalion passed steadily through the gloom until with blinding fury the storm broke on them, the air alive with water, lightning flashing around them with amazing power and rapidity. The march was a misery, but the column bore it, men and horses plodding ahead with their heads down. James dismounted to give Mémoire some relief and trudged alongside her, his boats soaked through, his oilskin cloak whipping around him. For a period that seemed to last forever, the rain came so hard that he had to turn his head to one side with his mouth wide open to breathe.

The storm lasted an hour or more, but as suddenly as it began the rain ceased, though the sky remained black and threatening. The next halt afforded them little comfort, as the ditches on either side of the road were full of water, the whole world dripping, soaked, and muddy, while the drenched men simply sat on the slick cobblestones until the word came to continue. The Inniskillings were not pleased with the situation, but neither were they unduly upset. That *sangfroid* had not yet fully permeated Ensign Blakeley, who found this, his first road march, a harsh lesson. His very being was soaked through, his blistered feet squelched in his flopping boots, and the dye of his coat had bled enough to turn his skin, shirt, and sword belt a very unmilitary pink. His lieutenant helped pull him to his feet, the battalion fell in, and the Inniskillings pressed on.

*****

More rain fell through the morning, but by noon the worst of the storms had blown themselves out. The brigade dragged itself through the western suburbs and entered

Brussels. While Ghent had been impressive, the centre of Brussels possessed an entirely greater element of grandeur. The Inniskillings, however, would have been more appreciative of the architecture if they had not been so wet and tired, their feet and legs aching, their backs and shoulders chafed by their packs and musket slings. The dignity of the city was also much diminished by the frequent scenes of panic, especially in the grand houses along the Regentschapsstraat where frantic civilians were hastily loading carriages, carts, and milk wagons with their precious belongings, everywhere the cry *"Les Français sont à venir!"* prodding them to further heights of hysteria. The poorer classes, evidently not concerned that the French would rifle their modest homes, sat in the cafés and watched the Redcoats pass, neither cheering nor cursing them.

James and Tom had decided their sore legs and the honour of the regiment required that they ride through Brussels. Thus Ensign Blakeley, his delicate feet lanced, wrapped, and cocooned in good English wool, marched with his platoon, and Mrs. M'Mullen, she of the lunar girth and happily quite recovered, strode alongside her particular friend Maggie O'Mara at the rear of the column. It proved prudent of Archibald to have adhered to the march orders regarding passengers in the baggage, as a Provost Marshal looked them over as they passed, and woe to the battalion commander who veered even a bit from the Duke's orders.

James allowed Corporal James Fegan to fall out and march in the rear, helping to tend to his two daughters. The girls were exhausted and feverish, and had to be carried by Fegan and his wife Marie. Several of the other wives took turns carrying the girls as well, but when they became too much of a burden James quietly told the massive Private Teady Murtagh to fall out to help Fegan carry the delirious children. Murtagh, a muscled veteran of twenty years' service who always had trouble finding a coat that fit, had never married, and whenever the topic was raised he'd quip, "As soon as I put my shako on, I know that it's my family that's covered, safe, and no worries." James noted that he carried Martha Fegan with great tenderness for miles, his greatcoat protecting her from the rain, and at times James thought that he heard Murtagh gently singing.

The column had been traveling eastward to reach Brussels, but once in the great city it turned to the south, and in the southern suburbs they saw evidence of Wellington's first battles against the French. Straw-lined wagonloads of wounded men, British, German, Dutch, and Belgian, sought solace in Brussels, the men tossed in together, pale, bloody, and ghastly in their agony. "Don't look at them, John," James said quietly to Blakeley, who had been staring in horror. "Keep your head down, and keep marching. Don't look at them, son."

The roads south of Brussels were far different from the roads that they had followed from Ghent, as they were choked with men and vehicles trying to join the army while panicked civilian wagons, carts, and carriages, as well as the wagonloads of wounded, tried to escape the fighting. The wagons and artillery used the cobble road, so the infantrymen were relegated to the muddy verges of the road, muddy and exhausting. In the press it was difficult to keep the company together, let alone the battalion, and there was no chance at all for the brigade to remain intact. When the rain began again the situation was nearly impossible.

At one sodden, mud-caked, congested crossroad, a squadron of dapper German Hussars attempted to force their way through the Inniskillings, while the Irishmen tried to stay together, pressing ahead to keep contact with the 40th. An impatient Hussar captain drove his mount into the packed ranks of Six Company, instantly inciting a multilingual melee of cursing, jostling, and subtle violence. He was dissuaded by Lieutenant Lockwood, who was seconded by Mémoire, who stood her ground against the German gelding with admirable aplomb.

The Inniskillings marched thirty miles on the 16th and twenty more on the 17th, but those last ten had been as difficult as they had ever known. There was unabashed chaos along the road south of Brussels, and the closer to the main army the column moved, the worse the congestion grew. The Inniskillings disdainfully eyed bands of leaderless soldiers, mostly Hanoverian, Dutch, and Belgian militiamen, who had gotten "lost" and who now did as they pleased, preferring the pleasures of the rear to the potential hazards of staying with their companies. There had been several instances of brutality and theft; James witnessed a Provost Marshal's drumhead court-martial of a young Dutch private who had struck a German officer. The terrified youngster was found guilty and was hanged with little ceremony in a stable yard beside the road. As horrid a sight as it was, James saw its necessity.

The rain stopped, at least for a while, and as the day wore into evening the road dropped into a great forest. Shortly after passing into the damp gloom, the Inniskillings were finally ordered off the road to rest and prepare their dinners. The men dragged themselves off the congested road and moved a hundred yards up into the woods, where despite the dampness they soon had their fires going in the surprisingly open ground between the massive trees. James stayed with his men as they wolfed down a few bites and gratefully rolled out their blankets. Soon Tom called him over to sit on the trunk of a fallen beech to share his scant dinner.

As James gnawed at the heel of a stale piece of bread, Tom said, "I am surprised that Doolan does not have you dining on quail and *foie gras*."

Deciding that no human teeth were capable of a successful assault upon the bread, James tossed it into the ferns and answered, "He ignores me in favor of Mémoire. If I were of a less noble nature, and less damned sleepy, I suppose that I'd be angry with him. But I doubt if even Doolan could scrounge a decent meal within twenty miles of here; too many hungry mouths, and it looks as if the commissary wagons have opted to take this campaign at their leisure."

They sat in silence for a while, companionably sharing the bottle of very average wine that Tom had stowed in his valise. The vastness of the forest softened the noise made by their seven hundred men, and it wholly swallowed the din coming from the still-crowded road below. The trees dripped, the ferns poised in great spreads of delicate, coiling leaves, and in the growing darkness, the forest silently ignored them.

James looked off into the woods where the massive trunks went on for what seemed an infinite distance, saying, "This must be much like the places men first lived, back when the world was young."

Tom nodded. "Very much like a cathedral, all these pillars, but a cathedral without walls, without limit."

James stretched, yawned enormously, and said, "I intend to sleep like the dead for a few hours; pray have Doolan call me if the world comes to an end."

Tom was yawning in reply when Major Archibald galloped up, agitated, and called the company commanders to join him. Lieutenants Massey and Reddock were already asleep, and had to be roused to join the group that clustered around Archibald.

James noticed the exhaustion in Archibald's face as he addressed them. "Gentlemen, General Lambert has spoken with the Duke. It seems that Bonaparte defeated the Prussians yesterday at Ligny. Thus finding his left flank exposed, the Duke found it necessary to withdraw the army to a ridge five miles north of here, and expects Bonaparte to attack in the morning."

A ripple of consternation and anxiety went the group. Archibald went on, "This forest in the army's rear would pose an obstacle if the Duke finds it necessary to retreat further, so our brigade is ordered to clear the road. The road must be completely clear: every wagon, every man, every horse, into the woods or into the ditch. It will take all night." There was a general groan of exhaustion and disbelief. "Mainwaring, as I recall from Spain, your Sergeant McCormick is an inveterate arsonist; pray give him a few shillings and a few men, and have him make torches for every officer, and a few spares. I hope that he may find some pitch hereabouts. That Wilson fellow has some French; send him along. Under all these damned trees it will be as dark as Satan's cellar, so we'll need those torches very soon. Keep them at it, gentlemen."

*****

June 18, 1815

My Dearest Brigid;

It is nearly dawn, and the French army is drawn up just a few miles from here. A few lines before the day unfolds. The battalion is quite done in. We have marched fifty miles in two days, and then worked all night in a driving rain to clear the road behind the army. In doing so we pushed hundreds of wagons and sutlers' carts into the ditches, and while most had been abandoned some of the drivers grew saucy, and were obliged to be knocked about. Very unpleasant duty, and while most of our men did well there were a few who took advantage and behaved badly. Many of the wagons held firkins or even full kegs of liquor, and in the rain and darkness nearly every one of our men managed to get into the rum. I am very unhappy with Sergeant Irwin, who opted to get wholly drunk and was insolent with Coakley; I shall have him broke as soon as we are done with the French. I doubt that there is one man in the company who is truly sober, or whose canteen is not filled to the brim with liquor. But I suppose that I cannot be too hard on them, as it is the only escape from this misery, and though the rain finally stopped around dawn we are all soaked, shivering and exhausted. Still, not one of them wandered off, and drunk or sober they are all present and willing to fight.

James had garnered a small chair and the corner of a table in an inn that was packed with officers, all of whom were bartering, in several different languages, for what little fare remained in the house. A captain of the Coldstreams bumped the table and nearly spilled James's ink. "Oh, I do beg your pardon, sir," said the captain with a cheerfulness that indicated that he had slept well the previous night, likely indoors after a hot dinner.

Wet, dirty, and exhausted, James muttered, "Not at all."

The captain, as much to himself as to James, said, "Not at all like dining at Black's, eh? But I do hope that they have some decent marmalade."

James stifled a snarl and returned to his letter. He sat and mused for a moment over the nature of men, of society, and carefully wrote,

Our battalion will fight. They are, on the whole, the most honourable of men, and I am intensely proud to be numbered amongst them.

But, pray, my love, do not worry about us, as the whole army is here, and I cannot think that even Wellington would ask our regiment to do much fighting. We are incapable of anything until we dry out and get some rest.

I am writing this note at the only inn in a village called Waterloo, while Tom is trying to get the cook to put together a decent breakfast. I shall leave it

with young John Blakeley, who is to stay behind and do baggage guard. Do not tell him, but I arranged with Archibald that John should stay in the rear, as he is such a decent lad, and I should feel quite bad if he got knocked on the head. You would like him.

We must wolf down our food and get back to our companies. Quickly, too quickly, I will tell you how I love you, and I promise to take care of the money and my family and this madness with Barr. First I shall do my duty, and then I shall come home to you, though hell should bar the way.

With Great Love,
James

"I wonder, Ensign Blakeley, if I might beg you to post this for me when the opportunity arises, please? A note home is customary before action, if you have the time, and of course you must leave another letter with one of your friends, to be sent in case of the worst."

"Certainly, sir, it would be my pleasure. But I hardly think that I need write home to tell them that I am to miss the battle while I command ten men and guard the battalion baggage."

"Oh, come, John, don't be so glum. It is an important assignment; every battalion detaches one officer to the rear, as everything we own is on those wagons, and we can't have stragglers or skulking civilians taking advantage of things and stealing us blind. But do write to your mother. It will be a comfort to her, when she hears about the battle, and imagines the worst."

Chapter Fourteen
Clonakilty

The front door of Fáibhile Cottage was a great, heavy thing that had been known to squeak at awkward moments, so Mary Lockwood had chosen to go out through the kitchen door. She was terribly excited and nearly equally afraid, as she had accepted a secretly delivered invitation from George Boffut to slip out for a midnight stroll. While she may have been naïve enough to misjudge that brutal young man's intentions, Mary was at least knowledgeable of the ways of her home, and as she crept into the dark kitchen she attempted to keep Sergeant quiet with a bit of stew meat. In doing so, however, she had not considered Sergeant's emotionality or Mrs. Cashman's suspicious nature. Sergeant was so pleased with his midnight treat that his wagging tail struck a table leg with great force and rapidity, waking Mrs. Cashman, who burst into the kitchen with a candle and a massive horse pistol that had last been fired in support of James II, and which most armies of the day would have classed as light artillery.

"Mary Lockwood, where in God's name do you think you're going at this time of night?"

"Oh! Mrs. Cashman... I am so sorry to wake you... I... couldn't sleep, and I thought that I might go..."

"Not one more word young lady, I'll hear no stories tonight. Just know this, Mary, as it's you I'm watching, and if I ever find you sneaking out at night, for whatever reason, I'll tell your dear mother the whole of it, and won't she have you in St. Maura's before you can blink, as a nun in the family is a grand thing, don't you think?"

While Mary Lockwood had few notions as to what that evening might have held for her, she certainly would not have believed that it would have included the contemplation of a life of celibacy. The shock that crossed her face was ready proof that Mrs. Cashman's shot had gone home. With Mary summarily, if quietly, returned to bed, Mrs. Cashman opened the kitchen door, holding Sergeant by the collar, half expecting George Boffut to be perched upon the garden wall like one of Satan's imps. While the kitchen garden was dark and silent, Catherine knew that Boffut was out there somewhere. *"Go dtachta an Diabhal thú,* George Boffut... may the Devil choke you. Won't you be disappointed this night... go on now, Sergeant." With that, Sergeant bound out into the darkness with a will, and Catherine had only reached her third Hail Mary before she heard fierce barking at the foot of the lane. She finished her Rosary and determined not to tell Mrs. Lockwood about all this. Brigid was a young woman with her husband away, with enough to worry about. Catherine returned to bed with a certain degree of satisfaction, but still deeply worried about the ways of dreamy young ladies, and of the evil men who pursued them.

*****

"Damn you, sir, have you no notion of standing at attention when addressing a superior officer?" Even at his advanced age, Colonel Simon was still capable of upbraiding a subordinate. "Have you puppies no concept of military practice, military courtesy? Is there a single yeomanry officer in the south of Ireland who knows his business? God damned amateurs."

Lieutenant Bookey recalled the lesson he had learned at the door to Fáibhile Cottage and hastily removed his shako, then stood as straight as his damaged ego would allow. Bookey considered Simon to be a doddering old fool, and likely a coward. But Simon was the senior yeomanry officer for the county and so, hoping to win his favor, Bookey had gone to the headquarters of the West Cork Yeomanry to report his suspicions of a Mrs. Lockwood, an avowed Catholic for all her airs, who had been disrespectful of a yeomanry officer.

Simon would have none of that; putting a finger in Bookey's face he said, "Mrs. Lockwood, sir, is the devoted wife of a serving officer, an officer on foreign service, an officer of many years' service in the regulars. The regulars, sir! A gentleman who has been fighting Frenchmen all across the continent, not chasing chicken thieves in Carrickbeg!"

Simon straightened his jacket, caught his breath, and went on with waning energy. "Now, as to your conduct since you have been seconded to my forces. You come from Wexford, and are unaware of how we do things here in Cork. There is an understanding hereabouts, sir, that has kept this county from degenerating into some God damned slaughter pen, an *abattoir*, as it were. The Government forces under my command use a light hand when dealing with the peasantry. The rebels seem to be equally cautious. We knock them on the head when we catch them, of course, traitorous vermin, but we don't ride about burning cabins and cutting down the rabble, and in turn the peasants don't lay hands on their betters."

Bookey still stood straight, but he did not veil the disdain on his face. "Certainly, sir, whether one is in Wexford or Cork, our goal is—"

Simon cut him off with, "You are at attention, sir!" but that drained away what little energy remained to him. He ran a hand through his thin white hair and continued in a tired voice, "If they should be driven to organize themselves, we would be outnumbered a hundred to one, sir, a hundred to one. If the rabble would rise it would be the Devil's own business to put them down again. We had a taste of that in '98. So you will perform the duties assigned to you, and no more." Simon had exhausted himself; he looked every bit the old man when he weakly waved at Bookey and muttered, "So, for God's sake keep your wits about you. You are dismissed, sir."

*****

Bookey was well mounted, though he did not ride well; he spurred his horse hard, and led his patrol of the Camolin Yeomen Cavalry at the gallop out of Clonakilty. They had been tasked with searching the hamlet of Carrigagrenane, where it was rumoured that a cache of weapons had been hidden. They searched every cabin, sty, and rick, and found nothing. They also manhandled and insulted the impoverished residents, who could do nothing but glare with unflinching hatred at the heavy-handed troopers. Dirty, frustrated, and angry, the patrol left Carrigagrenane, sullenly riding up Mill Road back toward Clonakilty. The road narrowed as it passed through a hilly, forested area, with thick hedges on either side. In other circumstances it would have been the perfect site for an ambush, though in this instance they found their way blocked only by a herd of sheep, driven by a stout boy named Kenny McElroy. The foul-tempered troopers ordered him out the way, and the boy was foolish enough to defy them. Bookey had the boy seized, and in what he referred to as a summary trial, the boy was found guilty of disloyalty and disrespect. He was taken up and flogged, each stroke cutting deep and drawing vain screams. Fifty strokes left him shattered, nearly dead, in the mud at the side of the road. Before they galloped off, several of the troopers took a sheep, throats cut and thrown across

216

the horses' rumps, the horrified mounts capering at the smell of so much blood.

*****

The sun had set two hours before, and the moon would not be up for another two. Silently approaching the house, the man with the musket took just a few steps at a time, then listened, listened: no dog barking, no movement at all. A few more steps; he could take the shot from there, but he had to make sure. The light from the windows streamed out, diamonds of leaded glass from the north side of the big house. A few steps more, and resting the barrel against a tree, he consciously relaxed in order to steady his breathing. Movement inside the house; there he was, now.

George Boffut was rarely a visitor to the Fort Dominion library, as his mother was the only person in the family who cherished the vast collection of leather-bound volumes. But George had heard from one of his friends about a title that might interest him, and as his parents were away in Dublin he locked the door behind him and privately spent the evening searching through the stacks, finally coming across the slim green volume. He carried his lamp over to one of the high-backed chairs that sat by the window, where earlier generations of residents had read first-folio Shakespeare, but where now George Boffut studied *The Memoirs of Fanny Hill*. He was flipping ahead, looking for the good parts.

The Royal Navy had trained John Cashman well, and it really was, he admitted to himself, a remarkably easy shot, especially as he was armed with a light hunting rifle stolen years before from one of the big houses. It was two weeks after Kenny McElroy had been flogged, and John's fourth night outside the house. Now that his chance had come he was surprised at how easy it was going to be. Calm, easy breaths, a slow pulse. A slow exhale and a gentle squeeze of the trigger just as he closed his eyes to preserve his night vision. The flash, the fire, and the lead ball sped through the darkness, shattering a diamond pane and tearing away most

217

of George Boffut's nose. John would rather have put the ball deep into his skull, but he had his orders.

The house had numerous servants, but none of them possessed a particularly bold nature (Boffut senior did not tolerate saucy servants), so John was pursued only by their cries and by the distant barking of the stable dogs, who, like the servants, were prized only for their timidity. George's screams for help went unanswered for some time, as no one could find a key to the library door, and by the time that George managed to stagger over to unlock the door his face was so horrid that the butler fainted dead away at the sight of him.

*****

Liam Collins and John Cashman took advantage of the gentle land breeze that carried their boat back into the usual fishing grounds. The curragh was rigged like every other small fishing boat in the area, except for the rifle that lay wrapped in rags at the bottom. At the least hint of trouble the weapon would be discreetly dropped overboard.

The pickup had gone smoothly, but Collins was still far from pleased. "Well?" he asked after a few minutes.

"It's done. The boy showed himself at the library window, plain as day. I was afraid the thick glass would deflect the ball, but it carried true and made a mess of him. Amazing simple. No pursuit at all."

"Good for us, sure, John, and won't your mamaí be pleased. But by noon the yeomanry and militia will be kicking in the door of every McCarthy home in Cork, thinking that this was their revenge for Boffut getting under that girl's skirts. This is the first shooting of a local Proddy in long years, and there will be hell to pay."

"Just remember," replied John, getting heated, "that it was your idea to hit back hard after those bastards flogged the McElroy boy. If I take the risk of doing the shooting, then by God I get some word as to who we target. It's you who is always preaching the way of it: one of our young men gets hurt, one of their young men gets hurt. If it just so happens that their young man has been threatening decent folks, so much the better."

"Decent folks, is it, John? What is it in your head, now, that has you thinking that the Lockwoods want shite to do with you? We're like ants to them and their kind. And you'll not be forgetting that it was Lockwood that saved the Westmeaths at Shannonvale, when they were ready to run like sheep, it was himself that stepped forward and rallied them, fighting like fecking Fionn mac Cumhaill and turning the tide. And here we are preserving his daughter's own virtue. It'll be angels flying out me arse, next."

John Cashman said nothing, as the tide in the Irish Sea turned, unseen, but gradually, relentlessly.

Collins, less harshly, went on, "So it cannot, cannot, become personal. The Movement has slipped into that *cac* before, and I say now that we must stay above it. All over Ireland there are bands of Whiteboys and Defenders and United men that don't do anything more than settle personal scores. But this is my group, I've learned how to run it, and we'll run it professionally. This is a war, a damned slow one, but a war, and we'll not pursue the private agenda of John Cashman, or his mother, for God's sake. So while we will never target the Lockwoods, we'll not do anything more to help them, either." Collins' voice grew thoughtful as he continued, "But God help them if things turn ugly; Lockwood had better come home quick, sword in hand, if Clerkin and his kind are loosed upon the land." A pained expression crossed Collins' face; he turned away and muttered, "It's always the women and children who pay for our madness."

*****

In the crimson serge coat of the West Cork Yeomanry, Colonel Simon trotted his favorite gray mare up Scartagh

Road at the head of twenty troopers. He had not felt so strong in years; the panicked pleas from the magistrate had come before dawn, and by midmorning his regiment was gathered and on the move. The attempted murder of the sole heir of an important landowner could be the first sign of an impending revolt. There was purpose in his life again, Corporal M'Vicar at his side, cavalry on the move, doing important work. He had patrols out everywhere, working in conjunction with the Camolins and the militia, doing all the dirty, unpleasant searches and interrogations that needed to be done but with which he preferred not to be involved. He allowed himself the more satisfying task of calling on the better families in the area, to reassure them and to perhaps impress some of the local ladies with his vigor and his manly dedication to their protection.

Fáibhile Cottage was in a state of turmoil early that morning, as news of the shooting had spread quickly. Mary, of course, was in histrionics at the thought of her beloved, for that is how she thought of him, laying wounded, while harsh oppressors who did not understand the beauty of true love denied her the right to fly to his side. Cissy, disgusted with her sister's complete lack of sense, spent her morning curled up with Jane and Elizabeth Bennet, while Lucy seemed content sit on the floor and howl without obvious motivation.

The boys, excited by all the activity, asked, "Mama, may we go into town to watch the soldiers? Scabs Butler says that every soldier in the county has stood to."

"Pray do not allow Mrs. Butler hear you refer to her son as 'Scabs'. But yes, you may go if you are home in time for dinner." Brigid sat on the settee and considered all that had happened. She was of two minds; while she was concerned that the Whiteboys had grown so bold, she could not deny that she was intrigued, even relieved, by their choice of target. She was also concerned over Mrs. Cashman's reaction to the news, as she had grown very nervous and tense, and

220

had taken to looking out the windows in the greatest state of agitation.

Fáibhile Cottage was further disturbed when Colonel Simon and his troopers reined in to halt at their garden gate. Mrs. Cashman quickly retreated to the kitchen, and made no move to answer the door. Eventually Mrs. Cashman absented herself entirely, and Brigid was forced to serve the colonel's tea herself. Simon put it down as typically incapable Irish servants, though Brigid was amazed at Catherine's behavior.

Simon, full of bluff bravado, stayed only a short while, as Mrs. Lockwood seemed preoccupied and not at all her typically charming self. After Simon and his troopers had ridden off, Brigid took a few minutes more to sit and contemplate the situation. Wide-eyed, suspicion slowly dawned. Brigid sprang to her feet and nearly ran to the kitchen, where Mrs. Cashman was sweeping the floor; she did not look up when Brigid came in.

"Mrs. Cashman," said Brigid with a break in her voice, "George Boffut has been shot and badly injured."

Intently sweeping out a corner, and still without meeting Brigid's eye, Catherine replied, "Sure and that's a pity. I shall pray a Rosary for him."

"Mrs. Cashman... Catherine, *a grah*... I must ask... do you know anything as to why... who might have done such a thing?"

The broom's pace quickened. "Sure it's those wild rebel boys, up to their old tricks, Missus. Tut, tut..."

Brigid drew closer to Catherine, and gripping her shoulder she said urgently, in Irish, "Can it be an accident, then, that the boy who wanted..."

The broom stopped, and Mrs. Cashman turned to Brigid with a spark in her eye, "What does it matter who does the deed, as long as it's the good that is served?"

"Catherine... we can't possibly be involved with this... there are..."

221

With a fierce anger that Brigid had never heard from Mrs. Cashman before, the older woman hissed, "Have you lost your sense, girl? Your mother is with God, so is it up to me, now, to remind you that we're Irishwomen? Irishwomen, the bottom of every ladder in God's own world. And yet still it's up to us, us! to protect our families, using God's tools or the Devil's. Our families must be protected, though you risk your own life, your own soul, to see it done. It's over now, our dear ones are safe from that raping beast, and we must never speak of it again. Never."

Catherine returned to violently sweeping the floor as Brigid drew back, her hand to her mouth, her eyes wild. "My God, woman, you may have put a noose around all our necks."

Chapter Fifteen

South of Brussels, Belgium

In the cool mist at the edge of the forest, the exhausted men were given thirty minutes to rest, and the family men were to say their goodbyes. Amongst the families there were no tears or long embraces, as it was considered bad form, as well as bad luck, to carry on. There was only a perfunctory acknowledgement of work that had to be done and some mild, understated admonitions to take care and watch out for one another.

Ensign Blakeley was at a loss as to what to do; Lieutenant Lockwood had gone forward to speak with Lieutenant Mainwaring, while Ensign Coakley, armed with a dirty scrap of paper, the stub of a broken pencil, and a soldier's vocabulary, was laying siege to a letter to his mother. Unconsciously, Blakeley assumed Lieutenant Lockwood's habit of wandering through the company as the men napped or tended to business.

"Good morning, now, Ensign *a grah*. Mornin', sir. Beg pardon, Your Honour, but as Sergeant Irwin has wrote this letter out nice for me, might I ask you post it home to my sister if I get snuffed? Thankee, sir. Mornin', sir. Looks like that old rain has finally dried for a bit, eh, sir? Mornin', sir. We'll miss that old rabbit of yours today, sir, Lord, yes. The great luck of the world he was, four rabbit feet with us wherever we went. Top of the morning to you, now, sir."

Blakeley came upon Mrs. Carmichael, who sat on a stump smoking her cob pipe with a practiced air. He tried to think of a polite way to avoid her, but at his approach she got to her feet and curtsied. As she was old enough, and certainly experienced enough, to have been his mother, Blakeley blushed and said, "Good morning, ma'am."

As she was speaking to an officer, Mrs. Carmichael took the pipe from her mouth as she said, "It's me hearing, sir, that you'll be standing baggage guard for us today, and on behalf of myself and the other ladies I'll say as how pleased we are to have such a good-natured gent with us while the Devil is afoot. Oh, beg pardon, sir, while I see to Liam Kelly, good fellow that he is."

Kelly had been lingering in the background, but now he stepped forward and said to Blakeley, "Beg pardon, sir." He then handed his purse to Mrs. Carmichael and said, "Will you be minding this for me, *le te thoil*, Abby *a grah*?"

As Mrs. Carmichael kissed Kelly's cheek, blessed him, and bid him good luck, Blakeley noticed several other purses on the ground at Mrs. Carmichael's feet. As Kelly returned to his mates Mrs. Carmichael caught the puzzled look on Blakeley's face and said with a smile, "An old custom in the regiment, sir. The married men will be leaving their valuables with their wives to make sure no nasty little Frenchman would be looting it if things go badly, while many of the bachelors will leave their purses with their friends' wives. If the battle goes well, the purse is returned, smiles all around. If our friend is captured, we'll be holding his money until he's freed. But if he is so foolish as to get himself killed, it's agreed that his friend and his wife should keep the money, with his blessing." As she stuffed the purses into her apron, Mrs. Carmichael grew very serious and added, "But you'll understand, sir, that by God I want to give these back, come tomorrow. A dead man's money brings bad luck, and it's the good luck we need now, the world as it is."

*****

The break was soon over. The companies formed up, and the families filtered back into the woods.

"Ensign Coakley, Ensign Blakeley, would you join me, please." They walked to their lieutenant looking tired, relaxed, and capable, and he paused briefly to look at them. For a moment he smiled down on them as if they were his own sons, then in a kindly tone said, "It looks as if we shall be having an eventful day." Turning to Coakley: "Peregrine, pray have the company check their firelocks. Ensure that the touchholes are clear and the flints fresh. Then we shall load blank, and discharge their firelocks in order to clear any moisture." For miles around, thousands of other soldiers from both sides were doing the same, those volleys impotent but hinting at the real battle that was to come, the smell of powder thick in the air, reminding veterans of battles past.

James handed Mémoire's reins to Blakeley, saying, "You'll take care of her for me, won't you, John?"

"You've decided not to keep her with you, sir?"

"Oh, goodness, no, son. And you should know that, by the way, if you had been studying the Regulations as you ought. Only battalion commanders stay mounted in action; the company commanders send their mounts to the rear. And that is just as well," he said as he patted Mémoire's flank, "as I wouldn't want anything to happen to her. And from a purely mercenary view, it would be madness to risk a horse worth eighty pounds for King and Country, when said King and Country will only compensate me for eighteen odd if she would get hurt. Off you go now, John. Do take care."

"Thank you, sir. Goodbye, sir." John Blakeley's heart was full and of considerable merit, but like most young men his head had yet to mature into an instrument fully capable of managing and conveying his feelings. Thus encumbered, and still swallowed by his oversized coat and shako, he led his ten men and the seven company saddle horses back into the Bois de Soignes to guard the baggage and to look after the battalion wives and children. There was no honour in the rear, no dashing romantic laurels to be won, but more than anything else John Blakeley feared that he had been deemed unworthy of the inclusive brotherhood he craved.

As James watched Blakeley's party move off, Doolan stepped up with a cylindrical portmanteau strapped to the top of his pack. "Now, never you mind about Mémoire, sir, as I've told that good Henry O'Hara all that he should know about how to care for her, body and soul, until all the unpleasantness is done with, and he being a good soul, I think, if a man can forgive his nervous nature, of which I am wholly capable, being bred a good Catholic, not to cast aspersions on those of other faiths, sir, begging your pardon, as somewhat of lesser worth, regarding chances at Heaven, in case of the worse, God forbid."

James continued to stare after Blakeley, saying flatly, "You well know, Doolan, that in most regiments it is customary for the officers' servants to stay in the rear. It is not too late to start that tradition in the 27th."

"Oh, now, sir, you'll not be toying with me so, with me taking such care of your every need. See here, now, on my own back I'm carrying this heavy load without a word of complaint, one! Half a dozen shirts, your good boots, an extra pair of uniform pants, greatcoat, four pairs of cotton stockings and three of worsted, and your own oilskin cloak. Let the heavens fall, you'll still have a clean shirt and dry stockings, and sure they might fall, with all these Frenchies about, and those nasty little Belgian civilians, lurking in a forest thick with trees that the Firbolgs might have called trees. Jesus, Mary, and Joseph, what a life."

Some of the servants preferred staying with their friends in the ranks even if battle was imminent, while some, including Diarmuid Doolan, though he would be loath to say so, also remained in the line out of a sense of duty to their officer. No matter what the motivation, choosing some men from the companies to act as baggage guard gave the officers an avenue to subtly remove to the rear men whose nerves would not ordinarily allow them to stand the strain of battle. There was no resentment directed toward those few, as everyone knew that some of the fellows could not take it, and no more was said as their names were called and they fell out for baggage guard.

Considering that tradition, James said, half to himself, "I should have thought to send Private Carter with Ensign Blakeley."

"That would have been a kindness, sir, Carter shaking like a leaf in a Connaught storm, going on about how he should have stayed with that soft posting with that Lieutenant Gooch in that stinking hell of a Gosport, the back of my hand to it."

Still half to himself, still staring after Blakeley, James muttered, "I shall send him off to help Kennedy and O'Donnell at the aid station; that should keep him out of the worst of it."

Doolan looked back to the rear as well, saying, "The boys would appreciate that, sir, as a nervous fellow tends to make everyone else nervous as well, don't they? So Carter will be out of the worst of it, but it's us now who are going to be in it, and won't we just have a time of it. Won't we just."

*****

General Lambert was like many generals in insisting that he get more sleep than his men, justifying that inequity with the contention that of all the men of the brigade he, at least, should have a clear head to make critical decisions in the coming battle. Thus, after six hours in a soft bed, he looked quite fresh as he and his aide trotted by and ordered the staggering Exellers, Lions, and Skins forward. In a long snaking column of quarter sections, the Inniskillings were directed to the far left of the Allied line, their feet dragging, marching as if in a nightmare, through the great army as it awoke and flexed its arms, preparing for battle. The fields were full of men; the brigade moved slowly past thousands of men, infantry, cavalry, and artillery, in coats of red, green, and blue, but all equally wet and filthy. James eyed them with something like hatred; while most of the army had gotten some rest during the wet night, the Inniskillings had not been off their feet for more than a few minutes in the past twenty-four hours.

To make matters worse, their move to the army's left was plagued by the thick mud that pulled at their feet, many of the men slipping and falling, other men tripping over them. The ground would not dry; dense clouds hung just overhead, the air still and humid, growing warm. James, making a deliberate effort not to get angry, did what he could to keep his company moving.

At one pause James looked about, and thought that in other circumstances the softly rolling hills, woods and verdant fields might have been beautiful. But in that muted light, packed with men, horses, and guns, nature recoiled, and men ruled the day.

The battalion had only just reached their post on the army's left when a staff officer galloped up with new orders. They were now to be posted in reserve, behind the centre of the army: in short, a position which they had passed one wet, filthy, exhausted hour before. With bitter resentment they marched back the way that they had come, their tearing frustration noted by the many units that witnessed their coming and going. As those units were populated with numerous wags, the 27th was bombarded with witticisms such as, "Lost your compass, there, boys?," and "Look, here,

Jocko, it's the Irish who have found a way to be paid by the mile, and won't they be rich by payday."

The stumbling battalion was directed to a hollow behind Mt. St. Jean farm, alongside the Charleroi Road. The countless hours of drill proved their value as the Inniskillings unconsciously formed column of companies at quarter distance, left in front, and in that formation they were at last allowed to lie down and rest.

As they rested the great battle began: all morning long they had heard the usual sporadic popping from skirmishers probing the enemy lines, but there now came the long, steady, continuous rumble of deliberate cannon fire. Low, stagnant clouds of powder smoke rose into the air and gave the cloud-scattered light a yellow-gray tinge.

In their hollow behind the lines the noise was loud, but not so loud as to disturb men who were beyond the point of caring. As the sounds of firing built to a continuous roar James noticed that the new men sat up and looked about nervously, while the veterans stayed asleep. It was another of the lieutenant's universal military norms: experienced soldiers knew the value of sleep, and would get it whenever they could, no matter what the circumstances.

The flow of wounded from the front began. The men who remained awake had no distraction from the tension other than watching the wounded stumble back, bloody and pale, which for men waiting to join the battle was poor distraction indeed. Still, the men they saw were only the lightly wounded, who could get to the rear on their own; the badly wounded lay in agony where they fell. Another universal military norm: no healthy men were to leave the ranks and assist the wounded until the battle was won.

*****

Most of the French cannon pounded the long low ridge behind which the Inniskillings sheltered, but a few shots skimmed the crest and bounded maliciously into the rear.

Eventually a chance twelve-pound ball thudded into their hollow, striking right between the prone ranks of Seven and Six, bouncing back to land square in the slumbering ranks of Four.

Two Six Company veterans were woken by the noise: Privates Lilley and Murray, friends through years of war, who lay side by side, their blankets caked in mud, both intent on sleep. Lilley rose up on one elbow for a moment, then settled back into his blankets grunting, "Looks like it hit about Four or so. I do wish they'd pipe down, so that a man might get his rest."

Without stirring Private Murray muttered. "Aye, it sounds like Four; they always was shrill bastards."

"Fucking sopranos, the lot of 'em."

"Good night, Sleabhac."

"Sleep well, Mamó."

Sleabhac and Mamó, Wilted and Granny, were their nicknames in the company, comrades and friends; only one of them would survive the day.

*****

While the men of the companies slept, chatted, or worried, their officers gathered at the head of the column and did much the same. There was one difference, however, in that it was the senior men who felt it their duty to stay awake, while their juniors felt no such compunction. It required only mild prompting from his lieutenant to convince Ensign Coakley to rest a bit, and that young gentleman was flat on his back in just moments, soon lost in stark, openmouthed unconsciousness. The officers who chose to stay awake found a spot to sit down at the edge of a low-hedged farm track, all at least a bit anxious, but each dealt with it differently. Some grew quiet, while others grew talkative. James Massey was known, and thoroughly accepted for, his nervous chatter, at one point saying, "By the end of the day some of us lieutenants will be scratching a captain's ass, for there will be wigs on the green." As there were only four captains present with the battalion that comment might have caused offence, but they had all heard the expression before. It was often proven true.

James and Tom found a comparatively dry bit of ground under a hedge, where they sat and looked back at the battalion. As the column was formed left in front, Pratt's Light Company was at the head of the column, followed by Tom's Seven, and James's Six, the others in descending order further into the hollow.

Gesturing to the air, James asked, "The light is very strange, don't you think?"

"I was just thinking that," said Tom. "Even sounds ring odd." He clapped his hands together, but the sound was strangely muffled. "It is as though nature is hobbled. No wind at all, this heat, this strange light, and the constant roar of the guns."

"Yes, hobbled, that is the word. When we would maneuver outside Ghent, the fields were that vibrant green, and from a distance the rows of red coats looked like a crop of poppies. But now it is all muted, almost just shades of gray. How very odd."

Tom, the minister's son, looked stricken by the thought that next came to his mind, and for a moment he kept it to himself, though he finally murmured, "If I were a man of greater parts, I should say that God had withdrawn his love from this place."

"I suppose that it is good that neither of us is necessarily of a superstitious nature." Again, a long moment of silence passed before James added in a hoarse whisper, "But I will confess, and I will say this only to you, Tom, and it is certainly very bad luck to say so, but I have the feeling that today is going to be a very bad day. Very bad, indeed."

Lieutenant and Mrs Lockwood

*****

With God's grace or without it, Lieutenants Lockwood and Mainwaring were dozing side by side when the drums barked out the order to stand to. They gave no further thought to fate, only shaking hands and wishing each other luck before they trotted back to their companies. Coakley was so mired in sleep that James nearly had to carry him back to Six.

In minutes the First battalion, 27th Regiment of Foot, was drawn up and ready for battle. It was just after one o'clock on the afternoon of Sunday, June 18th, 1815. Once they were awake, formed, and ready, they stood and waited. The excitement of standing to was quickly swallowed by the wracking tension of waiting, with no word as to what was to happen next, as the battle raged just beyond them.

Nearly an hour passed, and the tension grew nearly unbearable. James, always sensitive to the collective mood of his company, felt that their confidence had shifted; the men had already borne so much, and now there they stood ignored while another ball bounded amongst them and wounded two men. There was scattered grumbling from the ranks, and there was a growing sense that perhaps the generals had forgotten them, that the generals were incompetent.

"Let's fucking go!" called an anonymous voice from within the company.

Coakley called, "Silence in the ranks! Settle down, there!" The men did grow quiet, but there was still a perceptible air of nerves.

James left his post at the front right of the company, and strolled out to the front of the company. He was deliberate in that: he did not march, he strolled. He called out across the company, to a man in the far left files. "Private Moriarty!"

"Aye, sir!" called Moriarty in response, as every ear in the company turned to hear what the lieutenant was up to.

"I was just thinking; of all the men in the Company, I believe that you have seen the most action." Moriarty was a veteran of great seniority, twice wounded, a serious soldier, but whose complete illiteracy negated any hope of promotion.

Their conversation continued at a roar across the face of the company. "Sure and I've seen my share, sir!" called Moriarty.

"So, then, what was the first time that you were shot at?"

"*Wisha*, I don't think that anyone has ever shot at me a'purpose, sir, me being such an agreeable fellow!" This brought general laughter across the company, which was usually forbidden, but the lieutenant was having his fun.

With a laugh in his voice, James called, "Very well, then, Private, when was the first time that the men around you were shot at?"

"The first time, sir? Now, then, sir, that was when I first stood next to Kerry McIlhenny, a reprobate and a cattle thief, and sure and the Frenchies knew it, as he drew lead like no one I ever saw. That was at Nieuport in '94; no, I lie, sir, '93."

"Well, we're glad to have you with us today."

"Don't you worry, sir, we'll beat those Frenchies like we always do!" This was met with a rousing cheer, James, smiling, took his time returning to his post, exchanging some quick greetings with the men, squeezing a few shoulders, positive.

To their right, the hedge that bordered the Charleroi road became the company latrine, and as they stood waiting James noted that some men had to visit it quite often, others hardly at all. James searched his own mood and determined that he was a bit nervous, no, he thought, perhaps anxious was more the word, and certainly not afraid. And at least he had never had nervous bowels, which was some comfort, as he heard Private Evans once again ask McCurdy for permission to leave the ranks. In a rare instance of collective empathy no one made light of Evans's frequent latrine trips; every man could sympathize, as every man bore the same thoughts and the same fears, whether they allowed themselves to admit to them or not.

James caught himself begging God for an order to advance, but he quickly retracted that request, as it was certainly a sin of some sort. He held to no religious doctrine that would be recognized by any established church, but he did hold to a few basic tenets, however sporadically and irrationally applied, one of these being a conviction that he should not ask for God's aid in unimportant or selfish matters. Thus retreating from his initial plea for divine intervention, he contented himself with merely wishing for the order to advance; he wished it for himself and for his men, as standing, waiting, and wondering was certainly worse than moving forward and getting it over with. The noise coming over the top of the ridge gave little clue as to how the battle was progressing. All that came to their ears was an omnipresent roar, punctuated by closer, distinguishable volleys of musketry and individual cannon firing.

While many wounded men fell back past the Inniskillings, it was a horse that brought every man's heart to his throat. A brown mare wearing the saddle furniture of the 6th Dragoons came stumbling back down the ridge with the whole of the lower part of her muzzle shot away by a French ball. She was in agony, bleeding horribly, nearly all of her face from the eyes downward simply gone. Her appearance was so terrible that she had been driven away from several other regiments until at last she found her way to stand staring at Six Company. Several of the men called out in pity or horror, and as the 6th Dragoons was the only Irish cavalry regiment in the army, known as the Inniskilling Dragoons, the sound of Irish voices put a spark into the mare's fading eye and she drew closer, seeking some sort of comfort, some relief from her torment.

The horse was to the right of the company, only feet from James, every shake of her head, her every breath, throwing blood. James was aghast, horrified, and the only manner in which he could mask it was with furious anger. "Private Maddin! Fall out and tend to this God damned horse!"

In his youth Fergus Maddin had been apprenticed to a horse knacker, and that tenuous connection to animalia had eventually made him the Six Company expert on all matters natural. From rats to mad dogs, Maddin was the man who was called upon, and in this instance he gently stepped forward with his hands out, palms downward. He could not take the mare's bridle; there was no bridle to take. Neither could he coax it away with one of the apples that he had in his pack, as the maimed beast no longer had a mouth. "Ah Jesus... you poor dear, what have those bad men done to your dear face, *a cuisle*... you've never done anything to deserve such as this, have you, now? *Bí ciúin, mo grah, mo mheile stor*... be quiet, my love, my thousand treasures... *goitsa, anois*... come, now..."

The air around Six Company was alive with the sounds of distant firing, but it was Maddin's single musket shot from the edge of the field that made most of them jump. A moment after the shot, Archibald, who had been ahead with Lambert, Brooke of the 4th, and Heyland of the 40th came galloping back, obviously excited, too excited, and as he passed each company he called, "The battalion will advance! The battalion will advance!"

"We're for it now," muttered Doolan. Lieutenant Lockwood drew his sword to signal the company's advance; he absently noted that his hand was steady. Maddin, visibly upset, had to run to get back to his place in the line. As he trotted past, Lieutenant Lockwood said, "Thank you, Maddin," but not loudly enough for him to hear, as Maddin's mates called to him, some nervously, some not, "Hurry up, lard-arse! You'll not want to be missing this one!"

Chapter Sixteen

Waterloo

Like a series of six red waves, the companies of the 1/27th moved up the ridge, passing the 1/4th and 1/40th, being cheered, the Irishmen cheering in return. James wondered how it was decided that the Inniskillings would take the most exposed position, while the King's Own and the Somersetshires would deploy to their rear. Furious noise and banks of smoke boiled ahead; it was about a half a mile to their new position, the front of the Allied line. As they neared the front they came across increasing numbers of dead and wounded, bearing the white facings of the 32nd Foot, the yellow of the 28th, and numerous Scots with a blue and green tartan, Cameron Highlanders. James had some friends in the Camerons, but he saw no officers lying in the field.

The air was even hotter up there, still and hot, like putting his head in an oven. The smoke was everywhere, drifting thick above and around them in the motionless air, the light muted, a sickly yellow-gray. James would not allow himself to be distracted, instead concentrating on his company, making sure that they stayed in a straight line, at quarter distance, or about twenty-five feet, behind Tom's Seven Company. With his eyes continually trained to the left to monitor the company's front, James tripped over the body of a Rifleman, his dark green uniform making him hard to see in the grass. The Rifleman's eyes flickered, and instinctively James almost stopped to help him, but then continued on. Soon every man in the battalion had to step over dead and maimed men.

Several battered Hanoverian and British battalions withdrew to allow Lambert's brigade to take up position. As they crested the ridge James looked ahead and saw the French, untold thousands in perfect order, menacing beyond comprehension.

James averted his eyes and looked up and down the lines, where the battle raged all across the mile-long front. There was a great deal of firing, but most of it seemed to be coming from far off to their right, and while James heard some yelling from further back in the column his company had not yet taken any losses: they reached the top of the ridge unscathed. Archibald gave the order for the battalion to halt, and at last James had a brief opportunity to look around. The dense smoke covered much of the field, but from the crest of the ridge he could make out at least some of the ground.

To their front, the ridge sloped downward into a shallow valley, the French lines on the far side of the valley, perhaps six hundred yards away. He found that if he viewed the French with a professional eye they seemed somehow less ominous: masses of troops there, and a long row of artillery all across their front, but for the time being the guns were mostly silent, issuing only a few desultory shots. About fifty feet from the Inniskilling's position the road to Plancenoit ran across the face of the ridge, right to left, sunken into the hillside, bordered with thick hedges and brush. It was well below them on the face of the ridge, so the sunken road did not impede their ability to see the French. The unfortunate corollary to that visibility was that the French, especially the French gunners, could see them as well. Their position in the field at the top of the ridge offered no cover at all, but for those fortunate enough to occupy it the sunken road below them was an ideal defensive position. It was filled with British Riflemen, Grasshoppers, the French called them, squeezing off carefully aimed shots at the French skirmishers that haunted the knoll to their front.

The Charleroi road, also sunken as it crossed the crest of the ridge, ran from the French side of the valley and crossed the Plancenoit road just to their right front. It didn't require Wellington to explain to them that the Charleroi road was the perfect way for the French to launch themselves into the centre of the Allied line. Up to this point the road had been blocked by the German garrison of a large farm that lay a little further down and on the other side of the north-south road. But the farm was covered in dense smoke, the scene of heavy fighting, and the French were obviously determined to take it. The firing there continued unabated.

James found that he was no longer tired, or in the least bit frightened. He was interested. Wholly fascinated, since from the top of the ridge he could see more than just about anyone on the battlefield, as the lower-lying areas were thick with smoke. He clicked open his pocket watch: just past 3:30. Brigid had given him that watch on their tenth anniversary. He consciously told himself not to think about her, to think only of the present, to concentrate.

They were standing in what was once a rye field, but the passing of so many feet had trampled the thick stalks down and it looked as if they were standing on an India mat. He stepped back a few feet to get a look at Coakley, who was in his appointed post at the middle of the company, two paces back from the second rank. They exchanged nods, wholly meaningful nods: Coakley conveying nervous confirmation, James expressing grim confidence.

From the head of the column the drums called the company commanders, and James hurried forward. Tom was already there and they greeted each other with some relief. The other soon joined them; Barr was silent, his face waxy and completely without expression. Archibald quickly briefed them. "Here it is, now. A couple of hours ago the French launched a very strong infantry attack all across our centre and left. Our infantry stopped them, and then our heavy cavalry threw them back. But as usual our heavies went wild and got themselves mauled in return."

Pointing to the long line of French artillery, Archibald continued as each of the company commanders leaned forward to hear. "The French have gathered a Grand Battery there. It has been flailing this part of the line all day, and it is wearing us thin. That's why we were brought up, to—"

As if in response to Archibald's gesture, the French artillery picked up the pace of their firing, typically the precursor of another attack. A ball struck near the knot of officers, burying itself into the soft ground in a shower of dirt clods, as Archibald hurriedly pointed to the large farm to their front right. "That is La Haye Sainte," he called, "The French have been attacking it repeatedly, but the Germans holding it are doing very well. We are to support the Rifles to our front, but also ensure that the French can't advance up this road to our right. Captain Pratt, you will please deploy your Light Company to the right front, and work in concert with the Rifles." Another ball whirred just over their heads and struck deep into the column. Cries from behind them told them that they had been hit hard. "The 4th and 40th will support us, but we are to hold the juncture of these two roads! The Duke himself says that we must hold, as this is the centre of the line, and these damned roads are the key to the position! God bless us, but it will get right hot, right soon!"

*****

Archibald ordered the battalion to form line. To do so, every man in Tom's Seven turned to his left and the whole company marched far to the left, followed by Six, like clockwork, a hard-learned, critically necessary, organized, familiar clockwork. In line, the battalion presented a wider target, but a ball that struck them might claim just two or three men, not the twenty or more who might be hit when in the dense column of companies.

Six had just settled into the their new position, their ranks dressed, aligned with Seven to their left and Five to their right, when they took their first casualties: a ball struck the centre of the company, striking down Corporal Dean and Privates Curry, Hagan and Kenny. It knocked them down and scattered them like pins, the ball bounding within inches of Coakley, who dropped to the ground in startled terror. The men around them dragged the wounded back a few feet as Sergeant McCurdy calmly called, "Close ranks, there, close ranks!"

James looked over to check on Coakley, who recovered quickly, even though four men writhed in agony at his feet, blood and flesh scattered everywhere. Kenny's right foot was gone, while Curry's left leg was nearly completely severed. Dean's hand was crushed, and Hagan's head was bleeding badly, gashed to the skull when the ball had sent Dean's musket flying.

James again reacted with furious anger, calling, "God damn it! Private Mahonny! See to the wounded!" Regulations made no mention of medical care in the line, but several of the Inniskilling officers had a man in their ranks who could give some rudimentary care. Mahonny, who had grown up the only son of a Fermanagh midwife, had long before fallen into the role of Six Company aid man. That morning a prescient Lieutenant Lockwood had suggested that he stock up on green hickory sticks, and so armed he made belt tourniquets for Kenny and Curry, while the staggering Hagan and Dean were pointed back to the brigade aid station.

There was little time to look beyond his own company, but at one brief lull James looked over to see the lifeless Joseph Pratt being carried back from the skirmish line with a large part of his skull missing.

With relentless energy, the French artillery continued to fire. James had always found that standing still and being cannonaded was the most terrible trial that a man could be forced to bear, as there was nothing that he could do but stand and impotently contemplate the short odds of violent death. James tried to occupy his mind by carefully watching one distant French gun crew repeatedly swab out their piece, load, stand clear, and fire. Another of his hard-learned military maxims: if a man could see the ball coming toward him, then it really was coming toward him. Yet honour required that he could not flinch, no matter how clearly he saw it; men had been heckled out of the service for less. He eventually he saw one quite clearly, with increasing clarity and alarm: he did not flinch, but his belly muscles tightened in anticipation... the ball struck just feet in front of him and buried itself in an explosion of soil. He silently thanked God for the rain; if the ground had been hard the ball would have bounced and it surely would have killed him.

A moment later a shot struck the left side of the company, striking down the two Cunningham brothers, Peter and Teady, who had enlisted together and who stood side by side in the ranks, one losing his right arm, the other his left.

The rolling artillery fire filled the valley with even denser clouds of smoke, but James could see cavalry moving up just behind the guns. By their glittering appearance James knew that they were the French heavy cavalry: big men on big horses, with steel helmets, breast and back plates, and there were untold thousands coming forward. Moments later came the expected order: "Form square! Form square!"

The square formed by the Inniskillings did not adhere to the Regulations, the Regulations so often ignored by Ensign Blakeley, as the battalion had only seven companies present, not the ten called for. The Light Company was dispersed across their front, so their improvised square consisted of Six and Seven as the front; Five at half frontage the right side, Four at half frontage the left, Two and Three the rear. The square stood four men deep, the front two ranks kneeling with their bayonets bristling outward while the two rear ranks could deliver fire if any horsemen ventured close enough to risk the consequences.

Private Mahonny gave his lieutenant a significant look, and catching his meaning Lockwood called, "Drummer! See Sergeant Irwin and ask him to detail three men to assist Mahonny in pulling our wounded into the square." The change of formation had left Kenny, Curry, and the brothers Cunningham lying alone a hundred yards from the company. Those unfortunates would suffer from their wounds, and perhaps die from them, but they would not be left to do so alone.

James turned to watch the French heavy cavalry advance, the ground literally shaking under the pounding of tens of thousands of hooves. Like a sparkling wave, the horsemen crested the ridge and broke around the squares of Allied infantry. The Inniskillings, however, protected by the sunken roads to their front and right, suffered little from the horsemen. The first regiment of cuirassiers that wheeled right and advanced on Lambert's brigade came on in great style. In this case their appearance was duly noted by the Irish, indeed there came several knowing calls of admiration as they approached, but as the lead squadron came within sixty yards of the 27th the steady square fired with deadly intent. The squares of the 4th and 40th, deployed with the 27th like the squares of a checkerboard so that they did not fire into each other, joined in the volleys that swept the ridge. When the smoke cleared, the ranks of cuirassiers were in turmoil as the horses veered away from the hedges of bayonets. Dozens of men and horses lay dead and wounded as the French squadrons recoiled in disorder.

The cavalry reformed but held back, milling about out of range. Coakley excitedly asked Lieutenant Lockwood, "Why do they not charge again, sir?"

"Now that they realize that we know our business, they will not charge until we throw away our fire, and we will not fire until they charge. A stalemate, but one that we may enjoy while it lasts, as their artillery will not fire as long their cavalry is atop our ridge." The Irish had laid claim to that patch of Belgian hilltop, and they were willing to pay for it.

During the quiet of the stalemate, Private Ellis of Three Company nudged his neighbor, handed him his musket, and ran out into the no-man's land between the red square and the glittering horsemen. Ellis had seen a French officer fall, and he was determined to benefit by the occasion; the Frenchman's silver epaulettes were likely worth ten pounds, and if the officer had his purse on him Ellis could garner a year's pay in a day. Barr saw him bolt and suddenly came to life. He called Ellis back in a shrill, nearly hysterical voice, but his orders went unheeded as every man on the rear face of the square cheered or booed Ellis as he took his desperate chance.

A group of horsemen witnessed Ellis's attempt to loot their captain's body, and responded by loosing a volley of carbine fire. Ellis grabbed the epaulettes and bolted back, but was hit and fell dead fifty yards short of the square.

Private Toner, one of the new men, had been posted to stand by the veteran Privates Loughlin and Doolan, all watching the drama on the far side of the square. "Did ya see that!" cried Toner. "Those big Frenchies killed that poor man, so they did!"

"Serves the bastard right," said Loughlin. "If the Frenchies hadn't killed him, then Barr might have done for him. Dying for a ten-pound pair of epaulettes. A fucking shame it is, when these things aren't done proper, like."

"What is it you're saying, Lancelot Loughlin?" asked Toner, puzzled and angry, "When I took the shilling, Sergeant Maxwell told me that all was fair in battle, and loot went to the bold."

"Are ye daft, man," said Doolan, "listening to the words of a recruiter? A recruiter, a sergeant, and a Saxon, the unholy trinity of deception? These things have rules, don't they, it's not some goat-fuck free-for-all." Loughlin nodded wisely in agreement, and after looking to make sure that none of the officers were too near, Doolan went on, "There are rules, boyo. One: a decent fellow will leave the civilians alone. Oppression of the innocent is left to the English and their ilk. Two: thou shalt loot any Frenchman, whole, wounded, or dead, enlisted or officer, amen. Three: Ye might also go through the pack of any *dead* man who might be called 'friendly', though the Dear knows few Englishman shall call me friend, dead or no."

Diarmuid Doolan, drained of so much wisdom, found it necessary to take a long pull at his canteen, and as he was stunned into silence by its spectacularly effective contents, Loughlin proceeded with the edification of young Toner. "Four: it's considered a great sin to loot *wounded* friends, and to loot a wounded brother Inniskilling is a mortal sin."

"Capital crime, without benefit of clergy," choked Doolan.

Protected by the sunken road to their front, the front of the square had not been menaced by the cuirassiers, but a regiment of dragoons eventually came to attempt it. Seven Company had been allowed to stand while the cavalry had sense enough to stay clear of the road, but now from behind them Lieutenant Mainwaring called, "Seven Company! Kneel!" The men of Seven dropped to one knee and lodged the butts of their muskets into the soft ground, presenting a thick hedge of seventeen-inch long bayonets to the French horsemen. The two ranks of Six stood behind them, muskets at the ready.

Suddenly given a clear view of five hundred dragoons at two hundreds' yards distance, Peter Flynn swallowed hard and said, "Seven has their bayonets fixed; has Daidi forgotten to tell us to fix ours as well?"

"Don't you worry about Daidi, Flynn," said Doolan calmly. "You don't know shite."

Lieutenant Lockwood interrupted, calling "Six Company! Make ready!"

"You'll know, boyo, that there are bargains made, and if you make us a solemn vow on Saint Brigid, we'll let you in ours, as—"

"Six Company! Present!"

"—it's that some of us old timers that have agreed to pool and split any loot that we might come across, collective, as it were, share and share alike."

"Fire!" A hundred muskets loosed a sheet of smoke and flame. Individually they were inaccurate, but the collective effect of a hundred muskets throwing half-inch lead balls was devastating. Men and horses dropped, while wounded horses pitched and bolted in terror.

The dragoons fell back, but they were brave men. They reformed their ranks and came on again, determined. As they mounted their vain charge Doolan growled, "Here come those damned fools again," before he joined in the disciplined volleys that once again lashed the dragoons as they vainly sought a way up the ridge.

*****

When the frustrated, bloodied cavalry finally withdrew, the French artillerymen, rested and resupplied, instantly resumed their firing. The Inniskillings, still in their dense square, immediately began to take heavy losses. As James and Tom's companies comprised the front of the square they suffered dead and wounded at a staggering rate. Ball after ball shrieked around them. The balls that struck them mercilessly tore men to pieces.

The battalion had to remain in square for fear of a return of the cavalry, while the right side of their square watched over the critical road that ran past them and into the rear of

Wellington's army. The Irish suffered in place, dragging their dead and dying into the centre of the square, holding, holding.

James's focus, his entire view of the battle, was now restricted to the two hundred feet of frontage jointly held by Six and Seven. He moved constantly from one corner of the square to the other, encouraging to some men, demanding of others, as the case required, but despite their losses not one of their men ran. At first the drummers were tasked with pulling the dead and wounded back into the centre of the square, but soon both James and Tom were doing that onerous, heartbreaking duty as well. Most of the dead were horribly mangled, many of the wounded nearly equally torn. The lightly wounded could stagger off to find aid in the rear, but no one from the companies could be spared to carry the badly wounded men to the rear. Only the officers would be carried back to the aid station; it was unfair, but it was the way it had always been. Still, James felt a surge of black rage when he saw his moaning, shrieking, wounded lying in endless rows, and then Barr held up his hand so that Archibald could witness the scratch that a bit of shrapnel had caused. With that Barr fled to the rear, not looking back; as he ran off several surreptitious musket balls whistled after him, but again he escaped unharmed.

Eventually James ran to Archibald and said, "For God's sake, Major, you must have the men lie down. At this rate I'll lose every one of them."

Archibald was bleeding from several wounds. He looked stunned, almost overwhelmed, but he rallied and gave James a quick, lucid nod. James called to each of the four sides of the square, "Lie down, there, men, lie down! Massey, Elliott, get them down!"

Seeing the battalion go to ground, James for an instant imagined that every man was dead, and that only the officers had survived, staggered, swords in hand, over the broken bodies of their men. But now James could see that the number of officers was sadly diminished; Pratt of course had been carried away dead, and Barr had fled. But there were others now, dead or wounded: Campbell, Andrews, and Towne, at least, and several others were at least lightly wounded, still serving.

In the centre of the square was their island of bloody loss, their wounded brothers, and at the centre of that island stood the colours, the tall, unflappable Gerald McBride holding the King's Colour while Peter Elliott held the buff-coloured Regimental Colour, both massive flags limp in the still, hot air. But then a twelve-pound ball, never bouncing, flew into the centre of the square and smashed McBride to fragments and red mist, and the King's Colour, unhurt but with McBride's hand still clutching the staff, dropped slowly to the ground, as did the Regimental Colour as young Elliott, drenched in blood and flesh, dropped to all fours screaming, violently sick.

Archibald, shaken, spurred over to Six and hoarsely said, "Ensign Coakley, to the Colours, if you please." Coakley strode over and picked up the King's Colour with a shaking hand, then assisted Elliott to his feet with the Regimental Colour. They had been standing only a moment when a bounding shot struck Coakley, crushing his foot, and James ran to him, his arms outstretched, calling for Private Murtagh to carry the boy pig-a-back to the aid station.

James returned to his company, constantly moving, saying, "Stay down, men. It will be over soon enough."

A ball whirred past James, within inches of his head, and from the muddy ground Private Loughlin called, "For pity's sake, Your Honour, will you not be lying down, now?"

The concussion of the passing ball stunned Lockwood, but he managed to shake his head and motion Loughlin to stay where he was. The bombardment was a nightmare, a timeless nightmare in which more and more of his men were lost, and he could do nothing to save them. But it was a nightmare that did eventually come to an end. Some of their wounded had staggered to the rear, but the dead and most of his wounded lay in the centre of the square, the square that was growing weaker, slowly contracting, but still a shelter for the hurt. James also saw many of the wounded stay in the ranks, loyal to their friends, not wishing to leave them when things looked their worst.

The pace of artillery fire had dropped sharply, but the musketry from around La Haye Sainte, which had never slowed, now reached a crescendo. James stood still for a moment and watched, strangely detached, through gaps in the smoke as the fire of the farm's defenders slowed and then eventually ceased. Cheers rose from a thousand French throats as they broke into the buildings and bayoneted or drove out the last of the defenders.

That, then, was why the French guns had gone silent: with La Haye Sainte in their hands, the French infantry was now coming for the crossroads, and the thin centre of the Allied line. And they would be coming soon. James looked at his watch: nearly six-thirty. He noticed that his hands were covered in dirt and blood, and he frantically tried to wipe the filth from the watch. His bloody thumbprint on the crystal would not come clean.

Archibald, both he and his horse bleeding from shrapnel wounds but steadier now, came to James and Tom and said, "Gentlemen, sergeants will take command of the companies, and each officer will command a side of the square. Lockwood, pray see to our front, and Mainwaring, you take the left." Then Archibald asked, "How many have you lost, Lockwood?"

James was not sure that he could count them. Instead he saw faces, heard names. Nicholson had just crawled past, bleeding badly. Shaugnasey was dead, Maison beside him, his hip crushed. Keywood, Cassidy, Bampton, Toner, Montgomery, Curren. So many more. Beyond the harsh arithmetic of reason. "About a third," James eventually croaked, his throat parched, knowing that he had to say something.

Archibald spurred his horse to see to the other faces of the square. James rubbed his face with both hands, hard, and found himself standing next to Corporal Carmichael, who was clearly drunk. He was, however, a damned steady drunk, and he offered the lieutenant a pull from his canteen. "The best West Indies rum, sir, and never baptized, not if it's ever so." James took a long drink, the uncut rum burning, and he swallowed it down gratefully.

Determined to make the most of the lull, James moved through the remains of Six and Seven, leaning down to touch them as they lay bloody and exhausted, saying in a fatherly tone, "Up with you now, men, to your feet. The French are coming; here's your chance to pay them back. McCurdy, bring that box of cartridges over; we'll need them soon enough. Christ, Finney, get to the rear; you're not good to us with one hand, are you? Good man. Yes, Montgomery, I know that Shaugnasey is dead; I'm sorry, soldier, but we still have work to do. To your feet, men, to your feet. No bayonets... this will be a shooting fight, and no pack of God damned Frenchies can load and fire like you lot. Up with you, Reilly, we need you strong, we're counting on you. Form up, there, men, form up."

James found Doolan looking to the rear with a satisfied grin on his harsh face. "Would you look, now, Lieutenant *a grah?*" Surrounded as they were by that scene of horror, James and his men still managed a shaken smile when they saw Corporal Shanks, long forgotten in the rear, hobble up the ridge to join his mates in the ranks of Six Company. "Brúitín! Brúitín!" came the call, and even the desperately wounded took heart as he resumed his place in the ranks.

In the lull before the French infantry came, James was speaking with Archibald when Lambert, Brooke of the 4th, and Heyland of the 40th galloped up. They were quickly aghast. "My God, Archibald, it looks like a slaughterhouse here."

With empty eyes Archibald said, "Nearly all of my officers are dead or wounded."

"What may we do to help?" Brooke asked. "May I perhaps lend you a few of my subalterns, Archibald?"

"The sergeants of the regiment," Archibald said, "like to command the companies, and I would be loath to deprive them of the honour." It was a stiff, formal reply delivered in a heavy Scots accent, and despite his grief James felt a surge of admiration for Archibald.

Lambert stared down the slope and slowly said, "They are coming."

Their struggle with the stubborn Germans who held La Haye Sainte had caused the French great loss and disordered their ranks, but still the Frenchmen came on with great determination. They were not formed in ordered ranks, but rather came *en tirailleur*, a cloud of men who advanced in loose order. It was not a formation suited for a mass assault upon the crossroads. Rather, it was meant to attack the position with intense musketry, and the Frenchmen applied themselves to the task.

Just opposite the Rifles' position in the sunken road there was a small knoll over which the Rifles and a handful of French skirmishers had been dueling for much of the afternoon. But the knoll was now covered in swarms of Frenchmen who took advantage of every bit of cover. The green-clad Riflemen in their protected position along the road were very difficult targets, but on the ridge above the road the scarlet Inniskillings stood in the open, and the bulk of the French musketry was directed there, at perhaps a hundred yards.

With enemy infantry nearby the Inniskillings could not lie down to avoid the fire. The men on the front of the square, Six and Seven but all James's men now, stood and returned the French fire as best they could while the French musket balls maliciously whizzed past or struck flesh with a gasping thump.

The roiling smoke from hundreds of French muskets, from the Rifles, and from the Inniskillings soon obscured James's view, but still the firing raged on at a frenetic pace in the swirling gloom as he directed their fire at distant muzzle flashes. It was the fiercest musketry duel that he had ever seen: lethal, merciless, deliberate killing that lasted nearly an hour. The French on their knoll surely took losses, as did the Rifles in the road, but the Inniskillings standing in the open were cut to pieces. And still the Irish did not flinch, but stood and fired and fell with such blind determination that James nearly wept. To have seen him there one would think that James Lockwood had been born for such duty: roaring and cursing, an enormous man, filthy with dirt, gunsmoke, and the spattered blood of a hundred men who lay all around him.

The ranks which Lockwood commanded contained more dead and wounded than whole men. Fewer and fewer men were able to load and fire, at that juncture the one skill that James Lockwood valued above all others. Men from other companies came to stand with Six and Seven, firing steadily or suddenly dropping, bloody into the sodden earth. One of the new men, Private Patrick O'Boyle, froze standing in place, only staring, overwhelmed by the terror that surrounded him until Lieutenant Lockwood, huge and filthy, grabbed him by the back of his collar and shook him. "Private! If you do not care for those fellows shooting at you, shoot back, do you hear me, man, shoot back! *Scaoil, fear!* Shoot, man!" Rattled back to a semblance of consciousness, O'Boyle clung to the lieutenant's words as if they came direct from the throne of God, loading and firing as fast as he could, firing off every cartridge in his cartouche, then rifling the wounded for more.

In an act of desperation the French manhandled two six-pound guns up the road past La Haye Sainte, artillerymen and infantry frantically working together to bring the guns to bear on the square that defied them with such irrational obstinacy. The French infantry atop the knoll saw the massive brutes slowly being pushed up to their support. Taking heart, the Frenchmen picked up their rate of fire to cover the valiant men who exposed themselves to bring the guns up.

Through the boiling clouds of smoke Lockwood saw the guns, and roaring to his men he directed their ragged fire with the point of his sword. The Rifles along the hedge joined the Inniskilling in shooting down the gun crews while the French infantry did their best to suppress the British fire. One of the guns fired twice, the other only once, before their crews were shot down and the guns were abandoned where they stood. But the three shots, canister at less than two hundred yards, flailed the Irish square with horrid effect. Thirty or more of the remaining men fell, while wounded men were killed where they lay, and the dead were torn past recognition. And still no man ran.

The scattered Frenchmen could not physically force the Inniskillings from the crossroads, and their fire, as deadly as it was, did not break them. Their attacks, as valiant as they were, had failed. A few diehards, veteran sharpshooters, still held the knoll and La Haye Sainte, still maintaining a hot, accurate fire as the worst of the smoke cleared, but their officers called the French infantry back to their own lines, battered and disheartened. A few of the distant French guns, long silent while they watched their infantry struggle up the ridge, opened fire once again, but their fire lacked intensity: the French army was losing heart. The Inniskillings had won their part of the battle, and all across the front other Allied units had won their battles as well. From distant parts of the Allied line there came the sounds of cheering, full-throated joy, as the French army began to disintegrate. Only the handful of French sharpshooters remained on the knoll, and as a waft of breeze pushed the smoke away they saw the Inniskillings clearly.

Chapter Seventeen

Waterloo

In an odd moment of distraction, as the smoke, noise, and sudden, terrible violence seemed finally to be slowing, James saw a butterfly flitter past. It was the oddest thing that he had ever seen. He had always liked butterflies; it was amazing that such a delicate little fellow should have survived such a storm of cannon and musketry, yet there he was.

An instant later James Lockwood was down, spun to the ground as if he had been backhanded by God. He tried to get up, but his body no longer obeyed him. It was hard to breathe, impossible to think. A dozen men and more, half his company that was yet unhurt, scrambled toward him. Private Lancelot Loughlin was the first man there, bending over him, asking if he was all right, when a musket ball struck Loughlin in the temple, and he fell like a sack of potatoes. Doolan was there an instant later, rolling Loughlin aside, cutting away James's coat and shirt, applying a miraculously clean dressing. Tom was there too, his face anguished. No one wondered where in all this madness Doolan found a clean dressing, but there it was, over the round hole in James's

255

chest, the hole that pumped black-red blood in such ghastly quantities.

Pain. A constant pervasive pain, unlike anything James had ever known, interspersed with jets of agony caused by a breath, a cough, the tiniest of movements. Brigid would not have known him: his face gray, ashen, bathed in sweat, the eyes wild and panicked.

There was no bandage to apply to James's arm, so Doolan bound the remnants of the shirt around it, two ragged holes, in and out. James's world shrank to the narrow circle of gray sky above, and the occasional face that came into his field of vision, trying to reassure him. James had very few conscious thoughts, other than trying not to move, trying not to breathe deeply. Christ, the pain. Still, he could make out some of the voices around him. Tom, his voice breaking, yelling fiercely, "Sergeant Jameson, take command of the front face of the square! What, he's down? Who is next? McCurdy, then." Turning back to James, Tom had him placed on a blanket, yelling, "Doolan and Higgins, you will carry Lieutenant Lockwood to the rear. For God's sake don't drop him; get two more men. You two O'Neils, clap on there. Doolan, get him to Kennedy."

Tom had taken just two steps back towards his company when he was hit as well. Just as James was being lifted from the ground he saw Tom fall past him, his face covered in blood, and James gave a weak, unheeded cry of grief as the four Irishmen carried him away.

James never lost consciousness. Most of the trip to the rear was a gray haze, trying to bear the pain. As they carried him back, a musket ball tore away Doolan's left thumb, but still they went on. After an eternity the four men set him down, gently, but James could not stifle a brief scream as the pain jolted him. Higgins ran ahead to get Kennedy, as the lieutenant had gone blue, gasping for air, and Doolan promised to kill Kennedy as dead as Judas if he would not come. Doolan, a rag around his hand, spoke to James softly in Irish, the soothing tone incongruous in that harsh grating voice.

The four men clustered at the edge of a pasture that had been the bivouac of a cavalry regiment the night before, despoiled now by debris, manure, sodden campfires, mud, and trampled clover. Dozens of wounded men from several regiments were slowly, painfully, trying to make their way across the field. The battle had added the bodies of men and horses that had staggered back to die. But even that far from the lines there was risk, as occasional longs from the French artillery bounded across the field, digging furrows in the clover. Some of the men who were headed away from the fighting were unhurt, making a show of helping the wounded, others not bothering with that charade. "Look there, will you now, Charlie *a grah*," said Bernard O'Neil, "and see the smartest lads in the army, with sense enough to get themselves away from that crop of shite, joy."

Charles O'Neil disdainfully eyed them for a moment, replying, "Sure and it's true, then, the English got it right, the Irish regiment is made up of the most foolish men ever to walk the earth, as it's none of our boys who are taking the Dutch leave."

James lay on the blanket, motionless, his head turned to one side, and for a moment his eyes focused on a tortoiseshell kitten lying dead in the trampled clover. Beyond the pain, his mind grew strangely detached; the death of the kitten concerned him, and he was glad that his children had not seen it. Then Doolan came into his consciousness, words in Irish and English, lifting James's head, "A drink of whiskey, *uisce beatha*, the water of life, Lieutenant *a grah*, and another, for Saint Brigid's sake, and another, now, for blessed Patrick, and home." Doolan, always the superstitious rustic, washed the wounds with his whiskey, profligate with the last of his long-hoarded Donegal *uisce beatha*, faithful in its healing power, willing it to work. He held James's hand, muttering prayers, the O'Neils joining in, softly echoing, the plaintive ancient tongue like a song. "*A Naomh Mhuire, a Mháthair Dia, guigh orainn na peacaigh...*" James was fading, surrounded by the rough red-clad penitents, and then Kennedy came, bloody, running.

*****

When the Inniskillings took their post at the crossroads, Assistant Surgeons Kennedy and O'Donnell established the brigade aid post in concert with the medical staffs of the 4th and 40th regiments. Both the 4th and 40th had their surgeons present, and as Surgeon William Jones of the 40th was senior, he was technically in command. But as theirs was a medical organization rather than a strictly military one, there was an egalitarian tone to the small aid station. Both the surgeons addressed the Assistant Surgeons as "colleague", though only the surgeons and Kennedy could converse in Latin, the true sign of a university-trained professional.

The medicos had posted themselves in a rough cattle shed about two hundred yards back from the lines, halfway back to Mont St Jean Farm. The shed and the nearby fields were empty of their usual occupants, as the Belgians, long accustomed to the ways of hungry soldiers, had driven off their cattle at the first approach of the armies. Each of the three battalions of the brigade had also contributed two or three enlisted men to help the doctors, usually older men, otherwise reliable, who were like the baggage guard in that they were perhaps no longer suitable for battle. One of these was the ancient Private Robert Carter, whom James had quietly sent to the rear, for which Carter had thanked him with tears in his eyes.

Just minutes after the brigade went forward the casualties started to trickle back to the aid station. As the day wore on the trickle became a flood: Lions, Exellers, and so many Skins, maimed and bleeding. The surgeons were soon overwhelmed by both the number of wounded men and the severity of their wounds. They quickly lost track of time as the endless flow of horribly wounded men presented themselves. The trough that had once fed Belgian cattle was now used to hold the growing number of amputated arms and legs. Kennedy had just finished removing the arm of Private Terrance Devlin when Higgins burst into the shed.

"Mister Kennedy! It's Lieutenant Lockwood, sir, lying in the field itself, bleeding like a holy martyr, and I've come to beg you to come sir, or he'll die this minute."

"Lockwood, too, now?" replied Kennedy bitterly. "I suppose we have finally happened upon the battle where every damned one of us is killed. Very well, man, let me gather a few things, and I'll see what I can do."

Kennedy gathered up his pocket case of instruments and followed Higgins out into the field, followed by Private Carter with a handful of dressings.

"James, will you hurry now, sir?" asked Higgins, "That villain Doolan will have my very soul if we don't run like a pair of Clare thoroughbreds."

Kennedy, nearly exhausted by his labors at the aid station and further encumbered by his heavy, bloody apron, was in no mood to run anywhere. But he was fond of Lockwood, and with some further goading by Higgins he was soon trotting to the edge of the clover field where James Lockwood lay near death.

Doolan, buoyed by the approach of Kennedy, whispered to James, "It's Mister Kennedy himself, Lieutenant *a grah*. A Dublin-trained surgeon, and no man can ask better than that."

Kennedy knelt by James, all business, not noticing that his run from the cattle shed had left him gasping for breath nearly as loudly as his patient. A quick diagnosis: a through-and-through on the arm, the ball passed into the left chest. No exit wound. The arm had certainly slowed the ball, so it might not be buried too deeply into the lung. Doolan had kept pressure on the wound, which was good. The dressing was soaked through now, of course, but Kennedy had seen worse.

"What is that smell?" asked Kennedy absently. "Have you men been drinking?"

Kennedy and Lockwood had served together for years and each had a great deal of respect for the other, but at this juncture the patient was perfectly anonymous, and Kennedy could just as well have been tending to any man in the world. "You men, hold him down. I am going to probe for the ball. Do not let him move, at all, at all, or sure and he's a dead man." James heard him as well, and made every effort to hold steady, but the pain flashed so sharply, cresting in searing waves, that he twisted in animal agony, nearly throwing off the men who held him down. Kennedy leaned hard into James's bare, glistening chest, finally whispering, "There you are, you devil," as the tip of his probe clicked on the hard ball, deeper than he had expected. Kennedy ceased his probing, James panting as the pain eased to believable tolerances, but it exploded again as Kennedy inserted the ball extractor. "Hold him—hold him! Damn it, I've lost it. Where did you go now... ah there... hold him now, for all love —there! I have it!" Kennedy turned to the ashen men around him and held up the extractor, the ball and bits of cloth shining red in its jaws. There was more agony as Kennedy bound what bandage he could spare around James's chest, but his body was so drained that he could not fight it.

"James," said Kennedy into James's ear, "we are finished. The ball is whole, joy, not a fragment out of place, as clean a wound as I've seen, if deep. With the blessing, you should do very well. You must rest for a few minutes, and then I shall have the men carry you further to the rear. God bless, now."

Kennedy motioned the distraught Doolan aside, and as he dressed his thumb he said, "Listen, Doolan, the ball was lodged very deep, and it should really have killed him. Let him rest here a bit, then carry him back to the village, but there are so many wounded that I doubt you will find any shelter there. Do what you can, but even then he may not last the night. Maybe some rest here would be best, if ever—" Kennedy was interrupted by the pounding of a French twelve-pound ball that came whirling toward them, spending its energy in violent bounds across the field, throwing showers of clods with every skip. As it neared them it had very nearly spent itself, but it then hit the lip of the clover field and took a quick bound to the left, at man-height. That bounce was its last, but it struck Private Carter square in the chest, smashing the old fellow to the ground with startling force. Kennedy ran to him, finding him just alive, the skin unbroken, but massive bruises already blossoming, his sternum and nearly every rib fractured. The crushing wound left Carter in unspeakable pain, but there was nothing that Kennedy could do for him. "Hopeless. It would have been a mercy if it had killed him," said Kennedy bitterly, his voice just cracking. "I shall have the poor old fellow carried to the aid station, but he is not going to see Inniskilling again. Lieutenant Gooch will mourn him, but this is the day for mourning, the sorrow and woe. Get Lockwood out of here. Try to save him if ever you can."

Chapter Eighteen
Clonakilty

"We are the first ones here again, dear. But pray do not look so anxious; it will certainly come today. We have offered up so many prayers, God will certainly send word today." Anne O'Brian and Brigid O'Brian Lockwood stood close together, fiercely holding hands at the foot of the Post Office steps as an Irish rain misted down onto Clonakilty.

From across Bridge Street a well-dressed party emerged from the Bandon Arms, arm in arm, laughing loudly and shouting, "Huzzah, huzzah! Down with Napoleon! Long live Wellington, huzzah!" They too came to stand expectantly at the Post Office, and while they offered brief greetings to Brigid and Anne they chose to gather on the far side of the steps. Amongst them Brigid recognized the stylish Miles Beemish, though she was unacquainted with the wide-eyed, wide-bottomed brunette in a fur pelisse who clung to him with such tenacity. "Does it ever stop raining in Ireland? It makes my hair curl so!" cried the pelisse. "Still, I shall forgive you," she continued, "as the church bells and fireworks and bonfires have been such fun! Though I do wish that the common people would be more excited about the news. The Irish are so... what is the word? Ungrateful! Yes, ungrateful.

263

Such a victory! Down with Belgium! Long live the Royal Navy! Huzzah!"

Brigid was not so frantic as to completely forget herself, so it was in a controlled whisper that she said to Anne, "Oh, that fat little blockhead. I am sick to death of these fools prating on about their great victory, when they have risked nothing to gain it, made no sacrifice other than canceling their holiday in Paris. I shall strangle her with her own pelisse, the..." she only mouthed the word, "bitch."

Three carriages drew up nearby, their occupants loath to stand in the rain. Reverend Butler climbed out of his trap and called, "Mrs. Lockwood! Mrs. Butler has wisely chosen to stay out of the rain until the mail comes; would you and your friend care to squeeze in with her?"

"Thank you, Reverend, you are most kind, but my sister and I are perfectly comfortable in our cloaks, and the coach shall certainly be here any minute."

Brigid turned to Anne and absently said, "They have a cousin who is a lieutenant in the 32nd Foot, the Cornwalls."

"I am sure," said Anne, "that their concern for their cousin is very heartfelt, but we have been here every day this week, and to my certain knowledge you are the only woman seeking news of her husband. Wives and children should receive all due consideration, while these hangers-on," she eyed Beemish and his friends, "may quietly go to the devil. They and their cheering, waiting for more newspaper's talk of glory, when others here wait for news of the dead and hurt?"

Beemish and his friends continued their revelry; glasses were being passed around and raucous toasts made until Reverend Butler walked over and talked to them in muted tones. Suddenly shamefaced, several of the partygoers noticed the anxious faces in the crowd, though the pelisse continued her huzzahs until Beemish steered the group back to the Bandon Arms.

Over the next few minutes several more pedestrians arrived, draped in hoods and cloaks, adding a funereal air. Lord Bandon's black machine made a stylish entrance, the rain beading on its perfectly waxed surface, four chestnuts in the traces, four liveried coachmen up top, and the family coat of arms on the doors. Lord Bandon did not deign to step down.

Brigid looked up Bridge Street, stamped her foot, and said, "Why does it not come!" But she was soon distracted by the sight of one of her neighbors waddling toward the Post Office. "Oh, look, now, here's Mrs. Knox dressed in black and twisting a handkerchief. Can she know something?"

"I can't see how," whispered Anne, "unless a letter made it across quickly."

"She is always thinking the worst. We must pay her no mind."

"Sure, it's a bad omen, to wear black before the word. The Devil is waiting to pounce." They both crossed themselves, drawing a few looks.

The schedule called for the mail coach from Dublin to arrive at the Clonakilty Post Office every weekday at half two, and at precisely that time Post Master Jasper Hobgood stepped out to take his post at the top of the steps with no hat or cloak.

Normally the rain would have delayed the mail coach, as stretches of the road from Cork were not well drained, and prone to tenacious mud. But on that day the driver was well aware of the importance of his route, as he bore a copy of the *London Gazette* and its list of the casualties suffered by the officers of His Majesty's forces in Belgium. He snapped his reins with such earnestness that his jaded team took new life, arriving in Clonakilty only five minutes past their time. In the misty silence that followed their clattering arrival, the driver's assistant, a weedy old sinner with a rusty blunderbuss, muttered, "God save all here."

Two passengers climbed stiffly down from the mail coach, puzzled as to why so many people had gathered there. The driver dismounted with some ceremony and handed his leather pouch to the Post Master with a significant nod. After pulling the *Gazette* from the pouch, the Post Master stood at the top of his steps and called, "Ladies and gentlemen, the casualty list from the recent action in Flanders." Seeing Brigid's anguished face, he addressed Lord Bandon. "With your permission, My Lord, I shall favour Mrs. Lockwood with reading first from the losses of the 27th."

"Certainly not," sputtered Bandon. "We shall proceed according to the established order: by service, then by seniority of the regiment. It is tradition. The cavalry always take precedence over the infantry, and I have a nephew in the 18th Hussars, young Hesse. Hobgood, you will read the names from the 18th Hussars. Read them all, now, so that we might recognize any of Hesse's friends."

With an apologetic glance toward Brigid, Hobgood turned to the pages titled "Killed", and announced, "My Lord, the 18th Hussars suffered no officers killed." Then, turning to the pages listing the wounded, he said, "The 18th Hussars suffered two officers wounded, Adjutant H. Duperier and Lieutenant C. Hesse, severely. I am certain that we all wish to convey our sympathies to Lord Bandon, and offer our fervent hopes and prayers that his nephew Lieutenant Hesse will see a full recovery from his honourable wounds. My Lord, shall I now read from the next senior cavalry regiment?"

Bandon had lived a life typical to his class, in that he had rarely received any real reverse. For a moment it seemed that he had not heard Hobgood's question, until he muttered, "Do as you please," and rapidly retreated to his carriage.

All eyes turned to Brigid, standing very small in the rain, who could only look up at Hobgood and say with a break, a nearly hysterical break, in her voice, "Tell me quickly, Mr. Hobgood. Do you see him amongst the dead? I must know. Is he dead?"

Hobgood turned the pages, let his eyes scan down the page for a moment, and said with heartfelt relief, "No, Mrs. Lockwood, he is not dead." She exhaled a scrap of a scream and buried her face in her hands. He then read loudly, to Brigid and the crowd, "27th Foot, 1st Battalion—Killed: Captain Joseph Pratt; Ensign Gerald McBride."

A tormented whisper: "Oh, not dear old Joseph. And poor McBride was newly married."

Turning a few pages, Hobgood continued: "27th Foot, 1st Battalion—Wounded: Captain, Brevet Major, John Archibald, slightly; Captain James Towne, slightly; Captain Charles Barr, severely; Lieutenants R. Campbell, R. Andrews, G. Elliott," a painful pause, "J. Lockwood," a sharp gasp from Brigid, she would have fallen if her sister had not held her, as the Post Master continued, "I am terribly sorry, ma'am. T. Mainwaring, H. Price, P. Reddock, and Nicholas Pitts, severely; Ensign John Digby, severely; Ensign Peregrine Coakley, slightly; Ensign Peter Elliott, severely."

Brigid took strength in a brief irrational burst of denial, calling out, "Surely there is some mistake. That is nearly every officer in the battalion. Who have you not mentioned... Massey! James Massey! And that new boy, John Blakeley. They must have gotten the list reversed. Perhaps those two were wounded, and all the rest of them are well, quite unhurt? Surely they all can't be so hurt?"

She would not be consoled. After a flurry of blindly pushing people away, she ran off alone. She walked far into the hills before returning home, as she would not show her children shaking hands and tear-filled eyes.

*****

In the days following the battle, details of the great victory flowed back to Britain, all of which were analyzed by Colonel Simon and his old friend, Colonel Parker, formerly of the 55th Foot. They had been retired from active service for many years, but they were well-informed gentlemen, and still deeply interested in military affairs.

"Damn it, Duck," grumbled Simon, "you have gotten crumbs all over my *Gazette*. I was hoping to keep this, as a keepsake, like. And look here, a wine stain on the wounded of the 1/79ᵗʰ, you sloppy devil."

"Not to worry, Snooks," replied his aged friend, his hands quaking but with a grin on his face that evoked his mischievous youth. "As old as we are, it's likely that we'll both be dead before the week is out, and your keepsakes won't mean much then, will they?"

Simon coughed out a quick laugh, saying, "True enough, brother, true enough. But as I was saying, before you so cruelly maimed my relic, I was going to point out the name of one of my neighbors. He is numbered amongst the severely wounded, and will likely be amongst the dead soon enough, unless the sawbones are a good deal more capable than they were in our day. Lockwood, James Lockwood—that's him, there—wounded, 1/27ᵗʰ⋯ a great mountain of a fellow, quite good company... not a penny to his name; married for love, poor devil. You know his father, I think; Joseph Lockwood, up in Malahide."

"What, that miserable old bastard?"

"Yes, that's the one, loathed right left and centre, but this apple has rolled far from the tree. If you stay on awhile I shall introduce you to his wife, Brigid. Catholic as a cardinal, but a most charming woman. Lord, what a beauty. *Sans pareil*, I would say, if you had an ounce of culture in you. She has... well, at any rate, look at those casualties amongst the Inniskillings. Shot to pieces! If my calculations are correct—"

"I am sure they are," interjected Parker, who was well acquainted with Simon's fascination with figures of all natures.

"—then the Inniskillings took far and away the worst casualties of any regiment on the field. Any British regiment, at any rate, and we both know that the Germans, Dutch, Belgians, or Lilliputians, let alone the damned Frogs, cannot take a pounding like a British regiment. It looks as if the Inniskillings were critical in holding the centre late in the day. I can't tell you how I look forward to seeing the full casualty returns... if the Inniskillings lost that many officers, think of the losses in the other ranks. Lord, such a pounding. And they held, Snooks, and yet they held. Quite remarkable."

*****

"I beg your pardon, Mr. Hobgood, but the O'Brian sisters are waiting on the steps again."

"Thank you, Mr. O'Reilly," replied Hobgood. He and his assistant were sorting the canvas bag of correspondence that the mail coach had just delivered. "If you paid more attention to your work rather than looking out the window at elegant females, we might see our work finished before Michaelmas." Feeling that he had been too harsh, he went on in a more companionable tone, "I no longer need to consult my watch; they appear more regularly than the coach. They waited for the announcement in the *Gazette*, no matter the weather, and now every afternoon since, waiting for another word. Two weeks; a most distressing time for her, yet we cannot make letters appear from thin air."

The two postmen continued to snap envelopes into various boxes. Hobgood was not an emotional man, so he surprised his assistant when he threw up his hands and burst out, "The Post Office does not pay us enough to be the bearers of such news. How am I to deliver to her tidings of life and death? It is outrageous." With that, Hobgood came across a letter for Mrs. Lockwood, an official cover with a military postmark. He did not wish to appear hurried, but without another word he walked past his assistant and down the front steps. With a bow he handed the letter to Brigid and said, "As I was the man who announced the news of your

269

husband's wound, I now pray, Mrs. Lockwood, that I am the bearer of news of his recovery."

With a kind look, Hobgood returned to his work. Anne slowly, anxiously stepped away, and Brigid found that she had to grip the letter with both trembling hands.

> *Brussels*
> *10 July, 1815*
>
> *Madam;*
>
> *I am requested by a patient under my care, Lieutenant James Lockwood, 1st Battalion, 27th Regiment of Foot, to write this letter to notify you that he has suffered a wound to the arm and another to the chest, but that he is recovering* ~~*satisfactorily*~~ *quickly, and resting comfortably.*
>
> *As his attending physician I agree with the Lieutenant's request that you not leave your home to seek him out, as he is likely to be removed to Britain at any time, and he should further not be subjected to emotional distress. The Lieutenant insists that at this point I mention that he very much looks forward to seeing you, and any concerns regarding emotional distress come solely from the physicians who are only doing their duty to ensure his health and protect him from undue excitement. When known, the Lieutenant will write to you and notify you of his* ~~*final resting place*~~ *eventual place of recovery.*
>
> ~~*If there is a downturn in the patient's condition you will be noti*~~
>
> *As mentioned above, the Lieutenant is recovering, but is at this juncture wholly fractious, combative, and not satisfactory company. In fact*

he is exceptionally argumentative even in the composition of a simple letter. His servant is a further trial to this hospital and to this physician, a most forward, loquacious, insistent man.

Finally, as I address this letter per the Lieutenant's ~~bequest~~ direction, I note your home as Clonakilty, and I am prompted to beg you, madam, that should the opportunity present itself, to forward my regards to my uncle's family, Dr. and Mrs. Martin Kelly, of Bandon Square, Clonakilty.

Your husband wishes me to convey his ~~most sincere regards~~ dearest love, and I shall close with my own regards for a woman who must be the most patient of wives.

J.M. Kelly, M.D.

P.S. A hurried postscript, as I have many other patients to attend, but this fellow insists that I endanger the care of every other man on this ward by continuing to act as his personal scribe, and add his, I shall quote this exactly as not to further engender his wrath, 'very dearest love to all of the children, and tell them not to worry, and he shall see them all very soon.'

Brigid crushed the letter to her chest and jumped up and down like a child there in the middle of Bridge Street. Her sister leapt into the air as if shot out of a gun, and their embrace and tears of joy brightened many a face on the busy street. "*Mo cheol tu*, Mrs. Lockwood," whispered Mr. O'Leary, the butcher, with a broad smile from the door of his shop, similar congratulations being called to them as the two lovely women hurried back through town to share the news with the children, leaving a quite discernible trail of joy in their wake.

Chapter Nineteen

Dublin

Dublin's Kilmainham Hospital was styled after Les Invalides, and was thus a strictly military hospital. Tree-lined avenues cut its extensive grounds into neat geometric shapes, while its carefully manicured gardens, laid out with the precision befitting a military facility, were frequented by convalescents and their families. The hospital itself was a grand building in the classical style, featuring expansive, scrupulously clean wards and its own grand hall and elegant chapel, all built around a magnificent central courtyard. The lieutenant was comfortably ensconced in a small but brilliantly lit room on the top floor, while Doolan had talked his way into a prime berth in the attached enlisted barracks, as being a Waterloo veteran already carried with it a certain status, and to be a wounded Waterloo veteran granted heroic status without comment.

There had been a gradual transfer of both patients and hospital staff from the continent to the royal military hospitals at Kilmainham and Chelsea, and James was pleased that Kelly had been transferred to Kilmainham as well. James was aware of the fact that he had been short with Kelly on several occasions, and he was trying to make amends by not protesting his insistent prodding. He had a genuine regard for the doctor, who had tended to him since Doolan had gotten him into the General Hospital in Brussels. Kelly had an attentive, deeply lined face, a lean, strong frame, and hands of enormous strength, a working man's hands. James had recently been spooned a dose that lent a dreamy tone to his voice as he asked, "What say thee, Kelly? Will I live to see fair Cork again?"

Kelly straightened and said, "As to your arm wound, it is neither here nor there. The common butcher could care for such a wound. It is with this chest wound that our challenges lie, Lieutenant, for it is the wound to the body's core, its essential function, that requires our attention."

Kelly flipped through his notes, reading, "*Lieutenant Lockwood, aged 35. Wounded 18 June, admitted to Army General Hospital 22 June. Musket ball from perhaps a hundred yards distance. Extracted some minutes later by a battalion assistant surgeon. Stated that he had considerable pain, cough, and haemoptysis during the first twenty-four hours after wound. On admission, found wound of entrance between fourth and fifth costal cartilages four inches from left border of sternum. Inspection showed no retained debris or clothing in the wound, and the wound showed no mortification. There was some cough and a little blood-stained sputum. Progress was satisfactory. The sputum diminished rapidly and was nil by 20 July. Discharged to travel to Kilmainham 10 August.*"

Kelly then added, "*The wound continues to heal well, exuding only a minimum of pus, a laudable pus, but there is a recurrent fever that we have not yet fully conquered. The possibility of a progressive abscess is concerning.*"

James slipped further into a stupor as he laughingly asked, "Oh, what are you writing, Kelly? Does the power of life and death lay there in your wee pen?"

"*One wonders that the injury did not kill him immediately. But then a person of his size, this Mesolithic*

274

bulk, might be capable of absorbing more damage than those of a more elegant figure."

The doctor wrote on, and it was perhaps a blessing that James Lockwood could not look over Kelly's shoulder, as he would have found some of the notes regarding his future to have been less than encouraging.

*****

One advantage to being a patient in Kilmainham was a regular post, delivered by the postal clerk every day on a silver slather. For several days James was disappointed that no letter from home had yet found him. Yet a day did come when two letters arrived, the first from Chelsea, Britain's other great military hospital.

Tom was alive.

James stared at the letter for a moment, clearing his mind, and with tearing eyes he gently broke it open.

My dearest James;

I have heard from Kennedy that you are to be sent to Kilmainham, so I will address this letter to you there, in hopes that it finds you quite well. He also tells me that Doolan has been allowed to accompany you, which I suppose is (in some way, though I for one am at a loss to explain how) of some benefit to you.

I will repeat myself in hoping that you are feeling quite well. I was very concerned for you when I first saw you fall, as when they carried you off you looked decidedly punky. But it appears (as I have long contended) that you are born to hang, and will thus remain indestructible until that distant day.

Lieutenant and Mrs Lockwood

With the back of his hand James wiped his face and muttered to himself, "Dear old Tom, dear old Tom." Doolan, sitting by the door sewing the good buttons onto the lieutenant's only remaining uniform coat, heard him and smiled broadly without looking up.

You have doubtless read the papers proclaim that the battle was yet another stunning victory for British arms, though I for one remain unconvinced. If we have another such victory there will not be enough ground for the burials.

Kennedy's letter also contained some details as to our casualties. Since you were there until nearly the end of the battle, I believe that none of this will come as a surprise to you. But as stopping that bit of French lead may have clouded your memory, I am thoughtfully providing a brief summary of our friends:

<u>Archibald</u> took some shell fragments in the shoulder and side, but he stayed with the battalion throughout. He did quite well, don't you think?

<u>Pratt</u> you saw, killed early on. Poor fellow.

<u>Barr</u> had a scratch on the hand, the cowardly dog, and then a ball in the leg: more on him anon.

<u>Campbell</u> was shot in the chest, but will live to see Scotland again.

<u>Towne</u> took a ball in the thigh.

<u>Andrews</u> continues his charmed existence, hit three times but still draws breath.

<u>Elliott the Elder</u> shot through the leg... healing rather slowly: concerning.

<u>Price</u>, as you know, was struck by the remains of those poor fellows in Two Company. Who would have believed that a human jaw bone would make such a potent projectile? He has recovered

physically, but his spirits are still deeply affected. When you feel up to it, a note from you would do him a world of good.

Reddock was wounded by the same shell that peppered Archibald, but he has lost at least an arm, perhaps more before they are finished with him.

Pitts lost an eye to a musket ball; an ugly wound.

Digby was shot in the leg, but has since returned: his resilience is remarkable. Youth can on occasion be quite annoying.

Elliott the Younger lost a palm's worth of scalp to a musket ball and his wits are rather astray, but you know the only thing that Horse Guards values more than a volunteer is a heroically wounded volunteer. He shall likely be made field marshal and GCB by the end of the week.

Coakley of course lost a part of his foot. He apologizes very much for bleeding all over your good trousers, and sends his thanks for your tending him.

McBride you will remember (I cannot forget it, no matter how I try) was hit square by that ball and quite exploded. His wife is inconsolable, lost without him. She may return to Spain.

James felt a pang of regret at not having treated McBride's wife with more kindness. She was of common birth, not especially attractive, and her English was poor; yet she and McBride had been very attached to one another. She had never been accepted into the closed world of the battalion, and James's knowledge of Spain led him to conclude that her future there, the widow of a British soldier, would likely be difficult as well.

I am not sure how, but young Blakeley managed to get a shot across the neck as well. He must have come forward for some reason, and got knocked down for his trouble. But pray do not worry for him, as he is doing very well.

As for your devoted friend and correspondent, just as you were making your dramatic exit some mean-spirited Frenchman shot me, which I thought most unsporting, as it certainly was one of the last shots of the day. In the right cheek and out the left, knocking out a few teeth on the way. I wager that you were unaware of that little detail; my heroic phlegm is quite inspiring, don't you think? So if you should care to write to me, you will find me at Chelsea Hospital, restricted to liquids (thank God) and mush (damn all mush, and those who prepare it).

Assuming that you are ticking off the names, you will now find that only our dear Massey is whole and unharmed. He has always been the most fortunate fellow of my acquaintance.

You know as well as I the very heavy cost paid by the men of our companies. I confess that I do not sleep well, thinking of them, and wondering if perhaps I had failed them, so many dead and maimed, valiant fellows. Enough.

Lastly: I am sworn to secrecy by Colonel Pritchard, but as you are the soul of discretion, and a wholly interested party, I will tell you that Barr is relieved of his duties, under arrest, and is to face a court martial. Certainly neither you nor I should be surprised at the news, but I find my spirits much lifted, seeing some justice being found in this otherwise most disappointing world.

I shall forward more regarding the charges facing Barr as I am able.

Your Most Devoted Friend,
Tom

P.S. I have written to Brigid to ensure her of the insignificance of your wound, and of your animal strength and stamina. You will please not fail to convince that deserving woman that I am a man of discerning judgment.

P.P.S. My wound has rendered me quite horrible, but a young lady with whom I was acquainted in my misspent youth has come down with my sister to visit me. Her name is Julia; as lovely as when I first knew her, and very kind. I hope that you and Brigid will have an opportunity to meet her.

P.P.P.S. I forgot to mention that Barr's wounding was most curious. You and I both saw him leave the line very early with that ridiculous scratch on his hand. How he managed to get a ball in the leg is quite beyond me, as he made no effort to return to the line after Kennedy bandaged his hand.

James read through Tom's letter twice, so pleased to hear that he was alive, but the sudden shock of the memories of the battle, the suffering of his friends and his men, cut him deeply. It was if his wound, the pain, and the doctors' continual dosing had disconnected him from his former self, and suddenly Tom's letter threw open a door.

His mind was still not terribly clear, his thoughts and emotions in a muddle. He picked up the other letter, not recognizing the hand. The gathering clouds parted for a moment when he saw the name on the back: John Blakeley.

Lieutenant and Mrs Lockwood

Dear Sir;

I hope you are quite recovered from your wound, sir. I am quite well, besides a little scratch that I got in the rear. I mean, sir, that I got a slight wound on my neck in the rear of the army. I had long hoped to write, sir, but I am only now in receipt of your address at Kilmainham, and Major Archibald desires me to write and ~~appraise~~ tell you of the status of Six Company.

By the way, sir, I have still Mémoire with me. She is doing very well, and she seems to enjoy France. Please write to let me know what you would you like done with her. A captain of the Coldstreams is mad for her and is offering £100, if you should care to sell her.

Colonel Pritchard and the other three companies of the battalion have rejoined us here in France, sir. We Waterloo officers treat the fellows who missed the battle with such disdain; you would laugh to see my antics, sir; such fun putting on airs.

Before I forget, sir, I feel compelled to mention Captain Barr. Honour prevents me from saying as much as I would wish, but I beg, sir, that you be extremely wary of him. Since you and I last spoke, sir, I have become convinced that Captain Barr means to do you harm, but in good conscience I cannot say more.

I am currently in command of the company, sir, which you may find surprising, but there are so few men remaining that it is scarcely a larger command than the baggage guard. Since Waterloo we have seen very little fighting, and with the French surrender we are to camp outside Paris. Major Archibald has us standing watch over a little village near here, as the Prussians are behaving very badly,

280

and if we didn't keep them off they would rape and loot at every opportunity. They are most unpleasant fellows.

James knew that type of duty would please his men; they took pleasure in playing the hero, and doubtless the villagers would be grateful. He grinned a bit, thinking of how Lancelot Loughlin would woo the French ladies. But then James remembered seeing Loughlin die; Loughlin, Shaugnasey, Kelly, Lily... they were all dead. He suddenly remembered so much, his memories confirmed as Blakeley continued.

Knowing your attachment to the men, sir, here, please, are the casualties as best I can figure them:

Sergeants, four present: one wounded (Jameson)

Corporals, seven present: four wounded, one killed (Cavanagh)

Privates, eighty-six present: thirty-eight wounded, fourteen killed

The wounded are holding up well, sir, and they and all the other men desire me to tender their best regards. I have had the opportunity to visit some of the wounded, sir, and I am much stricken by their plight. When I was a boy I read of great battles and thought of the wounded as having a few heroic scratches and little more. Only now do I realize how horrible these wounds are. I was not prepared for the blood, the maiming, and the terrible pain that has to be borne. Many of the men, stout, strong men, did not die until weeks after the battle. We left most of the wounded at Waterloo, but we get periodic letters from Kennedy, who remained there with the Divisional Hospital when the army advanced. He has saved many of them. You may recall Private Carter,

Lieutenant Gooch's ancient servant: he died on 7 July, after much suffering, the poor old fellow.

Sergeant McCurdy is come in, to remind me that we march in ten minutes' time. He wishes that I send his hopes for your speedy recovery, and his heartfelt regards for your handling of the company during the battle. I shall quickly add my similar wishes, and close.

I remain, sir, your most obedient servant,

John Blakeley
Ensign, Six Company, 1/27th Foot

"Regards? After I led them to their deaths? Jesus, so many. So many." He closed his eyes and dropped the letter onto his chest. He was deeply ashamed of himself, as he had thought only of himself since he had been wounded, and had given scarcely a thought to his friends and his men. But above that, he was ashamed that he had survived, while so many of the men for whom he was responsible, *responsible*, were dead and maimed. After a moment he began to weep. Kelly stood watching at the door, but James did not care, the sobs wracking him, causing great pain, yet still they came. Doolan could not bear to see it, leaving the room in a fierce hurry with a tortured look on his face.

Concern that the lieutenant's emotional state might cause the wound to reopen prompted Kelly to order a hundred drops of the tincture of laudanum, and he resolved to keep the lieutenant in a state of incomprehension for some time, as he was determined not to lose this particular patient. He liked Lockwood, as far as his medical ethics would allow, if for no other reason than that gentleman's ability to cling to life with such determination. The wound was truly frightful, and it really should have killed him. The fact that it hadn't frankly puzzled him. As a physician, a wholly progressive, scientific physician, Kelly had few instances to consider God's hand in the affairs of men, but this was perhaps one of those rare, painfully rare, instances, and he privately drew some comfort from that contention.

*****

The fever returned. Dr. Kelly prescribed Jesuit's bark in heroic doses, but still James Lockwood burned, delirious and tortured. Reluctantly, Kelly ordered a massive dose of laudanum, and at last the lieutenant slept, deep in fever but at last at rest.

After long days at his bedside, Doolan left the lieutenant sleeping and went skulking down the broad steps into the lobby, the great sparkling marble lobby, convinced that its grandeur was only a suitable honour after the service that he and his officer had seen. He was going to check the post and to find a way to draw his rum ration when he felt a gentle hand on his arm, herself it was, saying "God and Mary to you, Diarmuid Doolan *a grah*." She kissed Doolan's cheek, adding, "Is it your thumb, now, Diarmuid, that is hurt, so? My seven blessings to you, and you shall have the thanks of me and mine as long as the sky is blue, for serving my husband with such loyalty."

He gasped and blushed deeply, as no one but Mrs. Lockwood called him Diarmuid, herself it was in all her caring and beauty, and he nearly wept with joy of the sight of her, the glorious sunlight filling the glittering lobby and lighting the air around her. Brigid Lockwood would confess to many faults, and if pressed James Lockwood might admit she had one or two, but in Diarmuid Doolan's eyes she was wholly flawless, and that shimmering light only reinforced his opinion.

Doolan saw her face shift when she grasped his arm and asked, "How is he, Diarmuid?"

"I beg, now," he said in his formal Irish, "dear gentlewoman, not to be downhearted, as he is much improved since the battle, God curse it, but a fever haunts him, and the doctors have given him Grainne's own potion, and he is sleeping a sleep that carries him far away."

Doolan led her up to the room, where she bolted to her husband's side but did not cry, only holding his hand and stroking his hair with the greatest tenderness. She did not take her eyes away from him for an hour or more, searching his face, until Doolan brought Dr. Kelly to see her.

Dr. Kelly was quickly conscious of Mrs. Lockwood's charms and evident good sense, but was not so in awe of her as to not to give her an honest assessment of her husband's state. "This fever is of grave concern, madam, grave concern. I have hopes that my bark will finally overcome its effects, and when the lieutenant returns to consciousness I will have no emotional turmoil, madam, on your part, or the lieutenant's. The battle has oppressed his spirits, and the news he receives weighs on him very much. I have dosed him, indeed I have heavily dosed him, and I will continue to heavily dose him, until that wound is no longer so vulnerable to damage from emotional turmoil. The alcoholic tincture of laudanum is the shield behind which he will heal, in body, at least."

*****

James was healthy and strong again, walking the most fashionable streets of Dublin in a finely tailored uniform, a captain's uniform. His companion was a gentleman of great standing, as tall as James, with dark hair and a handsome, deeply tanned face, dressed in the very finest suit, light gray, dapper and terribly fashionable. James was of mixed emotions; he knew that he had to be cautious, very cautious, but he was also intrigued, aware of the honour that he had been given to be allowed the company of this particular gentleman.

The gentleman was condescendingly polite, saying in a very friendly way, "I shall share a few minor truths with you, Lockwood. Do try not to scream." James could have sworn that his companion's coat was gray; now it was a dark brown. The hair was longer now, and the face was different, as well, was it not?

On the crowded sidewalk James and his companion were strolling rather slowly; an elegant, impatient woman behind them tried to push past. Without a glance James's companion suddenly threw an elbow that broke her nose and left her bloody and weeping on the sidewalk. None of the many pedestrians on the street stopped to help her. James was shocked, but his companion took his elbow and steered him along. As they moved on there were several wry smiles directed at them, and one man patted the gentleman on the arm and softly said, "Well done, sir."

"My position," said the companion as they continued their stroll, "allows me certain freedoms, as well as a unique perspective, a perspective far beyond the reach of those who roll about in the filth before their miserable little lights flicker out. What does that one fellow say? 'Nasty, brutish, and short'? Darling."

James was tempted, just tempted, to point out that one of the miserable little creatures had coined that darling phrase, but he thought better of it and said only, "I understand."

That dark, sharp, handsome face snapped to lock eyes with James. Black and blue. After a moment, the companion replied with a smile, "I believe that you do."

James had thus far said little, but he finally offered, "I beg your pardon, sir, but I confess that I am unsure as to how I should properly address you."

"Oh, that is perfectly understandable, perfectly understandable. So many of your kind have that difficulty." With a laugh he said, "I might suggest that my name is Legion, but that is a bit much for an afternoon stroll. Let us begin with 'Satan', I think, and we can build upon that as we go."

They had wandered onto one of the quiet shop-lined streets. Chatting, they stepped into an elegant little shop that

sold chocolates; Satan bought just one, not offering one to
James. James noticed that the chocolate began to melt the
instant that the Devil touched it. Languidly licking his
fingers, Satan handed the shop girl a five-pound note, and
demanded his change in coin. When the shop girl looked up
into Satan's eyes she recognized him even through his
disguise, a look of terror twisting her face. She crossed
herself, hard, and blindly handed over a pile of coins.
Annoyed, Satan scooped the coins into his pocket and guided
James back out into the street.

"I can't stand it when they cross themselves; it is so...
overt. A most odious cult. *Très vulgaire*. She is a perceptive
little slut."

"I'm certain she meant no harm, no insult," offered
James.

Satan paused, folded his arms, and his eyes went blank.
Coming back, he told James with a smile, "That was Mary
McCabe, born in Clogharinka, age nineteen, who will die in
childbirth one year, three days, and twenty-six minutes from
now. She is mortally afraid that she will be cast down to me,
and she has reason to be afraid, but not for the reasons she
thinks. How droll; He is so capricious, don't you think? Now
to the matter at hand." Reaching into his pocket, the Devil
pulled out the handful of change. Holding them in an open
palm, he asked, "What do you see, Lockwood?"

"Coins of the realm."

"Idiot meat-puppet. Here, see them as I see them."

Satan passed his hand over the coins; whereas before
they had been worn and dull, in an instant James was
amazed to see that several of the coins now gave off an
uncanny bright green glow.

"Do you see, it, Lockwood?" asked Satan hungrily. "It's
the lust, the greed. Several of these are quite fresh; they are
an opiate to me." With his free hand Satan picked out the
brightest coins, clamped his fist around them, closed his

eyes, and shuddered in ecstasy. James stared in frank amazement.

"This, then, Lockwood, is the first wonder which I will share; do you see, now, the wonders of money? There is magic there, and power! You have been sadly remiss in your pursuit of wealth; most disappointing. Your father, your brother, man! Follow their example. Your attachment to 'love' has blinded you to a gentleman's true duty. Here, Lockwood, witness this." Satan flipped a dull guinea into the gutter and pulled James into a doorway, gesturing for him to watch. After a moment a ragged boy spotted the coin and snapped it up with glee.

Satan stepped out, cuffed the boy, took the guinea back, and held it up for James to see. The coin now glowed with an intense gleam. "Oh, that boy wanted this in the worst way," Satan said huskily. His eyes went blank, and in a boy's voice he said, "Ah, Mam can get her own damned dinner, can't she. This is all mine, it is. My first bottle of the true *uisce beatha* and an hour, shite, a whole night with Molly O'Rourke. All mine, all mine." Turning to James, Satan dropped the guinea into his pocket and patted it closed, saying in a confidential tone, "I'll save that one for later."

Again Satan took James by the elbow and steered him further along, saying, "You see, I'm a deity of simple needs. The greed that soaks into money is enough to keep me happy for hours. But it has to be real coin, of course; paper money does not carry nearly the same essence of lust. Your laughable histories will tell you that the Fuggers were behind the advent of paper money, but I think it was what's-His-name, the kill joy."

James had been growing frightened, and though he had been paying close attention his attention began to drift, and he recalled something. Wasn't there something wrong? Yes, there was a hole in his uniform coat, red on red. He had been shot, but he couldn't recall under what circumstances.

Lieutenant and Mrs Lockwood

"Never mind that!" insisted the Devil, who seemed to be in a hurry now. "Come along now, and let me explain other mysteries to you, things that you've always wanted to know. Such bargains I shall offer! I, only I, truly know what you want, Lockwood, and for a pittance it can all be yours!" The Devil was less handsome now; his coat was black, and his voice carried an implied threat. James looked down and saw that his own coat was now his old lieutenant's uniform, stained with blood and mud, and he knew that he looked very out of place in central Dublin. A woman who looked a great deal like his sister walked past with a look of disgust on her prim face.

"I have an offer to make. Come with me, right now, sir," ordered the Devil with thinly veiled hatred and power in his voice, "or you shall suffer the consequences." Satan now looked very much like Charles Barr, furious and crazed, crying, "If you expose me, I expose you! That was your first bargain, and there are many more to be made, and I shall have you, Lockwood, I shall have you!"

James took two hesitant steps, following the Satan Barr further down that ornate street. But then, even though no one was near him on the once-crowded street, James felt an unaccountable sense of wellbeing. In a voice of quiet realization he said, "I am so sorry, but I just realized I must be getting home." Dublin, and the howling Devil, fell away, to other dreams, but none so dark.

The fever broke, and James drifted through the next two days as the laudanum relaxed its hold, and when he finally came to full wakefulness he was not surprised to see Brigid sitting at his side, watching him with a remarkable smile on her face.

Chapter Twenty

Dublin

Two weeks at Kilmainham allowed Brigid to establish a domestic atmosphere in James's room, in both appearance and routine. She quickly made friends and allies amongst the nurses and orderlies; her ability to speak Irish soon endeared her to those hardworking notables, and her management of her husband's care earned her a grudging acceptance from even the demigod staff physicians. The room became a miniature of Fáibhile Cottage, gleaming from floor to ceiling, furnished by pieces brought in for Mrs. Lockwood's comfort. A small feather bed and an elegant walnut desk were located and carried in by the attentive orderlies, who refused to take anything for their trouble, as it was for the lieutenant's lady.

The Lockwoods' days were taken up with chatting, reading, writing, and rest. James slept a great deal, but there was never a nightmare, his sleep wholly restorative. While James's sleep aided his recovery, Brigid grew concerned about his appetite, as he was not building back the weight he had lost since the battle. The hospital kitchens provided acceptable food at reasonable prices, but Brigid determined to visit the nearby inns and public houses, all of which did a steady trade with the hospital residents who desired, and who could afford, a more diverse menu. She finally came to an agreement with Mrs. Richmond of the Red Cow, who shared Brigid's notions as to what constituted a suitable menu for a convalescent. Thus, three times a day Doolan was dispatched to the Red Cow, returning with a basket of Mrs. Richmond's specialties, her Shepherd's Pie quickly being declared a work of genius.

James received several letters from his friends in the 27th, but most of his news of the battalion officers was pulled from the *Gazette*. While he tried to maintain an air of *sangfroid* in front of Brigid, she could not help but notice the gleam in his eye when he read the War Office news. His hopes of a captaincy and his own company were delayed but not dead, and the promotions and transfers throughout the army, particularly those inside the 27th, were of endless interest.

After Doolan brought in the latest edition of the *Gazette*, Brigid, who generally read her husband's mood with great accuracy, took a sip of her tea and casually asked, "Anything of interest, *a cuisle*?"

"Oh, I just happened to come across the War Office announcements." It would have been a miracle indeed if James Lockwood had not come across the War Office announcements, as he had torn through the *Gazette* with a noisy determination that would not have deceived a child.

"Any news of the Inniskillings?"

Giving up his façade of indifference, James eagerly read aloud, "Some good news, first. *War Office—August 26, 1815. 27th Foot, Lieutenant Rawdon Campbell to be Captain of a Company, without purchase, vice Pratt, killed in action.*' Good old Campbell got his company at last, which I am sure would have pleased Pratt."

Kelly had ordered James not to leave his bed. While he was feeling remarkably strong, James was still troubled by twinges of sharp pain. He winced, shifted his weight, and paused a moment to catch his breath before he continued reading, "Now, my dear, some even better news. *'Ensign*

John Blakeley to be Lieutenant, vice Campbell. Dated August 17, 1815.' Just think, such a youngster a lieutenant, though I imagine the weeks since the battle have matured him."

Brigid gave James the sparkling smile she used to cheer her husband and said, "You must be so pleased, *a grah.* I know that you are fond of him. And I'm sure that his mother will be very proud."

"She is entitled to her pride, certainly, though it appears that she helped Fate along, as John purchased his step. He's a good lad, and should do well; the men trust him, which is the secret of a successful company, as I believe I've mentioned before."

"Yes, dear, you have mentioned it once or twice." She had hoped to get him to tease her in return, but his face turned serious.

"John Blakeley has been in the army for all of six months, and he is made a lieutenant. I have been in His Majesty's service for eighteen-odd years, and, yes, a lieutenant as well, no further along than that boy."

Brigid did not know what to say, and before she could devise something both supportive and rational James turned back to the *Gazette* and continued, "The rest of the Inniskilling announcements are more of the usual damned foolishness. *'To be Ensigns, without purchase: Volunteer Abraham R. Marshall, vice McBride, killed in action. P. Montague Robertson, Gentleman, vice Blakeley. Dated August 17, 1815.'* Poor McBride came up from the ranks and they should have honoured his memory by bringing another sergeant up. There are a dozen good men to choose from, who deserve some sort of recognition for their service at Waterloo. Instead, in its vast wisdom the Army summons forth two young blockheads whose only experience in leadership consists of scolding kittens, whose only qualification is that they are gentlemen. My patience with gentlemen grows thin. God knows the title has been of little use to me." He threw the *Gazette* onto the nightstand in disgust, muttering, "P. Montague Robertson. What kind of God damned name is that for an infantry officer?"

*****

Brigid asked Doolan to pick up a bundle of flowers on his way back with their dinner, as she thought that the room lacked colour, not to mention cheer, and there was a girl who kept a booth on the corner near the Cow. Yet that afternoon, and for several days thereafter, he failed to do so, making only hollow, wholly unbelievable excuses; saying that his hands were full, weren't they, or the girl was not in the way, or that her flowers were no damned good.

After a week of such absurdities, pushed beyond all endurance, Brigid finally exploded, "Oh, fie, Diarmuid Doolan, for playing the fool, modest as a Dublin *gasúr scoile*, a schoolboy! To think that a soldier, a Waterloo man, would be afraid to carry a bundle of flowers!" She would hear no excuses about hectoring Home Service militia hounds at the hospital gates who would torture a man for weeks with comments about heartbreak, and him already carrying a wicker basket like a maiden. When Lieutenant Lockwood suggested, with great mildness, that perhaps Doolan might have a point, as the honour of the service had to be held above reproach, Mrs. Lockwood threw up her hands, let out of a screech of feminine despair, and stalked off to buy the flowers herself, muttering Irish phrases with which James was unfamiliar, but which made Doolan wince.

Once the Lockwoods' temporary address spread, they were soon the recipients of a gratifying flood of correspondence from family, friends, and comrades. Doolan, hoping to make amends for his failings as a florist, pursued the postal clerk with such tenacity as to make that fellow's life a burden. After each session with Mrs. Richmond's fare, Doolan would ceremoniously deliver their post, and James and Brigid would sip their tea and sort through the mail in a companionable manner. The children's letters were always read first, of course, followed by the balance of the post. They often updated each other with the contents of their letters, adding commentary as appropriate.

One afternoon James spotted a letter sloppily sprinkled with wax and written in a shaky, painfully familiar hand, and as he opened it he said, "A letter from my father; he has heard about my wound, and desires I inform him the next time that a battle is anticipated, so he might write to the Castle to have me transferred away from it. Come, that is thoughtful, don't you think, dear? I shall be transferred all over the globe, always kept a step ahead of danger, quite convenient, won't Horse Guards be amazed. He wishes that my wound will not interfere with my chance of promotion, as he confesses to be disappointed at my current rate of progress, as his neighbor, Mr. Grayson—you may recall Grayson, dear; one eye, fond of boys?—Well, at any rate, Mr. Grayson's nephew has been made Major in the Royal Corsican Rangers," adding softly with a hint of bitterness, "may it prosper him, commanding that pack of murderous banditti."

James spoke jokingly, derisively, but still Brigid knew that his father's comments cut deep. "Oh, my dear, I hope that you will not take him seriously. He does not know what he says... he cannot be well." Then, to herself, "The doddering old fool."

There followed a very conscious silence, as James read the letter again with a sharp, private sadness. Brigid looked at a letter from Mrs. Butler, not reading a word. James heard her sniffing, and he thought he heard a couple of tears strike her letter. He finally laid his letter aside, and said without looking at Brigid, "I don't know how I shall do it, but I will have to find a way to approach him about money. We cannot afford to continue to dine so well, and when we get home there are bound to be extra expenses. And if he so wishes my promotion then a few hundred will see me a captain in a heartbeat. But in the near term I shall write to have John sell Mémoire. As much as I love her we can't afford her; that hundred pounds and my pay should see us clear until I can address things with my father. I do hope he will not start harping."

"It is my fault," Brigid said softly, without looking up.

"Please, dear, do not say such things."

"If you hadn't married me, you would have been a rich man."

A hint of the lieutenant was in James's voice as he said, "The fact that my father cannot come to terms with the thought of his son, even if it is only his second son, marrying a Catholic woman, is no fault of yours." Then, in a conciliatory tone, he went on, "If he is fool enough to deprive himself of your company, that is his concern, but he will never convince me to ever regret one moment with you."

They exchanged a look of great affection, until she said with concern, "*A stor*, you should rest a while. You must not tire yourself."

James, who did look very drawn, said, "One more letter, if you please, honey. I had noticed one with an official looking cover. Yes, here it is; from a Major Lee of the Provost Marshal's office." He opened it with a serious look on his face, and was just beginning to read it aloud when a coughing fit racked him. Sharp, painful, explosive coughs made Brigid start for the door, but James regained his breath and waved her back to her chair, handing her the letter to read aloud.

Hôtel du Nord, Paris
October 2, 1815

My Dear Sir;
I am writing in reference to General Court Martial charges being brought against Captain

Charles Barr of the First Battalion, 27th Regiment of Foot.

Captain Barr is charged with several offences, only one of which requires input from you, sir, to wit: on 18 June of this year, at approximately six p.m., in the rear of the army during the Battle of Waterloo, Captain Barr was witnessed opening the trunk of Lieutenant James Lockwood, of the First Battalion, 27th Regiment of Foot. By way of explanation, Captain Barr offered he was going through the trunk in search of Lieutenant Lockwood's home address, so that Captain Barr might contact Lieutenant Lockwood's family regarding the wounds suffered by that officer, as Lieutenant Lockwood was well known in the battalion for his devotion to his family.

I am required by the rules of Courts Martial to inform you, sir, that, in contradiction to Captain Barr's statement, there is in evidence a sworn statement from Ensign John Blakeley of the First Battalion, 27th Regiment of Foot, that he witnessed Captain Barr destroying several documents from your chest.

Your comments are also requested, sir, regarding the relationship between Captain Barr and Ensign Blakeley, as both gentlemen suffered gunshot wounds while near the baggage, well to the rear of the army. Neither gentleman wishes to comment upon the circumstances under which those wounds were suffered, and the enlisted men who may have witnessed the incident deny any knowledge of the matter.

I need not point out, sir, that dueling is contrary to War Office regulation, especially during time of war, and for two officers of differing ranks to duel is looked upon with the greatest disapprobation.

If you wish to challenge Captain Barr's explanation and proceed with formal charges you will please reply to this notice no later than 1 December 1815.

I remain, sir, your most obedient servant,

W.E. Lee
Major, Provost Marshal

James and Brigid were aghast, aware of the opportunity that had been presented to them but also very aware of the danger.

"Can it be?" said Brigid, her eyes wide. "Can we finally be rid of Barr?"

"Rid of him?" answered James, still noticeably out of breath. "No, not truly rid of him, I think, but if he is convicted of these charges he would certainly be dismissed from the service."

"But then, if you respond and press charges, won't Barr turn on us, denounce us?"

"Yes," said James, his mind churning, "we cannot press any charges, as he would take that as a direct betrayal; I shall certainly write to decline the charges." James strained for more air, adding, "Our chances now depend on these other charges. If they can be proven, Barr may be dismissed, and, God willing, he will still keep his bargain with us. Without the army, I don't know where he would go, but he would be further away from us."

"And can the Provost be serious about Barr and John Blakeley dueling?"

For the past few days James had been doing very well, but Brigid now watched her husband go very pale as he said, "It seems that young John may prove... to be quite the lion. I pray to God that... he is careful with that bastard..." James began to cough again, savagely hacking, traces of blood in

Brigid's handkerchief as she held him, her voice echoing down the hall as she called for Dr. Kelly, for anyone.

*****

Two more weeks passed before Lieutenant Lockwood was given leave to return to Clonakilty. The news was very welcome to everyone but Diarmuid Doolan, who would not have minded a few more days with Mrs. Richmond of the Red Cow. Mrs. Richmond, who was in all other respects a rational woman, had grown fond of Doolan, and she was misty-eyed when Doolan came to pick up the last of the Lockwood meals. "I shall miss you, Doolan, though it must make the lieutenant and his missus, the dear woman, happy to be going home at last, God bless them, healthy and whole."

By most accounts Diarmuid Doolan was the least sentimental man in the United Kingdom, yet he seemed upset, and Mrs. Richmond hoped that he regretted leaving her. "Fare well to thee, Mary Richmond, *a stor*, as a soldier's duty calls him away when his heart might bid him stay, it's always the same, sure, it's a curse me being such a honourable fellow, loyal and true to my officer. And it's kind of you, *a grah*, to offer your blessing. But the news is not at all good, at all, at all, as Dr. Kelly himself told me the prognosis, it's a grand word, don't you think, now, prognosis?"

Doolan laid a few coins on Mrs. Richmond's bar. Carrying the basket he started awkwardly for the door, pausing only long enough to add in an odd voice, "The doctors told the lieutenant some days ago, but he didn't let on, did he, now, not a bit. It wasn't until this morning that the doctors talked to Mrs. Lockwood and me. He'll be doing well enough for now, and for a while to come, but it's after a time his lungs will fail him, and fail they will, no matter what the doctors might do, or how I love him, for I tell you that I love the man. They say that he shall fade like a Clare summer, and didn't it about break dear Mrs. Lockwood's heart, sure, as strong a woman as she is, yet she nearly broke at the news, not being able to bear it like myself."

Chapter Twenty-One

Dublin

Brigid Lockwood was in no way a flirt, and she was honestly wounded when anyone was so mean-spirited as to assume that she was. The perfection of her complexion and the flashing of her blue eyes were apt to draw lingering, admiring glances, while the elegant shape of her figure would prompt many men, and sadly many women as well, to believe that a woman of such beauty would utilize her appearance to advantage. Thus few of her errands to attend to business could be carried out civilly, instead drawing responses that ranged from dumbstruck admiration to open lechery.

Brigid anticipated such a trial on her call to the St. John's Road Post Master, but she was mistaken. She had gone there to reserve a chaise and four for their return to Clonakilty; in any other circumstances such a conveyance would have been an unspeakable luxury, but both she and Dr. Kelly had deemed it the only possible way to see Lieutenant Lockwood safely home. A voyage by sea was never considered, as the Irish coastal trade was primarily mercantile in nature, and the sea, always damp and often capricious, would guarantee neither speed nor comfort. When Brigid first suggested the hire of a chaise, James stubbornly maintained that he could manage the trip in the mail coach at a quarter of the cost. But the dirty, crowded, inconvenient mail was in no way fit for a convalescent, and so after some mild argument and quick, wholly fraudulent claims that they could certainly afford it, Brigid went to call on the Post Master. That gentleman, an aging, slightly nervous Mr. Miller, offered her a chair at his desk without even a hint of awe, condescension, or lust.

Mr. Miller thumbed through his ragged copy of *The Post-Chaise Companion*, saying, "It is, unfortunately, a considerable drive to carry you and your husband home, Mrs. Lockwood. Let us see; yes, the Dublin, Cork, Baltimore route for you. Some of the young pups in my trade might cry that my guide is thirty years old, and I confess that is a tad old-fashioned, even showing your home as 'Cloghnikelty,' but it is accurate, madam, accurate, to the rod! I scruple upon my honesty, so if I might beg you look here, please," showing her the appropriate page of the guide, "you shall see that it is every bit of one hundred forty-six and one half miles from Dublin to your Clonakilty. You can scarcely find another inhabited spot in Ireland so far from Dublin; inhabited by bipedal Christians, at any rate. Now, a chaise and four will cost two shillings tuppence a mile... times one hundred forty six and one half... carry the two... fifteen pounds, seventeen shillings and five pence, if you please. I realize that it is a tidy sum, madam, but a private conveyance offers what the mail cannot: speed, comfort, privacy, and prestige. I am so pleased, Mrs. Lockwood, to see a hero of Waterloo carried home in the style due to him."

For all his good will, the Post Master was evidently under the impression that Waterloo veterans had been liberally showered with gold rather than French shot, and it required a conscious effort for Brigid not to gasp aloud at the thought of spending the equivalent of two months of James's pay in such a fashion. For an instant, just an instant, she cursed herself for not playing the coquette, but still she reserved the chaise for dawn at Kilmainham in two days' time. Damn the cost; she and James were going home. She would have nothing to do with Dr. Kelly's prognosis. She was certain, *certain*, that once they were at home together no misfortune could ever touch them again.

*****

There were kind farewells, a long list of instructions from Dr. Kelly, and the excitement and anxiety typical of the beginning of a long journey. A pallet strewn with blankets and quilts was laid across the seats to form a bed for the lieutenant, Mrs. Lockwood sitting at his side. Some of the orderlies at Kilmainham had shared rumours of Whiteboys and Yeomen stirring up trouble in Munster, and Doolan was so convinced of their validity that he expected rabid mobs to assault the chaise the moment they passed south of Kilkenny. Doolan thus took post atop the box with his musket loaded and primed, only stern words from Mrs. Lockwood convincing him that he need not have the hammer back.

The Lockwoods resolved to save what money they could by taking their meals in the chaise, and not to sleep at any of the roadside inns. They instead impressed upon the post boys the need to switch their horses and press on, as the lieutenant needed to be in his own bed, and no other would do.

Just a few miles down the road from Dublin they rattled into Naas; in the early years of their marriage the Lockwoods had briefly lived there. Their return to the bustling town happened to fall upon market day, the narrow streets blocked with farm wagons and herds of livestock. As the chaise came to a halt in the crowded main street, James stirred and looked sleepily out the window.

"We are in Naas, my dear," said Brigid, looking wistfully at the streets through a light rain. "It hasn't changed much, has it? Look, there is Mrs. Toone's house. How good she was to us."

Weakly, James replied, "Yes, I remember her, the old lizard. She struck me with a broom once, and called me something unkind."

"Oh, pooh. If it had not been for her I doubt that either of us would have survived those first few months with Mary. What children we were, with a child of our own."

James had propped his head against the pillows so that he could watch the town without raising his head, his enormously painful head. "What has it been? Twenty-five years?"

"Nineteen, James. Mary is nineteen," said Brigid with a touch of annoyance with her husband, invalid or no.

South and west through the country. Ten miles past Naas all aboard were shocked at the number of beggars along the road, emaciated, ageless, androgynous figures in rags weakly calling for scraps. The senior post boy called back, "The taters are gone bad yet again, ma'am, and aren't they out in droves. It's right pitiful." James slept through the worst of it while Brigid gave away what little food they had left. The coachman pushed the team hard, the horses all too willing to get past those ghostly figures. Doolan watched it all from atop the box with a look of strained detachment, though he too tossed down his bread and cheese.

At Carlow the post boy, in fact a staggering fifty year-old, who was to drive the next stage was drunk, drunk even by army standards. As he crawled up into his seat a surprisingly strong male voice came from inside the chaise, "No, postillion, it will not do! You would have us in the Barrow before Ballybannon." As the driver was a former corporal of the Connaught Rangers, such a decidedly military voice instantly brought him to. "You are dismissed, sir. Find yourself a replacement, or by God I'll..." An hour or more passed before another driver came in from the Tullamore stage, and they pressed on, mile after mile, James growing weaker. Only his inordinate pride and a desire not to upset Brigid kept him from groaning with every lurch of the badly sprung chaise.

There was a long delay late the first night, as one of the horses had thrown a shoe. In the darkness the horse was awkwardly unhitched and led off to be shod by the sleepy, ill-tempered smith at Killamery. The chaise sat alone on the deserted road next to the ruined abbey there, and both Brigid and Doolan saw the ghost of a monk praying at the snake cross in the starlit ruins.

On, on, through the next day, rain, fog, and mud. In the thick, tangible darkness of the second night the driver lost his way in Cork city, and it was only the good sense of the experienced team that kept the Lockwoods from taking their breakfast in Fermoy. But at last Brigid began to recognize the road, and she could whisper to her anguished husband that they were almost home.

There are typically a few warm, clear days to be found in every Irish autumn, achingly beautiful days, and the memories of that sparkling afternoon would remain in the minds of the Lockwood children all the days of their lives. A cunningly laid dry stone wall surrounded their small front garden, and it was atop that low wall that the five children sat, anxiously waiting, unconsciously drawing strength from each other and from their massive black dog, who also waited in the reassuring manner of which massive black dogs are occasionally capable. The rosebushes that grew to such riotous glory framed them there, until at last they heard the rumble of a chaise at the foot of their lane. They were silent, staring, on the edge of tears until the chaise came clattering up the hill, both their mother and father leaning out the windows, calling and waving with fierce joy. Scartagh Lane, which over the past years had already sunk a few inches into the earth due to the tramping of Lockwood feet, suffered further as the children tumbled from atop the wall and pounded down to celebrate their father's return home.

The End

About the Author

Mark Bois

Born in Chicago and raised in Kansas City, Mark Bois is of Belgian and Irish ancestry. It is perhaps natural, then, that he would develop a fascination with the First Battalion of the 27th Foot, an Irish regiment, at the Battle of Waterloo. He would eventually return to school to earn a Master's degree in history, writing his thesis on the Inniskilling Regiment in 1815.

Amongst the dusty rosters and letters in the British National Archives, and then in the artifacts and records of the Inniskilling Regimental Museum, he found what he needed to write his thesis, but he also discovered the fascinating personal stories that provided the basis for *Lieutenant and Mrs. Lockwood*. Many actual experiences of the men and officers of the 27th Foot were pulled from those sources to be used in the novel.

Like Lt. Lockwood, Mark is the father of five, and has been happily married to their exceptional mother for more than thirty years. When not working, writing, or reading, he trains for indoor rowing regattas, where he enjoys only moderate success. He also builds furniture and remodels his house, though he is increasingly devoted to weekend naps.

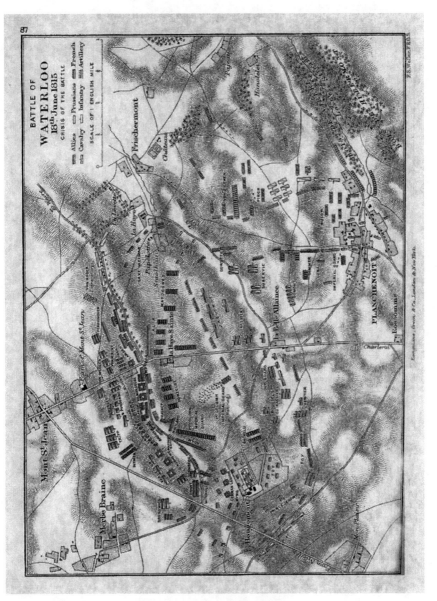

Old Map of Battle lines .
British to the North
French to the south

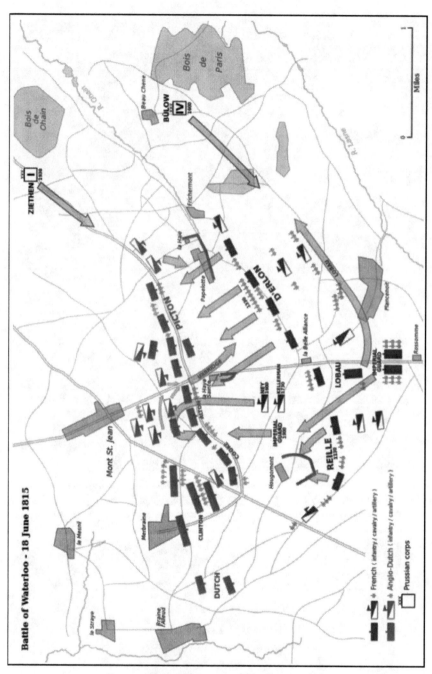

General positions of both armies

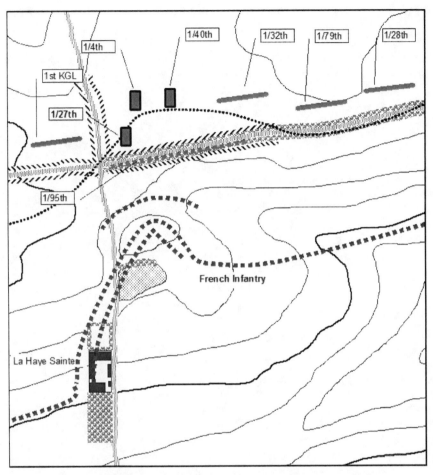

Inniskillings face off against the French

If You Enjoyed This Book,

Visit

FIRESHIP PRESS
www.fireshippress.com

Fireship Press books are available directly through our website, amazon.com, Barnes and Noble and Nook, Sony Reader, Apple iTunes, Kobo books and via leading bookshops across the United States, Canada, the UK, Australia and Europe.

Eastern Door

by

David More

Emigrating from 18th century rural Ireland, Billy Smithyman builds a new life in the New York frontier, a haven for himself and other immigrants. Billy's honesty stands out in the corrupt fur trade, and he earns the trust of formidable Mohawk war chief Emperor Marten. But powerful rivals in the colonial establishment resent Smithyman's success, and it wasn't only friends who came over form Ireland - Billy's most dangerous enemy has insinuated himself into the ruling class.

In the midst of the French and Indian War, Billy is appointed the amateur commander of a civilian militia and ordered to capture a powerful French fort and its garrison. Smithyman and Emperor Marten must outmaneuver a veteran French general, his well-trained army, their Native American allies, and a colonial consortium that finds more profit in war than in peace. *The Eastern Door* is the first novel in a breathtaking American Colonial History series that depicts the end of one civilization and the emergence of a new.

Fireship Press
www.FireshipPress.com

www.Fireshippress.com

HIS MAJESTY'S SHIP

BY

ALARIC BOND

A powerful ship, a questionable crew, a mission that must succeed.

In the spring of 1795 at the height of the Napoleonic Wars, *HMS Vigilant*, a 64 gun ship-of-the-line, leaves Spithead as senior escort to a small, seemingly innocent convoy. The crew is a jumble of trained seamen, volunteers, and the sweepings of the press; yet somehow the officers have to mold them into an effective fighting unit before the French discover the convoy's true significance.

Fireship Press
www.FireshipPress.com

www.Fireshippress.com
Found in all leading Booksellers and on line
eBook distributors

The Emperor's American

by

Art McGrath

Pierre Burns of Baltimore, Maryland was raised by his French mother to hate the English, but never thought he would be able to do anything about it. In early 1804, stranded on a French shore in the midst of Napoleon's Army as it prepares to invade England, Burns is given his chance when Marshal Michel Ney offers him a commission. Now in the uniform of a French officer, but still an outsider, Burns stands ready to battle his way to London, but it remains to be seen who his real enemies are—the English, his fellow soldiers who resent his presence, or even his American countrymen.

Art McGrath has explored a new region of the Napoleonic wars. Some Americans did indeed serve in the army of the Emperor, and served with distinction. McGrath conveys the style of the period and transports the reader to a time of adventure, when courage and integrity could make a world of difference. *The Emperor's American* is the beginning of a grand new series.

Fireship Press
www.FireshipPress.com

www.Fireshippress.com

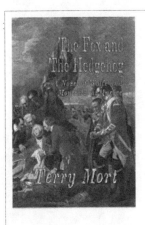

The Fox and the Hedgehog

A Novel of Wolfe and Montcalm in Quebec

by

Terry Mort

When the British defeated the French at Quebec in 1759, they guaranteed Britain's acquisition of Canada, but also unwittingly paved the way for the American revolution.

But this is a larger story than just the single day of battle on September 13, 1759. The final action was the culmination of a summer long campaign involving a series of engagements between the British Army, American Rangers and the Royal Navy on one side and the French Regulars, the Canadian militia and Indian allies on the other.

The two commanders, General Wolfe and Montcalm, could not have been more different, yet both were professional soldiers of the highest standards.

**For the Finest in
Nautical and Historical
Fiction and Nonfiction**

WWW.FIRESHIPPRESS.COM

Interesting • Informative • Authoritative

CPSIA information can be obtained at www.ICGtesting.com
Printed in the USA
LVOW12s2027270314

379184LV00002B/329/P